Newcastle Evening Chronicle

Also by Freda Lightfoot

Luckpenny Land
Wishing Water
Larkrigg Fell
Lakeland Lily
The Bobbin Girls
Manchester Pride
Polly's War
Kitty Little
The Favourite Child
Gracie's Sin
Ruby McBride
Daisy's Secret
Dancing on Deansgate
The Girl From Poor House Lane
Watch for the Talleyman
For All Our Tomorrows
The Woman From Heartbreak House
Putting on the Style
Fools Fall in Love
That'll be the Day
Candy Kisses

FREDA LIGHTFOOT

Who's Sorry Now?

HODDER

First published in Great Britain in 2008 by Hodder & Stoughton
An Hachette Livre UK company

First published in paperback in 2008

2

A CIP catalogue record for this title is available from the British Library

ISBN 978 0 340 89743 0

Typeset in Plantin Light by Palimpsest Book Production Limited, Grangemouth, Stirlingshire

Printed and bound in the UK by CPI Mackays, Chatham ME5 8TD

Hodder & Stoughton Ltd
A division of Hodder Headline
338 Euston Road
London NW1 3BH

1958

I

Carmina

It had been the worst Easter anyone could remember, a bitter Good Friday only brightening up as the weekend progressed. The weather was wet, cold and miserable with even some snow in the south. Trade on Champion Street Market had been the worst in living memory with rain dripping from the pink and white striped awnings down people's necks, forming puddles on the cobbles to soak the unwary. Temperatures were so low folk hurried to buy only the barest essentials before dashing home to their warm firesides.

Today, the Tuesday following Easter Monday, many of the traders were in the process of packing up early for the day, with only the hot-chestnut man doing brisk business.

Certainly no one was interested in buying ice cream and Carmina Bertalone had been excused work and sent to buy bread and Parmesan cheese from Poulson's. Papa issued a stern warning not to be late as the food was needed for supper. In any case, Mamma liked all her brood to be present before she began serving the evening meal and he well knew how Carmina loved to dawdle and chat to the boys.

Carmina sauntered along Champion Street, making

sure the hood of her scarlet duffel coat shielded her long ebony hair from the relentless rain. Usually she liked to feel its soft thick curls drifting over her shoulders, but Papa didn't allow this when she was working in the ice-cream parlour so today she wore it neatly secured in a pony tail.

She batted her eyelashes flirtatiously at Barry Holmes as he stacked boxes of apples and oranges in his van. Unfortunately, he was far too old to appreciate her charms. Jimmy Ramsay was old too but he still called out to her as she passed by.

'Tha looks a reet bobby-dazzler in that coat, chuck.'

Carmina purred with pleasure and rewarded him with a bewitching smile. She did *so* like to be noticed.

A crowd of people was demonstrating outside the market hall. They were marching right around the city gathering support for the New Peace Movement before delivering a petition to the Town Hall in Albert Square. Carmina paid them little attention, being concerned only in keeping her new black patent shoes dry. They had very high heels and were cramping her toes dreadfully but she wouldn't be seen dead in anything flat and frumpy.

She took a detour by Dena Dobson's stall in the market hall, not only to escape the rain but also to check if she'd any exciting new skirts in stock. She lingered long enough to try on one or two, even though she had no money to treat herself until she got paid at the end of the week.

'Save this red and black one for me, will you, Dena? I love these cabbage roses.'

Big Molly Poulson was wrapping the huge yellow cartwheels of cheese in their muslin cloths preparatory to stacking them away in her cold store by the time Carmina finally reached her stall.

'By heck, you Italians can get through enough Parmesan to sink a battleship,' she said, as she carved off a large block, much as she said every week. 'At least with yer mam's good pasta inside thee, tha'll not slip down t'gutter in all this rain.' She was clearly referring to Carmina's voluptuous curves, of which she was rightly proud.

Carmina put her head down against the deluge and hurried over to George's bakery to buy crusty bread to accompany Mamma's spaghetti. She was on her way back across Champion Street, dancing between puddles and trying not to slip on the slick cobbles in her high heels when she spotted her sister. Wiping the rain from her eyes she was about to call out to Gina to help her carry the load when she suddenly noticed she was not alone.

Carmina stopped in her tracks, shock running through her like a bolt of lightning.

She could hardly believe what her eyes were telling her. Her dull, stupid sister was talking to *Luc Fabriani*! How *dare* she? In an instant Carmina became oblivious to the rain; not even caring, for the moment at least, about her new shoes. Didn't Luc belong exclusively to her? At least he would if *she* had any say in the matter.

She stood stock-still, dazed with shock, the hood of her duffel coat falling back so that her hair was drenched in seconds but Carmina didn't even notice. Then someone bumped into her.

'Eeh, sorry, chuck, I didn't see you standing there. I nearly run you over.' It was Dorothy Thompson, more fondly known as Aunty Dot, rushing along wheeling a big pram with one of her foster babies tucked up inside. A small boy was perched on the end, and an older girl was hanging on to the handle.

'We're trying to get our errands done as quick as we can afore we get washed away.' Aunty Dot grinned. 'Not that I'm complaining mind, since the Good Lord chose to let the sun shine on us on Easter Sunday. It were a miracle. Lizzie and me took these nippers to Blackpool. Eeh, it were grand. We'd been saving up for months and we thought for a while we were going to be drownded, didn't we, chuck?' she said, addressing the question to the small girl. 'But it all turned out champion.'

Carmina didn't trouble to reply to the silly woman, she was too busy watching Gina with Luc.

Fists clenched, teeth gritted, she watched in mounting fury as her pathetically timid younger sister openly flirted with the boy *she* wanted most in all the world. No, not a boy, a *man*! Twenty years old and absolutely *gorgeous*!

'We saw the clowns and built sand-castles,' the girl, whose name was Beth, told Carmina, bright eyes shining at the memory of such joy.

Then her little brother piped up with some tale about riding in a big train and Carmina rudely ignored him too as she itched to escape their chatter, to run over and tear her sister away from *her* man.

Why a woman would willingly foster other people's children was quite beyond her understanding. Mamma had produced ten, plus one who'd died, which she couldn't understand either. Carmina wasn't in the least interested in babies. She'd had more than enough of their noise and smells to last her a lifetime.

Desperate to escape, she made some inane remark about being pleased the children had enjoyed their holiday and stepped back into the nearby pawn-shop doorway, leaving sufficient room for Aunty Dot to give a cheery wave and go on her way.

Carmina couldn't believe this was happening to her. She *needed* Luc. How dare Gina steal him from her?

Hadn't she been practically throwing herself at him for weeks now, ever since the day he'd callously told her it was all over between them and chucked her? So far none of her usual tricks and wiles had worked, and yet Carmina had convinced herself that this coldness he exhibited towards her was merely temporary, that she could win him back given time and persistence. All that was required was the right sort of inducement on her part. Carmina's velvet-brown eyes glittered wickedly. And how could she fail to persuade him, given her attributes?

Carmina freely admitted that she was passionate and quick tempered, her head constantly filled with wild schemes and dreams and forbidden deeds which she would impulsively put into effect without pause for thought. Her eyes blazed with wilful determination yet could melt a man's soul in seconds. Her wide seductive lips were eminently kissable and she had the kind of face which could transform itself in seconds from playful and sweetly kittenish to archly sophisticated or enticingly passionate.

Gina might be reasonably pretty, in a bland, uninteresting, *skinny* sort of way, but she had none of Carmina's voluptuous Latin charm. Without question the whole Bertalone clan agreed that Carmina was the beauty of the family.

How could Luc possibly resist her?

There had been a time a few months back when the two of them had been practically inseparable. The Fabriani family were one of the many rivals of the Bertalones, but far richer. Much to Carmina's disappointment, however, Luc was showing no signs of joining the family business. He worked on a building site, labouring on a development in Salford, and each day at five-thirty precisely she used to wait for him at the bus stop.

He would get off the bus, haversack swinging over one shoulder, all dusty and dirty in his working clothes, dark hair awry and grubby smears on his handsome face. Despite the grit and grime he had still looked incredibly sexy, acknowledging her presence with a non-committal grunt.

He would curl one arm about her neck, or capture her chin in his hand and give her a long passionate, tongue-in-her-mouth kiss right there at the bus stop before everyone. His mates would laugh and heckle and cheer him on but Carmina hadn't minded one little bit. She'd loved all of that. It had made her feel wanted, as if she belonged to him.

He'd never actually said that she was his girl, but she'd known it in her heart. Why else would he have made love to her? Admittedly, Luc wasn't the first boy she'd let go 'all the way' but he'd certainly been the most exciting.

His kisses were very nearly as passionate as the ones Burt Lancaster gave to Deborah Kerr in that movie *From Here to Eternity* which Carmina had seen at least three times when it came out a few years ago.

Now he was kissing her sister.

She saw how Gina shyly turned her head away when he tweaked a lock of damp brown hair, how she dipped her chin as he bent his tall, lean body to peep into her eyes. Gina had lovely eyes, they were her best feature: large and trusting, the colour of cinnamon, although she would beguilingly mask their beauty with a sweep of long dark curling lashes.

Luc was smiling at her, that lazy, cocksure smile he used whenever he sensed a new conquest. Carmina would have killed to be on the receiving end of such a smile.

Then, to her complete horror, he planted a tender kiss on the tip of her sister's small, snub nose, and another on her wide smiling mouth. In that moment Carmina felt physically sick.

She knew, in that instant, that she hated her own sister.

At just sixteen, fifteen months younger than herself and the nearest to her in age of the seven Bertalone girls, Carmina had always seen Gina as a rival.

Shy, and with something of an inferiority complex,

Gina was the one to whom her four younger sisters would be most likely to turn if they had a problem. In Carmina's opinion, she was her parents' favourite too, since she was so loving and affectionate, so special in their eyes. She'd suffered, and fortunately largely recovered from, a bout of polio. Now she exhibited the patience of a saint, always sickeningly determined to recognise the good in people, and to see their point of view.

Yet everyone marvelled at Carmina's own stunning good looks, particularly Gina, so how could her plain little sister *possibly* capture the attention of Luc Fabriani when she herself had so patently failed to do so?

Carmina's insides knotted with such jealous rage she could hardly breathe. If it was a sin to loathe your sister, then so be it. She'd say three extra Hail Marys at Mass on Sunday.

Despite the damp chill, her soaking hair and the misery of witnessing what she saw as a betrayal, Carmina couldn't tear herself away. There were several more sickeningly sweet and tender kisses in which Gina actually stroked the rain from Luc's handsome, angular cheeks before laughingly pushing him away. Then the girl turned on her heel and, head down against the slanting rain, hurried along Champion Street as fast as her limping gait would allow, up the stone steps into the Bertalones' tall Victorian terraced house.

In cold rage Carmina broke off a piece of the deliciously fragrant bread, tearing into it with her sharp white teeth while she contemplated revenge.

2

Amy and Patsy

From where she stood on the corner of Champion Street, Amy George could see Carmina Bertalone splashing furiously through puddles as she followed in the wake of her sister. The younger girl's face had seemed to shine with happiness, but Carmina's was another story. Sisters, Amy thought with a smile, recalling similar problems of her own. Almost as bad as a mother-in-law.

She shivered, soaked to the skin by the rain, auburn curls springing wildly out of control and a sneeze already tickling her nose. Yet she couldn't bring herself to leave. She was far too fascinated by the protest marchers.

The 'Ban the Bomb' banners were garishly painted in blood red lettering a foot high, declaring support for the Aldermaston marchers. These were the valiant souls who had walked fifty miles or more to make their protest. Some had started in Trafalgar Square, the rest walking from towns the length and breadth of the country to merge on the Nuclear Research Base in Berkshire, waving their home-made banners and singing to a skiffle band playing 'When the Saints Go Marching In'.

Amy had read all about it in the *Manchester Guardian*: how they'd collected more and more people as they walked, and any number of blisters; sleeping in school halls or on the floor of strangers' houses. Some people had given them food as they marched along, clapping and cheering them on, while others had heckled, jeered and booed them. It sounded so exciting, a real adventure.

In her heart, Amy secretly envied them.

Only once had she dared to rebel and that was when she'd run off to Gretna Green to marry Chris. What an adventure that had been! So romantic, even if they had come close to starving. Oh, but they'd been so much in love it hadn't seemed to matter.

Now, a mere few months later Amy rubbed her hands over her swollen belly and wondered just what she'd let herself in for. Chris was working in the bakery with his father now and she seemed to spend more time with her mother-in-law than her new husband: polishing the lino, cleaning out the new Baxi grate, ironing, or else sewing on endless buttons. Amy was not, however, allowed to darn Chris's socks as her stitches were considered to be too large and clumsy.

How had it all ended up like this? she wondered, giving a sad little sigh. Even their dreams of getting a home of their own had foundered. Chris insisted that the stress of moving was too much for her while she was pregnant. They seemed to be stuck with living over the bakery with his parents. Nothing ever turned out quite as one imagined.

The noisy crowd began to make its way between the

market stalls, singing and laughing in a happy, carefree sort of way. It seemed to be comprised mainly of students in college scarves and brightly coloured stockings, although there were some young mums pushing babies in prams. Many of the young men sported beards and the girls had frizzy hair and big round spectacles. Amy almost wished she needed to wear glasses or went to college so that she too could appear so cool and intelligent, and 'with it'.

They may well be idealist trouble-makers, but to Amy they seemed to be having such fun that she felt a strong urge to join in, despite her six-month bump. What would Mavis say if she did? Perish the thought.

She put a wet hand to her mouth to stop a hysterical giggle. Her mother-in-law was not the most tolerant or liberal-minded individual, ruling her household very much with a rod of iron. But then, even Amy's lovely new husband, Chris, would object too. And he'd be sure to tell her off if she went home soaked through, no doubt lecture her about taking proper care of herself and the coming baby.

Amy looked around for shelter so that she could watch events from a more sensible vantage point.

'Come and share my umbrella,' said a voice in her ear and Amy eagerly accepted, although her friend Patsy looked almost as wet as she did, silver fair hair hanging in rats' tails about her small elfin face.

As the two girls snuggled beneath it, warming each other against the cold, Amy said, 'By rights I should be helping ma-in-law peel potatoes for tea. And she'll give me gip if I drip water on to her clean lino.'

Patsy Bowman chuckled as she hooked her arm into Amy's. 'I should be helping Clara tidy up the hat stall but she's let me off to watch the demonstration. Look at you, as fat and round as a jolly robin, if a rather soggy one. You certainly shouldn't be standing out on the pavement in the pouring rain, that's for sure, nor peeling potatoes. Why aren't you sitting with your feet up being fed milk pobbies, or whatever it is a mum-to-be craves.'

'Because I'm bored out of my mind,' Amy said with feeling. 'Chris objects if I so much as lift a finger but Mavis is determined to turn me into the perfect wife and mother. She's teaching me all those little wrinkles my own ma failed to do, being the messy creature she is. Though to be fair, as Ma herself would say, she built up Poulson's to be the best pie makers in Lancashire, and has never claimed to be the best housekeeper.'

'Quite right! Why should women do all the scrubbing and cleaning?' Patsy agreed with feeling.

Amy giggled. 'I don't think Big Molly could ever be accused of doing too much scrubbing, except in her precious kitchen. Anyway, I have to do quite a bit for Mavis, although I don't really mind. I'm fit as a fiddle and if I sat about doing nothing all day, I'd go mad. Oh, but look at these people here, no younger than us and yet they're *free*. They're doing something worthwhile, not suffering heartburn and an aching back. Patsy, do you ever wonder if you've done the right thing by rushing into marriage so young?'

'I haven't . . . yet,' Patsy reminded her. 'Although it certainly seems to be approaching with the speed of an express train. Marc's mother seems to spend every evening stitching away furiously at my dress, the most glorious wedding gown you could ever imagine, not to mention seven bridesmaids' dresses for the Bertalone girls.' Patsy sighed. 'Sometimes, I envy you dashing off to secretly do the deed at Gretna Green. It would be so much simpler.'

Amy laughed. 'Don't you believe it. Exciting – yes, and utterly romantic, but also terrifying. I've never been so cold and hungry in my life! And we still had to come home, face our parents and resolve that dreadful family feud.'

'But it all worked out in the end, so why all this doom and gloom? I thought you and Chris were "love's young dream".'

'Oh, we are, only – well, you know what they say: marry in haste, repent at leisure.' Amy felt herself blushing. 'The honest truth is, it's his mother driving me up the wall, not Chris.'

'Ah, look why don't we grab a frothy coffee in Belle's Café and you can tell me all about it.'

'I – I'm not sure I have the time. I promised Mavis that I'd help with the ironing before tea, sitting down of course, and . . .'

'Amy, *so there you are*? What *are* you thinking of standing in the rain getting soaked to the skin? Are you quite mad?' And suddenly there was Mavis, bearing down upon them with the kind of expression on her face which made the day seem suddenly warm and mild by comparison.

'I'm coming, I'm coming,' Amy cried, and Patsy

could only watch in mystified disbelief as her sweet, stubborn friend, who had once defied her family to elope with the love of her life, scuttled obediently off to do her mother-in-law's bidding. Now what was that all about?

Alec Hall likewise had been watching the marchers pass by, a sardonic smile on his face. Poor fools! Did these young idiots imagine they could change the world with the help of a few banners and protest songs? War didn't go away just by wishing. And how could you ban something that had already been invented, already been used to decimate thousands of lives?

In any case, a great deal of harm could be done in ordinary warfare with guns and grenades. Would they ban those too? And would the other side obligingly do the same? Alec very much doubted it.

He'd seen action in two wars and the memories would haunt him for ever, particularly of Korea, the most recent. He'd been barely eighteen when he'd joined up in 1941, and a seasoned veteran when he'd been called to fight for his country a second time. There were times now when he felt like an old man, for all he was still five years short of forty. But Alec knew he should be grateful he was at least alive.

Strangely, people never asked him about the Korean War. Plenty showed interest in what he did in WWII but it was as if the Korean never existed. It was a war people preferred to ignore, or forget. So far as they were concerned the war, the *real* war, was over.

A population still weary from WWII had felt quite

unable to show interest in yet another taking place in some distant, inhospitable land, far from their shores. Life was good, the hardships and rationing behind them and they wanted to think of peace and the future, not remember the bad times, the worries and anxieties of loved ones who never came back. He and his colleagues returning from Korea were often treated with little more than indifference, as if people were surprised they'd ever been away.

Alec deeply resented this attitude.

The national press had been equally negligent, showing more interest in the Coronation and Sir Edmund Hillary's conquest of Everest, with far fewer column inches given over to the end of the war in Korea. Even the peace had been grudgingly made, signed on 27 July 1953, in a tiny, unknown village called Panmunjom.

Three years of bloody fighting, over two million dead, and for what? Less than three weeks after peace was declared England was celebrating with more fervour over winning the Ashes. By September everyone was drooling over reports of the wedding of John Kennedy to Jacqueline Bouvier just as if the war in Korea had never taken place.

Even today, five years on, the atmosphere between North and South Korea remained tense and unstable, yet the war itself was forgotten. Nobody cared. Where was the glory in that?

Alec's resentment bit deep. He could never forget. What happened in Korea was burned into his soul.

For all this group of young idealistic dreamers might

genuinely believe they were helping by making this protest about banning the bomb, what could they possibly hope to achieve? War was a necessary evil. Unavoidable! Besides, everyone was tired of the subject.

Even so, he tacked on to the end of the peace march. The last thing they wanted was another bloody war.

It was then that he saw her.

She was standing in the rain, like a showy bird of paradise in her scarlet duffel coat, rain dripping from her pony tail, ebony curls stuck enchantingly to her smooth young brow. Alec had often seen her about the market and had recently begun to notice that Carmina Bertalone was no longer a gawky schoolgirl but a shapely young Italian beauty.

His steel-grey eyes raked over her, taking in the swell of her delectable breasts, temptingly visible beneath the coat which she wore carelessly unfastened. He slowed his pace a little but even from this distance, several yards away, he could sense her passion and her fury, saw how her eyes blazed. He followed the line of her gaze, recognised her sister and watched more out of curiosity and amusement than actual interest, as the younger girl tenderly kissed her boyfriend then hurried away.

So that's how the land lay. Carmina Bertalone was jealous of her own sister.

Alec's gaze slid irrevocably back to Carmina, mesmerised by her beauty, marvelling at the wildness in those fabulous eyes, the length of her legs lashed by the rain in the short black skirt, and her bare feet in their silly high heels.

She emitted a little cry of rage, then began to tear clumps out of a loaf of bread with her sharp white teeth. Something hot and sharp pierced his heart, and in that instant the sound of the band and the chatter of the idealistic Peace Marchers seemed to fade to nothing more than an irritating buzz in his ears. Even his burning resentment over the perceived disinterest in his war career became of less importance.

Alec knew, in a moment of rare clarity, that he must have her. This girl would be his reward for services rendered to his country above and beyond the call of duty.

3

Carmina and Gina

It was so easy to lie. Carmina had discovered that people generally believed whatever you said to them, for no better reason than they felt obliged to do so, as if they could never imagine anyone deliberately telling an untruth.

Carmina felt no regrets about falsely accusing Luc Fabriani of two-timing her precious sister, even as she watched the colour drain from Gina's rosy cheeks and her lovely caramel skin turn to wax before her eyes. As was her nature, the poor girl didn't retaliate or object, didn't jump in with an argument but simply bit her lip and backed off as if the problem had nothing at all to do with her.

'I don't know why you're telling me this. Why would I care? He's nothing to me,' she innocently protested, which almost made Carmina smile.

'So how come you were wrapped in his arms a moment ago, out there in the street?'

They were standing in the hall, hanging their dripping coats on the hall stand, Carmina trying not to soak the bread and cheese as she did so.

'Seems a funny way of showing you don't care about someone, wouldn't you say? Anyway, you know that he and I went out together. Oh, for simply ages.'

Gina stiffly interrupted her. 'I thought it was only for a couple of weeks. Luc told me all about it, and that it's all over.'

Carmina ground her teeth together as she shook her head in pitying disbelief. 'So he didn't mention trying to kiss me the other day then?'

Gina gasped. 'He never did kiss you!'

Carmina was pleased the lie had at last ruffled her sister's maddening calm. 'I'm afraid so, love. He's girl-mad, didn't you know? He kissed *me* on Tuesday, Doris Mitchell on Wednesday, and Jane Hepworth on Thursday behind the market hall.'

Goodness, how did her imagination dream up all this stuff? Had she gone too far? She really would have to keep track, as one lie could so easily lead to another, a whole web of lies. Ah, well, in for a penny . . .

'*And* he asked us all to the dance, every single one of us, although naturally we all turned him down.' She lifted her nose in the air as if she wouldn't dream of going anywhere with Luc Fabriani.

'I don't believe you! He wouldn't . . .'

'. . . two-time you? Sorry, love, Luc simply isn't to be trusted, not where girls are concerned.' Whereupon, Gina's lovely cinnamon eyes filled with a rush of tears.

Unrepentant, Carmina raised a pair of finely drawn brows and casually shrugged, as if it were of no concern to her what Gina did, or felt. She tugged at the blue ribbon securing her pony tail to let her ebony curls fall about her shoulders, still beautiful despite being dripping wet, and smiled with feigned sympathy at her sister.

'You know I don't mean to be cruel,' she lied. 'I only want you to be happy, Gina, but Luc really is no good.'

Gina rallied, her fine mouth tightening into a firm line as it did when defending one of her younger siblings. 'That's not true! You're judging him like Mamma and Papa do, calling him a lout just because he plays in a skiffle group and wears his hair in a DA.'

Carmina made a little puffing sound. 'As if *I* would do such a thing? I *love* skiffle!'

She knew she shouldn't ask any questions, because of the pain the answers would bring, but felt as if she were burning up with curiosity and couldn't seem to help herself. Carmina took great care to keep her tone casual. 'Is that the first time he's kissed you? I mean, you haven't actually been out with him, have you?'

Gina glanced over her shoulder, a frantic expression coming into her face. 'Hush, Mamma might hear you. You mustn't say a *word*.'

Carmina's mouth actually fell open. 'You mean you *have*? You've been out on a *date* with Luc Fabriani?'

Gina drew a steadying breath. 'We've been seeing each other for two or three months now, although we've been careful to keep our meetings secret.'

'Two or three months! You've been seeing him for two or three *months*?'

'Since late January, yes. He asked me out at the New Year Social at the church, but I said no, at first.' A shy smile lit her face at the memory of how Luc had spent the whole of January trying to make her change her mind. 'I knew Mamma and Papa wouldn't approve, so we kept it a secret. They don't think I should have any sort of normal life because of . . . well, you know why.' Gina's quiet voice tailed away into silence.

'I don't *believe* you!'

'It's perfectly true. He's really nice, not the rebel Mamma and Papa claim him to be, although he says I've changed him. Luc says that I bring out the best in him, that I've made him almost respectable.' Gina smiled, blushing prettily and her cinnamon eyes took on a dazed, far-away expression. 'Anyway, I like him, and he seems to like me.'

Carmina's stomach clenched. The thought of Gina meeting secretly with Luc Fabriani for all that time almost made her want to throw up. Utterly sickening! It shouldn't be her stupid *sister* wrapped up in the arms of the hottest boy around, it should be herself.

She gave a mocking laugh and went in for the kill.

'You realise he's only after you because he knows how *desperate* you are for a fella! He thinks you'll be easy, that he can have his *wicked* way with you.'

Gina shook her head. 'You're wrong. He's not like that, not with me anyway.'

'So what *is* he like?' Carmina snapped.

Gina looked at her older sister, eyes bright with pent-up happiness as she combed strands of straight damp hair with her fingers. Then in the smallest of voices, said, 'He's sweet and loving, and really easy to talk to.' Her eyes darkened and once again she glanced over her shoulder. 'You will keep what I'm telling you a secret, Carmina, won't you?'

Carmina's entire body seemed to grow still as she agreed that of course she would, as she had done a thousand times before. It always amazed her that, in her innocence, Gina never seemed to realise that promises were only kept when it was in Carmina's interest to do so. Her sister had always been one for little secrets, hiding sweets in her handkerchief drawer, keeping a private diary, but this secret was totally unexpected.

'The reason I don't believe what these other girls have told you is that Luc has asked *me* to the dance. I haven't said yes, not yet. I explained to him that I'd never ever been to a dance before, not since my illness. But I do feel *so* much better and I'm trying to find the courage to try. I've agreed to let him know tomorrow.' Her cheeks flushed pink with excitement.

Rage roared through Carmina's veins as fiercely as a forest fire. This was too much to bear. Inevitably it awakened her cruel streak and she began to laugh.

'For goodness' sake, girl, can't you see he's having you on? Why would Luc Fabriani want to dance with someone as clumsy as you? He must be blind as well as stupid. I mean, you can't even walk properly, let alone dance, and you're not exactly mown out with offers, are you? I can't see them queuing round the block for the chance of taking *you* to the ball.'

Gina's pale cheeks suffused with a tide of hot colour. Since the polio she'd never entirely recovered her full strength and was thinner and smaller than she would otherwise have been, nowhere near as healthy and robust as the other Bertalone girls.

She favoured one leg, as it was now almost an inch shorter than the other, which gave her a slight limp. But at least she'd escaped wearing those dreadful callipers the doctor had once thought she'd need. They were hidden away in the back of a cupboard, a dreadful reminder of what might have been. She'd done all her exercises, made a determined effort to strengthen weak muscles, but it wasn't easy. Too much physical exercise could make matters worse, and cause excessive fatigue.

Mamma and Papa, and her siblings, were so delighted that she was walking at all, nobody commented upon her slight disability. Gina did her utmost not to be sensitive about it, although her awkward gait had given her something of an inferiority complex. And after so long confined to a sickroom, the real world seemed just a little scary to her.

But for Carmina to refer to this inevitable clumsiness was unforgivable and left Gina bereft of speech. Mostly, she'd learned to ignore her sister's jibes, putting them down to Carmina's uncertain temper, but this was too much.

When she managed to find her voice it trembled with emotion. 'That was a cruel and heartless thing to say.' Then she bit down hard on her lower lip and rushed upstairs to her bedroom without even bothering with her spaghetti supper.

Carmina was obliged to lie to Mamma too, explaining that poor Gina was suffering from a bad headache. Naturally, her mother dropped the serving spoon with a clatter and was for rushing upstairs after her precious daughter upon the instant. Carmina hastily reassured her it was simply the time of the month, and could she please have Gina's portion?

Allessandro, her greedy brother, objected, and any worries over Gina were soon lost in the usual mayhem over food and squabbles and general Bertalone chatter.

After talking long into the night with her sister, Gina finally acknowledged that Carmina was probably right and she made up her mind to decline Luc's invitation. No doubt he'd only asked her to the dance out of pity. She still found it hard to believe that he would want to take her anywhere. She didn't have one scrap of Carmina's beauty. Without doubt her elder sister was the glamorous one, the one who turned boys' heads. No one ever fell over their own feet watching her walk by.

While Carmina's hair fell into luxuriant dark waves, Gina's own brown locks were cut short and as straight as the falling rain. More often than not she pinned it out of the way with kirby-grips. Nor did she have her sister's curves. Clothes hung on her as if on a clothes peg, not a budding young woman. She despaired of ever getting breasts, of ever being seen as normal.

So why risk making a fool of herself before everyone? Despite her resolution Gina felt bitterly disappointed, wept silently into her pillow and slept not a wink. By morning she'd quite made up her mind. She couldn't possibly go to the dance. Carmina was right. She'd only make herself, and Luc, a laughing stock.

She sought comfort in the thought that they could perhaps still be friends, although she felt no longer able to consider him as a possible boyfriend, not now that she knew he'd kissed her sister too, and two-timed her.

But what did it matter? Surely she hadn't allowed

herself to fall in love with him? Gina didn't like to admit, even to herself, that she'd almost certainly been in danger of doing just that. He'd been so sweet to her, so unlike the Luc that Carmina had known and bragged about. He hadn't seemed dangerous and racy to her, not in the least.

But he needed to be told her decision and Gina really couldn't bear to tell him face to face.

Carmina generously agreed to personally deliver the note Gina agonised over and rewrote a dozen times before she was finally satisfied with it.

'Tell him I appreciate the invitation, but explain that I'm really not up to dancing, not yet,' Gina begged, and a great wedge of emotion blocked her throat so that she couldn't speak for a moment. She hated any reference to her disability, so having to use that as an excuse was a bitter pill to swallow. But not for the world was Gina prepared to admit that she'd heard about his betrayal.

'I'll make sure he understands,' Carmina reassured her with saccharine sweetness.

But then, of a sudden, perhaps caused by something in her sister's tone of voice, or a glint very like triumph, quickly masked, in her dark brown eyes, Gina instantly changed her mind. 'No! Give me back the note. I've changed my mind. I'll speak to him myself.'

'Don't be silly. Why upset yourself by seeing him again? No one else will know how he betrayed you, I swear it.'

'Perhaps I'm being too hasty. Maybe I should give him the chance to explain.'

Carmina was horrified. The last thing she wanted was for Gina to repeat to Luc all she'd said about him, showing her up for the liar she undoubtedly was. 'And make yourself look a complete fool by begging for him to like you? Don't be stupid! I'll put the letter into Luc's hand personally, and simply explain how dancing is not really your thing.'

'Thank you, but I'd rather do it myself. Give me the letter, Carmina. Please.'

The two sisters argued, almost came to blows over the scrap of paper, before Carmina tossed it to the floor in a 'why-should-I-care-what-you-do' gesture and flounced off downstairs. By the time Gina came down to breakfast some moments later she sensed at once by the chill in the atmosphere that Carmina had revealed her precious secret.

4

Amy

Amy was being instructed on how to make cold-water starch so that the collars of Chris's shirts could be properly stiffened. While conceding that today's young preferred attached collars, her mother-in-law insisted that all respectable men were expected to wear starched white shirts with collars ironed until they shone. The fact that her son did not care for them was quite by the way. Mavis was most particular about how things should be done.

She put mothballs in every parchment-lined drawer, folded her Viyella nightdress each morning into its satin nightdress case, brushed the crumbs from the table-cloth with a silver-backed brush and little dustpan especially for the purpose. Mavis liked things *nice.*

When she was young, Mavis's family had employed a young Irish maid from Donegal. She'd explained to Amy how the girl had needed to be taught proper table manners. 'My dear mother always insisted on the highest standards, as I do.' She made it very plain that she thought Amy too lacked certain values since she was a member of the dreaded Poulson family.

Mavis considered that she'd married beneath her in choosing Thomas George as a husband, and as she couldn't afford a maid and her son had foolishly made the same mistake, her new daughter-in-law would do very well instead. Amy was a useful, and free, alternative.

Mavis herself now did little more than flick a duster around, expecting her daughter-in-law to carry out the more mundane tasks under her careful supervision, hence the lesson in cold-water starch. Sadly, as usual, Amy's efforts were not appreciated and she found herself at the receiving end of yet another lecture.

She didn't protest, where was the point? It was far easier to comply. Any hint of rebellion always brought reprisals and Amy was a peace-maker, had spent her entire life mediating between various members of the Poulson household and was thankful to have escaped. Besides which she was a sensitive, caring girl who believed everyone should be happy and kind to one other, and would take almost any course rather than provoke an argument. She really had no wish to be at odds with anyone, if she could at all avoid it.

Yet there was a stubborn core of steel in her too, which had stood her in good stead over the years. Even the patient Amy had her limits, and Mavis was fast approaching it.

Since her soaking, Mavis had barely stopped berating her, as if Amy had done it simply to vex her.

'I really cannot imagine what you were thinking of.'

'I was interested in the march, in all those people who passionately believe they can make the government change its mind about nuclear weapons.'

'Absolute nonsense, how can such small-minded,

ordinary people know better than Mr Macmillan and his government what needs to be done?' she scoffed. 'What if the Russians should come and we aren't properly defended? We made that mistake in World War Two. We mustn't ever let that happen again.'

'But we weren't invaded in World War Two.'

'We might have been. We certainly had very little means of defending ourselves at the start of the war.'

'Yes, I accept that as a fair argument, but look what happened in Hiroshima. If we continue along that road, where will it all end? Isn't it time we concentrated on making peace?'

As ever, Amy made the fundamental mistake of imagining she could have an intelligent conversation with her mother-in-law.

'What would *you* know about such things? Foolish girl, you don't even have the sense to keep out of the rain. Goodness knows how you'll cope when the baby is actually born. Keep stirring that starch, child, we don't want it to go all lumpy. I really don't know what Chris will say when he finds out.'

Amy wondered how many babies she would need to produce before she ceased to be a child in her mother-in-law's eyes.

Mavis made a point of telling her son all about the escapade almost as soon as he walked through the door. Chris was so upset and worried at how the wetting might affect the baby that the moment they were alone in bed that night, he gave Amy a gentle ticking-off, almost as if he too saw her as a naughty schoolgirl who really should know better. He seemed to do that a good deal these days, usually instigated by some tale or other from his mother which more often than not was a huge exaggeration of the truth, or else far too trivial to matter.

The other day he'd looked at her straight-faced and said, 'Mother tells me that you turned all her lace curtains pink in the wash.'

'It was an accident. One of your luminous shocking-pink socks got mixed up with them. I rather liked the result, actually. It was a lovely shade of pale pink.'

Amy had instantly fallen into a fit of giggles and Chris had frowned at her reprovingly. 'You know that Mother considers her lace curtains to be the whitest in the whole street. You shouldn't be so careless, Amy.'

She'd naturally protested then but on this occasion, however, Amy was ashamed to admit that her beloved husband was probably right. She should not have been out in the rain getting soaked through. It was indeed a very foolish thing to do.

'It was just that I was so *bored*. I'll be glad when this baby *is* born and I can start living my life again. Why did you make me stop working for Ma? She could do with some help on the pie stall and we could do with the money to save up for a place of our own.'

'You know full well that I insisted you take time off from work because you were obviously tired and in need of a rest. Besides, I hope no wife of mine will ever need to go out to work just to put a roof over our heads.'

Amy cuddled up to him in the bed they shared in the back bedroom, the one where Chris had lived since he was a boy, kissing his tightly pursed mouth till it softened and opened to her.

'Stop being such an old fuddy-duddy. It was great fun watching that march. They were handing out leaflets,' Amy told him, between kisses. 'All about how we should walk for a weekend, a day, or even an hour if we're opposed to any government having nuclear weapons. Maybe I will.'

'Don't be ridiculous! I don't want you walking anywhere in your condition, or involving yourself with those sort of people.'

'What sort of people is that, Chris?'

'With people who sleep in church halls getting up to heaven knows what. They have no morals.'

Amy looked at him. 'They have a higher standard of morals than folk who click their tongues about the way the world is going and yet do nothing about it. My God, you're beginning to sound as snobby as your mother. Those people weren't just students and left-wing weirdos, there were also middle-class, professional people, the kind your mother might invite in for a dry sherry or afternoon tea. Some were young women pushing babies in prams. I almost went and joined them there and then. I want a safe world for our baby too, don't you?'

'Of course I do, but it's not our place to provide one. It's certainly not yours.'

Amy bristled slightly. 'What is my place then, Chris? If I can't have a home of my own, if I'm not permitted to work, am not allowed to join in an intelligent, non-violent protest about an important issue, what am I allowed to do? Wash your shirts, I suppose.'

'There's no shame in a wife washing her husband's shirts.'

'Of course there isn't, not unless I turn all your shirts pink, to match the lace curtains.'

He stared at her, horrified. 'You didn't!'

Amy could never be cross with him for long, if only because he was so very serious. Now she fell to giggling as she unbuttoned his pyjama jacket and peeled off his trousers. 'No, I didn't, the lesson today was in how to make a good cold-water starch.'

Chris groaned.

'Anyway, why would you care how your clothes are washed, so long as there's a clean shirt hanging in the wardrobe whenever you want one?'

All the while she provoked him with her teasing, Chris was beginning to respond to her kisses, quite against his better judgement, for she was too far gone in pregnancy for him to risk taking things any further despite Amy's insistence it wouldn't harm the baby.

But then Chris was a cautious man, not one for taking chances. It was only his desperate love for Amy and that dreadful feud between their parents which had driven him to do something as crazy as eloping to Gretna Green. And he hadn't regretted it, not for a moment, although it was a great help that his parents had agreed to offer them a home and employment on their return, since they were stony broke by then. Amy insisted they would have coped well enough on their own, but Chris wasn't too sure.

The bakery was a family business, his heritage in a way, so since he'd lost his job doing the milk round, he'd set his mind to learning the trade. Amy didn't seem to understand that he wanted things to be good for them, good and safe. No more risks.

But now his head was going all muzzy with desire. Maybe they might risk making love, after all, if they were gentle.

'Well then, could you at least beg her not to starch my collars,' he murmured in her ear. 'My neck is rubbed raw, as red as a turkey cock's,' and they both burst out laughing at this, although they had to stifle the sound under the covers so that his mother and father didn't hear.

It was a day or two later and, shoulders hunched against the April cold, Alec was making his way to his little music shop on the edge of the market hall. He still had the Peace Marchers' demonstration niggling away at the back of his mind, and he was also haunted by the image of a beautiful girl in a scarlet duffel coat.

The strains of Bobby Darin singing 'Dream Lover' reached him as he approached. Dreams! He had far too many of those, and they generally turned into nightmares. Day and night they played havoc with his mind.

But he mustn't dwell on memories, mustn't become obsessed. There was more to life than the war. His own father, for goodness' sake, had told him not to be a bore on the subject.

'Really, Alec,' he would say, in that commanding tone of voice he used when addressing what he considered to be lesser beings. 'I know you had a terrible time of it but stop being so damned self-pitying. You must learn to put the past behind you and start living again. Be a man.'

But then he'd never been a sympathetic parent even when Alec was a child. He would accuse him of being fussy and over-sensitive just because he preferred to play with the girls rather than other boys. Or of being too soft and namby-pamby, his favourite words. Alec's mother would insist that his father was only attempting to toughen him up so that he'd grow into a strong man. Where his father had failed, life, and two wars, had more than made up for it.

Even today, five years on, he showed little interest in Alec's excellent war record, constantly picking on him for being content with a small shop on an insignificant little market. He accused his son of having no ambition, and of not liking hard work. Nor were any of Alec's family and friends aware how badly the Korean war had affected him in that alien land.

He supposed his father was right in one respect, at least. Alec admitted that he wasn't the most astute businessman in the world. Classical music was his passion, and playing his favourite Mozart and Schubert was what engrossed him, not standing around for hours trying to sell complete rubbish to stupid teenagers.

Yet he was keen to make a decent living and hoped that Terry, his own son, had made them some much-needed profit this morning while Alec had enjoyed his usual breakfast of bacon and eggs in Belle's Café. The boy meant well but his head was full of that damned skiffle group he was in, so Alec very much doubted it.

As he pushed open the door, a young girl dashed

out and ran full tilt into him. She was carrying a record in its brown paper sleeve, and almost dropped it as they collided.

'Sorry! Hey, are you OK?' Alec put out his hands to steady her. It was Carmina Bertalone. Now here was one teenager he would be willing to find time for.

She looked up at him and laughed, velvet-brown eyes dancing. 'I'm fine. Who better to bump into than a handsome man?'

'I rather think I'm the lucky one,' he said.

She dimpled at him. 'Will you be playing the records during the interval at the dance on Friday night, Mr Hall?' Her lovely head tilted provocatively to one side as she innocently asked the question.

'I might,' Alec said, instantly dismissing his earlier plan to leave that to Terry as his gaze swivelled directly to her cleavage.

'See you there, then.'

He watched the provocative sway of her hips as she walked away, the flirtatious smile she flung back at him over her shoulder, the swinging gloss of her ebony pony tail. Standing there, smiling after her like some awe-struck schoolboy, he felt again that quiver of excitement, the familiar ache in his loins. Young girls were ever his weakness, but then didn't he deserve one, after what he'd been through?

5

Patsy and Gina

The Bertalone family's ice-cream parlour stood just inside the iron-framed market hall, a shining example of sparkling marble counter tops, huge mirrors, and brass and copper fittings. It was here that the ice cream was made, in a small, clinically clean room set behind the parlour. Patsy liked to help whenever she had a moment or two to spare during her dinner hour, if only because Papa Bertalone was such a kind man who had welcomed her into his family with open arms.

Not that she had much free time being almost fully occupied helping Clara on the hat stall, working on projects for her millinery course, or creating hats for her own clientele. Nevertheless, Patsy was anxious to be a part of this family she was about to join. She loved to watch Papa making the ice cream. He was so very proud of his small empire, and eagerly embroiled in expansion plans for a business started more than sixty years ago by his great uncle.

Today he was making peach gelato, and her mouth was already watering just watching him gather the ingredients together: ripe fresh peaches flown in from Italy, mascarpone and yoghurt.

'This tastes wonderful,' she said, nibbling a slice of peach.

Papa grinned at her. 'You come work with me in the ice-a-cream-a parlour and I teach you all you need to know about ice-a-cream-a.'

Patsy instinctively glanced across at Carmina who was just a few feet away serving customers, the rigid stance of her spine loudly proclaiming that she'd heard every word of her father's offer and resented it deeply. The girl would certainly not welcome Patsy's intrusion into her own private territory even though she frequently trespassed on hers, and claimed to be bored sick of serving ice cream. Patsy gave Marco a rueful look even as she picked up a knife and began to chop the peeled peaches into small pieces, as she had done many times before.

'My skills lie in a different direction. I love working with hats, and Clara needs me even more now that Annie has been forced to retire through ill health.'

Marco nodded sympathetically. 'The Higginson sisters have been good to you, I understand, little one.' He glanced across at Carmina's stiff back, then tapped the girl on her shoulder. 'It is time you take your turn on the ice-a-cream-a cart, Carmina.'

To Patsy he said, 'The ice-a-cream-a industry it see many changes. My uncle he have the horse-drawn cart, all brightly decorated with his name in curly gold lettering. I like to keep it, to see it stand proudly on Champion Street Market, a testament to the success of our family. Maria used to work in it, now it is Carmina's turn. Come along, girl, you will be late and your mamma she will want to be released so that she can do her chores before the children come home.'

Carmina cast Patsy a vicious look before stalking off, skirts swishing, to do as she was bid.

Now what was that all about? Patsy wondered.

Papa Bertalone watched her go with a sad shake of his head. 'She is wilful, this daughter. I worry for her. I worry for Gina too. Something is troubling her, I can tell, but I leave all of that feminine stuff to my wife. Daughters, pah!'

He shook his head in despair and Patsy couldn't help but smile, knowing he adored and worried about each of them.

'Sons are more sensible, more reliable. Soon you marry Marc and make him show interest in the ice-cream-a, *sì*?'

Proud though Marco was of his eldest son, Patsy was aware of his disappointment that Marc had chosen a different profession entirely.

Italians had been selling ice cream in Manchester ever since the first settlers came to Ancoats in the 1830s, driven from their homeland by poverty and a desire to better themselves. The area had come to be known as Little Italy because of the life the immigrants had brought to it, the typical Italian warmth, music and laughter, the gilders, carvers and instrument makers who had brought the flavour of Italy to the region.

'When did you first come to Champion Street Market?' Patsy asked now, wanting to distract him since he looked so gloomy suddenly.

'I open my first ice-a-cream-a stall here in 1938, just a year or so before I was interned.'

'That must have been painful, to be forced to leave what you had only just begun.'

Papa Bertalone gave a philosophical sigh as he peeled and pitted several pounds of peaches for the gelato with skilled fingers, Patsy working more slowly alongside.

'There was no sugar during the war so ice-a-creama was banned. I couldn't have carried on with the business anyway. There was some anti-Italian feeling, it is true, thanks to Mussolini, and my family they were put under the curfew, but I have no regrets.'

He lifted his hands, dripping in peach juice, as if to appeal for her understanding. 'Why would I blame the authorities? They had no choice but to lock me up. I was one of the enemy, though not through any fault of my own. I have no quarrel with them. The camp on the Isle of Man, it was humane and civilised. We were not too badly treated and I survived. Many who had to fight in the war did not, so what right have I to complain? I am proud to be Italian, and content to have brought up my family in this famous Lancashire town.'

Patsy knew that many of his fellow countrymen had attempted to disguise their identity by anglicising their names. Marco had never pretended to be anything other than what he was, a proud Italian. He and Carlotta had followed other family members to Manchester from a small town in southern Italy that nobody had ever heard of. Young and newly wed, they had fallen in love with this fine city, and with the warm, cheerful Mancunians who live here.

'Now times have changed and as well as Uncle's old cart, I also own two motorised ice-a-cream-a vans. I buy them so that I can expand the business for the sake of my sons.' He shook his head in a gesture of despair. 'But do they care? Allessandro and Giovanni are too young and Marc shows no interest. We waste the wages of a driver when my own son could be earning the money, for you, for the bambinos you will have together.'

Patsy wagged a gently admonishing finger. 'Hold on a minute, don't expect one of those any time soon. I'm in no hurry to be a mother.'

'Every woman she wants to be the mamma.'

Patsy laughingly shook her head. 'Designing and making hats keeps me fully occupied, *and* creatively fulfilled, thanks very much. I'm young yet, remember. Maybe in a few years, when I'm twenty-five or twenty-six, or even thirty, I'll start to think about kids.'

Papa Bertalone looked shocked. 'Thirty! But you would be too old for babies by then.'

Patsy laughed. 'I don't think so. There's plenty of time.' Judging it wise to change the subject, she asked him what made Italian ice cream so special.

Marco frowned, fully aware he'd been sidetracked, and said rather irritably, 'The best ingredients, what else? We use real fruit – fresh and ripe. We use creama, butter and, with some recipes, eggs. With these we can produce the finest ice-a-creama. There is none better in all of Manchester than Bertalone ice-a-creama, so much flavour, so good to lick.' He grinned and Patsy laughed again.

'I agree. Bertalone ice cream is the very best ice cream in the world,' and on an impulse she hugged the old man. But it seemed that even when you did have a family, life was still full of problems.

If asked, Carlotta would have agreed with her. As she made breakfast for her brood Mamma announced in brisk Italian, 'Gina, I am very disappointed in you. What were you thinking of? You are certainly *not* going to any dance. Papa and I won't hear of it. In any case, dancing would not be good for you.'

Gina cast a furious glare in her sister's direction but only twin spots of colour high on Carmina's cheekbones revealed any show of guilt over the fact she'd reneged on her promise to keep her secret.

'Why wouldn't it?'

Gina longed to live a normal life, to be free to do as she pleased like other girls. She adored her family, loved her siblings but envied them their freedom. Maria, the eldest, was the only Bertalone girl to be married. Antonia at twelve was the clever one while Lela was the complete opposite, never quite seeming to understand what was going on around her but happy for a cuddle if there was one going. Marta liked to organise and constantly made lists. She was determined to play an important role in the family business one day, while eight-year-old Gabriella was as much of a tomboy as her twin brother Giovanni.

They all enjoyed school or work, had friends and hobbies, played out in the street till it was quite dark, and never ailed a thing. Yet somehow Gina felt hedged in by restrictions, by doom-laden prophesies of what might happen to her if she walked too much, worked too hard, or stayed out too late.

She'd certainly worked hard on her recovery, still went to the public swimming baths twice a week, not to swim but to go through a carefully designed programme of exercises. She'd been fortunate to find a woman doctor who was forward thinking enough to suggest it.

Gina accepted her limitations. She had problems with lifting and carrying things. Her arms and elbows weren't too strong, but she had learned to 'read' her body, to judge when to stop an activity. If she noticed the onset of twitching or pain, or a reduction in control of the muscle, then she would rest. Yet too much inactivity was equally bad for her. It was vital that she keep mobile. Her condition was considered to be stable but, particularly with the right leg, she had to watch out for excessive fatigue.

Oh, but she felt good about herself inside, almost stronger for having come through it. OK, she was a little nervous, deep down, of going out into the wider world, but she was tired of being protected. Gina wanted to live a little.

'You know very well why,' her mother was saying, as she had a thousand times before. 'You are not like other girls. It worries me that you won't see that you have special problems.'

'You shouldn't worry so much, Mamma. I had poliomyelitis, we can't change that fact. But I'm making a good recovery so why won't you let me go out and enjoy life a little more, like other girls? I'm sixteen years old, for goodness' sake!'

'I can't let you because it would make you sick again. You know the doctor said you must not get too tired.' Her mother made a little huffing sound as she tipped porridge into Gina's bowl. 'Now eat up every scrap. We need to put some flesh on those bones, to keep those muscles strong. In any case, the Fabrianis they are big rivals of Papa, they do their utmost to damage his business. You know this, so how can you even think of going with that Luciano? He is nothing but a hooligan.'

'That's not true. Luc isn't a hooligan.'

'Stop this, Gina. Don't your mamma and papa know best what is good for you?'

'I'm not so sure,' Gina muttered into her porridge, but no one heard her. The Bertalones were not good at listening. Mamma was weeping and wailing over disobedient daughters while her siblings were rushing to put forward their own point of view on the subject. And of course they were all saying how much they loved and cared about her, suffocating her with their concern.

Carlotta wagged an admonishing finger in Gina's face. 'Let me tell you, girl, even if you are ever fit enough to consider marriage, it will not be to a man your papa and I do not like.'

Gina sighed. She might have pointed out that it was surely more important for *her* to like the man concerned, rather than her parents. Instead, she said, 'It's just a dance. No one has said anything about marriage.'

'*Dio*, I should hope not!' her mother cried, clapping her hands to her breast.

Gina escaped to her room but the subject came up yet again when Papa came home for his dinner. And he was clearly ready to firmly back her mother's stance.

'Why you not tell your mamma you go out with this boy, huh?' he demanded to know, and Gina had no answer. 'You see him how many months? One, two . . . more?'

'Since January.'

'*Since January*?' Carlotta threw up her hands in horror, letting out a string of rapid Italian in her distress. 'All this time you lie to me and keep secrets from your own mother. My child! My baby! *Mamma mia*! That settles it, you will stay in on Friday and help me with the sewing. When you are well enough to do this stupid rock 'n' roll, never mind start the courting, I will tell you.'

'Until then,' Papa declared, 'you will do exactly as your Mamma says, *sì?*'

Gina knew when she was beaten. She loved them both far too much to ever stand against them. Even so, she hated the look of pure victory on her sister's lovely face.

6

Gina and Carmina

Gina was not allowed out of the house for the entire week. Carlotta decided that her daughter must have been over-taxing herself, as she'd become far too emotional and tearful of late. She was instructed to rest, and largely confined to her room which had come to seem like a prison to her after the long years of her illness. Sometimes, in the afternoons, Mamma allowed her to come downstairs for a little while to play with the children, since it was Easter week and the school was closed.

It was no life for a sixteen-year-old girl on the brink of womanhood.

Gina guessed that a part of her mother's reasoning was the fact that these restrictions would also allow her to keep a better eye on her wayward daughter. Carlotta kept on lamenting how she had never expected Gina to be the one to cause her problems, how she had always been the good girl.

'Such an angel you were! So much the sweet charmer. Never a worry, not until . . .' Then her mother would wring her hands in despair over the unmentionable shame of her illness, and reach for her rosary to say thanks to the Virgin Mary that she'd been spared.

Gina endured it all in silence, occasionally stealing glances out of the window, whenever Mamma wasn't looking, in the hope of catching a glimpse of Luc.

She hoped that he would come knocking on her door and demand she be released from her prison. Of course, he didn't do any such thing. How would he dare to confront Papa or Mamma? This was no fairy tale and she was no Sleeping Beauty.

But she ached to see him, longed to have the courage to stand up to her parents and demand more independence now that she was reasonably well again. But how could she defy them when they'd devoted years of their lives to nursing her?

They wanted only what was best for her and Gina knew that she had to win them over gradually. She felt convinced they would come to trust her and cease to worry about her quite so much if she demonstrated sufficient common sense and maturity. Then she would be free, to start living as she so longed to do.

Except that she did wonder if all this nurturing and sheltering had made her too trusting and naïve. Was Carmina right when she accused her of not understanding how the world worked, or how boys really treated girls?

Gina had never been given the opportunity of a normal upbringing like her siblings. She knew nothing of the rough and tumble of school-life. She was an innocent, spending her days in a kind of bubble, protected by her loving family from the harsh reality of everyday life.

Was she a fool then to trust Luc?

Gina was haunted by the thought that what Carmina

had said about him might indeed be true. Was he guilty of two-timing her, of kissing other girls? Gina desperately wanted to believe that her sister's accusation was a result of malicious gossip, of which there was plenty in Champion Street. Otherwise how could she go on loving him?

It tormented her that she couldn't get out of the house to ask him for herself but since Mamma remained adamant that she stay in her room, in the end Gina was driven to writing him a letter. There seemed no alternative.

She chose her words with painstaking care and asked Carmina to deliver it for her, impressing upon her sister the urgency of giving it to Luc personally, without telling a soul, and to ask for a reply.

'Tell him that I need to talk to him. I *do* want to go with him to the dance, I *do* like him, and it's not my fault that I'm not allowed to go. Can I trust you to do this for me?'

'Of course you can trust me!'

Carmina had apologised for revealing Gina's secret meetings, and begged for forgiveness. The two sisters had made up, in a fashion, and Gina didn't feel she had any alternative but to trust her. It was vital that Luc get this letter and her younger sisters would only blab to Mamma right away, even if they managed not to actually lose the darned thing.

Besides, Carmina might be mercurial and quick tempered but she was the sister closest to Gina in age. They'd been quite close before her illness, and Carmina was the one who'd always shared her room.

When Gina had been frightened that she might never walk again, it was Carmina who'd cuddled beside her in bed in the middle of the night, reassuring her that she would indeed get well. She might claim that it was the only way for her to get any sleep but Gina knew her sister hated to show any sign of weakness. She would also run up and down stairs fetching hot-water bottles, romance novels from the library, fascinating titbits of gossip, or sneaking up extra treats such as Pringle's chocolate mints that Mamma didn't think were quite good for her. So how could she not trust her?

For days Gina waited for Luc's reply, but none came.

Once, she saw him crossing the street, weaving his way between the stalls, and her heart started to race. He was coming to the house. She waited, ready to hurry down the stairs as fast as she could were he to drop a reply to her note through the letterbox.

He stood for a moment looking up at her bedroom window. Embarrassed to be caught spying on him, Gina quickly stepped back to hide behind the curtains. After a moment, he thrust his hands in his pockets and walked away, shoulders hunched. He hadn't posted any letter.

In that moment, Gina knew, in her heart, that it was all over between them. He obviously could offer no defence to Carmina's accusation. He was guilty as charged and there was no alternative but to forget Luc Fabriani. She must put him right out of her mind.

Carmina picked up the dish of rum tortoni she'd just finished making and threw it at her brother. To her enormous irritation, he ducked and the glass dish shattered into a dozen pieces on the marble countertop, the ice cream splattering everywhere. Now she would have to clean it all up before Papa returned from his errands. But Carmina did so hate to be crossed.

'I *won't* work this afternoon, so there! I have some errands to do and I *must* get ready for the dance. If you won't stand in for me, then Patsy will have to do it instead.'

It being Friday and pay day, she was anxious to pick up the red and black cabbage-rose skirt she'd reserved from Dena, perhaps buy a blouse to go with it. Carmina never could keep money in her pocket for more than five minutes, although she'd made sure to put aside a few shillings for the dance tonight.

Patsy smiled pacifically, well used to Carmina's tantrums, and, reaching for a fresh dish, began to fill it with rum-flavoured gelato for the bemused customer.

'Sorry, but I have my course this afternoon, so can't help, love. I only popped in to ask you to remind Mamma that I'll be a bit late coming for supper tonight.'

Two afternoons a week on Wednesdays and Fridays, following a busy morning on the Higginson sisters' hat stall, Patsy attended a milliner's course at the local tech. The moment it was over she rushed to see Marc, her fiancé, in the tall terraced house on Champion Street where all the Bertalones lived noisily and happily together.

'Well, you'll just have to cancel it for once,' Carmina snapped. 'Aren't you even listening to me? This is *important*.'

Patsy took a breath, privately congratulating herself

on how well she could hold her own temper these days. A skill she would need once she was married into the volatile Bertalone family. 'I'm sorry, but we all have our duties and responsibilities to bear and my class is important too.' Far more important, Patsy privately considered, than a dance. 'You'll just have to manage as best you can.'

Carmina stamped her foot, having no intention of allowing her wishes to be so casually ignored. 'Don't you dare tell me what to do! You aren't in charge here, and I *have* to get ready for the dance. It's *vital* that I look my best tonight.'

She pulled the ribbon from her loosened hair and tied it up again, the curls rippling as if with a life of their own, and was instantly distracted by her own flattering reflection in the huge mirrors that lined the walls of the small icecream parlour. She began to preen herself, fiddling with the ribbon, teasing the kiss curls on her smooth brow.

Patsy thought the girl looked utterly bewitching, as always, particularly since her cheeks were suffused with hot temper. 'Why is this dance so important? Who are you going with?' she pleasantly enquired as she scooped up a generous portion of ice cream for the poor, patient customer.

The woman had quite lost interest in her treat as she listened avidly to what was going on, not wishing to miss a word of this fascinating conversation.

'She's going with my mate, Arnie,' Alessandro interrupted.

Carmina glanced at her brother in open contempt.

'I'm going nowhere with *boring* Arnie, even if he is your best friend. He has pimples and is far too young for me.'

Alessandro looked stricken. 'He's nearly sixteen, only a year younger than you, and he's doing something about the pimples. Besides, you *promised*! He's told everyone you're his date. It would be cruel to dump him. He'll be devastated!'

Carmina shrugged, the gesture eloquently expressing that she was well accustomed to breaking young men's hearts.

She was all too aware of her attraction to men. She could see the admiration in their eyes, the glint of excitement when they looked at her, even in older men like Alec Hall, let alone all the boys who would be eager to ask her to dance tonight. She'd noticed at once that he was smitten, positively salivating over her. It amused her that he probably hadn't even considered attending the dance until she'd suggested it. Which gave Carmina a delicious sense of power.

Oh, and didn't she enjoy that? Carmina loved men, so long as they appreciated her properly, which Luc Fabriani clearly did not. He would pay for his negligence, if she had her way.

Perhaps that was where older men had the advantage. They were far less concerned with themselves.

'For your information I've promised nothing! I *hinted* that I might be prepared to go with your friend, that's all.' She had, of course, done exactly the same with half a dozen other slavering hopefuls.

'You mean you kept him dangling in case you didn't get a better offer.'

Carmina stamped her foot so hard this time the brass scoops and spatulas in the dish beside her began to rattle. 'Of course I got a *better offer*. I've had dozens of offers, any number, and when I make up my mind which one I intend to accept, you'll be the first to know, little brother.'

It occurred to her in a moment of inspiration that she might well be able to take advantage of all this interest in her to make Luc jealous. Except that none of these plans would work if she didn't have ample time to get ready. It was vitally important that she stun him with her beauty tonight, and make him forget all about her stupid little sister.

Alessandro started mocking her about how she would soon be too fat to attract anyone, if she kept on eating the way she did, and Carmina retaliated with fury.

Patsy considered intervening in the quarrel which seemed to be escalating out of control but elected instead to persuade the long-suffering customer to sit at one of the little marble-topped tables while she finished preparing the Tortoni Sundae. The woman chose one close enough to the counter to hear the rest of the argument.

Alessandro pulled a face. 'As if the rich and handsome Luciano Fabriani would so much as glance in *your* direction. No wonder he asked our Gina to the dance, and not you. She's a sweetheart and you're a *witch*!'

Carmina's temper reached boiling point, but she could hardly refute the accusation without revealing that he had indeed once fancied her and then chucked her. That would be even more shaming. However, she'd devised a plan which tonight would have him eating out of her hand, she was quite sure of it.

She flicked her pony tail and a sly smile curved her sultry mouth, her mood changing as swiftly as a black cloud passing over the sun. 'Luc only asked Gina because he was afraid *I* might refuse him. He isn't Gina's type. It's me he really wants. I *shall* be with Luc tonight, make no mistake about that.'

A figure appeared in the mirror beside her, arms folded in typically censorious fashion.

'Oh, no you will not, *mia carina*. Haven't I already made it clear, that boy, for all his money and his fine looks is no good. He is not for Gina, not for you, not for *any* daughter of mine, so do not think for one moment that your father or I will allow it. And if you don't clean up that mess this instant, you won't be going to any dance either.'

'Mamma, I didn't hear you come in.'

'No, too full of yourself, I think.' Plump, homely Carlotta flung up her hands in a gesture of fretful despair then she held them out to Patsy as if begging for sympathy.

'Was any woman more harassed by daughters than I? Why did I ever imagine that to have seven was a blessing?'

Patsy suppressed a giggle and concentrated on scattering roasted almonds over the double scoop of rum ice cream, trying not to catch her eye.

Thirteen-year-old Alessandro snorted with laughter. 'Just as well you have three fine sons to make up for it then, Mamma.'

Carlotta flung her arms about her son, hugging him with flamboyant fervour while she showered his face with kisses, then slapped him playfully about the head, making him cry out in protest.

'You boys are the bane of my life too, always doing the bickering and the fighting, leaving your clothes all over the floor and never coming to meals on time. Was a mother ever more burdened?' she asked of the bemused customer.

Alessandro, who had heard it all before, kissed his mother soundly on one round pink cheek and grinned. 'Best thing to do then is to get some of us married off, and where better to start than with Carmina? She's the one who means to marry Luc. Poor Gina won't get a look in.'

'What nonsense you talk, boy? Who say she marry Luc? I will hear no more about this stupeed young man. *Sì*? None of my girls marry without Papa say OK.'

Carmina made no reply. She twitched her bouffant skirts, feigning indifference as she checked that her stocking seams were straight, that the low neck of her pale blue broderie anglaise blouse showed off her prettily rounded breasts to perfection. Taking a lipstick from her skirt pocket she began to apply it with painstaking care to full, pouting lips. 'I shall marry whomsoever I choose, when I'm good and ready. It's for me to say, not Papa.'

Carlotta snatched the bright pink lipstick out of her hands. Grabbing a cloth with one hand and her daughter's pony tail with the other, she began to scrub at her mouth, oblivious to her squeals and protests. 'No daughter of mine will look like a slut.'

Patsy delicately decorated the Tortoni Sundae with maraschino cherries and chocolate chips.

Alessandro stood for a moment longer listening to the screams of his mother and sister as they railed at each other, watched by a growing crowd ostensibly queuing for ice cream while clearly revealing by their smirking expressions their enjoyment of the floor show in the meantime. Satisfied with the trouble he'd caused, he slipped silently away.

Patsy stopped drizzling chocolate fudge sauce to rest a gentle hand on her future mother-in-law's arm, respectfully pointing out that they had an audience.

'*Mamma mia*!' Carlotta cried, noticing the curious onlookers for the first time and slapping her recalcitrant daughter once again for causing her so much embarrassment. 'See how you shamc me! Where is Alessandro? Why isn't your brother serving the ice-a-creama? See how you drive him away with your tantrums? Go wash that muck off your face and get back to work this minute. There will be no dance for *you* tonight either. You can stay home with your sister.'

Whereupon, Carmina snatched up the second dish of rum Tortoni that Patsy had painstakingly managed to prepare for the accommodating customer, and flung it after the first.

7

Amy

Amy wasn't the only one constantly under siege from Mavis. Her husband was more often the subject of her censure. After a long morning's work in the bakery, the poor man only had to set foot in the living room behind the shop for Mavis to start spreading newspapers all over her precious carpet rug, complaining bitterly about the dusting of flour emanating from his clothes.

'Can't you ever think to wipe them on the mat?'

'I did wipe them.'

'Not enough. You've brought half the bakery in with you. There's flour everywhere.'

Mavis was nothing if not houseproud, constantly plumping up cushions, getting Amy to polish the big mahogany dresser till you could see your face in its waxed surface, every ornament carefully placed upon its own crocheted mat which she called a doily. She had even had her curtains hung pattern side to the street so that folk could admire them.

Thomas would massage his hands, red and swollen from all the kneading and pounding he'd been doing that morning, and say no more.

No matter how careful he was not to upset her, she

loved to find fault, to contradict and criticise him in front of others, making him look like a right gormless idiot. And if he didn't hang his coat on the right hook, line up his slippers by the hearth just so, or committed the ultimate sin of leaving his pipe and tobacco pouch tucked down the crack of the cushion in his wing chair, she'd go spare. His life wouldn't be worth living for days.

Thomas was not a man who cared for battles, particularly with a wife who always managed to win.

On the rare occasions he did come out on top, she'd make sure that he lived to regret it. She would barely speak to him for days and put him on what Thomas called 'hard rations'. Where was the point in engaging with an enemy who didn't play by gentleman's rules?

Come to think of it, he could do with them Peace Marchers in this house, though she'd take not a scrap of notice of them either.

She was a woman with her own way of going about things, was Mavis.

When she was in one of her moods, he'd eat his dinner in silence then retire to his bed for an hour or two, catching up on the sleep he missed by having to be up before dawn to bake bread.

After his rest he would put on his cap and old tweed jacket, make himself a flask of coffee and go off without a word to dig his vegetable patch, or sit in his little wooden hut and contemplate life. Sometimes he would stop off at Lizzie Pringle's stall on the way to buy a few mint chocolates, his favourite.

The allotment was Thomas's pride and joy. That was

the place he most liked to be. Now that Chris was in the business with him, he tended to spend less time in the bakery and more hours growing his precious vegetables: radishes and beetroot, carrots and cos lettuce, raspberries and gooseberries. Thomas had even won prizes for his leeks. The allotment was his sanctuary – much needed with a wife like Mavis. He dreamed of retiring altogether and spending all his time there.

On his return she would make him sit in the backyard until he'd stripped off to his long-johns, no matter if there was a bitter north-east wind blowing.

'I don't want no nasty bugs and spiders in my house.'

Funny how she always referred to it as *her* house, except when bills needed paying when it was *his* business. Mavis found it demeaning to live behind the baker's shop, had complained about their lack of privacy almost daily throughout their married life.

'If we had a proper house . . .' she would say, whenever she launched into one of her complaints.

'If I didn't have to listen to that shop bell jangling all day my nerves wouldn't be half so bad,' was another.

There were times when Thomas didn't like himself very much, only too aware that he should stand up to his bullying wife more. And he the man who'd done battle royal with Big Molly Poulson, flinging custard tarts and lemon meringue pies at each other on one occasion, as part of a feud that had lasted for most of his adult life. Not that he'd been the cause of it, but Big Molly held him accountable for something his older brother had foolishly done years before.

He dreaded to think how Mavis would react if he

ever did make a stand against *her*. He'd waved the flag of truce so many times it was threadbare, so happen he should consider marshalling some big guns instead.

Amy watched all of this in sympathetic silence, her heart going out to the beleaguered Thomas for he was surely a saint.

Chris maintained that his father had lost all self-respect by allowing himself to become hen-pecked. Amy had some experience of this with her own father, yet Ozzy had a way of going his own way, of standing up to her big noisy mother without actually appearing to. Chris's father was quite another matter. Firm enough with his son, but putty in the hands of his over-bearing wife.

Amy felt she was in danger of falling into the same trap: doing as she was told simply for peace.

Their sex life too had been severely hampered by living with his parents, cramped in the back bedroom where Chris had lived as a boy, his old comics still lying about and his cricket bat standing in the corner. It had been difficult enough for them to consummate their marriage in the first place, but then she'd quickly fallen pregnant and all plans for moving had been put on hold.

Since coming to live with the Georges, following their marriage just a few months ago, Amy's patience had been stretched to its limit. She'd discovered that her mother-in-law was generally right about most things, at least in her own opinion.

Mavis seemed to delight in proving how useless Amy was as a wife, constantly finding fault with her efforts as she had done over the starch incident. There were a whole string of tasks she was forbidden to do for her own husband, like darn his socks, or fold his shirts since his mother obviously knew best how he liked them done. She wasn't even allowed to make his dinner without a stream of advice and criticism.

Today she was being taught how to skin and joint a rabbit and deal with the heart, kidneys and the suet surrounding each. It might, as Mavis insisted, be a vital part of the cooking process, but Amy wasn't enjoying the task one little bit.

She was wearing a large apron over her print maternity smock and pants with the button-up flap at the front, and it was all smeared with blood and other unmentionable mess.

When they were finished, the pastry mixed and rolled to Mavis's satisfaction and the rabbit pie standing on the Formica-topped kitchen cupboard ready for the oven, Amy was quite certain she wouldn't be able to eat a mouthful.

'Now go and change, and see that you wash your hands thoroughly,' Mavis scolded, as if she were still a child needing to be told such things.

'I've nothing else to put on. My other smock is washed but not yet dry enough to iron.' Amy glanced at the clothes-horse laden with clothes that stood by the kitchen range.

'Don't you have a decent skirt to wear? Or a dress that fits?'

'Yes, but those are for best. We're saving our money for the baby and for a home of our own. What's the point of wasting it on clothes I'll only wear for a few months?'

'We always changed for dinner when I was a gel,' Mavis snapped.

'I really don't think Chris would expect me to.' Not just for rabbit pie, Amy thought.

'It's important for a woman not to let herself go, even when she's married.'

Mavis was always impeccably well groomed, in a sensible, wholesome sort of way. She claimed not to slavishly follow fashion, although Amy would often see her poring over the photographs of models in her *Woman's Weekly*. Even when she was ostensibly 'doing the housework' she would be smartly attired in twin-set and pearls, a clean frilly apron tied about her waist which she changed for a fresh one every single day.

She always wore dark red lipstick on her small tight mouth, and attempted to cover the wrinkles on her sagging cheeks with Goya face powder. Her natural wavy brown hair was worn in a neat pleat at the back of her head. It was slightly greasy as she washed it only on Fridays with Silvikrin shampoo, and visited the hair-dresser once a month for a trim. She would tell Amy off for washing hers too often, or at the wrong time of the month. Mavis was full of dire warnings and old wives' tales.

'Chris seems happy enough with me the way I am,' she would protest.

'Well, let me tell you men can very quickly start to look elsewhere if you don't take proper care of your-self, girl.'

Amy tried not to giggle at the thought of the beleaguered Thomas daring to look elsewhere, much as he might suffer at his wife's hands. Yet there was a resentment building up inside herself over this constant litany of advice and put-downs. Somewhere inside her head a voice was screaming to be let out, but Amy knew better than to allow these dangerous emotions free rein. She went quietly upstairs to examine her meagre wardrobe.

Amy felt desperate for some peace, a place of their own, for things to be perfect when their first child was born. She knew in her heart that something must be done to improve their lives. Quite how she was to achieve this minor miracle, she really didn't know.

It was one day when she was out and about in the market that Amy spotted a young man carrying a clipboard. She overheard him asking people if they would sign his petition for peace. He was obviously one of those Ban the Bomb people and, inspired by the spirit of the marchers, Amy went over and offered to sign. He looked pleased.

'Hey, I know you. It's Jeff Stockton, isn't it? Weren't we in the same class at primary school?'

The young man grinned. 'Amy Poulson, as I live and breathe.'

'Amy George now,' she said, patting her swollen belly. 'Good to see you again, Jeff.' They shook hands, his grip firm.

He was tall and lanky with pale grey eyes, a long bony nose, wide smiling mouth and untidy brown hair.

Quite attractive really, considering how he'd looked as a boy.

'I remember you in those awful grey short trousers, your socks always falling down . . .'

'. . . and a plaster over one of the lenses on my glasses because apparently I had a lazy eye.' Jeff laughed, pushing his spectacles back up his nose. 'Lot of good that did. I remember you with pigtails, frizzy and ginger.'

'Auburn, if you don't mind,' Amy corrected him. 'You got your scholarship, I seem to remember, and went to the grammar school?'

Jeff nodded. 'Now, I'm studying to be a teacher myself, but I'm on my Easter vac.'

Amy was impressed. 'Were you part of the march the other day? I saw it come through the market. You all looked very wet, but then so was I, standing in the pouring rain watching.'

'We were all soaked to the skin, but it was worth it. We made our point and got hundreds of signatures. You should have come and joined us, Amy. You'd have been very welcome.'

'I got an earful from my husband as it was, for being so daft as to wet the baby's head before ever it gets born,' she ruefully admitted. And then after a fractional pause, 'I would like to help though, if there were something I could do which didn't involve marching in the rain while pregnant.'

'Are you serious? We're desperate for volunteers. You could help with this job for a start, or making posters, or writing letters to the press. There are any number of things that need doing.'

'Don't ask me to write any letters but I'll give you a break with that clip-board, if you like. Go and warm yourself up with a frothy coffee and a toasted tea cake in Belle's Café. I'll still be here when you get back.'

'You're sure?'

'Absolutely. I've nothing else important to do right now. Go on, you look all pale and pinched around the gills.'

'Great!' Handing her the clip-board with its sheaf of papers filled with lines of signatures, Jeff strode away, then just as quickly bounded back. 'You are sure about this, are you? I don't want you getting into trouble with your husband again.'

'Go on, take your break, then afterwards you can tell me more about your campaign.'

'Thanks, Amy. You always were a good mate,' and he ruffled her untidy hair before dashing off.

What have I done? Amy thought, overcome by her own daring as she watched him stride away across to the market hall and the fuggy warmth of Belle's Café. Oh, dear! She didn't care to imagine what Mavis would have to say about her joining the Peace Movement.

Mavis was at that precise moment crossing the street on her way to buy a nice piece of haddock for her husband's tea. Thomas enjoyed it poached, with a dab of butter. But she hadn't missed this little exchange between her daughter-in-law and the young man.

8

Patsy and Carmina

Patsy could hear the noise long before she reached the house. Even as she tripped up the very same steps on which she used to watch the Bertalone girls in their rainbow-coloured dresses kiss goodbye to their mamma and papa every morning, she could hear the shrieks within.

Yet another squabble.

She was eager to see Marc and give him a kiss at the end of a long day spent apart. On the days when she attended her millinery course, he usually arrived home from his job at Kendals department store a little before her, so Patsy expected to find him just as eagerly waiting for her. Often he would meet her at the end of Champion Street and she'd been disappointed to find he wasn't there waiting for her this evening. But then he might have been late home himself.

She took off her coat and hung it on the hall stand then walked into the living room. Everyone called out a welcome: Mamma Bertalone hugged her, Alessandro pretended to box with her, as he was off that evening to Barry Holmes's club. Gina gave her usual warm smile but Carmina glanced coolly across at her then flung herself on to Marc's lap, effectively preventing him from getting up and coming to kiss his fiancée.

Despite her disgraceful behaviour that morning, Carmina evidently had every intention of going to the dance. She sat on Marc's knee humbly apologising for breaking Papa's best glass dishes, contriving to put the right degree of sincerity into her voice in an effort to win over her big brother's support. Sweet-talking her way out of trouble as she had done all her life.

'It was Alessandro's fault and Patsy made things worse by interfering.'

'Hey, I was only trying to calm things down between the pair of you.' Even though she knew it to be unwise, Patsy couldn't resist leaping to her own defence. She hated to think that Marc might assume Carmina's assessment of their dispute was accurate.

'You're always interfering in matters that don't concern you,' Carmina snapped. 'Yet you aren't even *family*, so keep your nose out of my affairs.'

'Carmina!' scolded her mother. 'That is no way to speak to your *cognata*.'

'She isn't my sister-in-law,' Carmina yelled. 'Not yet!'

'As good as,' Marc quietly put in.

Carlotta gabbled something furiously in Italian that Patsy didn't understand but which made Carmina flush bright red.

She was grateful for Carlotta's support as she seemed to have found a particular rival in Marc's sister. Carmina was jealous of the fact her big brother had a new love in his life, viewing Patsy as some sort of competitor for his affections, which was ridiculous. Surely the love of a sister was vastly different to that of the woman you intended to marry?

Mamma put down her sewing to frown at Carmina, and speaking in her halting English, said, 'How can you go to the dance? You have the tantrum in front of everyone. You break Papa's best glass dishes.'

'Carmina is quite right. I shouldn't have spoken,' Patsy said, rather stiffly. 'The matter has nothing at all to do with me.'

'She stay home with Gina. They both naughty girls.'

Gina was seated in a corner, hemming a pink bridesmaid's dress by the light of the standard lamp. She glanced up at mention of her name but made no comment. Like a bird in a cage, her dream of freedom was a fragile thing.

Looking at her, Patsy's heart filled with pity. It was too easy to overlook Gina, to forget that she was even there, which was unfair. She was a young girl, after all, like any other. And she did wonder if Carmina had had a hand in her sister being banned from attending the dance. The two certainly didn't get on.

Carmina, delighted by Patsy's apology, yet sensing a coolness in her brother's tone, judged it wise to manufacture a few tears. 'If you tell Papa, I will *die*! Why does nobody love me?'

The ploy worked as Marc put his arms about her, assuring Carmina that of course he loved her, they all did, but that she must learn to guard her quick temper and not be nasty to people.

Marc cast Patsy an anguished 'what are we to do with her?' kind of look; shrugging his shoulders in that expressive Italian way. 'I'm sure Patsy didn't mean to interfere,' he said, attempting to placate his sister.

'Yes, she did. She's always doing it. All I needed was enough time to get ready but she absolutely refused to help, even though I begged and begged her to, and explained how *important* it was.'

Patsy was still watching Gina, saw how the big cinnamon eyes seemed to widen, the lovely dark eyelashes fluttered as if with surprise, before she dipped her chin to concentrate on her sewing. A tear dropped on to the pink satin and, horrified, Gina wiped it quickly away. Patsy longed to say something, but dare not.

'If it *is* so important,' Marc was saying, 'then you should behave better. You must earn the right to go. When Papa finds out how rude you have been to his customers, he will agree that you must be punished.'

'Oh, but please let him punish me in some other way. I *can't* miss the dance, really I can't, Marc. I'll scrub the steps, fill the coal bucket every morning, wash up for a week, *anything*.'

Marc laughed, knowing how much his beautiful, spoiled sister hated menial household tasks.

Carmina flounced off his knee in a huff. 'Stop laughing at me, I've bought a new outfit, shoes, bag, everything!'

'So have I,' Gina said, but not one of her noisy, quarrelsome family heard her.

'You cannot always have what you want, much as you might wish to,' Marc gently pointed out, still sounding highly amused.

Carmina allowed the tears to fill her big brown eyes

and slide down her cheeks. 'Papa will understand. He knows that all my life I have *desperately* wanted friends.'

She began clasping and unclasping her hands in a display of heart-rending anguish, her wide, sensual mouth down-turned in an agony of self-pity as she went first to her mother to beg forgiveness, then back to her brother. She beat his broad chest with small clenched fists, sobbing as if her heart was broken.

All the younger children watched in awe and admiration. Giovanni and Gabby paused in their game of Sorry!, Lela let her dressing-doll flutter to the floor and Marta stopped sticking stamps in her album. Patsy too thought it a fine show, and, judging by the glances mother and son were exchanging, it was producing the desired effect.

Carmina twisted their heart-strings one more notch. 'For so much of my childhood I felt like an outcast because my beloved papa was held prisoner, interned for no better reason than his nationality. No one would even *speak* to me for *years*.'

'Don't exaggerate,' Carlotta scoffed. 'The people of Manchester, they good and kind to we Italians. Not like the stupeed government. Your papa, he the one to suffer most. He the one locked up in that bad camp, and you just a child.'

'But I felt so alone. Now, at last, I have found some friends and you're all trying to spoil things for me.' Carmina sank on to a stool and put her head in her hands in a gesture of utter despair. 'Oh, it's so unfair. Why do you all treat me so badly? I don't understand.'

Patsy half expected violins to start up and was

beginning to find great difficulty in keeping a straight face throughout the entire over-dramatised performance.

'You would keep me a prisoner too, like Gina, over one broken dish.'

They all looked across at Gina and smiled at her sympathetically, as if it was taken for granted that she must stay in.

'Two dishes,' her mother robustly reminded her.

'Two,' Carmina grudgingly agreed. 'But how will I *ever* find a man to marry if I'm *never* allowed to go out?'

Gina quietly remarked, 'How will *I* ever find a boyfriend either, if I'm never allowed to do anything?'

'You are sick,' Carlotta said, dismissing her with a sad shake of the head. 'The boys and the marriage they are not for you, my precious one.'

Marc drily remarked that Carmina's complaint might be something of an exaggeration since she was always out somewhere with these friends of hers. Patsy could tell that he was weakening, unable to bear the dispute for much longer. No more could she. Carmina's tantrums were always emotionally draining.

'I'll work extra hours tomorrow,' Carmina promised, ignoring Gina and offering Marc her most ravishing smile. 'And I'll bring you a cup of tea in bed every morning.'

'All right, all right,' Marc laughed. 'Enough! Let us settle this matter once and for all, without bothering Papa. Perhaps if you say sorry to Mamma, she will forgive you and allow you to go to the dance.' He glanced enquiringly up at his mother who let out a heavy, resigned sigh. Carmina squealed with delight.

Instantly flinging off the mantle of contrived self-pity she flew about the room, this time giving excited little hugs and kisses all round. Carmina had got her own way yet again.

The argument had ended almost as quickly as it had begun, typical Bertalone behaviour. They were never cross with each other for long, never held grudges. Now Mamma was serving out the lasagne, Marta was busily laying the table, Antonia was curled up in a chair reading a Chalet School book, Lela cuddling her father and Giovanni and Gabby were happily working on an Airfix kit in a corner, content with each other's company and ignoring everyone.

Once supper was cleared away Patsy sat with Mamma, helping her to embroider flowers along the hem of her wedding gown.

'You can begin your penance by clearing away the dishes,' Mamma said, attempting to sound stern while Carmina rained kisses upon her plump cheeks.

Carmina happily collected up the plates but on her way to the kitchen she passed close by Patsy and somehow contrived to trip over her own feet. A fork slid from the top of the pile of dishes and dropped on to the white satin wedding gown, staining it with a splash of orange pasta sauce.

'*Mamma mia*!' Carlotta cried, leaping up to rescue it while Patsy sat paralysed with horror. 'Don't fret, don't fret. It is only a small stain and we can cover it with some appliqué flowers. No one will notice. It was an accident.'

Patsy looked up into Carmina's artfully contrite expression and knew it had been anything but. Her new rival had deliberately taken her revenge for Patsy's alleged interference.

9

Carmina and Gina

Carmina was jubilant. She'd got her own way and here she was bopping to Elvis Presley's 'Hound Dog'. She spun about making her can-can petticoats swirl to reveal long shapely legs. She felt daring and wonderfully attractive.

Some of the girls were in stiletto heels, others in bobby sox, jeans and Sloppy Joe sweaters. Carmina was wearing the skirt she'd bought from Dena Dobson: polished black cotton printed with red cabbage roses, her favourite colour. Her white blouse, with its neat Peter Pan collar, strained over her full breasts, cinched in at the waist with a three-inch-wide black patent belt that matched her new strappy shoes and clutch bag. She felt young and beautiful, aware of boys' eyes hungrily watching her, dazzled by her own power.

A queue of ardent admirers was already hovering in the hope of claiming her as a partner. Unfortunately, Luc wasn't among them, but Carmina meant to win him too, one way or another.

It was all so exciting. She'd danced every dance so far, played by Terry Hall and his skiffle group. The Hand Jive, The Stroll, lots of bopping and rockin' 'n' rollin', and of course the sexy Cha Cha. Arnie had bought her a milkshake, Jake Hemley had told her that she looked the mostest and she'd even smooched with Kevin Ramsay, who must be twenty-five at least, although only so that she could let Luc see how much in demand she was.

As she made her way back to her friends Carmina spotted him. He was weaving his way through the crowd, making a bee-line straight for her, and her heart quickened. She'd known all along that it was herself who Luc Fabriani really fancied, and not Gina at all.

He was wearing a draped blue jacket with long lapels fastened with a single link button, and smartly tailored black trousers. He looked incredibly sexy and fashionable but unusually conventional, not nearly so cool or with-it as she remembered. His hair, almost black, was flicked up into an artfully disordered quiff, although he seemed to have shortened his sideburns.

He reminded Carmina of the dreamboats in her magazine, a pin-up every bit as exciting as Ricky Nelson and Troy Donahue whose pictures she had stuck to the wall of their bedroom. Gina was more of a Pat Boone fan.

Folding her arms, she looked him over from head to toe. 'What happened to the leather jacket and the black turtleneck sweater? You never used to go out without them?'

'Gina doesn't care for them.'

Carmina felt as if he'd struck her. She couldn't believe that he would actually change his appearance to suit any girl, let alone her boring sister.

'Has she not come then?' he asked, looking around

as if half expecting to see her. Carmina went quite cold inside. This was not what she wished to hear. Tilting her head provocatively, she fixed him with a radiant smile.

'Doesn't really care for dancing, not with the leg . . . you know. Anyway, why would you want the monkey when you can have the organ grinder?'

She saw Luc wince slightly at her caustic comment so that she almost regretted saying it. But then he surprised her even more with a sharp retort of his own.

'She never seems to let it stop her doing stuff as a rule.'

'Depends how much she wants to do whatever it is, I suppose,' Carmina snapped right back. 'She didn't seem too bothered about missing this dance, or you for that matter. In fact, Gina asked me to tell you that it's all over between you. She wants to finish with you, as you really aren't her type.'

Silence. Had she not found it so incredibly hard to believe, Carmina would have said he looked stunned, and deeply disappointed.

Carmina stepped closer, fluttering her eyelashes as she flicked him a flirtatious smile, allowing him ample opportunity to catch a whiff of her favourite Max Factor Primitif perfume that she'd almost drenched herself in before coming out. She thought it so delicious and romantic he'd surely instantly forget about Gina and be quite unable to resist her.

Luc glowered down at her, deep creases etched between those dark enigmatic eyes. 'Why?'

'Sorry?'

'Why would Gina want to finish with me? We were getting on really well.'

Carmina gave a little shrug. 'She seems to think you've been a naughty boy, which I'm sure you have. When did you ever stay faithful to a girl? You certainly never were to me.' That had been a big bone of contention between them at the time they were going out together, the way Luc was always off chasing some bit of skirt or other.

'I've changed. For the better, I hope. Perhaps I've matured. OK, you and I had a bit of fun, but what I feel for Gina is different. She's special, at least she is to me.'

Carmina thought she might vomit all over his polished winkle-picker shoes.

Oh, God, but he was so handsome, so assured, so *dangerous*! His mouth was full and so very kissable that Carmina longed to reach up and taste it, but that wasn't what *nice* girls did, was it? She must try to remember to play hard-to-get. That was the best way to catch him.

'Spare me the hearts and flowers,' she said, and tossing him a careless smile, spun on her heel and walked away. Otherwise, she might well have hit him. Anyway, if she knew Luc Fabriani, he'd soon come running.

Gina sat at home alone in her room and thought of what might have been, indulging in a bout of uncharacteristic self-pity.

She was bored with sitting with her family night after

night listening to some orchestral concert or operetta on the wireless. Tired of sewing. Tired of being brave.

Had things been different and she hadn't developed poliomyelitis when she was ten years old, she could have been attending her first dance this evening, with a boy she liked a great deal, might even be growing to love. She would have been the one getting dressed up to go out, the one putting on lipstick, and the new skirt and top she'd secretly bought for herself from the small allowance Papa gave her.

Instead, she felt as if she were being dragged back into childhood, back to those bitter dark days of pain and suffering.

Carmina was the one going out into the world, as always. The one who was allowed a normal life to enjoy herself while Gina wasn't permitted to do anything: no boy-friend, no dances, not even a job.

She'd tried playing chess with Antonia but her mind wasn't on the game. Marta had made an effort to keep her company, helping her to reorganise Gina's collection of Whimsies. These were little porcelain animals: a hedgehog, tortoise, frog, rabbit, owl, dogs and farm animals which family and friends had bought her over the years to add to her collection whenever she'd been facing yet another operation, or having a hard time. Somehow the cheery little figures had offered a kind of comfort. Not tonight.

Gina was all too bitterly aware that while she sat listening to Marta chatter away as she rearranged the ornaments on the shelves Papa had made specially for the purpose, Luc was dancing with some other girl, kissing someone else, someone who was normal. He probably hadn't even given her a thought.

As the evening progressed Carmina became quite certain that Luc was watching her, giving her the kind of measured look any girl could interpret. Maybe he was thinking better of his declaration of devotion to the antiseptic Gina.

Exciting little shivers rippled down her spine as she imagined Luc's glorious dark eyes blatantly undressing her, examining every luscious curve, the olive tone of her skin, the sheen of her hair. She came over all hot and bothered at the thought of his hands following the same track. He was within her grasp, Carmina was sure of it.

And then to her complete delight he came over. 'Wanna dance?'

'Sure.' She answered with a casual disinterest, as if to imply she really didn't care one way or the other.

It was a Johnny Mathis number, 'The Twelfth of Never', the kind of song where you barely moved an inch, which was exactly what she'd dreamed of night after night for *weeks*.

'*I'll love you 'til the poets run out of rhyme. Until the Twelfth of Never and that's a long, long time.*'

Oh, if only he would love *her* like that. He was holding her quite loosely, and he seemed to be miles away, deep in thought, no doubt wondering how he could get her to go out with him again without losing face.

Carmina pressed herself closer so that she could feel the hard heat of his body searing through her blouse right to her bare flesh. Her can-can petticoat bunched a little around her bare thighs and he adjusted his position slightly to accommodate it, which allowed Carmina the opportunity to slip one of her legs between his. It was the most thrilling moment of her life.

He cleared his throat. 'You reckon Gina doesn't fancy me any more, then?'

Not Gina again! Carmina could hardly believe it. She really had no wish to be constantly reminded of her dratted sister. She nestled closer against his broad hard chest, breathing in the exotic scent of his after-shave.

'My sister is such a home bird. Doesn't care to go out much at all, not since she had the polio. She's so *boring!* Not in the least bit interested in boys, or films, music, dancing, whatever. She loves to sew and knit, listen to the wireless, that sort of stuff. Not like me.' And Carmina awarded him her most entrancing smile.

Luc seemed unusually thoughtful. 'She enjoyed the flicks well enough when I took her.'

Carmina swallowed her silent fury. 'I'm sure she was only being polite. She's like that, is darling Gina. Hates to hurt a person's feelings. She did confide in me that you'd been seeing each other *secretly*, which proves it was against her better judgement.'

There was a silence, and then he looked down at her as if from afar, a hardness to his gaze she'd never seen before. 'It's not true that I cheated on her. Who told her all those lies, I wonder?'

'I really couldn't say.' Carmina smiled up at him in wide-eyed innocence. 'I can see you're upset. Just as well I'm here, to cheer you up.'

He gave a snort of disbelief. 'And will you also confide in her that I danced with her sexy, glamorous sister?'

'Possibly not. Are you going to tell her?'

They regarded each other for a long moment, then he allowed his chin to rest against the pulse that beat in her temple and went on swaying to the music. So *delicious*!

When the dance was over he nodded briefly and walked away. Carmina's heart sank as she went drearily back to her friends.

During the supper interval Carmina wandered over to speak to Alec Hall, as she'd promised she would, feeling the need to boost her confidence with a little gentle flirtation. She'd most carefully manipulated this situation so that everything was in place to execute her plan yet felt suddenly overcome by uncertainty over the outcome. Would Luc succumb? Could she make him want her as much as she wanted him?

Carmina almost laughed at her own foolishness. Of course Luc would succumb. When had a man ever been able to resist her? She was turning soft, that's all it was.

There had been one scary moment this week when Gina had pressed her to deliver a letter. She'd very nearly weakened and done as she was bid, feeling just a little sorry for her fretful sister, as she had so many times in the past. But one glance at Luc's darkly handsome good looks as he crossed the market towards her, and she'd felt no compunction at all about dumping it in a nearby litter bin.

She felt rather like a cat who would purr and rub against people so that they might stroke her and make her feel good about herself. But Carmina could just as easily stretch out her claws and cruelly scratch them, or walk away with her nose in the air, tail swishing, completely independent.

Carmina quite liked this trait in herself, but playing a game of cat and mouse with Alec Hall might sharpen her skills nicely.

The room was hot and crowded, but even so she pressed herself close against him, ostensibly to read the label on the record he was sliding on to the turntable but really so that he could appreciate the soft swell of her breast.

'"At The Hop" with Danny and the Juniors. Great, I like that one.'

Alec felt strangely at a loss for words as he drank in the sight and smell of her. She was like a ripe peach, soft and round in all the right places, ready for the plucking. And he was most certainly the man for the job, so why did he hesitate? Because she was so young, and no doubt a virgin? That had never stopped him before, certainly not with his lovely Joo Eun who had welcomed him as if he were a hero.

Carmina batted her eyelashes and smiled, really rather enjoying the way he gazed at her, apparently struck dumb by the attention she was giving him.

He had the kind of eyes which seemed to look right through to her very soul, a hint of derisory appreciation in their steady, penetrating gaze, yet contriving to reveal nothing of his own feelings in their smoky-grey depths. He possessed the kind of mature good looks that would appeal to any young girl: charming, debonair, cultured, and that most enticing turn-on of all . . . experienced.

He cleared his throat, hurried to put on another record. 'I'd ask you to dance only I'm on duty.'

Carmina shrugged, which jiggled her breasts and brought his eyes flicking over her and then quickly away again. 'Maybe later then, when the main band comes back and you're off-duty?' She didn't miss how his eyes brightened at her suggestion.

'OK.'

'See you,' and she swung about on her high heels and sauntered elegantly away, deeply aware of his eyes following every sway of her hips. She dearly hoped that Luc had noticed too.

10

Carmina

The moment the band came back Carmina saw Alec weaving his way across the dance floor towards her, and her heart sank. She hadn't meant it about dancing with him. She'd just needed reassurance of her own power. Then, as luck would have it, Luc got to her first. One minute she was giggling with her friends over what remained of the plated sandwiches and sausage rolls, the next he was standing beside her, his gaze burning into hers. He didn't even ask her this time, just jerked his head and took her hand, as if he wanted to resist her, but couldn't.

Carmina meekly followed him on to the dance floor, with only one backward glance of triumph to her neglected friends.

This time it was a jive to 'Rave On', a Buddy Holly hit, and she had no trouble at all in keeping up with him. Luc had rhythm, never missed a beat, his hands sure and certain, twirling and catching her, spinning her round then holding her close to his chest making her heart race, and sweat break out between her breasts. She wondered if he were as aware of her as she was of him.

The music ended and for one dreadful moment she

thought he was going to walk away a second time. In desperation, she flapped her hands to fan herself, 'It's hot in here! I feel a bit faint.'

A second's pause and then he said, 'Let's get some air.' His voice sounded gruff, almost angry. Snatching hold of her hand, he began to pull her through the crowd.

Carmina's heart soared. She'd caught him at last. He didn't need air any more than she did. She knew exactly what he wanted, but then didn't she understand men perfectly?

Once outside in the back alley Luc took out a packet of Gold Flake and lit up while Carmina leaned back against the wall, revealing the long white curve of her throat. She'd surreptitiously unfastened the top three buttons of her blouse so that he could see right down into her bra, should he have the inclination. He'd always rather liked her breasts.

Licking her lips with the flick of her pink tongue, she gazed up at him through her lashes. After a moment, annoyed by his inattention, she asked him, 'Aren't you going to kiss me?'

He looked at her, saying nothing.

'I'm a much better kisser than our Gina. But then you know that, don't you?'

When still he didn't respond, she pushed herself forward and slid her arms about his neck, nibbling tantalisingly at his full lower lip with her sharp white teeth. He swore softly under his breath and for one dreadful moment she thought he was going to shove her away.

'You're a real hell-cat, Carmina Bertalone. Did anyone ever tell you that?'

'And you're a wolf.'

With one vicious movement he flung the cigarette away and kissed her savagely, exactly as she'd hoped he would. The sensation was electrifying, even the taste of the beer he'd drunk earlier filled her with a strange pulsing excitement. Carmina could scarcely breathe, nor did she want to. His tongue was in her mouth, his hands on her bottom, squeezing her to him. The next instant he flung himself off her, and swore loudly this time.

'Satisfied now? Is that what you wanted, a bit of rough?'

'Isn't it what *you* wanted when I suggested we come out for a bit of fresh air?' she teased.

'Drat it, no, it damn well isn't! I asked you outside because I wanted to tell you about how it is with me and Gina, and to ask you to – leave – me – alone.' He punctuated his words, seeming to hit her with them one by one.

Carmina laughed. A rowdy group of revellers burst out of the door of the dance hall, and with the first drops of another rain shower starting, said, 'OK, so you want to talk. There's precious little privacy here, and I really don't want to ruin my hair, so why don't we sit in your car for a minute? We'd be much more comfortable.'

He glowered at her as if debating whether he could refuse. 'Only if you'll listen to what I have to say.'

'Of course I'll listen. Where did you park it? Come on, it's raining hard now and I'm getting soaked.'

* * *

He owned a beat-up old Morris which he kept going with spare parts from scrap yards. He and his mate, Jake Hemley, were often to be found with their heads under the bonnet, tinkering with the engine. With the rickety doors locked to stop them falling open, rain washing the windscreen and their breaths steaming up the inside, Carmina felt as if they were in their very own private little world.

A memory of the letter Gina had so painstakingly written flashed into her mind, but she dismissed it instantly. She was glad she'd dumped it in the litter bin.

Carmina almost laughed out loud at the thought of her loyal sister sitting obediently at home while she was the one tucked up with Luc in the intimacy of his car. If it had been her, she'd have defied Mamma's rules and slipped out to speak to him personally. She'd have climbed out of the kitchen window, if necessary, and sneaked off to the dance anyway. Gina was a fool to herself, and Carmina was tired of running errands for her.

'Go and keep your sister company,' had been Mamma's constant cry. 'Go fetch her a library book, take her some sweeties. Talk to her. She gets lonely stuck on her own in that bedroom.'

Nag, nag, nag, and all because the girl was sick. Her own needs always took second place to her pathetic sister and Carmina became sick and tired of waiting on her, of being seen as the problem child. Gina was the one who was the nuisance, not her. Carmina had no wish to deny the girl the joys of a wonderful recovery yet nor did she want Gina to move in on *her* friends, *her* life. Luc was hers. She should have known that and left him well alone. Besides, Gina wasn't wise in the ways of the world and should learn not to be so stupidly naïve and trusting. The silly girl didn't deserve him, and shouldn't be allowed to have him. Nor would she, if Carmina had her way.

But she must tread carefully.

Carmina adopted a sympathetic smile. Luc sat hunched in the driving seat as if he carried the entire woes of the world on his shoulders. She forced a softness into her voice as she gently rubbed his arm. 'I realise you must be disappointed about Gina. You're bound to feel a bit let down, and confused, but she is adamant, I'm afraid. It's over.'

When he said nothing Carmina edged closer, attempting to remind him of their previous encounters with the taunting challenge of her gaze. 'Seems to me that kiss didn't feel like one from a man wishing to simply talk about my sweet virginal sister. I mean, if you and I got together, it wouldn't be the first time, would it?'

Luc wished, in that moment, that he'd never allowed Carmina into his car. He wanted to walk away, to run as fast and as far as he could away from what she was so clearly offering. He'd no wish to be reminded of the reckless risks they'd once taken.

Both angry with the world, frustrated by life and by their own inability to control it, they'd indulged their lust without thought for any consequences. Fortunately, he'd been lucky and got away with it.

There'd been something about Carmina that had

appealed to the old Luc, to the rebel who had refused to conform. She was feral and exciting with a wildness about her that still appealed to the devil in him, to the part which hated his family for trying to mould him to suit their own needs instead of his.

He'd made many mistakes in the past, and Carmina was one of them. But if he'd done stupid things, was it any wonder, bearing in mind all the hassle he was getting at home?

He'd hated driving the ice-cream vans, hated everyone thinking him well off and spoiled when the truth was very different. Since he'd refused to comply with his father's plans for him, Luc had only the low wages he earned as an apprenticed builder, and he must pay board and lodging out of that. His father barely spoke to him these days and his mother would never take Luc's side against her husband.

More than anything Luc longed to be a chef, and maybe one day own his own restaurant. He was saving up hard to pay for a course in cookery at the local tech, though he couldn't imagine ever being able to save up enough to buy himself a business. His father absolutely refused to help, had dismissed the idea as a waste of time and money when there was a perfectly good ice-cream business for him to inherit.

The real problem was that Luc was an only child. All his siblings had died at birth or as a result of miscarriage, which meant his father had invested all his hopes and dreams in Luc.

Gina was the first person he'd been able to actually talk to about these problems without feeling stupid or embarrassed. Here he was, a supposed rich kid with a tough reputation and all he wanted to do was cook and win the approval of his dream from his family.

He couldn't explain why he'd chosen the quiet sister. Gina was lovely but without Carmina's luscious charms. Yet she was the one who had somehow captured his heart. He loved her softness, the radiance of her, as well as the way she made him feel good about himself, as if he were a different person, someone worthwhile instead of being at odds with the entire universe.

Put simply, he adored her.

And he'd foolishly imagined that she felt the same away about him. Obviously he was wrong. She'd probably only listened to him out of pity; had agreed to go out with him because she felt sorry for him. Gina was that sort of person: kind and caring, sympathetic to the troubles others had to endure because of her own problems. But it was obviously no more than that.

He could well appreciate that she might feel too shy or embarrassed to tell him all of this to his face, and to admit that she thought things were moving too fast between them.

He'd spotted her hiding behind her bedroom curtains, and could understand now why she hadn't come out to speak to him. She was sick and tired of him and had really wanted him to go away and not bother her any more.

Carmina's soft mouth was moving over his, insistent, demanding. She was loosening his tie, sliding her fingers down his chest as she slid open each shirt button, stirring some need in him that he really didn't like but simply couldn't resist. She wasn't the kind of girl any man could resist, not for long.

Luc hated to admit it to himself but his blood was stirring. Just the feel of her moving against him set his senses racing, his lust merging with the deep hurt and anger he felt over losing Gina. If only she hadn't finished with him . . .

Carmina cupped one hand around the bulge in his trousers, and with a soft chuckle at his reaction, began to unbuckle his belt.

Out in the alley a figure stood huddled in a doorway, watching. He'd seen the young couple dash to the car, and it didn't take much imagination to work out what they were getting up to behind those steamed-up windows. One day, he'd have some of that, he thought, as he walked away.

Back in the car Luc suddenly came to his senses.

'Damn you, Carmina!' He jerked himself free of her and flung open the car door. 'Get out! You and me are finished, remember? Even if I can't have Gina, I certainly don't want *you*.'

She slapped him across the face. Hard! Had he been less well brought up he might have slapped her back. Instead, he pushed her out of the car and drove off, leaving her standing alone in the pouring rain.

11

Patsy

The rows of canvas-topped stalls lining Champion Street were well attended today, being a Saturday, positively humming with people. Patsy loved the vibrancy of it all, the strings of brightly coloured beads hanging on wooden pegs, the piles of striped tea-towels and checked tablecloths, the buckets of yellow daffodils, scarlet tulips and blue iris at Betty Hemley's flower stall, brightening a dull day. She bought two tea-towels and tucked them away in her bag with a smile. Something else for the bottom drawer.

Patsy tried to buy a little something each week to put into it, however small: a rolling pin or a pair of pillow cases; Tala kitchenware or a Prestige pan to add to her set when she was feeling a bit flush.

An auction was taking place on Abe's stall and Patsy wandered over to see if there was anything else worth buying for their future new home. He was selling a roll of lino, slapping it hard to attract attention.

'Wife says I'm that generous I throw me money about like a man wi' no arms. Today, I'll break the habit of a lifetime and give away a strip of stair carpet to go with this roll of lino. I can't say fairer'n that, now can I?'

Patsy laughed, sorely tempted to make a bid, but since she didn't know where she and Marc would be living, whether they would need lino, or even have any stairs, she firmly kept her hands in her pockets.

In any case, she really shouldn't be dawdling around the stalls dreaming of weddings and new homes. She had work to do: hats to finish for her special customers, as well as the normal round of work on the hat stall.

She dodged a boy on a bicycle delivering bread for Thomas George, waved to Carmina who was browsing through records and chatting animatedly to Alec Hall. She didn't wave back, but stood laughing up into his face, leaning against him. Patsy wondered why the girl never chatted to her in such an openly friendly fashion, then forgot all about her as she stopped to admire some sequinned fabric on Winnie Holmes's stall.

'This'd mek a champion hat, one of them natty little head-hugging numbers,' Winnie suggested.

'You might be right,' Patsy agreed. 'Or I could use it to add a sequined band to a velvet beret. I'll give it some thought.'

Patsy never grew tired of wandering through her beloved market, searching out hidden treasures, finding ideas. It had been her favourite occupation ever since the first day she'd arrived when she'd recklessly nicked a pie off Poulson's hot potato pie stall, but that was when she hadn't eaten for two days.

She never went hungry these days, thank goodness, and Big Molly was still on speaking terms with her, although it had been a close-run thing for a while.

* * *

Arriving at the hat stall rather later than she'd intended, Patsy apologised to Clara and got on with sewing some grosgrain ribbon on to her latest creation. Tongue stuck in the corner of her mouth, she gave the work her entire concentration while Clara served customers.

Later, Clara set a steaming mug of tea down on the table beside her. 'Time for a brew.'

'I've finished this one, anyway.' Smiling, Patsy snipped off the thread and held the hat up for Clara to examine. 'What do you think?'

She'd finished off the fashionable pill-box made of imitation leopard skin with a velvet bow in a toning dark brown.

Clara smiled. 'I rather think it might suit Carmina.'

'Goodness, I hope she doesn't spot it then, or she might demand a large discount.'

Patsy picked up another hat, one comprised largely of petals and leaves, and began to search through the big wide drawers for a silk scarf to team with it before she put it out on display. The drawers were stuffed with reels of ribbon, hat trimmings, millinery wire and hat pins, horsehair bows, silk flowers and feathers. She seemed to spend her life tidying them out and still they were a muddle.

'We need more drawers, a whole new set. I can never find what I'm looking for.'

'Leave that for a moment, Patsy, and drink your tea. Besides, there's something I wish to discuss with you.'

Patsy did as she was told and sipped the hot tea, which was more than welcome on this cold spring day.

She frowned, troubled by Clara's sombre tone. 'Is Annie bad again?'

'I'm afraid so,' Clara said. 'She's not been herself this last twelve months, not since she had that heart attack, if you remember?'

'I remember it well. It was last summer, the day Marc took me to his sister Maria's wedding. Could she be overdoing it, do you think?' Annie was a stickler for wanting to oversee everything herself: the buying, the displays, how customers should be dealt with, and most particularly of all, the accounts.

Clara nodded, her usually soft mouth tight with worry. 'I'm certain she is. However, I think I've finally persuaded her to retire, even though she isn't yet sixty. It's so sad, but quite the best thing, I believe. If she does agree, then I'm not sure I could manage the business on my own, even if I wanted to. I wondered, therefore, if you'd be interested in taking her place.'

Patsy looked stunned, as well she might. It wasn't so very long ago that she'd been a mere apprentice on this stall, and even that job had been in doubt for a while. Now Clara seemed to be offering her much more and she felt a surge of panic.

'Hey, I couldn't do Annie's job. I'm not good with figures.'

'It's not the accounts which worry me, as Annie could continue to do those from home. It's the stall itself. You've said yourself that it needs updating. I don't have your flair for choosing the right hats for today's cool cats, as you like to call yourselves. Not that hats are worn as often as they were in my day, so it's even more important that we choose, or make, the right ones for the wedding market, social functions and the like.

'Also, if Annie retires early through ill-health, I would want more time to spend at home, to look after her. I'm too young to consider retirement myself, of course, but I wouldn't mind reducing my hours to part-time, perhaps two or three days a week, or afternoons only. Whatever suits you best. What I'm offering you is a partnership.'

Patsy was stunned. 'Lord, I don't know what to say.'

'Because you're horrified by the idea, or thrilled by it?'

'Oh, the latter, of course, I'm thrilled. Delighted! I never expected this though, not in a month of Sundays. I'm hugely flattered. But do you think I'm up to the task? I mean, it's not just about choosing the right stock, is it? It's about getting the right price, bargaining with suppliers. Making a profit! Although I think we could expand and find other things to sell, like this line of scarves we've tried which have gone really well.' Patsy began to feel quite excited. 'We could also try a little haberdashery, maybe gloves, or stockings and those new tights.'

Clara laughed. 'There you are, you see, full of ideas, as usual.'

Patsy grinned at her. 'If you're really serious, I accept. I'll snatch your hand off, in fact.'

Clara laughed. 'Well, I must say I'm delighted too. That's a huge weight off my mind. But you are sure? I mean you can take time to think about it, talk it over with Marc, if you like. I did wonder, with the wedding coming up, if you might feel you don't want to be too involved in the business in the future.'

'Why would I? I love what I do,' Patsy assured her. Babies would come soon enough, but Patsy was ambitious and there were things she wanted to do first. Having a business of her own was one of them.

'I've dreamed of this,' she confessed. 'Can we drink to it?' and lifting her mug of tea they did just that.

The next day, being a Sunday, Marc and Patsy were walking down Lower Byrom Street, arm in arm, taking their usual afternoon stroll. Puffs of white cloud sailed high in a sun-filled blue sky, exactly the kind of spring day when two lovers might dream of a future together.

Marc was suggesting they marry in the summer but Patsy was thinking less about the wedding and more about Clara's startling offer. Should she mention it to him now? She couldn't quite judge what his reaction would be, since he seemed keen for the wedding to take place as soon as possible. Which thought reminded Patsy of the 'accident' Carmina had had with the fork and the resulting stain on her gown. It made her wonder what she might be taking on by marrying into this family. Not that she would mention a word about the incident to Marc.

Patsy might adore the Bertalone family but she didn't envy Amy being obliged to live with her in-laws. She and Marc intended to rent a house or flat of their own right from the start of their married life together. If they could save enough they might even put down a deposit on a new one. They were going to do things properly, so Amy's words about marrying in haste and repenting at leisure surely wouldn't prove correct in their case?

She was very content with her lot although she wished Marc would understand how difficult Carmina could be with her at times.

'I was disappointed that you didn't come to meet me after my class, as usual, on Friday,' Patsy casually remarked, trying not to sound grumpy and childish and failing miserably.

'Sorry, but as you could see I was embroiled in a family argument over that flipping dance.'

They reached the old graveyard where once St John's Church had stood, and paused beneath the overhanging trees so that Marc could sneak her a kiss.

Patsy smiled up into his eyes. 'I try so hard to please her, but Carmina seems to resent everything I say. I do worry, sometimes, if I'm ever going to be a real part of your family.'

'Of course you are,' Marc said, kissing her some more. 'Once you stop being jealous of her.'

Patsy couldn't help but let out a small gasp of protest. She understood why the pair were particularly close. Maria, the oldest Bertalone girl, was grown-up and married. Patsy had attended her wedding with Marc last summer. And as the eldest required to help Mamma she had appeared more like a surrogate mother than a sister to Carmina. Gina seemed to be rather secretive, a girl who preferred her own company, but then much of her youth had been lost in ill health so she'd been little company for her older sister. The four younger girls were always together, and Alessandro and eight-year-old Giovanni were great friends. Which left Marc. He was Carmina's big brother, able to offer protection should she need it.

'Carmina is the jealous one, not me. She winds you round her little finger, constantly asking you to do something for her, fetch and carry this or that, solve all her problems.'

'She's my sister,' Marc quietly reminded her.

'And I'm your fiancée.'

'So you are.' Infuriatingly, he took her into his arms and kissed her more passionately this time, pushing her back against the churchyard railings. Patsy melted, as always. He was so gorgeous, so tall and strong, so kind and loving. And so sexy. How could she stay mad with such a man?

Patsy had been used to seeing Marc Bertalone around the market, going to and from the tall terrace house but the first time he spoke to her was still a red-letter day in her heart. She'd fallen for him at first sight. Not that she'd let him know that, of course, at the time.

She'd called in at Alec Hall's music shop to buy herself a Frankie Vaughan record and suddenly there he was, crooning a Johnny Ray number: 'Here I am – broken-hearted', and chatting her up with that delicious smile of his while she'd stood dry-mouthed, heart racing, quite unable to think of a sensible thing to say.

He'd looked so handsome, like a demi-god, those magical Bertalone brown eyes alive with merry laughter; hair neatly cut and slicked into a crinkled sea of waves.

Patsy still loved the way some curls sprang stubbornly forward, and he had the kind of classically oval face you would expect in an Italian, lean, with high cheekbones and a perfectly straight Roman nose.

And now, unbelievably, they would soon be married with a home of their own.

She'd been grateful for the home the Higginson sisters had given her, right from when she'd first come to work for them on their hat stall; a bewildered and rebellious young orphan neglected and abandoned by her foster parents. They'd made her a part of their family, Clara in particular becoming almost like a mother to her. Even Annie had warmed to her in the end, and, in her turn, Patsy had made a valiant effort to curb her cheeky spirit, her 'sauce' as Annie called it, and her sense of bitter resentment against life. She'd learned to accept herself for what she was, thanks to the sisters teaching her to have faith in herself and her future, to look forward instead of back.

Marc's love too had convinced her that she had a future after all, and that she was beautiful inside as well as out.

Yet with no real knowledge of who her own real parents were, Patsy dreamed of being part of a big happy family, still needing to feel that she belonged somewhere.

It was true that Papa Bertalone was friendly enough, as was Carlotta for all she had limited English and Patsy knew even less Italian. Communication between the two women wasn't always easy for all they got by well enough with smiles and little mimes when words failed them. Other members of the family seemed slower to accept her, perhaps influenced by Carmina's prickly attitude, although Marc said that was only out of shyness.

'If you're really concerned about getting to know my family . . .' he was saying now, pausing in his kissing to allow them both to catch their breath . . . 'maybe you should give up this millinery course. You could learn Italian and work in the ice-cream parlour full time so that you can get to know them properly.'

Patsy stepped away from him, filled with alarm. 'Marc, what a thing to say! I *love* making my hats and there's still so much I need to learn. Besides, Clara needs me on the stall now that Annie isn't well, you know she does.'

This was the moment. She should tell him now about Clara's offer. But Marc smiled in that lazy, relaxed way he had, as if he knew that despite her protests she'd come round to his way of thinking in the end.

'As a good Catholic wife you'll soon be pregnant anyway, and staying home with a baby, so why waste your time on learning stuff you won't need?'

Incensed, Patsy began walking away from him. How could she talk to such a man? Couldn't he understand that she felt a fierce pride in her work? And a strong objection to this threat to her independence, again recalling Amy's words with a shiver.

'I'll tell you when I'm ready to produce. This is a discussion I've already had with your father, and as I told him, it won't be any time soon.'

Hurrying to catch up with her before she turned

into Liverpool Road, Marc grasped her arm and pulled her to a halt. 'You talked about *babies* to my father?'

'Only in passing,' Patsy said, smiling despite her show of temper. 'You know how he is. Family and children are his life.'

'Don't I know it?' Marc put his arms about her and nuzzled into her neck. 'I do so love it when you're angry. You have such passion. Even so, I hate us to argue.'

Since Patsy had no wish to argue with him either, she happily resigned herself to more kisses, which attracted quite a few whistles from passers-by.

Later, as they sat in their favourite place on a bench by an old lock on the River Irwell, she asked him again, 'Will your family ever come to love me, do you think?'

'Of course they will. Alessandro loves you already. The twins, I'm afraid, are completely wrapped up in themselves but the girls are getting to know you, little by little. They will soon love you too.'

'And what about Carmina?'

Marc chuckled. 'That little madam is a law unto herself but *I* love you, sweetheart, and always will. What more could you wish for than to be my adored wife?'

'Nothing,' Patsy said, as she sank back into his arms. But that wasn't strictly true. She still hadn't told him that she also wanted to accept Clara's offer and take on the hat stall.

12

Amy

Thomas George was considered by Amy's mam, fondly known as Big Molly by all who knew her, to be the leper of Champion Street. He had never, personally, done anything to cause her offence save for being born into the George family.

The feud which had separated the two families and nearly destroyed Chris and Amy's hopes of marriage had lasted for years, ever since Big Molly had been a young woman herself.

It all had something to do with Big Molly's sister being badly treated by Thomas's brother, Howard, but memories were long and some hurts never could be forgotten. This was the reason Chris and Amy had eloped to Gretna Green, in order to escape the bitterness of the family feud. There were times when Amy still felt trapped by it, as if Mavis were punishing her for these old wrongs.

Yet strangely, it was Chris's father, Thomas the leper himself, who proved to be her greatest ally.

One evening, as they were washing up together in the kitchen, he suddenly said to her, 'You can't stay here, lass. She'll strangle the life out of your marriage. You must get away before it's too late.'

Amy was so startled she almost dropped the tea cup she was drying, completely taken aback by his remark. There was no doubt in her mind that it was Mavis to whom he was referring, but he'd never before displayed such animosity towards his wife.

As if that wasn't surprising enough, he glanced over towards the kitchen door then went to push it closed before coming to whisper in her ear.

'I know what she's like, how she deliberately makes your life a misery by having you working all hours when really you should be putting your feet up. I've told her you need to rest, but I'm the last person she listens to. You should move into a place of your own before it's too late.'

Amy looked at him, bemused. What was he saying? What on earth did he mean? 'Too late for what?' she asked.

'For you and Chris to be happy. She poisons everything she touches, that woman.'

Too shocked to think clearly, Amy gabbled something about Chris not wanting to put any strain on her by moving house while she was pregnant. 'In any case, I'm not sure we could afford to rent a place of our own just yet.'

'Yes, you can.'

Again he glanced towards the kitchen door as he handed her a plate to dry, dropping his voice still further to a confidential whisper. 'Believe me, it's important you get out of here. I've put the word out that yer looking fer a place. I'll let you know if I hear owt.'

'Oh, goodness, I don't know. Do you think we should . . . ?'

'Now don't get all flummoxed. You have to stay calm when you're carrying. You need a place of your own, love. Remember, I might not always be here to stand up for you.'

Now Amy really was alarmed. 'You aren't sick, are you?' She didn't share her mother's contempt for this man. On the contrary, she felt rather sorry for the old man, seeing him as a fellow sufferer at Mavis's hand.

'Nay, I'm not going to die, if that's what yer thinking.' This quiet man who usually barely spoke more than half a dozen words to anyone now grinned from ear to ear and gave her a conspiratorial wink. 'But one of these days I might do summat, shall we say, a bit daring like.'

At which point the door opened and Mavis herself marched in. 'Have you two not finished that washing-up yet? Goodness me, look at all those bubbles. You've used far too much soap.'

Mavis prudently saved left-over pieces of soap and put them in a small plastic cage which could be swished about in the washing-up water. Unfortunately, Thomas had been so busy talking he'd rather overdone it and bubbles were everywhere.

'What a waste! Really, I can't trust you to do anything properly.'

Thomas took his hands out of the water and carefully dried them on a towel. 'Best do it yourself then, so you can be sure the job's done right,' and walked out of the kitchen.

It was the first hint of rebellion Amy had ever seen in him, and, following on their most interesting conversation, and that last enigmatic remark just as they were interrupted, she couldn't help wondering why. What on earth was going on? Thomas was behaving very oddly, very oddly indeed.

Amy thought no more of this unsettling conversation, finding that her life had quite livened up just by getting involved with the Peace Movement. Jeff Stockton, the old school friend whom she'd met when he asked her to sign his petition, had invited her along to a meeting and she'd gone, just to see what it was all about.

There'd been a speaker talking about the threat to Great Britain's security, how if it chose to follow the nuclear route, this would ultimately lead to the destruction of mankind. It was all very depressing, particularly with the baby coming. Jeff and his girl friend Sue didn't agree with her.

'We need to understand what's going on so that we can fight back. Youth must have a voice. It's our future they're messing up, after all.'

Amy went to more meetings, carried along by the rhetoric, by the sheer passion and energy of these people. These were often held at the Friends Meeting House or the Rechobite's Hall, but for some reason she couldn't quite bring herself to tell Chris where she was going, feeling sure he would object. She would pretend that she was going over to Patsy's, or to see Lizzie Pringle. It wasn't really a lie, Amy told herself; well, only a white one.

Ever cautious, her husband wasn't at all the sort of man to get involved in demonstrations. He was turning into a replica of his father: a family man with a small-business mentality. He certainly wanted his world to be safe, but he trusted the government to make sure of that for him. And as a tried and true conservative, he saw the new Peace Movement as far too left wing for his taste.

Amy, on the other hand, wasn't the least interested in politics, either left or right. She focused entirely on that one important word: peace. She interpreted this in a simplistic way, as a safe future for her child. And if this new movement was full of students, journalists and intellectuals, making her sometimes feel a little out of her depth, that was simply her own lack of education showing. Mixing with such people could surely only be a good thing.

Besides, with the state of housing in Manchester the way it was, that's what the government should be spending their hard-earned taxes on, not nuclear missiles to start yet another war. Amy spent every waking moment longing for a place of their own.

And with the cold war she was fighting with Mavis, peace, like privacy, seemed like a distant dream.

But then one morning when Amy was pegging clothes out on the line, Thomas came creeping down the back stairs from the bakery above and spoke to her once more in hushed conspiratorial tones.

'There's a two-bedroom house come empty down the bottom of the street, just next door to the pawn shop. I've spoken to the landlord, and, thankfully, it's not that Billy Quinn but an old mate of mine. He says it's in a bit of a mess so he's not asking too much. You must take it, lass. I'll help you fix it up, give it a daub of paint and such like. You choose the colours, I'll wield the brush. You won't recognise the place once we've given it a wash and brush-up. Just don't tell Chris it were my idea, that's all I ask.'

It was a week or two later and Amy was so excited she couldn't wait for Chris to come home so she called in at the bakery during his dinner hour, begging him to come with her there and then. 'There's something I want to show you. It won't take long.'

Chris was tempted to refuse, to protest that he'd left some dough proving and must bake several dozen currant teacakes this afternoon, but Amy looked so lovely with her fly-away auburn hair, her patient, loving smile. And she was all round and cuddly with the child she was carrying, *his* child, that he'd really no wish to upset her.

'Very well then,' he conceded with a gentle sigh. Yet he felt compelled to put in a reminder that life wasn't all girlish fancies; that he was a family man now with responsibilities. 'Make it quick, whatever it is.'

Amy bit back the protest that she too had responsibilities, producing his son or daughter for one thing. It irritated her sometimes the way Chris had started talking to her as if she'd turned deaf, blind and stupid simply because she was pregnant. Sometimes she would do battle with him over this condescending attitude but today she swallowed her pride and hurried him along

Champion Street, drawing to a halt on the corner by the pawn shop.

'Here it is.' She did a little flourish with her hands, rather as a conjuror might produce a rabbit out of a hat. 'See, I've found us a house to rent. What do you think? Isn't it wonderful?' She carefully stuck to her promise that she wouldn't reveal his father's part in the deal.

Chris stared at the small terrace house, utterly dumbfounded. Several long seconds ticked by before he spoke. 'I thought we'd agreed to do nothing about that until after the baby was born?'

'I changed my mind. A woman's privilege. A *pregnant* woman's privilege, anyway. Oh, Chris, think of it. Wouldn't it marvellous to have our own place? Once this little one is born I'll be far too busy to have time to move house then, and I can't wait until it's four, five or six months old. We need a place of our own *now*.'

Chris continued to look doubtful as she fitted the key in the lock and ushered him inside, the scowl on his face deepening.

'Even supposing we could afford the rent, what with a baby coming an' all, how could you begin to manage a house in your condition, without Mother's help? Look what silly things you do. How would I know that you could manage on your own?'

'I'll take good care to wash your pink socks separately,' Amy told him, straight-faced.

The corners of Chris's mouth twitched as he tried not to smile. 'It's not only that. I don't want you lifting anything heavy, or trying to cope with things you know nothing about. How could I be sure that you'd be sensible and take proper rest of an afternoon? Keeping house might look easy when Mother is around, but she is far more experienced than you, love.'

'Oh, thanks a bunch. You mean because my own mother's home is an untidy mess?' This was undoubtedly true. The Poulsons' abode always looked a complete shambles with clothes and dog hairs scattered about everywhere, but Amy adored her mother and really didn't like anyone, outside of the family, to criticise Big Molly.

'I meant nothing of the sort. I'm saying that Mother has the skills, and you don't.'

'As a matter of fact your mother has taught me a great deal, for which I'm truly grateful, even if I don't always care for the way she does it. But having said that, she and I have entirely different ideas about how things should be done. She insists on using only a brush and dustpan to clean the carpet while I'd prefer a vacuum cleaner. She uses hard soap and a scrubbing board for your soiled white baker's overalls. I'd use Omo. I'd even rather like to buy a washing machine. It's not a crime to want to be modern. We're a different generation.'

'I know, love, but Mother likes things to be done in the traditional way.'

'Don't I know it!' So long as she has someone willing to wield the brush and shovel for her, Amy thought, although she didn't say as much out loud.

According to the gospel of Mavis, cleaning must be

done not only in a particular way but also in a certain order. There was a strict daily routine in which the carpet must be swept and the furniture dusted. She maintained windows must be kept closed while this was going on so that the dust didn't fly around too much, and would scold Amy should she dare to open one to rid the room of stale air.

Then there was the weekly clean which, in addition, required rugs to be hung on the washing line and given a good beating; awkward ledges, picture rails and shelves wiped down with a damp cloth, windows cleaned and last of all, the furniture polished to perfection with beeswax.

Most important of all was the annual spring-clean. This had been carried out only recently, an exhausting task which Amy could well have done without at this stage in her pregnancy. The big carpet rugs had to be rolled up and floorboards scrubbed; curtains taken down and washed, drawers and cupboards emptied, disinfected with a weak solution of bleach and everything put back in a tidy fashion.

And once all of that was done, a fan of newspaper was set into the cleaned fire grate for the summer. No more fires would be allowed until the autumn, no matter how cold or wet it might be as the chimney might belch out soot and smoke and make the room dirty again.

Poor Thomas's life was a misery while all of this was going on and he would retreat, yet again, to his precious allotment.

Chris was saying, 'Besides all of that, this place is a

mess, a real dump. How could we ever make it decent enough to live in? I don't have the time and you aren't fit to do the job.'

'I'm sure your dad would help. I'll ask him. We *need* our own place,' Amy insisted. 'I've already spoken to the landlord and we *can* afford the rent, simply because the house does need so much work doing to it. But a lick of paint will work wonders. Oh, come on, Chris, do say yes. I want us to be in our own home by the time the baby comes.'

'I know, love, so do I, but . . .'

'No buts!' Amy kissed him, a sweet, lingering kiss. 'And we'll only be at the end of the street so I can still ask your mother for advice, should I need it. Which I'm sure I won't,' she hastily added.

'Well . . .' She could sense that he was weakening.

Amy led him upstairs into the empty bedroom, hugging his arm close as she outlined her plans, saying how much better it would look with new wallpaper, a rug on the floor and home-made curtains at the window.

'It'll have to be a second-hand bed, I'm not having anything to do with this never-never business,' Chris warned her.

'I've a bit saved up for a new bed,' Amy told him. 'And a bed is all we do need at first, isn't it? We can get other things later, a bit at a time.'

Her bright eyes twinkled so cheekily at him he fell to laughing and kissing her, as he always did. A moment later he was happily agreeing to her plan, if only because it would be so good to have the freedom to make love to his lovely wife in private without being conscious of his mother listening behind paper-thin walls.

'He agreed,' Amy told Thomas in jubilation that evening as once again they were doing the dishes in the back kitchen.

'You didn't tell him I had owt to do with it, did you?'

Amy assured the old man that she hadn't broken her promise. 'I did say I'd ask you to help us do the place up though, since Chris is working so hard learning his new trade, is that all right?'

'Aye, course it is, chuck. I've already said, I'll be happy to help. I'll pop round tomorn and have a shufti, then we'll decide what needs doing.'

'Oh, I'm so thrilled! Should I tell Mavis, do you think, or leave that to Chris?'

Thomas was thoughtful. 'Nay, leave that to me, love. I'll fettle it.'

13

Carmina

Carmina eagerly returned to her daily routine of meeting Luc at the bus stop on the corner of Hardman Street. Night after night she would patiently wait for him. Sadly, he was not pleased to see her. Now, when he got off the bus, instead of wrapping a casual arm around her neck and kissing her, as he used to do, he seemed embarrassed that she should be there. He would walk right past as if he hadn't even noticed her. Carmina didn't like being ignored and vigorously protested.

'What's wrong?' she asked, miffed that he should be so distant.

'Nothing,' he growled, striding away from her at such a speed she had to half run to keep up with him.

'I'm not angry. It was just a bit of a tiff. I've forgotten it already.'

She'd far from forgotten it, but Carmina certainly had no intention of letting Luc know how hurt she'd been by his rejection. Maybe he was playing hard to get, but he'd certainly wanted her, for goodness' sake. Any fool could tell that. And she was even more determined to have him. Couldn't she always twist a man around her little finger?

If her mother had told her once, she'd told her a thousand times to be a good girl, to respect herself then others would respect her in turn. Carmina wasn't interested in respect, only passion. Mamma also said that once a boy had had his wicked way with you, he dropped you.

Not that she'd ever listened to her mother's advice. What did *she* know?

Carlotta still listened to Perry Como and Glenn Miller, and spent all her time cooking and washing dishes. She didn't approve of today's world, of bad boy Elvis the Pelvis, of loud rock 'n' roll and the new earning power of the young. She believed that today's teenagers had too much money and too little discipline. Her mother was old-fashioned, still with one foot in the past, constantly reliving the war years, or forever harping on about how things were different in Italy when she was a girl.

Carmina saw herself as the future, free to do as she pleased now that she was seventeen, nearly eighteen. She intended to be Luc's girl and she would do whatever was necessary to get him.

She'd almost had him that night at the dance, but then he'd chickened out at the last minute. Carmina felt cheated and annoyed with him. Why wouldn't the daft fool admit that he wanted her as much as she wanted him? Hadn't she longed for that moment, dreamed of it for weeks ever since they'd split up? She'd ached to be in Luc Fabriani's arms again, and all her careful planning had seemed to be working beautifully until he'd no doubt been hit by a bout of guilt over her stupid sister!

'You haven't taken up with our Gina again, have you?' She hadn't meant to blurt out this worry, but somehow couldn't get her head round the complex emotions she was experiencing.

Yet Carmina didn't really think that could be the case as the silly girl was still moping about looking like a wet weekend. Besides, wasn't she herself far more lovable and desirable than her sanctimonious sister? Hadn't she proved this by the way Luc had kissed her? 'She'd never have you back, you know,' Carmina finished, wanting to drive home her point.

Luc spun about, his face an angry crimson. 'Why wouldn't she? Because you've poisoned her mind with more of your lies?'

'They aren't lies.' Carmina put back her head and laughed. 'You can hardly claim to be the faithful boyfriend *now*, can you? You were gasping for it, so don't pretend otherwise. Although I can't imagine what Mamma and Papa's reaction would be if they learned you were dangling both of us on a string.'

'I'm not dangling anyone on a string.'

'Of course you are. You have both Gina and me panting for love of you, you lucky brute. Unfortunately, you aren't one of Mamma and Papa's favourite people. Apart from the fact your family are business rivals, they're very protective of our Gina. She's still sick, as you know.'

'She looks fine to me.'

'What would you know about it?' Carmina almost told him that Gina did feel a bit below par this week, but changed her mind in case it should spark off some sort of stupid sympathy in him. 'Anyway, Papa may seem soft but actually he's quite strict. He likes to be in control, just as he would be in the old country.'

It had been almost midnight when Carmina had got home after the dance. Having persuaded her father to let her stay out till eleven o'clock, she knew she'd be in trouble for being late. Her cheeks had been flushed, her eyes glazed with the fury of frustrated passion, and her chin a suspicious raw crimson from rubbing against Luc's roughly shaven skin.

Papa had eyed her keenly over the rim of his newspaper as she'd hurried in. 'You're late. Where have you been all this time, girl? Your mamma she is worried sick.'

'Just at the dance. I'm sorry, Papa, I forgot the time. It won't happen again.'

His old eyes had softened as Carmina kissed his brow. 'See that it doesn't. And don't be late for work in the morning.'

'I won't, Papa, I promise.'

Carmina had escaped to the bathroom to get ready for bed and to splash cold water on her burning face before she faced Gina.

As expected, her sister had still been awake when she'd climbed into the bed next to her. 'How was it?' Gina had asked, in a small sad voice. 'I expect you danced every dance.'

'I most certainly did,' Carmina agreed with a happy sigh.

'Who was there? Did you see Luc?'

'Only briefly. He was with someone. Don't know her name.'

'A girl?'

'Yes, a girl. You don't think a boy like Luc Fabriani would go to a dance alone, do you? Stop fretting about him. He isn't worth it, and you didn't miss a thing. It was all very boring.' And turning on her side, she'd snuggled down into her pillows and, despite her failure to seduce him, nursed the memory of Luc's kisses with secret delight. Her oh-so-innocent sister would have fifty fits if she'd the smallest inkling of how close Carmina had come to stealing him from her.

And now, over a week later, she was even more determined to succeed. She'd get him next time for sure.

'Gina doesn't know about us, or what nearly happened in your old banger,' Carmina admitted.

'I pray to God she never does. That was a mistake, a bad one. It won't happen again. Anyway, there is no *us*.'

He was again striding away from her, turning the corner into St John's Place where he lived in a fine Georgian terraced house with his parents, the polished brass knocker and letter box on its porticoed door probably cleaned by some maid this very morning. Carmina would dearly like to be invited in for tea, but doubted they'd reached that stage. Not yet.

'Oh, I think there is,' she insisted. 'Very much so.'

He paused to glare at her. 'I was a stupid fool to allow you to push things so far.'

'So it's all my fault now, is it?'

'You know it was.' He almost shouted the words at her, his voice hard with accusation.

Carmina gave a brittle little laugh. 'You were panting

for it. Couldn't help yourself, because you know how much you like me really.'

'I do not!'

'Oh, yes, you do! And you still are gasping for it.'

'I was stupid to believe what you said about Gina wanting to finish with me. In fact, I intend to speak to her and put her straight about some of these lies of yours.'

He set off across the road as if he meant to carry out his threat there and then but Carmina snatched at his arm and dragged him to a halt. They were both breathing hard, she quite out of breath trying to keep up with him. 'If you do that, you'll be sorry.'

'Why? Who'll make me sorry?' There was a hard brightness in his gaze that sent a shiver of longing down her spine. He excited her when he was angry. He looked so *dangerous*!

'*I* will.' She shook back her dark hair so that it rippled over her shoulders, brown eyes blazing a challenge. 'Admit it, you really can't resist me. I'll tell her how passionately you kissed me, what very nearly happened between us. I won't spare her a single detail. I might even embellish things a little.'

She watched with pleasure as the colour drained from his handsome face.

'You wouldn't dare do that, not to your own sister?'

'Watch me.' Now she softened her stance, trailed a finger over his full mouth. 'There's a way to keep me quiet though. If you're so keen for me to keep my mouth shut, then meet me tonight down by the canal bridge at seven, and don't be late. You and I have some unfinished business.' Then she left him standing in the middle of the road, a car peeping its horn at him as she sashayed away, hips swinging.

Carmina managed to avoid speaking to Gina as Mamma carried supper up to her room on a tray, claiming the poor girl still needed to rest. How she did fuss! But then later, just as she was creeping out the door, her mother caught her.

'Where you go? Who you go with? Not seeing a boy, I hope?' Then reverting to her native tongue, Carlotta asked if Carmina too had secrets like her younger sister?

Carmina widened her eyes in an expression of outraged innocence. 'Now why would I?'

'Are you sure?'

'Mamma, are you accusing me of being a liar?'

'I only accuse you of being a silly young girl, as we all were once.' Carlotta jabbed a finger in her own ample chest. 'I am your Mamma. It is my job to protect you. You must be a good girl, understand?'

Carmina rolled her eyes and let out a heavy sigh, having heard all of this a thousand times before. 'Of course I'm a good girl. Don't you trust me, Mamma?'

Then catching sight of her own reflection in the hall mirror she tweaked a few kiss curls here and there, ran a damp finger over each plucked brow. Her face was bare of make-up but she carried lipstick, green eye shadow, mascara and powder compact in her pocket, ready to put on the minute she got out of the house. Her mother didn't approve of her looking like a floozie, but what she didn't see wouldn't hurt her.

Carlotta was wringing her hands in despair. 'Why won't you listen to your mamma? Don't think I don't know what is going on. I hear you danced with that Fabriani boy, that you too follow him about like the little lamb.'

Carmina was stunned. 'Who's been telling tales?'

Carlotta merely folded her arms, and her lips. Gossip wasn't hard to pick up on this market. Alec Hall had casually mentioned the dance, and Winnie Holmes had filled her in on the other details, which she'd no doubt gleaned from her customers. 'He is no good. He has the record with the police.'

Carmina snorted her contempt. 'Nonsense! OK, so Constable Nuttall gave him a clip round the ear once for doing a bit of shop-lifting when he was a kid, so what? That's not exactly a criminal record, is it?'

'He bad boy. In any case, he not love you, he love Gina. But he can't have her either . . .' Carlotta had resorted once more to broken English in an effort to make her point.

Carmina sighed and pouted her lips as she mentally tried to tune out her mother. It was true that so far Luc did seem more interested in talking about her dratted sister than any future for them, but she intended to change all of that. His relationship with Gina was now over and done with, she'd make certain of it. Luc Fabriani would very soon be absolutely besotted by her, putty in her hands.

Her mother, however, was too old to understand any of this, Carmina thought. Listening to only a fraction of Carlotta's dire warnings, she titivated her hair, reached for her coat from the hall stand and tried to nod, or say 'Yes, Mamma,' whenever it seemed appropriate.

'. . . men of that sort they like bad girls as playthings but if you make-a mistake, who would marry you then?' Carlotta was saying, then lifted her hands to pat her own cheeks in a gesture of helplessness. '*Mamma mia*, you would be *ruined*.'

'It isn't like that these days.'

'It is, if I say it is.'

'Nothing bad is going on, I swear it.'

Carlotta scowled as she helped Carmina button up her coat, wrapped a scarf about her neck and pulled a warm fluffy wool hat over her abundant curls, not entirely convinced by her daughter's air of innocence.

Yet she was all too aware that pushing her too hard could easily backfire and the silly girl would do the exact opposite of what she told her, simply to be perverse. These teenagers, as they now called themselves, were a complete mystery to her. Far different from her own youth when her father had found her a good man to marry, and a wise choice he had made in her beloved Marco.

'You *are* still a virgin?'

'Of course I am,' Carmina lied, flushing with embarrassment as she rushed for the door. She couldn't quite recall when she'd first given up that so-called prize. Two years ago? And either Tom Salmon or Jake Hemley had been the lucky winner. She couldn't quite remember, but what did it matter? Carmina didn't have any time for this holier-than-thou-mustn't-talk-about-sex attitude. Really! Mothers!

Carlotta sighed over a changing world and kissed her daughter soundly on each cheek. 'Then see you stay that way or your papa he will take the whip to you.'

Since Papa Bertalone would never lift so much as a finger to hurt any of his adored children Carmina ignored this threat completely. She kissed her mother in return and told her that she was only popping round to chat to Amy George as, being pregnant, she didn't get out much at the moment. Then she walked straight down to the canal where Luc was waiting for her near Princes Bridge, as instructed.

They stood in the chill of the evening by the River Irwell, hands in pockets as Luc promised he would offer no defence of his supposed ill conduct, indeed dare not do so now that Carmina had turned the lie into a truth. OK, so he had indeed kissed her, albeit savagely and in anger, briefly tempted because he felt convinced he'd lost Gina. But how could he explain all of that to Gina? And would she believe him? He very much doubted it. She would indeed feel betrayed, for all he had backed down at the last moment.

Carmina swished at a few nettles, wishing there was somewhere more glamorous and private she could take him, wishing he'd brought his car, but preened herself over having at least partially achieved her object.

She was anxious to get things back to how they'd once been between them. Unfortunately, when she pressed herself hard against him and tried to give Luc a French kiss, ready to tantalise him into further indiscretions, he shoved her roughly away.

'Get off, Carmina. I've already told you this has got to stop. You're out of control.'

'Cheeky monkey!' Carmina deliberately laughed off the remark to prove that she'd no intention of taking offence this time either. 'And there's me thinking that I was your girl.'

'Not on your sweet life. I've promised to keep my mouth shut but you and me are still history. How much plainer can I make it?'

Carmina smiled her most brilliant smile. 'Sweetie, what *you* have to realise is that you can't have everything in this world, and I'm not going to allow you anywhere near our Gina, not ever again. You and she are never going to be love's young dream. Get that idea right out of your head. If you were ever to take up with her again, then I'd have to enlighten her on a few interesting facts, wouldn't I? Only you and I know the truth of what went on in that car, of how far things went, or not, as the case may be. It's your word against mine, isn't it? So if you want me to keep *my* mouth shut, I need a little more attention from *you* in return.'

Luc's expression went blank with shock. 'That's blackmail!'

Carmina widened those bewitching velvet-brown eyes as she gave a casually expressive shrug. 'Well, would you believe it? I never thought of it that way, but do you know, you're absolutely right.'

'You *bitch*!'

Carmina put back her head and laughed. 'You always were good with the sweet talk, Luc.'

14
Patsy

Patsy stepped off the bus and smiled to find Marc waiting for her. He'd been quite diligent in that respect lately. Relieving her of the heavy bag in which she carried the books and materials for her millinery course, he slipped an arm about her waist and kissed her.

'You look all flushed and pretty.'

'Must be love, or the cold breeze, one or the other.' She smiled.

'I'll go for the first, if there's a choice.'

Tucking her arm in his, they strolled along Champion Street, content in each other's company. 'We're like an old married couple already,' Patsy teased.

'There's nothing wrong with that. Can't wait for the big day myself, so long as it's not too big. We have to be careful or Mamma will invite half of Manchester.'

Patsy chuckled. 'I don't care what she does so long as at the end of it, you and I are man and wife,' and reaching up she kissed him again, just to prove how happy she was.

'You must be nearly at the end of this course,' Marc idly remarked as they headed for Belle's Café by mutual consent. They often liked to enjoy a quiet moment together over a frothy coffee before facing the rest of his family.

'Nearly, yes. It finishes at the end of May. It was quite difficult but I've enjoyed it and learned so much.'

'Hello, you two love birds,' Belle called to them, as they strolled in. 'The usual?'

'Thanks.'

Belle brought over two brimming cups of steaming coffee and set them down, her long crimson nails clicking on the saucers as she did so. Folding her arms, she regarded them both with candid interest, clearly ready for a chat. 'You look like you've swallowed a silver farthing, Patsy, your face is all lit up and shiny.'

'It's the heat of that mucky, sweaty bus,' Patsy quipped. She and Belle had never been what you might call close friends, and she certainly wasn't in the mood for small talk today, not when she'd made up her mind to tell Marc about Clara's offer at last.

'I reckon it must be love, beaming out of you like a sunbeam. I hope I get an invitation to the big day. When is it to be?'

'August,' Marc said.

'Some time in the autumn or winter,' Patsy replied at the same moment.

'By heck, make up your minds. If you don't agree about owt else, you two need to agree about the day of your wedding at least,' and Belle went off chuckling to herself.

Marc was frowning as he picked up his coffee and took a sip, then licked the frothy moustache from his upper lip. 'Why did you say that? If we find somewhere to live we needn't wait till the autumn.'

Patsy shrugged, her hands clenched tight under the table. 'What's the hurry? We still haven't found anywhere yet, and neither of us has much time to look. I certainly don't, not with Annie ill. At least, not till I've finished this millinery course. And I've started lessons in Italian with Antonia. She's surprisingly strict for a twelve-year-old, and even gives me homework. I don't seem to have a minute to myself these days.' She laughed.

'As I've already said, you don't have to go on with this hat-making malarkey. You could give it up. You probably won't use half of it.'

'Of course I will,' Patsy retorted. 'It's my job. By the time I'm done I doubt there'll be any kind of hat I couldn't make, including a straw bonnet, should I feel the urge.' Her laughter this time sounded a bit more forced. 'Actually, there's something I need to tell you, something exciting.'

'Oh?' Marc sipped his coffee as he glanced at her, a slightly wary expression coming into those brown, Bertalone eyes.

Patsy felt she'd contained her excitement for long enough. She was itching to share her good news, felt all shining inside. Belle had been right about that, even if she couldn't possibly guess the reason. 'Clara has asked me to become a partner.'

There was a small silence. 'A partner? On the hat stall, you mean?'

Patsy chuckled, her cornflower-blue eyes glowing. 'Yes, on the hat stall. What else could it be? Annie needs to retire through ill health and Clara has offered me a stake in the business in her place. Isn't that marvellous?'

Marc set down his cup with a clatter. 'I'm not sure. Will you have time? I mean with the wedding and everything.'

'Carlotta seems to have it all in hand. Besides, as you were saying just now, we don't want a big affair as it's only one day. Once that is over life gets back to normal, doesn't it?'

'Not exactly, we'll be married. You'll be my wife, with a home to run and a whole new life to lead.'

'True, but I've no intention of stopping work. Why would I, when we need the money so much and I enjoy it?'

'You may have to, once the babies start coming.'

Patsy took a breath before replying. 'Look, I know I agreed to convert and become a Catholic but there are some things . . . about your religion . . . that I don't quite agree with. Birth control for one. We've had this out before. I'll have a baby in a year or so, when I feel ready. There's plenty of time. I'm not yet twenty, remember.'

'They say it's best to have your children when you're young, so that you can be young with them.'

'I think I'd like to enjoy my own youth a bit more first, before I start shaping someone else's, if you don't mind.'

'And what if I do – mind, I mean?'

Patsy hadn't even touched her coffee and knew she couldn't pick it up at that precise moment as her hands had started to shake, so she'd be sure to spill it. Even the smell of it made her feel sick. She could hear her heart knocking against her ribs, drumming in her ears, and she thought the image of Marc's implacable face would live with her forever. Marc Bertalone, the man she loved more than life itself, suddenly seemed like a stranger to her, all cold and distant.

'Why would you mind?'

'Perhaps because I want my wife not to have to work quite such long hours. You know I've been promoted recently, to top window dresser in Kendals, so we won't be too hard up. Some men wouldn't want their wives to work at all. I'm not like that, but I don't want you overdoing it, Patsy, or committing yourself to something you can't possibly keep up once you have other responsibilities.'

Patsy took a moment to sort out her thoughts before answering. 'I understand what you're saying, Marc, but, like you, I'm ambitious and I love my work.'

He scowled at her. 'I'm not suggesting you stop work altogether. Just do part-time, perhaps a couple of mornings a week.'

'I don't want to work part-time. Nothing gives me greater pleasure than making hats.' Patsy wondered if she looked as pale and sick as she felt. Marc's reaction had been worse than she'd feared.

'But you don't have to take on the running of a hat stall to do that,' he coldly insisted. 'You could continue to make hats at home.'

She stifled a sigh, struggling now to hold on to her temper. 'I know I could work from home and maybe I will, one day, once we do start a family. But until that day arrives I'm quite keen to learn more about running a business. This is a marvellous opportunity Clara is offering me. I'd be a fool not to take it up. Believe me, I would like children, a real family to call my own, one day. But not now, not yet. There are other things I want to do first.'

'So being a wife, a mother, comes second to being a businesswoman, does it?'

'No, I'm not saying anything of the sort. I just want to enjoy what I have a bit more before . . .'

'. . . I trap you into marriage?' Marc stood up. 'Well, if you're going to postpone having babies, maybe you'd prefer to postpone the wedding too.'

'Marc, what is this? Why are you being so difficult all of a sudden?' Patsy gazed up at him, her mouth falling open in amazement.

'You made this decision without even discussing it with me. That tells me a great deal. It tells me you aren't really committed to our marriage.'

Patsy shook her head in disbelief. 'It tells you that I'm an independent, free-thinking girl, which is why you fell in love with me in the first place.'

'Yes, but from August, or some time in the autumn or winter, or whenever you can find the time to marry me, that will all change, won't it?'

'No, it won't change. Why should it? I'm me, and you're you. We can be married and still be individuals, surely? And for goodness' sake sit down, Marc, everyone is staring.'

Marc sat, but his face remained stony. 'Perhaps I'm overreacting,' he conceded.

'I think you are.'

'But I would like to have been consulted.'

'Did you consult me when you took the promotion?'

'That's not the same thing, and you know it.'

Patsy sighed, pushing her untouched coffee away. 'I never saw you as a chauvinist, Marc, so don't start now. I've no wish to quarrel with you because I love you.' She took hold of his hand, holding it between both her own, feeling its warmth, its strength. 'But give me a little space to breathe, please. If you're wanting a good Catholic wife who'll give you ten bambinos as your mamma did for your papa then you're marrying the wrong girl.'

He looked sharply at her for a second and then the frostiness in his expression melted away. 'Dammit, Patsy, you know you're the only girl for me. Is it wrong to want a replica of you, a smaller version?'

'I think you'll find one of me quite enough to deal with for now,' and lifting his hand to her lips, she kissed his fingers one by one. His eyes glimmered at her, telling her he wanted to take her some place and kiss her more seriously. But he still didn't offer his congratulations on the partnership, and there was the very slightest coolness between them as a result.

15

Carmina and Patsy

Alec Hall always seemed to know the moment she walked into his shop. Even before he scented that familiar and intoxicating perfume, he would experience a prickle of recognition, an instinctive awareness that she was close by. He was never wrong. There she was now, riffling through the latest bunch of records. God, she was coming over.

'Can I listen to "I Beg of You", please? I just love Elvis.'

'It's doing well this month.' As he reached for the record from his stock Alec was wondering how long he could keep her talking. 'Do you go dancing every weekend?'

Carmina manufactured a look of boredom. 'If I feel like it. I'm pretty busy, you know. And my parents are so strict they don't always let me go, and if they do I have to be home by eleven at the latest.' She pulled a face.

'I'm sure they're only trying to protect you, and I don't blame them, lovely girl like you.'

'They're just being mean and old-fashioned.'

He gave her a sympathetic smile. 'I expect they can't

quite accept that you're all grown up and not a child any more.'

Her eyes seemed to darken as she vigorously nodded. 'That's it *exactly*! Oh, how understanding you are.'

Alec's brain fogged as he gazed into those melting brown eyes and all he could think to say next was, 'You can go into the booth now. I'll play the record for you.'

Alec swore softly to himself as he watched her sashay across the floor, swinging her hips in that tempting, beguiling way she had. What was the matter with him? Couldn't he keep her talking a while longer? He was behaving like some tongue-tied schoolboy. And no wonder. How long was it since he'd had a woman? Any woman, let alone one as young and stunning as Carmina Bertalone. Too long!

Save for one or two disastrous episodes best forgotten, the last time must be five years ago when . . . no, best not to remember that either. Yet the image of another young and beautiful, much-cherished face, rushed into his mind nonetheless, heedless of common sense.

There wasn't a day passed when he didn't think of her . . . and remember.

How could he ever forget the vivid happiness whenever she looked at him, always smiling, always laughing. His precious Joo Eun, his silver pearl. And that's what she'd seemed like to him, a treasure beyond price at just fifteen. So young, so perfect. There was nothing, to his mind, more special, more perfect than a young girl, a virgin. He'd been so utterly besotted that he'd even married her, gone through a form of marriage anyway, out there in the wilds of Korea.

He could still mentally trace the high sculptured cheekbones, her wide luscious mouth, the huge eyes beseeching him to stay. But he hadn't stayed. The moment peace had been declared he couldn't wait to get home, certain she'd follow him. Only she hadn't. She'd stayed behind and he'd lost her.

'Mr Hall.' Carmina had opened the door of the booth and was calling across to him. 'I can't seem to get the earphones to work.'

Alec ignored a customer waiting to pay for a selected record and went right over. Joo Eun had been shy, her behaviour bound by tradition. Yet here was one girl who showed not a care in the world for boundaries of any kind. What she'd got up to in that car with Luc Fabriani didn't take much imagination, certainly enough to turn her poor mother's lovely black hair quite grey.

It was cramped and warm in the tiny booth with the scent of Carmina's Primitif perfume overpowering his senses. He edged in beside her and began to check the earphones. 'They were working fine half an hour ago.'

'Maybe it's me,' she said, in her little-girl voice. 'I'm hopeless with anything mechanical.'

He looked down into her face, into a pair of fascinating, darkly fringed eyes which were anything but innocent, one eyebrow slightly raised as if to provoke him. Alec recognised the game she was playing. 'These things can be tricky,' he conceded, instinctively going along with it. 'That's a pretty dress you're wearing, Carmina. Blue is definitely your colour.'

He could have kicked himself. What sort of stupid remark was that? *Blue is definitely your colour.* What had happened to his wit, to the seductive charm which had once won over women, young girls in particular, with no trouble at all? Worn out by age and cynicism, no doubt.

'Thanks.' She seemed pleased by the compliment nonetheless, her cheeks going a little pink and her mouth drooping into a tantalising pout.

Alec had a sudden urge to kiss her, to rip open the pretty buttons of her shirtwaister dress and explore the luscious beauty beneath. Sweat broke out on his brow just thinking about it. He was burning up inside, in torment. He had to get out of here before he made a complete idiot of himself. This wasn't the place for making overtures of that nature, not with customers waiting.

'There you are, I think you'll find it OK now.' There'd been nothing wrong with the earphones, but then he'd known all along that there wouldn't be. So had she. He turned to leave but Carmina seemed to be in his way and they bumped into each other, the fullness of her breasts pressing softly against his heated skin.

'Oh, sorry,' she giggled.

Alec felt a tightness in his chest. This was a dangerous sport she played. Did she have any idea where it might lead?

'You weren't doing the records last Friday,' she said, putting her mouth into a little moue of regret. 'Will you be at St John's school this week?'

'I might.' His voice cracked. 'I'll try.'

'Try hard, Alec,' she whispered. 'I can call you Alec, can't I, now that we're friends?'

He nodded, for the life of him quite unable to respond.

'Good. I'll look out for you.' Then she took the earphones from his nerveless fingers and clamped them to her head, giving him a teasing smile that carried a world of meaning.

All Alec could do was escape while he still had some of his dignity intact, deeply aware of an embarrassing flush about his neck and jaw as he hurried to the counter to take the money off Patsy Bowman for a 'Whole Lotta Woman' by Marvin Rainwater.

But the girl's outrageous behaviour had given birth to a small thread of hope that perhaps life might still have a few surprises in store for him, after all.

On Sunday mornings Carmina was expected to put on her best clothes, complete with hat and gloves, and attend Mass with her parents and brothers and sisters.

Even Patsy went regularly to church as she was having lessons with Father Dimmock, Papa having persuaded her that it would be a good thing for her to embrace the Catholic faith if she was to become a member of the Bertalone family.

'I don't mind turning,' Patsy had told him. 'It's the same God, and if it makes you all happy, I'm quite happy to convert. My foster parents never bothered much about church and I'm not sure who my real parents were, although . . .' She'd paused, searching for some sort of explanation of how she felt about the confusion over her identity, but couldn't quite seem to find the right words. It was a long and complicated story and she really didn't feel like talking about it. Papa Bertalone had interrupted her with a gentle hand on her arm.

'It isn't important who you *were* my little one, only who you are *now*, and what you might become . . .'

Patsy had smiled at him. 'That's what Clara always says.'

'She was ever a wise woman.'

Patsy had come to church with the family ever since, though she couldn't yet take a full part in the Mass. Today, she was happily chatting to Carlotta and Gina, Marc hovering nearby. He was always seeking ways to touch or kiss her, even if it was only to put his arm about his fiancée as he led her into church.

The sight of their evident happiness in each other, and Patsy's cheerful, friendly attitude, almost made Carmina want to throw up. Why did the girl have to be so reasonable, so helpful? Carmina had no desire for a stranger to join the family, or to come between herself and Marc. She liked things exactly the way they were.

Except, of course, that she would be getting married herself quite soon, if things worked out right.

Carmina glanced across at Gina marshalling the younger children into line, making sure they had their missals, their socks pulled up, their hair all tidy. What a little mother hen she was. Yet still a secretive one. The sisters had rarely exchanged a word recently and Carmina felt she had to watch the girl like a hawk, just to make sure Luc came nowhere near her.

Of course, once Luc had stopped fighting the

inevitable, Gina's little crush on him would no longer matter. It would be in the past, buried. And since Luc was not only a Catholic but also Italian, Carmina was quite certain she could persuade her parents into accepting him, in the end. It was simply a question of timing, and good planning.

Today, as luck would have it, she saw him the minute they came out of church. There he was, lounging on a wall smoking a cigarette. Carmina ached to boldly walk over and give him a kiss, or maybe say: Papa, this is my boyfriend. Surely the fact that he was here proved that he wanted to be with her. And like all good Italian Catholics, the Fabrianis never missed Mass.

But then Carmina noticed that Gina was watching him too, which instantly filled her with fury. It was imperative the erstwhile lovers be kept apart. Once they started exchanging sweet little confidences, who knew what might go wrong with her plan? She was about to go over to drag Gina away and make sure she had no opportunity to speak to him when a hand grasped her arm.

'Don't even think about going over. Mamma is expecting us all to hurry back for lunch, and you'll only ruin a lovely family day.'

Carmina spun about, her face crimson with rage. 'Who are *you* to tell *me* what to do, Patsy Bowman? You've no right to lecture me on *family*!'

'I'm your friend, I hope. I saw you eyeing up Luc and thought you might be considering going over to speak to him. I wouldn't advise it. Papa would be cross and Mamma would only get upset. I'm just warning you that I don't think it would be wise.'

'You know *nothing*!' Carmina hissed, aware that Papa was indeed glancing her way, puzzled by the angry sound of their voices.

'Don't play the innocent with me, Carmina. I know you're chasing after him. Leave well alone.'

Carmina gasped. 'Unlike you, I don't need to chase a man. I only have to crook my little finger and they all come running.'

'I'm only too aware that you love chasing men, Carmina. You can't seem to help yourself. You were certainly in that record booth with Alec Hall a long time the other day, for instance. Few of his other customers get such close attention.'

'Now you're being ridiculous. Alec Hall is *old*. I wouldn't look twice at him.'

Patsy smiled. 'No, but I suspect you enjoy having him look at you, admiring your charms.'

Carmina bridled, eyes darkening dangerously as she hissed at Patsy, 'Shut up! How many times do I have to tell you to keep your interfering nose out of my affairs?'

From the corner of her eye Patsy saw Luc get up off the wall and go quickly over to Gina. For some reason this surprised her. Gina had never seemed the sort to defy her parents. Nevertheless, the pair were certainly talking earnestly enough now, uncaring of who might see them together.

Thinking Carmina might defy her and go over to interrupt them, Patsy grasped the girl firmly by the arm and began to steer her along the church path, away from Luc Fabriani.

Carmina had noticed too and struggled furiously to release herself from Patsy's iron grip. 'Let me go!'

Patsy gave the girl a little shake. 'Listen, you know how Papa feels about the Fabrianis and Gina is already in trouble over him. You order *me* not to interfere but that's exactly what *you're* doing. Gina is nuts about him, so leave well alone.'

The girl came rushing past at that moment, at a lolloping run, to join her parents and siblings ahead of them on the path. Carmina wrenched herself free and stalked off after her, pert nose in the air, making it abundantly clear that Patsy had overstepped the mark yet again.

Carmina didn't go directly home to share in the usual Sunday lunch. She couldn't bear the thought of family chit-chat, of being forced to be polite to Gina, or to Patsy, neither of whom she had the patience for right now. They were so self-righteous, so sure of their own boring judgement on what was right and wrong, wasting no opportunity to point out how she couldn't have what she most wanted in the world.

They were so wrong! She could have whatever she wished. She'd known that from the moment her own brilliant beauty had blossomed, and men, even Papa, would softly smile and give in to her every whim. Why should Luc Fabriani be any different?

Furious that he should have the temerity to ignore their agreement and speak to Gina, she wanted time alone to think, to calm herself, to readjust her plan. She needed to walk in the fresh air, and, ignoring her mother's pleas, set off towards the canal.

'That girl is such a trial to me,' she heard Mamma say in despair, but Carmina only quickened her pace.

There were times, like now, when she felt very much an outsider, as if nobody cared one jot for her feelings.

She rushed along Liverpool Road, slipped down through the canal basin past narrowboats painted in bright reds, blues and greens, then crossed beneath the Bridgewater Viaduct heading for some wasteland where, it was claimed, lay buried an old Roman Fort. She was hoping to find some peace and quiet since little work would be taking place down on the Wharves today. Once or twice she glanced back over her shoulder, thinking that she heard footsteps following her. She waited a moment thinking it might be Luc, come to say he was sorry for ignoring her.

No one appeared, but then most people were in church or at home with their families, as she should be, Carmina supposed, still burning up with rage. She must have imagined the footsteps as there was only the sound of a passing goods train clanking overhead.

Because this area had once offered a good viewpoint of the River Medlock and was on the direct route to Chester, the Romans had apparently selected this ground as a site for a fort. Not that there was much evidence of it now among the weeds and rubble. Close by, where once the Medlock had flowed, the Bridgewater and Rochdale Canals had been cut through the red sandstone. Carmina flung herself down on a grassy hump with a sigh and put her head in her hands.

What was she to do? Luc was ignoring her, still chasing after Gina. How could she make him see that she simply wouldn't take no for an answer?

Perhaps she was worrying unduly and he'd really only been saying goodbye to her, making it clear that Carmina was his girl now, and that it was all over between them. She might have found out if Patsy Bowman hadn't got in the way.

How could he possibly love Gina? She was so insipid, so *plain* by comparison to herself. Carmina was quite sure that Luc was only being nice to the girl out of pity. He felt sorry for her, that's all.

If only Gina wasn't on the scene at all.

16

Gina and Carmina

The market was strangely silent, deserted since it was a Sunday. There were no striped canvas awnings flapping in the wind, no voices shouting out the glories of their wares. No women in headscarves haggling over the price of Jimmy Ramsay's brawn. No banter and chatter. It was as if the beating heart of Champion Street had for some reason stopped. Gina's own heart didn't seem able to keep to its normal rhythm either, not since the moment Luc had approached her outside the church.

'I need to speak to you urgently,' he'd whispered. 'It's so long since I've seen you. Can we meet at our usual place? Please?'

She'd turned away with a little shake of her head, but Luc had blocked her escape.

'Gina, listen to me. Things aren't what you think. I want to explain something to you. Please do this for me. Meet me later this afternoon, if only for what we once were to each other.'

She'd wanted to refuse his request. He'd betrayed her, after all, by two-timing her with other girls. Carmina had explained all of that to her. He hadn't even responded to her note of apology when she'd been confined to her room by an over-protective mother.

But then Gina made the mistake of looking up into his dark eyes and found herself quite incapable of saying no. She'd glanced along the church path, saw that Carmina was arguing with Patsy, as usual, that Mamma and Papa were well ahead with her younger siblings in tow.

'All right, I'll see you later, but I can't stay long. Not like before.' And she'd run from him then, in her hobbledehoy fashion, afraid that if she lingered, she might weaken and throw herself into his arms.

Now here she was, still wanting to do exactly that. They were standing together in the shade of the old copper beech in a quiet corner of Buile Hill Park, their favourite spot on what had once been a regular Sunday afternoon jaunt in the last month or two. They'd take a bus to the end of the road, then stroll around the park, hand in hand, laughing and talking the whole time. It had felt wonderful to escape Castlefield, to go to a place where nobody knew them and they could kiss and cuddle far away from nosy neighbours and prying eyes.

Despite her reservations, Gina had tried to make herself look nice in a new green plaid chemise dress. It had a button-through collar and was belted over the hip above a pleated skirt. She wore her black patent T-strap shoes to go with it.

A pale late April sun was slanting across the grass, radiating around them, lighting his glossy black hair, making his olive skin glow with health and vigour. Luc's eyes were a dark blue, almost purple, but for some reason today they looked dull and lacklustre, as if he gazed into some far distant place where she couldn't quite reach him. Yet he had never appeared more handsome, more attractive.

Feeling her knees start to weaken Gina took a step back, not wishing to seem needy. 'So, what was it you wanted to explain to me?'

Luc shuffled his feet in the dusty soil, looked out across the vista of lawns where young couples strolled with babies in prams. A child was throwing a ball for a yapping dog, a boy flying a kite. He thought the museum might be closed today but there were several young people playing tennis on the courts, and a few old men happily enjoying the delights of the bowling green. He could hear a band playing and wished he could take her somewhere really quiet and private, where he could persuade her with his kisses, which would surely be far more effective than the pitiful excuses crowding his mind.

Luc cleared his throat, took a steadying breath. There was only so much he could say and she looked so cold, so unfriendly, not like his sweet Gina at all. But he had to try, or his dreams ended right here.

'I believe Carmina has been telling you lies about me.' He looked into her face, small and pinched and pale, and waited for her reaction. When none came, he continued, 'I hear she's been spreading rumours about me, saying that I've been seeing other girls. I need you to know, Gina, that it isn't true.'

Gina gazed up at him from beneath her long lashes, saying nothing, not daring to hope.

'And if she said I went with someone else to the dance, that was a lie too. I hoped and prayed you'd be there. When you stood me up, I was devastated. I missed you, and had a miserable time. Then Carmina said you'd chucked me. I don't know why you decided it was all over between us, but if it's anything I've done, you just have to say what it is and I'll do my best to put it right. I'd do anything for you, Gina, anything!'

'I don't understand. Carmina said I'd finished with you? I never told her to say that. Anyway, I didn't stand you up. I sent a note.'

He looked at her blankly. 'Note? I never got any note.'

'I gave it to Carmina. It said how Mamma and Papa insisted I stay in all week, because I was over-tired. Of course, they'd also found out we've been secretly meeting and didn't approve.' Gina pulled a face. 'I wrote to explain all of this and Carmina promised faithfully that she'd . . .'

Gina stopped speaking and they stared at each other.

'She never delivered it,' Luc said, his voice hard. 'Surprise, surprise.'

Gina swallowed, and feeling suddenly confused and vulnerable, left him standing by the tree and went to sit on a nearby bench. She clasped her hands tight in her lap to gather her strength. Could this misunderstanding be all Carmina's doing? She'd believed in her sister, had trusted her implicitly. Clearly she'd been a fool to do so. Had Carmina not given him the letter out of carelessness, or sheer malice? And why would she do such a thing? Gina picked at the pleats of her dress with troubled fingers, trying to sort out the muddle in her head.

'You know what this means, don't you?' Luc said, coming to sit beside her. 'This split between us is caused by Carmina, not me.'

Gina looked straight into those dark hooded eyes. She wasn't quite ready to accept this fact, not quite yet. Nor was she prepared to defend her sister. Not until she'd talked to Carmina and asked her about the letter.

'So who did you dance with then?' she asked, returning to her earlier point.

Luc sighed. This was the question he'd dreaded most. It was sheer torture to him that now he did have to lie, if he was to have any hope of winning Gina back. He combed agitated fingers through his hair. 'I can't remember. Nobody who mattered. It's you I want, Gina, you know it is.'

But Gina wasn't letting him off the hook quite so easily. She edged away, leaving a little distance between them. 'Did you dance with Carmina?'

There was a small silence, then Luc said, 'I might have done, briefly, I don't remember.'

She gave a bitter little laugh. 'Now that *is* a lie. Nobody can dance with my glamorous sister and not remember.'

'I needed to ask her about you. We only talked about *you*.' That part at least was true.

Gina looked unconvinced. 'Carmina tells me that

you and she used to go out together, so what went wrong? Which of you broke it off?'

'I did, when I met you.'

'But how do I know you don't still fancy her?'

'Because I fancy *you*. How can I convince you, Gina? The minute I saw you at the church's New Year Social, I had eyes only for you, not for your sister.' He was looking at her now as if he couldn't bear to tear his eyes away. 'It took weeks for me to convince you that I was serious, if you remember, and I'll go through it all over again, if necessary. I just hope it won't be.'

Oh, she wanted to believe him, badly. Gina longed to accept his word but felt compelled to ask one more question. 'So it's not true then that you asked Carmina to go to the dance before you asked me, or that you've kissed her?'

This was turning out to be even worse than he'd imagined. Luc felt sick. 'No, I certainly didn't ask her to come to the dance with me.' He made no mention of the dangerous kisses in the car later.

He didn't even know if it was possible to win Gina back without Carmina ruining everything, but knew he must try. It was at least true that he never had asked Carmina to the dance. He'd cursed himself a million times since for his weakness in letting things go so far, but he'd believed that Gina really had dumped him and he'd felt bereft, so hurt and angry inside. Thank God he'd managed to resist Carmina in the end.

Now he was convinced Carmina had lied to him too, and he'd no intention of allowing a stupid mistake to ruin his chances with Gina. For that reason she must never hear of what had gone on in that car, not if he had to walk through fire to keep Carmina from blabbing.

'Have you seen her since the dance?' Her eyes were wide and clear as she asked the question, determined not to show her pain.

He recklessly slid one arm along the back of the bench. 'No, she follows me about sometimes, which I hate. It's you I want and only you. I hate to say this, since she's your sister, but Carmina is a compulsive liar, and she can't seem to get it into her head that I'm not interested. OK, we had a bit of a fling once, but it was all over between us months ago. Believe me, I don't give a fig for Carmina, only you. Why would I want to kiss her when I could have you?'

Then he tilted up her chin and if his words didn't quite convince her, his lips most certainly did.

Gina breathed in the familiar scent of him: Lifebuoy toilet soap, the oil he put on his hair and something that was indefinably Luc. It was some moments before the kiss ended and then she leaned against him with a little sigh.

'Oh, Luc, I thought I'd lost you.'

'Never, not while I live and breathe, no matter what anyone tries to do to us.'

The late afternoon sun was glinting on the waters of the canal as it slid slowly beneath the railway arches. The narrowboats bumped gently against the quay and somewhere in the distance Carmina heard a clock strike, and the shunt of a train. Five o'clock already. She must have fallen asleep but now hunger was beginning to overcome her sulks and she thought that if she didn't go home soon, she might miss tea as well as Sunday lunch.

She dreaded facing Gina, who would no doubt be bursting with happiness, having at last spoken to Luc. Carmina would have given anything to know what had passed between them in that conversation outside the church. Anything.

'Hello, Carmina, had a good sleep?'

Carmina started as Alec Hall flopped down beside her. She'd been so engrossed in her own thoughts, she hadn't heard him approach. 'Hell, you scared me half to death, creeping up on me like that. What are you doing here? Have you been watching me?'

Alec smiled. 'I thought you looked in need of a bit of company. Unless you're content simply to admire the scenery, of course?'

Carmina pouted provocatively at him. Alec Hall might be a bit long in the tooth but he always made her feel good about herself, offering the sort of admiration she most desired. 'I couldn't bear to go home and play happy families. Sundays are so *boring*!'

Alec chuckled. 'I can see that wouldn't exactly be your thing.'

He brushed a stray curl from her cheek, a surprisingly intimate gesture which startled Carmina. Usually he looked too afraid to touch her, treating her with gentlemanly deference. Not that she minded too much. She was feeling particularly raw and rejected after seeing Luc and Gina together, and, even more than usual, felt in need of proof that she was still attractive to men.

She pretended to frown at him. 'I think you've been following me, you naughty man. I thought I heard someone a while back.'

'Would you mind if I had?' Alec softly asked as he edged nearer.

He ran the heel of one thumb down her bare arm, making Carmina shiver. The sensation wasn't entirely unpleasant and she dimpled a smile at him, stretching herself as a cat might when it wants to be stroked and petted.

'Depends why you did it.'

'Maybe I like following you. You are rather irresistible.'

Carmina almost purred with pleasure, then tucked her feet beneath her so that her short skirt slid up her long shapely thighs. She made a show of smoothing it down again, giving him a seductive little smile as she saw his eyes darken. He was entranced by her, she could tell. Why couldn't she have this effect upon Luc?

'I saw how upset you were over Luc Fabriani talking to your sister. Why do you bother with him, Carmina? You're the kind of girl who needs a man, not a boy.' The back of his fingers brushed her cheek and Carmina jerked away, not quite liking this perceived criticism of the man she adored.

'Luc is man enough for me.' She made as if to get up but Alec prevented her from moving by capturing her head with one hand, his fingers now combing through her soft curls.

'Do you know how very lovely you are, how bewitching your eyes, how luscious your mouth? Yes, I expect you do. Your many boyfriends will tell you that all the time. But I'm not a boy, Carmina, so it means more when I say it.'

'Does it?' She felt strangely mesmerised by his closeness, by the way he was looking at her so steadily with that steely gaze of his. She could see the wrinkles fanning out beneath his eyes, the deeply etched lines between nose and mouth. He didn't look quite so alluringly handsome close to, his age being far more in evidence, yet he was still attractive in a compelling sort of way. 'Why would that be, I wonder?'

'Because I have more experience.' Closing the short distance between them, he gently nibbled at her lower lip. Carmina pushed him away, excited by his daring and yet shocked by it.

'Hey, what the hell do you think you're doing?' It was fine when she was the one doing the flirting, but he seemed a bit too full of himself today.

Alec didn't seem to hear her. He gave a throaty chuckle, pulled her close again and began to kiss her more thoroughly. This time Carmina did not resist. Instead, she found herself responding. His tongue rasped against her teeth, moving and teasing, stirring a burn of desire somewhere deep in the pit of her belly. She arched her body against his, relishing his kisses, making no protest when he cupped her breast.

But then he slid his hand between her legs and she jerked away, giving a little cry of protest.

'Don't play the virgin with me, Carmina, because

unlike your trusting mamma, I know that you aren't.' The next instant he was pushing her back on to the grass, dragging apart the buttons of her blouse with clumsy fingers. 'I know what you and Luc Fabriani got up to in that old banger of his after the dance. Not quite the behaviour of a nice, well-brought-up girl, is it?'

She was struggling to catch her breath, to capture his busy fingers. 'You were spying on me? How dare you! You're wrong. We didn't do anything.'

He gave a low chuckle. 'Then it's time you found out what you're missing.'

She tried to stop him, gasping for breath as she tussled vainly to free herself, but he was too strong for her, too determined. Her hair was all over her face, her breasts open to the cool breeze and her skirt half way up her thighs, all dignity quite gone.

'I've told you to stop. What the . . .'

But her protests were stopped by his mouth clamping down upon her own, hard and hungry. Carmina could feel the weight of him on top of her, the bulge against her bare leg. He pulled up her skirt the last few inches and ripped off her panties. Then he was thrusting into her with an urgency that would have made her gasp, had she been able to. It was like a horror movie. It all happened so fast that she couldn't move, couldn't even think.

He lifted his mouth from hers for a brief second to give her a leering grin, but did not pause, his breathing ragged as he pounded into her.

She might have screamed then, only Carmina

couldn't believe this was actually happening, that she could have so entirely lost control of the situation. He had her pinned down with her arms splayed out above her head, making revolting animal noises as she lay helpless beneath him in complete shock and agony. The pain was terrible but he made no concession to her whimpers and cries, presumably taking them as some sign of enjoyment on her part.

Yet something overwhelming was happening to her. A curl of raw, fierce emotion was born deep inside her belly, neither fear nor revulsion but the hard burn of desire. With painful clarity Carmina knew in her heart that she'd provoked this situation. She'd asked for it with her flirtatious teasing, and her allure.

And now, to her shame, she was revelling in it. The excitement of his lust had fired her own.

She tried to bite him, snapping and snarling like a bitch on heat, and when he released her hands she didn't claw at his face, as she might have done to protect herself. Instead, Carmina clutched him tightly to her bare breast, scratching him all down his back, raising them both to new heights of passion. Minutes later she gave a sigh almost of regret when he slumped from her to roll over on to the grass.

'Oh, that was good, Carmina. Did you enjoy it? I certainly did. Dammit, you're a little whore, you really are.'

That was not at all what she'd wanted to hear.

Fury rose in her throat like bile. She suddenly felt incandescent with rage. Sobs shook her body, tears began to roll down her cheeks and she slapped and beat at him with her bare hands, clawed at his laughing face with her nails.

'How dare you do that to me without my permission! You raped me. You goddammed *raped* me!

Alec began to laugh. 'Don't be ridiculous! You were as desperate for it as I was. That wasn't exactly a virginal kiss you gave me. You've been sitting up and begging for me to do that ever since that day you bumped into me on your way out of my music shop back at Easter time. And I dare say you'll want it again, and again. You and I, Carmina, are one of a kind. It's as if we were meant for each other.'

17

Amy

The little row of white tubes on the gas fire in the bedroom popped one after the other as Thomas put a match to light them. Mavis, seated at her dressing table in her Viyella nightdress, spun about at the sound.

'I don't think a fire is necessary, since we're going to bed.'

'It's like an ice box in here, and if you're going to sit about half dressed you'll catch your death,' Thomas said.

Mavis at once reached for her silk quilted dressing gown, then went to turn off the gas tap. 'The bill is big enough.'

Thomas shivered as he dropped his trousers to the floor. Making a small clicking noise at the back of her throat Mavis rushed to pick them up and put them on a hanger in the wardrobe, giving her husband a filthy look as she did so.

'I were going to do that. But if you like waiting on me, do you want to hang up me shirt, an' all?' He held the garment out to her.

'Don't be facetious.'

Mavis returned to her dressing table and took out her hair-pins, dropping each one with a little ping into a china tray. 'Do try not to wake me when you go down to the bakery before dawn, will you please? You make such a noise, falling over your own feet I shouldn't wonder, and I need my sleep. I really wish we had a proper house, with three bedrooms, then I wouldn't be disturbed at all.'

'I'll try to creep out quietly, love,' Thomas agreed, as he did every night. 'Anyroad, I won't be doing it for much longer. Once our Chris knows the ropes, I intend to take a well-earned rest.'

Mavis looked at him in disbelief. 'You mean slope off down to the pub instead of working?'

'I mean it's time I retired.'

'Oh, that old chestnut,' she huffed. 'I'll believe that when I see it.'

Thomas waited until his wife had put in her curling pins, encased them in a brown hair net and climbed into bed beside him. Putting on her spectacles, which she never wore in public, she picked up her *Woman's Weekly*.

Usually, Thomas was happy to leave her reading while he drifted off to sleep. It never took him long, sleep capturing him the minute his head struck the pillow; the result of a hard day's work in the bakery or at the allotment. Mavis would give him a few nudges with her sharp elbow if he started to snore, before finally switching off her own lamp and settling down as far from him as was humanly possible in the double bed they'd shared throughout their married life.

Tonight, however, he was feeling pleased with himself that for once in his life he knew something she didn't.

Thomas cleared his throat. 'Has our Chris mentioned the latest plans to you?'

From behind her magazine Mavis gave a small sigh. Engrossed in a romantic serial she really had no wish to listen to her husband prattle on about business matters, some new cake recipe or whatever it was that consumed his tiny brain. 'I've no idea what you're talking about.'

'Oh, hasn't he told you?' Thomas said, milking the moment for as long as he possibly could. 'I fully expected him to mention them, since you and him are like that much of the time.' He crossed two fingers and grinned across at her.

Mavis struggled to contain her patience. 'Well, are you going to tell me or not?' she snapped, when it finally ran out. 'What plans are these?'

'His plan to move out.'

Thomas felt rather as if he'd dropped a hand grenade then stood back to watch as it took off. He wasn't disappointed. His wife's face looked as if it was about to explode. Her *Woman's Weekly* dropped onto the green quilted eiderdown, quite forgotten, as she jerked upright in bed and almost screamed at him.

'*Move out*?'

'That's the general idea. I felt sure he would've told you.' Reaching over, Thomas turned off his own bedside lamp, plumped up his pillows and settled down to sleep. 'Night, night!'

'Don't you dare start snoring in the middle of a conversation. Why is he moving out? Where is he going?'

Thomas closed his eyes. '*They*, not him. Our Chris is a married chap now, Mavis, with responsibilities, which he's taking very seriously. Him and Amy have decided they need a place of their own, for when the babby comes. They've taken that house next door to the pawn shop.'

He might just as well have said brothel. Mavis was appalled.

'The *pawn shop*! My son is going to live next door to a pawn shop? *Never*! I won't allow it.'

Thomas chuckled softly into his pillow. 'I doubt you can do owt to stop it.'

'I certainly can. I simply won't hear of it, do you hear me? I shall put a stop to this nonsense first thing in the morning. They can't possibly move until that baby is safely born. I won't allow it. Do you hear me? *I will not allow it*.'

Thomas answered her with a loud snore.

'I really can't think why you would choose to move out. It's so much more convenient for you to live here, above the bakery, particularly since you and your father have to be up before dawn each day.'

Chris sighed. He'd expected this reaction from his mother, but was determined not to be pressured into backing down. 'Amy feels we should get a place of our own before the baby comes, and it's no more than fifty yards down the street. I don't think I'll have any trouble getting to work on time.'

'Next to the pawn broker? I never thought a son of mine would stoop so low.'

Chris chuckled. 'It's still here in Champion Street, Mother. *You* live above the shop, with market stalls opposite.'

'More's the pity. I'm *still* waiting for your father to find me a decent house to live in. I hoped for something better for my only son.'

Chris smiled to himself and couldn't help glancing about him at the impeccably decorated, well-furnished terraced house he'd always called home. Not a table-mat out of place. Even now, laid up for breakfast after they'd completed the first baking, the kitchen table was covered with a hand-embroidered tablecloth, the toast neatly arrayed in a silver rack and his eggs and bacon on blue and white Cornishware. Yet somewhere deep inside, his mother clearly harboured a deep resentment against his father.

He wondered if perhaps she wasn't just the teeniest bit jealous, perhaps of their youth and evident love for each other, if not the home he and Amy had chosen to live in. 'I think that's for us to decide, don't you. We're happy and excited about our new life together, and starting a family. Be pleased for us.'

'Of course I'm pleased, dear, but you're my only son, I want the best for you. I never wanted you to go into the business with your father in the first place.' She dabbed at her eyes with a lavender-scented handkerchief, although there was no sign of tears.

Chris decided to tease her out of her ill humour. 'You wanted me to stay as a milkman, working for the Co-op Dairy?'

'Don't be daft. I wanted you to get a good job, or

perhaps start a business of your own. Not rent a poky little house next to the pawn broker.'

'We all have to start somewhere. I'm sure we'll survive, as you have. You and Pops seem to have done all right for yourselves. There's a new Hillman Minx parked outside, remember.'

'You wouldn't *believe* what I've had to put up with,' Mavis objected, at which point Chris decided it would be politic to escape. He'd heard her list of complaints many times before, and it was a long one. He put his knife and fork neatly side by side on his plate, as he'd been taught to do from a boy, wiped his mouth on his napkin, then kissed her papery soft cheek. It smelled strongly of the powder she used, even at seven o'clock in the morning. 'Stop fretting, Mother. You're going to be a grandma soon, concentrate on that. It'll be great!'

She called after him as he fled back to the bakery, but Chris pretended not to hear.

Amy had fewer opportunities for escape. Throughout each long day as she ironed shirts, polished the brasses, cut ham sandwiches for lunch then spent the afternoon struggling with knitting a pair of socks on four needles under her mother-in-law's strict supervision, Mavis never let up for a moment.

'I can't think why you would want to take Chris away from his family. We've made you very welcome, despite your disastrous start to married life together, of which we strongly disapproved, as you know. We've even provided a brand new three-quarter bed and somehow squeezed it into Chris's old room. Although what more do you need to do in a bedroom but sleep?'

'There wouldn't be room for a cot,' Amy pointed out.

'Don't be foolish. Cots, and babies, are very small. Absolutely tiny. And everything is done for you here. How on earth would you manage on your own when the baby comes?'

Amy judged it wise not to respond to this, nursing her happiness close to her heart that at least escape was in sight.

'Chris has certainly never said anything to me before about wanting to leave home.'

'It's quite usual, when boys grow up.'

Mavis bridled. 'He's always been very happy here. This is his *home*.'

'He's a married man now,' Amy quietly reminded her. 'And soon to be a father.'

'Exactly, but I would have thought it was a wife's duty to fit in with her husband, and not the other way around,' Mavis snapped.

Amy swallowed her irritation and patiently smiled. 'We've been very grateful to you for letting us stay here all these months. But it's time for us to have our own home now that we're starting a family. I would think you'll be glad of the extra space, once we move out.'

'It would make far more sense if Thomas and I moved out to the suburbs, and you and Chris took this house.'

Amy glanced up from her efforts to turn the heel and stared at her mother-in-law in surprise. 'Is that a possibility?'

'It would be if I had any say in the matter,' Mavis snapped. 'Thomas, however, is a law unto himself. If he ever sat still longer than five minutes I might manage to have the matter out with him. He promised me years ago that we'd move out of Champion Street. Of course, a promise from a husband, you'll come to see, my dear, means nothing. Men are selfish to the core. It suits him to live over the bakery, and close to that dratted allotment, even if he is contemplating retirement. Never gives a moment's thought as to whether it suits *me*. Please do make me a cup of tea, dear, my head is thumping.'

And Amy, whose legs were aching as she'd scarcely sat still all day herself, obediently went to put the kettle on. So that's the nub of the problem, she thought. Mavis has fixed her sights on a new house out in the suburbs and Thomas is content with things exactly as they are.

18

Gina and Carmina

Weeks had gone by since Gina and Luc had made up their differences beneath the old copper beech. Following the occasion when her parents had seen him at church, she'd half expected them to remark on how smart he'd looked, how polite he was, but they'd said nothing.

Every Sunday following that day, Luc had made a point of saying good morning to each of them. Good manners had driven them to reply in the end, and once or twice her mother had even smiled at him. Gina had rather hoped that this politeness might soften their attitude towards him.

To be fair to them, when Gina had finally admitted that she was seeing Luc again, her parents made no attempt to stop her. But then Gina had been very firm, determined to stop pretending, to stop being secretive.

'You can say what you like,' she'd informed her parents. 'I'm sixteen years old and I like him, so there.'

They would watch in silence as she got ready to go out, making no comment beyond asking for the usual assurance that she wouldn't be late home.

'I won't be late,' Gina would cheerfully say. Then she would kiss them on both cheeks and leave, smiling to herself as she saw Mamma bite her lip, itching to ask where Luc was taking her.

In fact they rarely did anything particularly exciting on their dates, as they didn't have much money. Most evenings they would walk by the canal or in the park if the weather was fine and they could afford the bus fare, content simply to be together. Sometimes they went to the pictures, and once to a dance, although Gina spent most of her time giggling as she simply couldn't get the hang of rock 'n' roll.

'I don't have the balance,' she mourned.

'We can smooch though, which is far more fun,' Luc told her, holding her close in his arms as they danced cheek to cheek.

But if her parents seemed to be mellowing a little, loving her and wanting her only to be happy, as all Italian parents did, her sister was barely speaking to her.

Carmina had been in a sulk for weeks, even more moody than usual. She told Gina that she thought her quite mad. 'Luc is no good. You're acting like a fool still going out with him. He betrayed you, for God's sake!'

'Ah, but he didn't,' Gina insisted. 'I realise now that was only one of *your* lies. I also know that you never did deliver that letter I gave you. Don't think I don't understand what game you're playing, Carmina. You want Luc for yourself. But you can't have him. He's mine now, so forget him. Choose one of your other many admirers.'

The fury in her sister's eyes had almost taken her

breath away. Carmina had looked as if she were about to strike her and Gina had felt a momentary, and very foolish, stab of fear. This was her sister, for goodness' sake. Instead, Carmina had clenched her fists and stormed out of the house. She'd hardly spoken a word to Gina since.

But neither Carmina's black moods, nor her jealous fury, could quench the love that was growing between Gina and Luc. They were happy together, content in each other's company despite the cloud of disapproval still hanging over the young couple, one they longed to eradicate.

Gina badly wanted Luc to be fully accepted by her parents. She longed for their approval, and one day, unable to keep her joy to herself any longer, told her mother straight out that she loved him.

Mamma huffed and puffed, threw her hands up in the air as was her wont, declaring a girl of sixteen couldn't possibly know her own mind. Gina asked how old she'd been when she'd married Papa.

'Eighteen, a very *sensible* eighteen. Nearly two years older than you are now.'

'But I'm not asking to marry him . . .' Gina very reasonably pointed out, '. . . not yet, anyway. I only want your approval that I can continue to see him and go out with him. Besides, how will you know if he's suitable if you won't meet him? I'm sure your father made an effort to get to know Papa before he agreed to your marrying him.'

'These important matters were dealt with differently in my day.'

Gina smiled. 'Of course they were, but you still fell in love with Papa, didn't you?'

And so, at last, Luc was invited to visit.

It was May and he was to come to Sunday lunch. This was the day Gina had dreamed of for so long: the day she was to bring Luc to meet her parents. She really didn't know how she'd finally succeeded in persuading them. Sheer persistence, perhaps.

Gina gave him strict instructions not to wear his leather jacket, or his tight trousers, but to choose something smart and conservative. 'And no lime-green socks or crêpe-soled shoes.'

'For you, anything,' he'd promised.

As she let him in, excitement churning her stomach, Gina saw that he looked very smart indeed in a navy suit with sharply creased narrow trousers, a Burtons Special, with a pale blue waistcoat and toning silk tie. He'd even had his hair cut. Checking that neither of her parents had followed her out into the hall, she quickly gave him a kiss.

'You look wonderful, so handsome, so respectable,' she giggled.

'So do you.'

Gina was wearing a simple grey pinafore dress in the fashionable princess line, and a pink gingham-checked blouse with a white pique collar. 'Mamma made it for me, as she loves to sew. At least with this style she can't put in sleeves of a different colour. She's so thrifty, likes to use up every scrap of fabric.'

Luc risked kissing her again while she laughed at

the memory of the rainbow-coloured dresses she'd worn as a child, and her younger sisters still wore.

'Are you ready to face the music? They're all waiting for you.'

He drew in a deep breath. 'I think so, although I'd much rather stay here and look at you.'

Gina pushed her hair from her face. She'd left out her kirby grips and it kept falling over forward into a careless bob. 'I can't think why you would want to. I'm not beautiful like Carmina, and you mustn't ever look down at my legs.'

Luc cupped his hands about her face. 'You are far more beautiful than your sister. Carmina's beauty is like an overblown rose, yours is still unfurling like a new bud.'

'Oh, Luc,' she murmured, kissing him again because she simply couldn't resist him when he spoke to her with such love in his voice. 'I can't believe this is happening, that they're willing to meet you properly, at last.'

'How could they not when I'm such a nice guy?' And they both fell to giggling.

Then Gina glanced quickly at the living-room door, dropping her voice to a whisper. 'Carmina's in there too. We had a bit of a ding-dong about her not delivering that letter, and all those lies she told about you. Yet another row. She hasn't spoken to me since but . . .'

'Gina, what are you doing out there? Where are your manners? Bring your visitor in.' Mamma's voice called out to her, sounding stern.

'I'm ready if you are,' he said, and holding hands they walked together into the living room as if they were going before a judge and jury instead of Gina's loving family.

It was the longest meal Gina could ever remember. At first no one spoke, Papa and Mamma eyeing Luc as if he were a specimen on a slab. Giovanni and Gabby giggled and whispered together, Marta told him where to sit, next to Gina but opposite herself. Carmina simmered in sulky silence at the end of the table. Only Marc and Patsy weren't present, as they were eating with the Higginson sisters today.

Antonia bluntly asked why Luc didn't get himself a better job than that of a builder's labourer.

'Antonia!' Mamma chided in shocked tones, but then listened avidly for Luc's reply.

'I'm not a labourer,' Luc explained with a smile. 'I'm an apprentice builder, learning the trade. It wasn't my first choice, that's true, but it's a good trade to have at your fingertips. There's plenty of work for builders right now.'

Gina said, 'Luc loves to cook and would like to own his own restaurant one day.'

'Cooking is good,' Mamma said. 'Why you not train to be chef?'

'I need to earn a good living first,' Luc put in. 'My father does not approve so it is no more than a dream at present. And dreams are all very well, but it is reality which pays the rent.'

Papa said, 'Very true,' and even Mamma murmured noises of approval. 'Your father he want you in his ice-a-creama business, *sì*?' Papa asked.

Luc conceded that he did. 'He is sad that I am not interested, as I am his only son.'

Papa Bertalone gave a grunt of annoyance. 'Then your papa and I have something in common, after all. Marc is not interested in the ice-a-creama either. He has the good job though, so I must accept that.'

'But you have other fine sons,' Luc pointed out. 'And many clever and beautiful daughters.'

'Don't count on me,' Alessandro hastily put in. 'I'm going to be an engineer and make lots of money.'

'I shall be a policeman when I grow up,' piped up young Giovanni. 'Or a soldier.'

'He likes uniforms,' his twin sister explained. 'So I might do the same.'

Antonia said, 'I hope to be a teacher, and Carmina is going to marry someone rich, isn't that right, Carmina?'

Carmina shrugged. She hadn't spoken a word so far and Gina cast her sister an anxious glance, praying she wasn't going to be difficult on this special day.

'You see . . .' Mamma sighed, smiling proudly at her offspring . . . 'how they disappoint us.'

'I shall go into the business with you, Papa,' said nine-year-old Marta.

Papa smiled at her and tweaked her curls. 'Then I shall just have to be patient and wait for you to grow up. And what about little Lela who is sitting so quietly beside me. What is it you want to be, my precious?'

Lela hugged him. 'I want to be with you, Papa.'

Everyone smiled at this simple ambition, but then Marco's face darkened as again he addressed Luc. 'Why your father get his drivers to take their vans on my rounds? He want to kill my business?'

'Papa,' Gina cried, appalled by the sudden turn in the conversation.

Luc frowned. 'I wasn't aware they were doing that. Would you like me to mention your objections to him? Perhaps the drivers have done this without telling him.'

Papa snorted his disbelief. 'Your papa no fool. He know what go on.'

'I'll speak to him.'

A small silence fell, no one quite knowing what to say. Gina thought it was as if Papa had been gearing himself up for an argument and when his comments were met instead with reason and politeness, all the air went out of him, rather like a punctured balloon. Gina and Luc exchanged a secret smile.

They ate breast of chicken in a delicious tomato and basil sauce and when the meal was over Luc helped to carry the dishes into the kitchen and offered to wash up, which Carlotta absolutely refused to allow.

'No, no, this is women's work. Gina and Carmina will help me.'

The younger children were sent out to play while the older ones helped Mamma clear away and then settled in a corner to read or draw, or continue working on a jigsaw. Papa got out the chess board and challenged Luc to a game. Gina was thrilled, as she interpreted this as some sort of acceptance on her father's part, if not entirely approval. It was but an opening gambit, however.

Papa came at last to the point. 'So what are your

intentions with regards to my daughter? We worry much about Gina because she is special, not like other girls.'

'She is special to me too,' Luc said, and Marco eyed him suspiciously.

'She has been very sick,' Mamma said, wiping her hands on a tea towel as she came in from the kitchen.

'Mamma!' Gina cried. '*Papa*!' But neither of her parents were listening.

Luc said, 'I know, and I'm delighted to see that she is better now.'

'She still needs special care,' Marco explained. 'She gets tired easily. Doing too much, staying out too late, is bad for her.'

'I understand.'

Gina hated it when they discussed her as if she were an object, as if she weren't sitting here listening. 'Luc doesn't want to hear all of this,' she protested.

Mamma flapped the tea towel to shush her. 'He must know how things are. You are different from other girls.'

'Stop saying that! I'm not different, I'm *not*. I've no wish to be different. I can walk, I could earn a living if only you'd let me. I might even learn to dance one day, if someone can teach me.'

Luc smiled as he squeezed her hand. Seated in the far corner of the room, Carmina made a small sound of disgust in her throat. Everyone ignored her.

Papa sternly remarked, 'And she is a good girl. Her mamma and me want her to stay that way.'

'*Papa*!' Gina was appalled and deeply embarrassed that he should presume to say such a thing.

'So do I,' Luc said, sending her a reassuring smile.

'Gina and I are good friends. Isn't that enough, for now?'

Papa seemed a little nonplussed by this sensible answer. 'So you not wish to marry my beautiful daughter?'

Gina cried, '*Stop it*, Papa! That's enough. This is Manchester, not Italy. You don't ask such questions, not so soon. We just want to see each other, to go out, and would so like your approval.'

Carmina, who had remained silent throughout the entire meal, spoke up at last. 'He can't possibly marry Gina.'

They all looked at her, surprised by the fact she had even spoken, as much as at her choice of words.

'Why could he not?' Mamma wanted to know, since no one else seemed willing to ask.

'Because I am pregnant with his baby, so Luc will have to marry *me*.'

19

Gina and Carmina

'You *slept* with her?'

'No, I didn't, I swear it,' Luc insisted, his face scarlet with embarrassment and barely controlled rage.

Papa Bertalone had generously allowed the young couple to slip quietly away to talk, following the uproar resulting from Carmina's announcement.

'Mamma and I will speak to Carmina. I think you have some explaining of your own to do with Gina.'

The pair were sitting on a folded market trestle amongst the building works by the market hall. Not the place Luc would have chosen to open his heart but Gina refused to walk any further with him.

His worst fears had been realised. Carmina had taken her revenge for his rejection by accusing him of seducing her. And he was not in a good position to deny it. He'd already admitted that they were together in his car, in a tight clinch. How could he prove that he hadn't gone all the way? He really didn't know how to cope.

Carmina had carried out her threat. It was her word against his, and why would Gina believe him? Carmina was family.

Now Gina listened to him white-faced, saying

nothing as he reminded her how he'd believed she'd finished with him. He tried to explain how Carmina had attempted to seduce him, but didn't feel his story came out quite right. The explanation sounded lame and insincere, as if he were making excuses.

'You swore to me that you'd never even kissed her. Why did you lie?' Gina asked, the pain in her voice almost more than he could bear.

'I didn't want you to be hurt. It was all a mistake, a bad one, but it meant nothing. It wasn't important. Nothing really happened, I swear it.' He grasped her hands but she tugged them away.

'Not important to you perhaps, but it was to Carmina. And is to me.'

'I hoped you'd never find out. I wish to God you hadn't. I swear I never wanted her. I don't care about Carmina, it's you I want. You know that in your heart, Gina.'

'So why did you make love to her?' The question seemed to be torn out of Gina against her will, but Luc's angry response was instant.

'I *didn't*!'

'Carmina says you did.'

'Then she's lying! Why do you believe her and not me?'

'Because she's my *sister*!'

Gina couldn't take any more. She got up and began to walk away, her limp never more pronounced than in this moment of acute distress. Luc rushed after her to grab her by the arms.

'What can I do to convince you it didn't happen?'

'Of course, it happened. She's *pregnant*, Luc. *Pregnant*! You're the one who's lying.' Panic and misery made her voice sound shrill, even to her own ears. 'I believed you the first time when she accused you of two-timing me. I can't believe in you any more. I can't *ever* forgive you for this.'

She ran from him then, sobbing as if her heart would break. Luc let out a howl of anger and frustration. He set off after her, calling her name but Gina ignored him, only trying to run faster and Luc stopped, realising he was making things worse by chasing after her and he'd no wish for her to fall.

He put his hands to his head as if he would tear his hair from his scalp, the truth of her words finally sinking home. He felt like a man drowning, floundering in deep water, gasping for air. He'd lost her. All his hopes and dreams, his plans for a bright future with the girl he loved were as ash in his mouth. A moment of stupid folly had cost him everything.

Later that same afternoon, Papa Bertalone paid a visit to the Fabrianis to discuss the matter in full, addressing the problem rather as he would a business proposition. Carmina had made her announcement, her charge against the boy, Marco explained, and how could Luc deny it?

Marco pointed out, in no uncertain terms, that he wanted no shame reflected upon his family. Their son had deeply offended two of his daughters; both Carmina and Gina were heartbroken, their young lives in ruins, and reparation must be made. If Carmina was expecting his child then there was only one possible solution: Luc must do the honourable thing and marry her.

The Fabrianis made no difficulties. They agreed with Marco's view of the situation and assured him that their son would indeed do the honourable thing. He would marry the girl, and with all speed.

Luc protested but the two older men ignored him, leaving him to stand before them white-faced as he was accused of bringing shame upon the entire Italian community and they made decisions on his future. He watched in silent anguish as his mother sobbed into her handkerchief. He tried again to put his side without entirely accusing Carmina of being a slut, but his words fell on deaf ears.

'I only kissed her, I swear it.'

But nobody was listening.

'You will marry the girl and there's an end to the matter,' his father told him. 'And if you are upset over getting the wrong daughter, you should have thought of that before you dropped your trousers. Serves you right, you stupid boy! Perhaps you will think twice in future.'

So much for family sympathy.

Luc ran up to his room, slammed and locked the door. Then sitting on his bed he picked up the photo Gina had once given him, holding it in shaking hands. It showed her leaning against their favourite tree in the park, the wind lifting her short bobbed hair, a glow of happiness in her cheeks. She looked so heartbreakingly lovely he could hardly bear to look at it. In that moment he stopped being brave and became a boy who had just lost the love of his life.

Carmina was triumphant. The fact that Gina had sobbed her heart out into her pillow all night didn't trouble her in the slightest. All was fair in love and war, wasn't that how the old saying went? Besides, hadn't she suffered too? Carmina thought that she deserved this victory after what she'd been through.

It had taken her days, weeks, to get over the shock of what Alec Hall had done to her. She'd considered reporting him to the police, except that would be far too embarrassing. They'd ask her a lot of personal questions, like why she'd let him kiss her in the first place, why her skirt had been half way up her thighs.

Carmina knew it was partly her own fault for teasing and flirting with him, although not for a moment had she meant it to go so far. She still couldn't quite work out how the situation had got so out of control. She wouldn't so much have glanced in Alec Hall's direction had Gina not stolen Luc from her. Her sister was really the one to blame. She'd started this war.

Carmina rather liked the sound of the word. War! Because that's what it was. A battle for the love of one man, and she intended to be the one to win, no matter what weapons she needed to use, what lies she had to tell.

Now Gina was sitting up in bed, her breakfast abandoned on the bedside table.

'Ooh, aren't you going to eat that?' Carmina asked,

and picking up a sausage began to nibble on it. 'Waste not, want not. Anyway, I suppose I'm eating for two now.'

Gina looked at her, her lovely cinnamon eyes filled with tears. 'You did this deliberately, didn't you? You knew that I loved him, and that Luc loved me. You just wanted to spoil things for me. I realise now that's what you most enjoy doing. It's what you've done all my life, pretending to be friendly and sisterly and really being entirely selfish. You positively enjoy taking advantage of my stupid innocence.

'I remember you wanting to play with my doll because you'd broken yours, and you'd turn down the corners of my favourite books, even when I asked you not to. Whatever game we were playing you always had to win. Things had to be done *your* way, to suit *you*. It spoiled things for you when I got polio, didn't it? You couldn't boss me around any more.

'Then when you heard I'd been seeing Luc, you were so furious you said he was only going out with me because he'd think me *easy*! You claimed to be trying to protect me, when all the time you were planning to grab him for yourself. This is the meanest trick you've ever pulled, Carmina.'

'You're right, I did want him. Because he's *mine*! Luc belongs to me. I had him before ever you laid eyes on him. Did he tell you *that*?'

If it were possible Gina's face paled still further, yet what did it matter what had happened before she'd met him? It was the fact he'd been with her sister while supposedly still going out with her, that's what hurt the most. He'd told Gina that he loved her, yet had *sex* with her sister. Even if it was during a period when he'd wrongly believed Gina had finished with him, how could she ever trust him again? And how could she ever trust Carmina?

'I know you never gave him that letter, as I asked you. You lied to me about him two-timing me, then made it come true by seducing him yourself.'

Carmina gave a merry little laugh. 'Don't be naïve. Luc wouldn't have allowed himself to be *seduced,* as you quaintly describe our *love-making*, if he hadn't fancied me rotten.'

Gina winced. It seemed worse to think of it as love-making, rather than crude sex. 'What made you *do* such a stupid thing, anyway? Why do you insist on behaving like a slut?'

Carmina almost snarled. 'Don't you dare call me a slut! Don't speak to me like that. You'd never make him happy, never in a million years. You're pathetic with your limp, and your soppy doe-eyes, your anxious-to-please expression and your so-sweet nature. Girls like you make me sick. I've hated you all my life, even if you are my sister.'

Carmina almost spat the words at Gina, burning up with envy, the spiteful jealousy that had haunted her since her sister had been born, and reached a new depth when she was struck down as a victim of polio. Once, she'd almost wished it had been her who was sick, so that their parents would shower attention upon her instead.

'Just because you've been ill, you think you deserve

extra pampering. You've had Mamma and Papa, and *me* for that matter, waiting on you hand, foot and finger for years. No doubt you imagine you can get that kind of treatment from everybody, Luc included. You just love being the centre of everyone's universe. Well, it's time you stopped feeling sorry for yourself and got out into the real world where the rest of us live, instead of this cotton-wool paradise where Mamma has kept you safe and warm!'

Gina sat immobile throughout this vicious attack, too shocked even to consider interrupting. She and Carmina had had some spats over the years, as all sisters do, but this one was the worst yet.

When Carmina finally ran out of breath, she quietly asked, 'So that's what you've thought of me all these years, is it? And I'd foolishly believed that you helped me through my illness out of love, because we were sisters.'

'Huh, as if I cared. You're a pathetic, self-pitying, useless, ugly *lump*!' Carmina screamed, getting carried away now by her own invective. 'Luc would have come round to the same conclusion in the end, believe me. I told you from the start he was only using you. Haven't I been proved right?'

The door flung open and Mamma stood there, her face creased with worry, eyes wide with alarm. 'What's going on here? What all this noise about?'

'Nothing, Mamma,' Gina said. 'Carmina has decided to move in with Antonia and Marta. At least until she and Luc get married. I can't see how she can possibly continue to sleep in here with me.'

Carmina marched to the door. 'An excellent idea. I'll move my stuff out later.'

Carlotta cried, 'Where you go, madam? Stay here, you and I need to talk. There are matters to be discussed, things to be done.'

'Not now, Mamma,' Carmina snapped. 'I need some air.'

Hugging herself with quiet glee Carmina left Gina to the ministrations of her frantic mother and walked out of the house. She really did feel in need of fresh air, to escape the stifling tension. Out in the market, it was a perfectly normal Monday, a busy day with the stall-holders optimistically preparing for a good week's trading ahead.

It was unfortunate that Gina had become so attached to Luc, but it was her own stupid fault. She, Carmina, had been his first love, she told herself, rather romantically. Luc belonged to her by right. She'd been determined from the first moment she'd seen them together, kissing, to win him back. Now Carmina had got him, she meant to keep him all to herself.

Old men in flat caps and mufflers stood in a huddle by the ancient horse trough as Carmina strolled over to buy a morning paper from Les, who was gossiping with them. He carried a placard, something about United losing in the Cup Final to Bolton Wanderers. Judging by the loud argument going on this news had upset many of the old men and she strolled away again, uncaring.

Carmina sat on a bench and opened the paper. Papa had told her not to come in to the ice-cream parlour today, not until Mamma had spoken to her. What he meant by that, Carmina had no idea. Nothing her mother said now could make the slightest difference. The Fabrianis, and Luc, had accepted the inevitable.

Even Gina realised there could be no other solution.

Maybe she should start looking at flats, Carmina thought, glancing at the small ads. They'd need somewhere to live. She spotted Amy George across the market, looking plump and ripe as a fat plum, ready to give birth very soon by the look of her. Should she go over and talk to her, ask for some advice?

Carmina chuckled to herself at the very idea, deciding that would perhaps be a touch premature since the whole thing was a figment of her imagination. There was no baby, no pregnancy. How could there be when he'd never really touched her? The idea had come to her on the spur of the moment. She'd wanted to say something, anything, to spoil the sickening happiness of that pair of twittering love-birds.

Oh, but it had all worked out better than she could have hoped for. She was feeling mighty pleased with herself as she wandered over to the hat stall to see Patsy. 'You might be needing to make a hat for Mamma soon,' she said, a mischievous glint in her velvet-brown eyes.

Patsy glanced up from sewing a veil on to a kingfisher-blue felt. 'Oh, is she going somewhere special?'

'She might be going to a wedding. In fact, I'm certain she will be. I can say no more at present. I'm sure you'll hear the whole story soon enough. That's pretty, do you make bridal veils and stuff too?'

'A Juliet cap you mean? I could, if someone wanted one,' Patsy said, a crease forming on her brow as she tried to detect exactly what it was Carmina was hinting at.

'Interesting, well, must dash. Mamma is waiting for me back at the house.'

'Not working today, then?'

Carmina gave a little smile that twisted one corner of her full mouth. 'Not today, there are family matters to attend to. Which is why they wouldn't concern you.'

Patsy smiled. 'Like it or not, Carmina, I will be family soon.'

A customer appeared at that moment and Patsy was distracted, putting down her sewing to attend to the woman. Irritated by her response, Carmina moved away and, as she passed a display, spotted a silk scarf draped beside a flowery hat in a pretty shade of blue, her favourite colour. Maybe she would buy it for herself? She deserved a treat after the strain of these last weeks. Glancing over her shoulder she saw that Patsy was busy helping the customer to try on hats.

She felt that familiar wave of jealousy towards her future sister-in-law. Marc was rarely around now to give Carmina the support she'd always been able to rely upon before that girl had appeared on the scene. More often than not he was with Patsy, deep in private conversation or gazing lovingly into her blue eyes.

Carmina recalled how the other girl was always on at her, criticising her over something or other. She'd warned her against speaking to Luc at the church, even accused her of flirting with Alec Hall. Which was the very reason she'd taken herself off for that walk and, as luck would have it, Alec had followed her. So Patsy was as much to blame as Gina for what had happened that day on the site of the old Roman fort. Interfering busybody!

Carmina slipped the scarf from its stand and tucked it quickly into her pocket. Yes indeed, she deserved a little treat. And why should she pay for it? If Patsy wanted to be a member of the family so badly, why should she need to?

Not that she'd know who had taken the scarf, if Carmina somehow forgot to mention it.

'Bye, Patsy,' she called, as she strolled away.

A boy careered past on a Vespa scooter; a young mum struggled along with two children in tow, each one carrying a placard around their necks which said: *Think of the children. No more bombs!* People jostled between the stalls, paying the protesters no attention.

Carmina thought, if she had a bomb, she'd blow her stupid sister out of existence. War! That's exactly what this was.

20

Patsy and Amy

Patsy noticed that a scarf had gone missing some time in the late afternoon but did not associate its disappearance with Carmina. She'd dismissed the girl's visit from her mind along with the mysterious hints of some wedding or other. Then Marc arrived at closing time and told her the whole sorry tale, which instantly banished any lingering concern about the scarf. Dealing with shop-lifting was, after all, a familiar problem in retailing, and insignificant by comparison to losing the man you loved.

'Oh, no, poor Gina. How has she taken it?'

'How do you think? She and Luc had been seeing each other secretly for months apparently, since January. But then Carmina stuck her nose in, told some lies and upset the entire apple-cart. I don't have all the details, but for some reason Luc believed Gina had dumped him and the damn fool couldn't resist Carmina's charms.'

Patsy said, 'She'd make sure of that, the little minx.'

Marc frowned. 'It's not quite fair to put the blame entirely on Carmina. It takes two to tango.'

'Yes, but what poor bloke could resist if Carmina offered herself on a plate? He'd need a will of iron and the sexual urge of a gnat.'

Marc smiled, put his arms about Patsy and hugged her. 'My own sexual appetite is stirring again. Have you changed your mind yet about when *we* marry? I'm not sure I can wait until August, let alone the autumn. Give a chap a break, love,' he said, nuzzling into her neck.

Patsy chuckled softly. 'Down, boy, down. There's a great deal to be attended to besides that lovely wedding dress Carlotta is making. Finding somewhere to live for a start.'

'Let's go and look at flats tomorrow. They're building some new ones out Salford way.'

Patsy screwed up her nose. 'That's a bit too far from the market.'

'It's an easy walk over Princes Bridge, or we could take the bus.'

'Tomorrow's no good anyway. I'm off to Preston to see a new supplier. The scarves have been a great success so I'm keen to expand into other accessories: gloves, stockings, little evening bags perhaps. Seems the right way to go and Clara's just letting me get on with it, not interfering in the slightest. At first I felt shy about making decisions and changing things, but I'm really getting the bit between my teeth now, trying out new lines, determined to make something of this business.'

Marc groaned. 'Why does the hat stall always have to take precedent over anything to do with us?'

'Because it's how I earn my living. Stop grumbling and give me a kiss. You can eat at our place tonight, Clara is making macaroni cheese.'

'They're lovely those two. Real ladies. And I'm aware that they've been good to you, but I can't wait for us to have a place of our own. It would be wonderful with just the two of us for supper,' he said, running kisses behind her ear and making her giggle.

'That's because you've never tasted my cooking.'

'It's what comes after supper that's important. Once we're married . . .' he murmured, pulling her tight against him so he could move his hands over her back and through her hair . . . 'I could have my wicked way with you every single night. You wouldn't fancy letting me have a little taster in advance, I don't suppose?'

'Don't push your luck, mate. Anyway, I would think one shotgun wedding in the family is enough. Come on, all this talk of food is making me hungry.'

It was Saturday afternoon and Thomas was listening to the Sports Report on the wireless. He was sitting with his eyes closed, his feet, encased in thick woollen socks caked with dried mud and grass, were propped on a stool before the fire. At first sight it might be imagined that he was asleep, but there was no sound of snoring and he didn't miss a single result from the droning voice of the announcer.

Mavis, putting on her hat preparatory to visiting a friend for their usual Saturday afternoon tea and trip to the pictures, thought this an appropriate moment to announce her own news.

'I've had a word with that friend of yours about the house next to the pawn shop and told him Chris won't be wanting it after all.'

'Doncaster – three, Manchester City – two.'

Thomas opened his eyes and looked at his wife. 'What did you say?'

'I see no reason for him to move out just now, not with the baby coming. How on earth would they manage?' Mavis slid a long hatpin into her felt hat, anchoring it firmly to the tight marcel waves.

Thomas felt anger curl hot and sour through his veins. 'What have you done now, you stupid woman? It's got nowt to do with you.'

'It's got everything to do with me. I'm his mother.'

'If you haven't noticed, he's a married man. He's got a wife now. When did we ever ask my mother, or yours for that matter, in our younger days, afore we did owt?'

'That is quite different.'

'Oh, and why would that be?'

'Because houses were easy to come by in those days. And I was extremely capable, from a good family, with standards to be proud of. Besides, your mother and father moved out of here and you moved me in, above the bakery, promising at the time, I seem to remember, that one day you'd buy me a better house away from the business. I'm still waiting.'

'And because I've let you down, *in your eyes*, you'll punish my son, is that the way of it?'

'Don't be ridiculous!' Mavis put on dark red lipstick with angry little stabs. 'It's quite impracticable for Chris and Amy to move out. How that girl would manage to run a house on her own, I don't care to think. She can't do anything unless I explain to her, in words of one syllable, how to carry out the simplest domestic chore.

She's certainly not capable of looking after a husband single-handed, let alone a baby.'

Thomas glowered at his wife. 'I reckon that's for Chris to decide, not you. You can't go interfering in his business like this, it's not your place.'

Twin spots of colour showed high on her cheeks as Mavis headed for the door, her voice as sharp as a razor blade. 'Well, it's done now. Your friend, the landlord, told me he had another prospective tenant lined up, and a good thing too.' She flounced off but then bethought herself and was back in a flash for one last parting shot.

'And I'll thank you to remove those mucky socks.' Whereupon she left the house, closing the door very carefully behind her so that she didn't chip the paintwork.

Thomas missed the end of the football results as he comprehensively listed every swear word he could think of. He'd never been in the army, being too young for the first war and too old for the second, but there were some suitable words in his vocabulary nonetheless, of which Mavis was not aware. He used every one of them now.

Drat the woman! Why did she always have to poke her nose in and interfere?

Mavis spotted her daughter-in-law out in the street and took great pleasure in informing her too that the landlord had changed his mind and let the house to someone else.

'What?' Amy was shocked and deeply upset by this unexpected news. Her dream of a happy life with her darling Chris shredded in an instant as she contemplated months, years perhaps, of further intimidation at Mavis's hand. 'When did you learn this? And why didn't anyone *tell* me?'

'I'm telling you now,' Mavis tartly informed her. 'It's for the best, Amy, so please don't make a fuss.' And turning on her heel, she once again beat a hasty retreat before further questions could be asked.

Amy was distraught. It had taken months to find this house, miserable though it might be. What hope could they possibly have of finding another before the baby was born? And the thought of living in that cramped little bedroom with a small baby filled her with dismay. She could see it all quite clearly. Mavis would complain if it kept her awake by crying; she would object to nappies filling her clothes line; to having baby equipment litter her lovely sitting room. Nothing would be quite right. And Amy and Chris would have not one scrap of privacy in which to enjoy their child.

Chris was equally upset, and later that evening, having packed a distressed Amy off to bed, railed at his mother, demanding to know if she'd had a hand in the man's decision.

Mavis robustly denied this, offering a lengthy explanation about how she'd run into their prospective landlord quite by chance, and he'd passed on the unwelcome message.

'It was all a mistake. Your father got it wrong, as usual. The man had forgotten that he'd already agreed to let the house to someone else. Never mind, you're perfectly comfortable here, and quite right too that you should stay in your own home with the baby due in just a few weeks.'

Chris was unconvinced by his mother's explanation. He always knew when she wasn't telling him the complete truth. She could never quite look him in the eye. His father sat tight-lipped throughout her long-winded tale, a look on his face which revealed he could say more, had he a mind to.

'If you've influenced this man any way, Mother, I won't be responsible for my actions.'

Mavis gave a trilling little laugh. 'Dear me, how very dramatic. You should be grateful you have such a loving home, unlike some people I could mention.'

'If that's a dig at Amy, then you're quite wrong. Big Molly absolutely adores her, for all she was as much against our marriage as you were at the start. The Poulsons have a very happy home, as a matter of fact.'

'Utterly chaotic!' Mavis said, with a curl to her lip.

'Chaotic or not, I'm sure she'd welcome her daughter home in time for the birth of her first grandchild, if asked.'

This was by no means a part of Mavis's plan. She'd assumed her son would bend to her wishes, as he had always done when he was younger. Nothing had been quite the same though, ever since he'd taken up with this Poulson girl.

'I really don't think that would be wise . . .' Mavis began. 'That house isn't even *clean*, not at all a fit place to bring a child into.'

Thomas gave a low growl at the back of his throat. 'That's enough, Mavis. You go too far. Whatever vendetta we might personally have against the Poulson family, or the fact they are untidy, noisy, messy people, you have to admit that Big Molly's kitchen is as bright as a new pin. She must clean it half a dozen times a day at least. She made pies in it all through the war, and for years after, without managing to kill off a single soul with food poisoning.'

'By a miracle.'

'In any case we're not talking about the Poulsons here, we're talking about our Chris, and it's time he set up on his own.'

'I don't think so,' Mavis said with a sweet smile. 'He's stopping at home.'

Days later Thomas came to his son. 'Don't worry, lad, I've had another word with my friend Jim, your future landlord. There was a bit of a mix-up about letting the house but I've sorted it all out, *and* paid a month's rent in advance. We can set about cleaning it up first thing in t'morning if tha's a mind.'

'Well, really,' said Mavis, cheeks flushing bright pink. 'When did all this happen? And why didn't you tell *me* you'd spoken to Jim?'

'I'm telling you now,' Thomas said, his face deadpan. 'Aren't you pleased? It's good news for our Chris, wouldn't you say?'

'Thanks, Dad,' Chris said, pumping his father's hand in heartfelt relief and gratitude. 'Amy will be pleased as punch.'

'Of course she will, poor dear,' Mavis agreed, through gritted teeth.

21

Gina and Carmina

'He's here again, Gina. He comes every day, and it's you he wants to see.'

'Well, I don't want to see him.'

Carlotta put her hands to her mouth to smother a little sob. How could life play such cruel tricks? She'd changed from being fervently opposed to Luc Fabriani to finding herself almost pitying the boy. You could argue that the problem was of his own making, so why did she let his evident misery trouble her?

Because of Gina. It was her daughter's plight which broke her heart.

This wasn't what she'd planned for any of her daughters. Her hopes for Gina had admittedly faded years ago when she'd been struck down with the polio, as so many other children had been in the early fifties. Carlotta had decided that the poor girl must be protected and kept at home, for her own good. Now she wondered if perhaps she might have made a mistake. If she hadn't kept her home from that silly dance, then this might never have happened.

Carlotta wrung her hands together in utter despair. What was a mother to do? How could you tell what was best for your child? Oh, but she'd fully expected

Carmina to find herself a man of stature and importance in the community. Her beauty alone surely merited that.

Not that Carmina had ever been an easy child, forever creating problems both at home and with her teachers. The girl was far too arrogant for her own good. Carmina had hated school and refused to pay proper attention to her lessons, being far more interested in chatting up the boys. Unlike Gina, who had railed at the fact she was missing so much school work through ill heath, and Antonia who always had her head in a book, Carmina wasn't the least bit interested in learning, even in cookery and needlework. It had taken her two whole years to make a cookery apron.

She would often be late home, having been kept in on detention. Eventually the teacher would come knocking at their door to complain about their daughter's rudeness, or wild behaviour. She'd ask why none of the letters she'd sent home, requesting they call in to discuss Carmina's problems, had received a response.

Carlotta would shrug, pretending not to understand when really she guessed that Carmina had probably thrown them all away.

The girl had not passed her eleven-plus and had left school at the earliest opportunity, the moment she turned fifteen. This had upset Papa as he believed education to be important,

Their last remaining hope for Carmina's salvation had been for her to make a good marriage. And now look what had happened. Perhaps Papa had been somewhat prejudiced against the Fabrianis, as they were being entirely supportive over this, but in her heart Carlotta knew that this marriage was wrong. She knew her own daughter too well, that the poor boy hadn't stood a chance against her feminine wiles and scheming ways. Carmina had filled his head with lies over her sister, and, with the lust of youth, he'd been putty in her clever little hands.

And broken Gina's heart as a result.

Luc did not love Carmina. He loved Gina. That was clear enough to her, if not to the girl herself.

Carlotta groaned. Daughters, what problems they created. 'Luc says he needs to explain something to you.'

'I have heard all his explanations,' Gina said, not lifting her eyes from the book she was supposedly reading, although she hadn't turned a page in a good half hour, by Carlotta's reckoning.

'Sometimes explanations are difficult. Things happen between a man and a woman, and men are so *weak*.' Carlotta spread her hands in a helpless gesture. 'Look at your sister. Could any man resist her?'

Gina did now raise her eyes. They had dark bruises beneath each, and the expression in them jolted her mother's heart by its very coldness. 'Quite! Would you really wish me to be involved with a man who cannot keep his hands off my beautiful sister?'

'*Mamma mia*, that is not what I meant, oh my darling girl . . .'

Carlotta embarked on a string of rapid Italian and Gina leapt to her feet to avoid being swept up into her mother's suffocating embrace. 'It's all right. I can cope, so long as people don't feel sorry for me all the time,' and she limped swiftly from the room before her defences crumbled away entirely.

From her bedroom window Gina watched as Luc walked away, hands in his pockets, shoulders hunched. He looked so utterly dejected and miserable she ached to run after him. She almost felt sorry for him. To be compelled to marry her volatile, selfish sister was not a comfortable prospect for any young man.

When he reached Lizzie Pringle's Chocolate Cabin, he half turned to look up at her window. Gina stepped quickly back behind the bedroom curtains, rather as she had done on the fateful day when she hadn't gone to the dance and he'd betrayed her. If only she'd slipped out to speak to him then, had somehow found the courage to challenge him about the lies Carmina had told about him. If only she'd explained that she did indeed care and desperately wanted to be with him.

Instead she'd hesitated and foolishly trusted Carmina to deliver her letter, afraid of upsetting their parents. Although that hadn't been her only reason.

Gina knew she'd been filled with insecurities and fear, half believing the poisonous words her sister had poured into her ear. After all, why would he want to take her, a person with a handicap, to a dance? What handsome young man would want to be seen out with a girl with a limp? Doubts had assailed her, her inferiority complex coming to the fore. Gina had believed Carmina must be right when she'd said that she really didn't have the experience of life or men to fully appreciate how he was using her. Rightly or wrongly, these concerns had made her reluctant to defy her parents, and she'd lost him as a result.

Now, as Luc finally disappeared from view, Gina felt restless, quite unable to tolerate staying in the house a moment longer. She reached for her coat and hobbled down the stairs then slipped out to find Amy, not even telling Mamma where she was going. Gina felt desperate for someone more her own age to talk to, someone who wouldn't preach or lecture, or regard her with sad, pitying eyes.

Carmina, working on the ice-cream cart, had been watching Luc for some time. She'd made it her business to follow him everywhere and keep track of what he was up to. Today, she'd spotted him talking to her mother, noted how he gazed up at her sister's bedroom window. Then as he crossed the street she begged Alessandro, who happened to be around, to take over serving for ten minutes, claiming she needed a break. He complained, as he always did, but she was already rushing after Luc.

She fell into step beside him, slipped her arm into his as if she had every right to do so.

'Hiya, how are you on this lovely sunny day?'

Much to her irritation, he shook her off. 'This isn't going to work,' Luc growled.

'What isn't?'

'This stupid plan of yours. Whatever little scheme you've got bubbling away in that clever head of yours is a complete waste of time. How can it when you and I both know the truth. We didn't have sex and you aren't pregnant.'

Carmina chuckled. 'I think we'll be married long before that can be proved.'

'You'd only regret it. You'd hate being married to me. It wouldn't work.'

'It'll work if I say it will,' Carmina airily assured him, pouting provocatively. 'You surely aren't going to do the dirty on me and leave me to bring up an illegitimate child all on my own, just like the notorious Dena Dobson?'

'There is no child, and I don't love you, Carmina. I never did. Once, months ago, we had a bit of fun, nothing more. I should never have believed your lies, never let you worm your way back. I'm damned if I'm going to spend my life paying for a moment's weakness. All I did was kiss you, and that was just a stupid mistake.'

'Ah, but some mistakes have to be paid for. And it was rather an important one, after all.' She smoothed a hand over her flat stomach.

Luc stopped walking to glare down at her, a cold hard glint in his dark blue eyes. 'Now you're coming to believe in your own fantasies. OK, so you've managed to get both families on your side, but what good will that do? Even if you succeeded in forcing me to marry you, holding the proverbial shot-gun to my head, as it were, you can't force me to *love* you. I've no intention of ever sleeping with you, Carmina, married or no.'

Carmina laughed, her luscious brown eyes wickedly

teasing. 'Oh, I think you will. You wouldn't be able to resist.'

Luc was appalled by the mess he found himself in. How could people believe her lies? How had he allowed her to lead him by the nose, like some stupid stud instructed to perform on demand? But he hadn't quite, had he? There'd been no performance. He must keep reminding himself of that fact.

He used to wonder why it was he'd fallen for the quiet sister, and not the gorgeous, adventurous one, particularly when he'd been a bit of a rebel himself, once upon a time. He didn't ask himself that question any more.

Carmina Bertalone was poison, as dangerous as an unexploded bomb.

'I *can* resist you, Carmina, and will continue to do so,' he coldly informed her and strode rapidly away, calling back to her over his shoulder. 'Accept it, Carmina, I'd always be pining for my lovely sweet Gina.'

Carmina stood in the middle of the street, rage running through her like molten fire, furious that he'd rejected her yet again. She was humiliatingly aware of people watching her, of sniggers from his friends hanging around on the street corner. Bitter disappointment churned in her stomach, making her feel violently sick. Why wouldn't he accept that it was *her* he really loved, and not Gina at all? Gina was boring, pathetic, a *cripple*, for God's sake!

If her sister had appeared, right at that moment, Carmina wouldn't have held herself responsible for her actions.

Luc had to be made to see where his best interests lay.

'Don't I just *love* it when you play hard to get,' she shouted after him, then winked provocatively at his mates and flounced off in the opposite direction, just as if it were nothing more than a lovers' quarrel.

Amy listened in silence as Gina poured out her heart. 'You don't have to say anything,' Gina warned, when her story was told. 'I don't want you to say how sorry you feel for me, how sad it is, how much Luc loves me or any of that rubbish. If he really had loved me, properly and faithfully, my sister wouldn't now be carrying his child.'

'Oh, Gina, I don't know what to say. It's just so awful. I can't imagine how you must be feeling. I'd kill Chris, if he did that to me. But then, Carmina is not someone anyone would welcome as a rival.'

Gina sighed. 'I wish I'd a gold sovereign for everyone who's said that to me, in one form or another.'

Amy was perched on an upturned packing case in the half-painted living room, Chris and Thomas having gone over to the Dog and Duck to wet their whistle on a welcome pint, as Thomas put it. Gina paced the room, too strung up to be able to sit still for a moment.

'It's true though,' Amy said. 'Once that sister of yours has her claws in a man, she's like a tiger, never lets go. You have my deepest . . . Oh, sorry!'

Even Gina managed to smile at her near slip.

'Do you want him back?' Amy quietly asked.

A moment of silence before Gina finally let out a

trembling breath. 'I don't know. I really can't decide how I feel about Luc right now. I feel . . . very . . . muddled.'

Amy chewed on her lip, which she often did when she was thinking hard. 'Look, what you need is something to take you out of yourself. Keeping busy, I find, may not solve problems but certainly helps to keep one's mind off them.'

Gina couldn't help but smile at her friend, who looked positively blooming with her rosy cheeks and gleaming hair, bright eyes and hands moving protectively over her swollen stomach and the baby she carried. 'What possible problems could you have?'

'Oh, believe me, living with Mavis is no picnic, far more dangerous than a nuclear bomb,' and both girls giggled. 'But I'll admit my problems are as nothing by comparison. Still, there must be something you can do to take your mind off Luc and allow yourself time to heal.'

'Perhaps that's part of the problem, I don't have anything to do. Mamma has never let me get a job, or even help in the ice-cream parlour. Now I'm not sure what I could do. I'm certainly not trained for anything, and my education was virtually non-existent.'

'What about hobbies?'

Gina shook her head. 'When I was ill with the polio I was in quite a lot of pain, or going through some difficult treatment or other. I wasn't really in the mood for hobbies. There were times when even reading or doing a jigsaw exhausted me. I had a lot of physiotherapy to flex my muscles which is quite painful and hard work, and exercises at the swimming baths. They even put me in a funny sort of machine to warm my muscles and help prevent cramps. Then there were a couple of operations on my feet, which required long stays in hospital. It was all worth it in the end, of course. They got me walking again, and I've had hardly any problems for months now. So long as I never want to run the four-minute mile, I'll be fine. But all I can really do is help Mamma with the sewing, fairly basic stuff though.'

'Can you operate a sewing machine? I mean – if you don't mind my asking – do you have problems with the treadle?'

Gina shook her head. 'No, that's not a problem, so long as I don't do too much.'

'Then there's your answer. Go and see Dena Dobson and ask her if she's in need of a new machinist.'

Hope lit in Gina's sad, cinnamon eyes. 'Do you really think she might be?'

'You can but ask. What have you got to lose? Dena is lovely, and knows what it is to be up against things, having gone through torment herself over the death of her brother. She might be able to give you a few hours, at least.'

Dena instantly offered three mornings' employment a week. 'It might be more some weeks, if we've got a big order in, or we're coming up to a fashion show. If you feel up to it, that is, Gina. I recommend you start with just a few hours and let's see how you get on. Joan Chapman usually organises the team so talk to her if you want to increase or change your hours. Welcome on board, love, I reckon I'm going to need all the help I can get in the coming months if trade carries on as good as it is.'

Even Mamma was pleased, kissing her on both cheeks. 'Splendid! We can see the light at the end of the tunnel now, *sì*?'

'Not quite, Mamma, but it's a start, isn't it? It's a reason to get up in a morning. Dena says I can start first thing tomorrow.'

Carlotta clutched her daughter to her bosom and hugged her tight. 'I would like to smack that little madam's silly face. She's brought shame and disgrace upon us all, as well as heartbreak for you, my lovely girl.' She cupped Gina's cold pale face between her warm hands. 'But you will survive, my little one, because you are strong. Stronger inside than out, *sì*? And there are other fish in the sea. You will find another young man.'

'I don't think so, Mamma. Who would have me?'

'You mustn't say such things, child. Carmina isn't the only one who is beautiful, you are too.'

'But it's Luc that I love.'

Carlotta's soft brown eyes filled with tears. 'I make bad mistake keeping you two apart.'

'Don't, Mamma, you'll have me crying too,' and mother and daughter quietly wept in each other's arms.

22

Amy and Patsy

The CND meetings, dry as they so often were, had been a welcome relief, representing an escape from Mavis's tyranny and litany of complaints.

Amy had sometimes struggled to understand what the speakers meant by their convoluted arguments, or to show proper interest in news of the latest rally or protest vigil. She'd found their vision of infinite destruction and the ultimate annihilation of man a trifle depressing, particularly in her current condition. Nevertheless, she'd felt as if she were taking part in the birth of a new political movement and had readily agreed to stand on street corners and hand out leaflets.

Once, she'd painstakingly addressed a couple of hundred envelopes to MPs and newspaper editors; working on them secretly in their bedroom while Chris was at the bakery and she was supposed to be resting.

She'd been glad of the distraction, anything which took her from under Mavis's thumb, if only for a short time. Amy had looked forward to the meetings for that reason alone, irrespective of any higher moral reasons. But now that she was so near her time she'd been forced to call a halt to the activity and was missing them badly, not least the new friends she'd made.

'I'll be back later,' she'd assured them. 'I'll probably be glad of the diversion after a month or two of dirty nappies, but for now I can't walk to the end of the street without needing a crane to first hoist me out of the chair.'

Jeff and Sue had laughed, told her she exaggerated and that she looked marvellous, but they'd understood her predicament and promised to keep her informed of progress.

So here she was, like a beached whale, confined to sewing curtains for their new home. But the thought of being entirely free from Mavis in the near future filled her with excited anticipation. It would be so wonderful to have Chris all to herself at last, and not be lectured or criticised by her mother-in-law over every little thing she did.

She'd bought some cheap cotton off-cuts from Winnie's stall, and taken careful instructions on how to make them. Amy didn't possess a sewing machine but as this was her first attempt at curtain-making she was content to sit and hem and stitch the ruffle-tape on by hand. At least that way she felt in control.

Sometimes Gina came round to help and the two girls would sit and quietly sew together, sharing problems and secrets.

'Have you spoken to Luc yet?' Amy would ask, and Gina would shake her head.

'What is there to say? If he prefers Carmina to me, so be it. I can't blame him for that, can I? She's my sister so I should be happy for her. What about you, are you looking forward to moving into your new home?'

'Can't wait.'

Then Mavis came in and hovered over Amy, issuing instructions. 'You aren't leaving enough heading for the tape. Have you measured the window properly, allowed for fullness in the curtains?'

'Yes, Winnie explained all of that to me.'

'Cheap fabric never looks good. You should have spoken to me first. I could have lent you my winter curtains, a lovely plush velvet.'

Amy tried not to wince, remembering the dusty brown curtains they'd recently taken down. 'I didn't want anything too dark. I want it to look all bright and cheerful,' she explained, admiring the orange and blue maze-like pattern of the cotton sateen.

'They are lovely and bright, aren't they, Mrs George?' Gina said.

'Some people really don't have any taste,' Mavis replied with a disapproving sniff. And the two girls stifled their giggles, put their heads down and kept on sewing.

Patsy had never worked so hard in her life. This morning, as on every other, she'd swept all around the stall, then got on with dusting and tidying her stock. It was important to keep it clean and bright, and displayed in a way which was attractive to the customer.

She knew every hat and hat-pin, every scarf and marcasite brooch, every bunch of shiny silk cherries or pair of kid gloves.

Patsy had spoken to the bank manager and arranged a small overdraft to enable her to expand her lines.

Since then, she'd visited any number of warehouses, plus one or two fashion fairs, where she'd ordered a small range of gloves, stockings, scarves, some neat little clutch bags, and other accessories. She was even trying a few beads and bangles.

Oh, and she was so excited. It was such fun to feel that she was in charge of her own business, free to do as she pleased without Annie breathing down her neck. And Clara seemed happy for her to get on with things, issuing only a sensible warning that she should fix a budget and stick to it.

'Never be afraid to try something new, so long as you feel it's right for your customers. But try out one or two samples first to test the market. And never overstretch yourself by attempting to expand too fast. Since we buy only in cash from wholesalers and not the manufacturer, you can always go back for more if something sells well, but you can't send it back if it doesn't.'

All good advice which Patsy took on board.

Clara hadn't even made any protest when Patsy had suggested they reorganise the central workroom, perhaps add a curtained alcove to offer the customer a little privacy.

'You do what you think best, love. I have every faith in you.'

Patsy hugged the older woman, overcome by emotion. 'You're like a mother to me.'

'Indeed, I hope so.'

Patsy depended upon Clara, and even the grumpy Annie, far more than she cared to admit, as she'd never known her own mother. Even her foster parents had rejected her, once they'd had a child of their own. That sense of being unwanted had affected her badly for years, made her angry and rebellious, unable to trust anyone.

Now, she had a good life, a good man, and a family of sorts in the Higginson sisters. Everything was going well for her at last; except for the fact that she was still troubled by shop-lifting. Whoever was doing it was persistent and clever, as Patsy could never link the loss of an item with any particular customer.

She kept a careful watch, had even put up a mirror so that she could see most of the stall without moving from her chair were she to be busy sewing. That was the real danger. The stall occupied quite a large block of space on three sides, the fourth butting on to Marion's Ribbons and Lace stall, and Patsy would become so engrossed in her work that she'd forget to keep a proper watch.

It was so much easier when Clara was with her, as they could take it in turns to patrol the length of it. But Clara was more often than not absent these days as Annie had been unwell for weeks and her sister was very concerned.

Number 22, the little house where the Higginson sisters had lived since they'd come home from France during the war, became permeated with the sour-sweet smell of sickness.

Patsy did what she could to help with the endless cleaning, the scrubbing and disinfecting, the washing of linen; the fetching and carrying of beef tea or barley water to Annie who lay like a withered leaf in the

Victorian iron bedstead. Later, Patsy would carry the tray away again as the poor lady rarely ate a scrap no matter how much care Clara took over the preparation of the poached salmon or the soup which she made specially to tempt her.

And then one morning before it was quite light, Clara came to Patsy's room and told her that Annie had gone.

Patsy sat up, blinking owlishly in the light cast in from the stairs, wanting to ask gone where, before sleep fell away and reality hit home. Annie was dead. That crotchety old woman with a heart of gold had finally gone to meet her maker, and, sadly, few would grieve for her, save for her beloved, distraught sister and one orphan to whom she had given a home.

Thomas had at last opted for semi-retirement, considerably cutting down the hours he spent at the bakery. He'd even temporarily abandoned his allotment to devote long hours to helping Chris and Amy renovate and restore their little house. He declared he was happy to make a few sacrifices to help them on their way. And very glad of his efforts they were too, as the house made a depressing picture. The walls were running with damp, much of the woodwork was rotten, and it stank of rot and damp and vermin.

Mavis had been horrified when she was taken to view it. 'I won't have my s— any grandchild of mine . . . being brought up here. Ten shillings a week for this? You've been robbed! I've seen drier cellars.'

For once Amy had to agree with her, although she did notice how she had very nearly said 'my son' before quickly changing it to grandchild. Just as if Amy's comfort were of no consequence at all.

'What's the alternative?' she very reasonably pointed out. 'There aren't enough decent houses to go round. They say two fall down every day in Manchester, too rotten to stand up any longer. As for a new council flat, we'd be old and grey before ever we got to the top of the list. We think it's up to us to make our own way.'

'But not here, not in this hole,' Mavis snorted. 'As I've said countless times before, I can't see why you need to move at all.'

'Nay, it's not that bad,' Thomas said, ever the optimist. 'I've seen worse. It's got potential.'

It had two rooms downstairs, a front parlour which for the time being would have to be left empty for lack of furniture, and at the back was the living room. Beyond this was the scullery with an old-fashioned shallow brown-stone sink and slop-stone. The hot water was provided by the back boiler, set behind the Lancashire iron range which must have been there since the house was built a century ago.

'By heck,' Thomas had said when he'd first clapped eyes on it. 'We had one of those once. My mother used to black-lead it every week.'

Amy looked stricken. 'Oh, no, am I going to have to do that too?' The joy of owning their own home was suddenly beginning to pall. The task of making the house habitable seemed enormous.

'Nay,' Thomas assured her. 'We could have it out in a jiffy but then you'd have no hot water, unless we rewire the place and put in one of them new-fangled immersion heaters?'

Amy gave a rueful smile. 'We can't afford, not with a baby to provide for.'

'Well, then, it'll have to stay where it is. I'll give it a lick of black enamel paint so it don't need more than a wipe down.'

Thomas put on his overalls and got right down to the job there and then. He chipped away old plaster, removed rotten shelves, skirting boards and picture rails. He knocked out an old Victorian fireplace in the back scullery.

'How about we build on a bathroom, since you've not got one upstairs?'

'We can't afford one of those either,' Amy said, in something of a panic as he broke through the outer scullery wall with his sledge hammer.

'Don't fret,' Thomas cried, like a man possessed. 'I'm just going to put up a lean-to on the back of the house, to link it to the old outside lavatory. It won't be no palace but at least you'll not risk catching pneumonia every time you go for a pee.'

He did all the work himself, Chris working alongside his father whenever he could be spared from the bakery, acting as labourer under Thomas's patient instruction.

'Plastering is no more difficult than icing a cake, well not much anyroad,' he explained to his son. Thomas was an enthusiast, willing to have a go at anything, whether or not he had any experience in the task.

'Except for the fact the surface is considerably larger

in dimension, and vertical,' Chris groaned, as yet another trowel-load of plaster fell with a plop to the floor.

The two men worked tirelessly at all hours of the day and night: mending kitchen cupboards, putting new hinges on doors, repairing broken sash windows, scrubbing away black mould. And once all of that was done they gave the old walls a coat of size, then started on the painting and distempering.

Amy wasn't allowed to do a thing except brew endless mugs of tea for them both, and choose the colour of the paint: jasmine yellow and white, she decided. She'd also chosen a wallpaper in a vibrant abstract design as she wanted their first home to look modern and cheerful in jazzy colours. Mostly she was happy to sit and watch the two men work, knitting matinee jackets and baby bonnets. She was getting very near to her time so was thankful for an hour or two of peace in her day when she wasn't at Mavis's beck and call.

23

Carmina and Gina

It was a week later when, as Carmina walked into the house, Carlotta took off her apron and reached for her coat. 'You come with me, madam.'

'What? Why? Where are we going?'

'You will see when we get there. We have a visit to make.'

It was perfectly plain that her mother wasn't taking no for an answer, so with a weary sigh Carmina allowed herself to be shepherded back out of the house and marched along the street.

She was feeling in a sour mood anyway because she hadn't seen Luc for days; hadn't, in fact, set eyes on him since their quarrel last week when he'd sworn never to love her. Foolish boy! He hadn't meant it, of course, not deep down. He was in a sulk because he believed she'd trapped him. Men didn't know what was good for them. He'd soon see that they could have a wonderful life together if only he would stop fighting her.

Carmina hadn't even spotted him at the bus stop lately, although she'd been there waiting for him, without fail, every single day. He must be taking a different bus, or getting off at a different stop, she thought, furious that he could avoid her so easily. She was particularly cross today as it was a Friday and she'd hoped to persuade him to come out of his sulk and take her to the dance. He was absolutely potty about her deep down, she was sure of it. He just needed to get rid of this guilt he felt over abandoning her stupid sister. And Carmina had no intention of allowing him to escape his responsibilities.

She almost giggled at this thought, for in reality he had no responsibilities. He owed her nothing. But since she'd told the Big Lie almost two weeks ago, Carmina had come to half believe in it herself.

'Where exactly are we going?' she repeated in her most irritable voice, as her mother steered her across the busy street.

Carmina decided it must be something to do with the wedding, perhaps they were going to see Dena Dobson to get her to make the dress. She had her heart set on something short and lacy, ballerina length with a nipped-in waist. No one could accuse her of not having good taste.

But they walked on without stopping. Where on earth were they heading? To Betty Hemley's flower stall perhaps? Carmina wanted something exotic and romantic for her bouquet. White lilies, perhaps. They'd be rather grand, with a sprig or two of orange blossom for luck.

Betty smiled and looked faintly puzzled as they swept past, for there was nothing Carlotta liked better than a little gossip with the flower seller. She swore that was how she'd learned most of her English. There was certainly little that went on in Champion Street which Betty Hemley didn't know about.

People were turning to watch as they hurried by and Carmina began to feel uneasy. She could see Alec Hall staring at her with open curiosity from the doorway of his little music shop. She'd managed to avoid him this last week or two, but might well have run to him now were it not for the iron grip her mother had on her arm. And there was something unsettling in this purposeful walk.

They finally came to a halt outside the door of Doc Mitchell's surgery and panic hit her like a smack in the face.

Carmina felt as if she might actually throw up. 'I'm not going in *there!*'

'Oh, yes, you are, my girl. When you have baby, you need examination, to make sure all is well.'

There was a roaring sound in Carmina's ears, like the hum of a thousand angry bees. She couldn't think for the noise. It had been easy enough to lie, to make up this tale which had successfully brought Luc to heel when all other methods had failed, but this man would see the truth at once. He was a *doctor*, for heaven's sake!

She tried to back away. 'It's too soon. I don't need to see any doctor yet.'

'You think your mamma not know about babies? Have I not had enough to make me the expert? The sooner you see the doctor, the better,' and Carlotta thrust her daughter through the door.

They clattered up a long flight of stairs then each took a seat in the small, stuffy waiting room. Here, Carmina was condemned to wait her turn behind a queue of people with the usual coughs and colds and sniffles, stomach complaints or with faces etched with concern over something more serious. Someone new would arrive and people would shuffle along to make a space for them on the wooden benches, or indicate with a glance or a flick of the hand, who was the last in line. Eyes would assess the newcomer, inwardly trying to guess the reason for their visit, before returning to reading one of the tatty magazines or crumpled newspapers heaped on a small table.

But Carmina was almost glad of the wait since it gave her time to think. She'd had her period, as usual, just two weeks ago, would the doctor be able to tell? Surely not.

The grubby walls with their brown anaglypta wallpaper and faded posters about '*breast being best' and 'get the proper immunisation for your child*', seemed to press in upon her. Carmina hadn't bargained on this, not quite so soon, and desperately strove to think of a way to escape.

'I'll just pop back home to the toilet,' she whispered to her mother, but Carlotta showed her the door to the ladies right there, before her. It didn't even have a window large enough for her to crawl out of. In any case, it was on the first floor with a fifteen-foot drop or more over the rooftops below. Even the view made her feel helpless, trapped.

So it was that Carmina found herself undergoing a

most thorough and embarrassing examination, Doc Mitchell's wrinkled old face growing increasingly puzzled as he prodded and poked.

Finally, as she sat beside her mother, humiliated and deeply angered by this complete loss of dignity, he sighed and smiled kindly, addressing his remarks to her mother, just as if Carmina weren't even present.

'It's possibly too early to be certain, but I can see no sign of a pregnancy in the girl. Rest assured, I think you might be worrying unnecessarily.'

Carmina made a valiant attempt to hang on to the make-believe. 'Excuse me, but I certainly *am* pregnant. I know it. I feel it instinctively as a woman does. Why, I've even had morning sickness, and can't stand the smell of coffee.' With so many younger siblings, Carmina was no stranger to the symptoms of early pregnancy.

The old doctor looked into her eyes, a calculating, professional glance that seemed to probe right to the heart of her. His gaze was like a knife scraping away the veneer of the fabricated tale she'd created, to reveal the worm of truth beneath. Carmina's heart almost stopped beating. Could he tell she lied, just by looking into her eyes? Mamma always said a woman could sense when her own daughter was pregnant; was that why she'd brought her here? Was she about to be unmasked?

The doctor asked when her period had been due, if anything was worrying her, or if she'd been feeling off-colour in other ways. 'Maybe you've eaten something which doesn't agree with you.'

'I have not!'

'Well, I'd say from this initial examination, that you are not pregnant, Carmina.'

Carlotta clapped her hands to her cheeks in relief. 'It ees the miracle, doctor. My daughter, she is not going to shame us, after all?'

'She wouldn't be the first to bring such grief to her parents, Carlotta, and I'm sure you'd survive. Nevertheless, I see no signs to cause you any undue alarm. Bring her back to see me in a month if she still hasn't had a show,' and a bemused Carmina found herself ushered out of the surgery by her delighted mother.

Outside on the pavement, Carlotta hugged her recalcitrant daughter tight, and reverted to her native tongue, the words pouring out of her in a rush of ecstatic relief. 'Thank goodness you made a mistake, and you are not pregnant at all. Your life will not be ruined, and we can tell Luc that he doesn't have to marry you. Oh, and what a blessing for poor Gina! Now we can only hope she can find it in her heart to forgive his infidelity and the two of them can start afresh.'

Carlotta wagged a finger in her face. 'As for you, madam, I hope you have learned a big lesson from this scare. If you are bad girl and forced to marry a man who doesn't love you, you will never find happiness.'

'Luc *does* love me. He was only flirting with Gina, and feeling sorry for her. And I had him first, remember.'

Carlotta gazed at her daughter with a sad expression in her brown eyes. 'He haunts the house every day looking for her, like a man possessed. Accept it,

Carmina, it is Gina he loves, not you. If you make him marry you, he will hate you all his life. Leave him be, Carmina. Find another man to love.'

She grasped her daughter's shoulders with both hands and gave her a little shake. 'And you listen to what your mamma tell you about respect in future. You be the good girl, next time, *sì*?'

Carmina was thinking, next time I'll have to be much, much cleverer.

'I'm not sure it's possible to start again, Luc. How can I simply pretend that this didn't happen?'

The pair of them were sitting in the parlour, the door firmly closed in order to give them the necessary privacy to discuss this delicate issue, but Gina was all too aware of the rest of her family keeping quiet in the other room.

She'd resisted long and hard the pressure to speak to him, her parents surprising her by their insistence that she at least give the boy a chance. In the end, partly because she simply had to be sure she was doing the right thing in turning her back on her love for Luc, she'd finally agreed.

Now that he was actually here, seated beside her on the sofa, Gina could hardly bear to look at him. She clasped her hands between her knees so that they weren't tempted to reach out and touch him. She could sense his discomfort, his embarrassment and anxiety, and knew if she were to look into his eyes she would be lost.

'I don't know what more I can say, Gina. It isn't

true, none of it. Surely you can see that now. I can't tell you how much I regret letting things go as far as they did. I shouldn't have believed Carmina when she told me you'd chucked me. If I'd got your letter, it might all have been different. It's you that I love, Gina, believe me. What more can I say?'

The power of his emotion almost overwhelmed her, yet how could she be sure? How could she trust him?

'My sister is very beautiful. If she crooks her little finger one more time, will you fall again for her charms?'

He took Gina's hands in his own, tenderly stroking each finger. '*No*, I swear it. I swear it on my life. Look, give me a chance, at least. I'm not asking for you to make any long-reaching promises. Let's just make up and start seeing each other again, and see what happens. Perhaps, in time, I can convince you that I'm sorry for what happened, and for what *almost* happened, and you'll come to trust me again.'

Gina stared at their joined hands, then pulling away began to pick at a thread on her pink Capri pants. 'I'm not sure.'

'Can't we at least be friends? Please? I told you once that you would never lose me and I still stand by that. If you want me, that is.'

She looked at him then, straight into the soul-searching depths of his blue eyes, as dark and mysterious as the sea itself and felt such a wave of love for him it almost swamped her. Could she even bring herself to turn away when she loved him so much, or was it already too late? He might look, and sound, completely sincere, but was it safe for her to love him, or did she risk being hurt all over again?

Gina's mind was in turmoil and when still she said nothing, those same dark eyes became clouded with anxiety. 'Gina, please say you'll forgive me.'

She swallowed, except that her throat seemed blocked by emotion. She thought of all the times in her life when she'd needed to dig deep into herself to find the strength to go on, to harden her heart against the pain. She did that now. 'I'm not sure I *can* believe in your so-called innocence. It's your word against my sister's. Who am I supposed to believe?'

'But you admit that Carmina tells lies.'

'Sometimes, yes.'

'Well then?'

Could all this talk of a baby have been another deliberate lie? Surely not. Even Carmina wouldn't go that far, for how could she possibly have got away with it? Even if Mamma and Doc Mitchell hadn't found her out, it would soon have become obvious that there was no baby, that there never had been. Probably she'd been so anxious to get him, she'd imagined herself pregnant, when really she was only a bit overdue with worrying herself into a stew. Clearly not pregnant at all. A silly mistake. But that didn't prove she hadn't had cause for concern.

Gina said, 'I don't believe she would make up a tale over something so serious, so important. I think this time you are the guilty one, making excuses for your bad behaviour.'

A spasm of pain flickered across his face and, despite

herself, Gina's heart went out to him. Perhaps it wasn't entirely Luc's fault. Where was her compassion? Mamma said men were weak, and how could anyone resist her scheming, beautiful sister when Carmina had set her heart on something she wanted? She should perhaps feel just a little sorry for him.

'I think I understand why it happened. Carmina is hard to resist. Maybe . . just possibly . . . and I'm not making any promises . . . but I might be prepared to be friends again. No more than that for the present. No kissing, no cuddling, nothing of that sort. We take things slowly and see how things go.'

His expression was instantly transfused with joy and Luc captured her hands again and brought them to his lips to kiss them. 'I'll spend my entire life making it up to you, Gina, I swear.'

24

Gina and Patsy

The entire Bertalone family were delighted with the good news. As the young couple emerged from the front parlour, Luc's arm wrapped about a shyly smiling Gina, everyone cheered. Carlotta clapped her hands with joy.

'All is going to be well. Oh, what a relief! I am a happy Mamma again. Carmina is not in trouble and has promised to be a good girl in future. And Gina is happy and content with Luc.' She rushed over to kiss them both in her fervent Italian way.

Papa shook Luc by the hand, then slapping a firm hand on his shoulder led him away from the knot of excited children. 'You will behave with more respect with my daughters in future, young man?'

'*Sì*, Mr Bertalone, I will, I swear. You have my word on it.'

'I won't have Gina hurt. She is very special to us, all our children are. They are *mia famiglia*. I have the *amore di un padre*, a father's love for them all. But Gina is extra-special because of the problems she has had to surmount.'

Luc was nodding. 'Like I told you before, Mr Bertalone, she is special to me too. She is so kind, so gentle and sweet, so sensitive and generous. I feel fortunate that she is prepared to try and repair our friendship. She has even agreed, with your permission, to come to the dance with me tonight. I will take good care of her, I promise, and have her home in good time.'

'Dancing is hard for her. You make sure she don't get too tired.'

Papa Bertalone nipped the bridge of his nose while he tried to work out how best to say what he needed to say. 'And you will take better care over this problem with Carmina? She has always been a little wild. That girl she act first, think later. I'm sure there is no real harm in her but she is *bellissima*, and like all beautiful women a little vain, *sì*? So vain she expect the world to be dropped at her feet. Do not let her steal your world, the one you wish to share with Gina. You behave. Understand me?'

'I understand, Mr Bertalone. I will take better care.' What else could he say, if they all chose to take Carmina's word and not his?

Gina was trying to hear what it was that Luc was saying to her father, but she was too far away, the sound of their voices drowned by her chattering siblings.

And then for some reason everyone stopped speaking and Luc's voice seemed to ring out clear and strong in the small living room. 'Gina has given me another chance and I've no intention of ruining it. Nothing and nobody will make me spoil things between us ever again. I have learned my lesson.'

He glanced across at Carmina as he said this. She

was sitting white-faced with fury in the corner, not joining in the general hub-bub.

She couldn't quite believe what she was hearing. How dare Luc deliberately drop her and go back to her sanctimonious sister? Carmina felt again that spine-tingling hatred for her sibling who had managed to rob her of everything she'd ever wanted in life: her parents' approbation, the full and undivided attention she deserved, and now the man she loved. She'd watched in disgust as her brothers and sisters crowded around to wish the reunited pair well. How could they all be so damned *happy*!

They should have been congratulating herself and Luc on their coming nuptials, not Gina. Instead, all her efforts, all her plans and schemes, had come to nothing. Her feelings, even her place in this family were given no consideration at all. Now Papa was opening a bottle of wine, declaring they had much to celebrate as family honour had been restored.

'Come, Carmina,' he called to her. 'Come and be happy with us.'

When still she didn't move from her chair to join in the celebrations, Carlotta marched over and gave her daughter a nudge.

'Stop sulking. Come and tell your sister how sorry you are, and that you won't do anything to spoil her chances ever again. Tell her!'

'It's all right,' Gina said. 'I'm not asking for an apology.'

'Just as well, since you won't get one,' Carmina bit back.

Carlotta patted her own plump cheeks in despair. 'What am I to do with her? Papa, make your daughter say that she will be the good girl and behave. I want no more lies.'

Papa Bertalone attempted to look stern, not easy with Lela cuddling up on his lap begging for a sip from his glass, and Marta and Gabby playing marbles at his feet. He'd had a hard day in the ice-cream parlour and was really far too weary to deal with any more female angst and emotion. All he wanted was his supper, a little snooze, and some peace in his life.

'I have spoken to Luc, my love, man to man. You have spoken to Carmina. Enough has been said, Mamma. Let this be an end to the matter. Gina and Luc will either make a go of it, or they won't. It is up to them now.'

Only the expression in her sister's hard glare warned Gina that the matter was very far from closed, certainly so far as Carmina was concerned.

Carmina went to the Friday night dance, despite having no partner, her friends complaining that they'd never known her to be in such a foul mood. They kept well out of her way while Carmina made a complete exhibition of herself dancing and necking with boys who were perfect strangers to her, and in full view of everyone. She seemed more reckless than ever, as if she had something to prove.

How could Luc treat her so callously? One minute prepared to do the decent thing and stand by her, the next giving her the cold shoulder and making up with her dratted sister. To add insult to injury Carmina caught a glimpse of him across the dance floor with Gina in his arms.

She felt as if she were burning up inside, wanted to walk over and push the stupid girl away. What right did she have to steal the man Carmina had planned to marry herself? Selfish little bitch!

The lovebirds were doing a slow waltz to 'Blueberry Hill', so Gina's limp didn't show too much. Luc was holding her close but, come to think of it, they didn't give the impression of being lovebirds at all. They weren't exactly dancing cheek to cheek. Gina wasn't even looking at him. She had her hands resting loosely on his shoulders, holding him away from her at a safe distance, while she gazed about at the other dancers. She was clearly not at all happy to be there. And Carmina could tell by her manner that she still hadn't forgiven him.

When the dance ended they left the floor, but Carmina noticed that they didn't hold hands. Luc tried to take her hand but Gina quickly pulled it away. Oh dear, he was definitely still in the dog-house.

Carmina smiled to herself. How long would a boy like Luc put up with such treatment? Not long, surely. And she'd be ready and waiting when he grew bored.

'Are you enjoying yourself?' Luc asked and Gina gave him a little nod of agreement.

'Would you like a lemonade or something?'

'No thanks, I'm fine.'

Luc took a breath. He hadn't expected it to be easy

but trying to get a smile out of her, let alone any sort of conversation, was proving impossible.

'Carmina's over there, why don't you go and dance with her,' Gina said.

Once upon a time she would have been thrilled to be at a dance with Luc, but now she felt awkward with him, and conspicuous on the dance floor with her limp, as if people were looking at her and wondering why she danced in that funny way. 'She keeps glancing across. I think she must be feeling a bit low now that you've called the wedding off.'

'Don't tell me that you're feeling sorry for Carmina now?'

Gina still didn't look at him. 'I'm saying that you're free to ask her to dance, if you wish. You don't have to stay here with me.'

With an exasperated sigh, Luc took Gina firmly by the shoulders and turned her to face him. 'Look, if you keep talking about Carmina like this, it isn't going to help us to forget what happened, is it? You have to stop being so concerned about her, and stop believing every bit of rubbish she says.'

'She's my sister.'

'I know she's your sister but can't you see what she tried to do to us? It wasn't a mistake, all this talk about a baby, it was another of her lies. She wouldn't recognise the truth if it jumped up and bit her.'

Gina scowled, hating herself for behaving this way but quite unable to help it. They were huddled in a corner of the dance floor now, speaking to each other in furious whispers above the noise of the music. Elvis

Presley was belting out 'All Shook Up', and people were glancing across at them in curiosity.

The room was hot and crowded and Gina felt harassed and uncomfortable, wishing she'd never come and was safe at home in her bedroom. What had possessed her to imagine she could go through with this, and pick up where they'd left off? Hadn't Luc destroyed everything they'd had together by sleeping with her sister?

'She says you were rampant for her, wouldn't leave her alone. Maybe Carmina too was fooled into thinking you cared for her, just as I believed you loved *me*. Wrongly as it turns out.'

'I *do* love you.'

'But not enough.'

'Oh, Gina, let's stop arguing, let's just try to be friends.' He touched the swathe of hair that fell forward over her face, tucked it behind her ear. 'One day, I hope you *will* believe me, but I accept that maybe it's too soon right now.'

An awkward silence fell between them, one in which Gina realised the band was playing 'Bye, Bye Love', an Everly Brothers hit. It seemed so appropriate that for a moment she feared she might start to cry. It entirely echoed the terrible despair she felt.

Perhaps Luc realised this for he gently took her arm. 'Come on, love, those words aren't meant for us. Let me show you how to do the hand jive, which we can do sitting down. It'll cheer you up. No more quarrelling, we're here to have fun, remember?'

And to Gina's great surprise, even though she was

upset over the heated words they'd exchanged, felt vulnerable and nervous because in some mysterious way Luc seemed almost like a stranger to her now, she did indeed start to relax a little and have fun. She even had a go at the cha-cha and found she could do it rather well. Luc said she'd be an expert dancer in no time.

Not that she believed him when he said that either, not with her lolloping gait. He was just being kind, and she'd really no wish to be an expert in anything. Gina simply wanted him to love her, as she'd once fondly imagined that he did. He swore that his feelings hadn't changed, but how could she believe anything he said after all that had happened? There'd been so many lies told, Gina no longer knew who she could trust.

Bored and temporarily short of partners, having refused several candidates because they were too tall, too short, had spots, a big nose or simply weren't Luc Fabriani, Carmina had been sitting in a corner sulking for some time when she suddenly noticed that the band had gone off for a break and Alec Hall was setting up his record player in their place.

An image of their encounter on the supposed site of the old Roman Fort flashed instantly into her mind. She no longer thought of it as rape, only too aware of her own foolishness in flirting with him. Things had simply got out of hand, and, OK, so he'd taken advantage of her, in a way. He'd rushed things instead of making sure she was entirely willing. Yet there was something appealing about the man. His casual assurance that he could do with her as he pleased excited her. Carmina had discovered that she rather liked a man who knew how to take control.

She liked his smoky-grey eyes that seemed to devour her, even the derisory smirk when she said something that amused him.

A burn that could only be desire started up deep inside her at the memory of his passion, his intense hunger for her. That's all it had been; not wickedness, not a violation, simply an unstoppable, unquenchable need to possess her.

Carmina rather liked that too. So thrilling! So dangerous!

She fluffed out her hair, smoothed her circular skirt over her bouffant petticoats and strolled over to say hello.

25

Carmina

Alec Hall looked oddly out of place in his black velvet jacket and pink dickie-bow tie with a carnation in his buttonhole, but she smiled at the way the light came into his eyes as he saw her approaching. Carmina had forgotten that she'd once thought him an old-fashioned fuddy-duddy. He was simply a man who liked women; a man who fancied her like mad.

Rumour had it that he'd been married twice; his first wife dying when a V2 bomb dropped on his house, the second someone he met when he was out in Korea who'd either tragically died or deserted him. A bit of a ladies' man, our Alec.

'I wondered when you'd come over,' he said, as soon as she reached him. 'I knew you wouldn't be able to resist.'

Carmina couldn't help laughing. 'Don't flatter yourself.'

'I wouldn't dream of it. I'm flattering *you*. You're the most beautiful girl in the room.'

His words were balm to her bruised pride, exactly what she needed right now: a man who appreciated her charms.

'Cigarette?' He was offering her a Capstan full

strength. Carmina didn't smoke but she thought, what the hell, and took one. It made her cough and it was his turn now to laugh.

'I think you need a bit more practice.'

'Maybe I do, but then I am only seventeen, so I'm needing practice in all sorts of things. Maybe I just need a good teacher.'

He looked at her steadily, one eyebrow raised as he slid another record on to the turntable, then gave that little smirk. 'Maybe I should apply for the job.'

'Maybe you'd get it.'

'That's a lot of maybes.'

Carmina shrugged. 'Well, it's up to you, isn't it?'

'Is it?'

'I'm a bit disappointed in you though.'

She was delighted to see that his face fell. 'Why, what have I done? Look, if it's about what happened the other week, I can only say I read the signals wrong. I'm sorry. It won't happen again.'

'It certainly won't.'

'Next time I'll be the perfect gentleman.'

Carmina stared at him. 'Next time? Now you are flattering yourself. All I meant was that you once said you'd come and ask me to dance when the band came back, but you never did. You forgot all about me.'

'How could anyone forget you, Carmina? Once seen, never forgotten.'

She moved closer, so that she could look directly into that steady, penetrating grey gaze of his. 'Why don't you ask me tonight then? If you did ask me . . . to dance, I mean . . . I might be more amenable this time.'

Both of them were breathing quite deeply as they each considered the underlying meaning beneath her casual remark. After a moment Alec gave her a slow smile. 'OK, how about the first one after the band comes back?'

Carmina shook her head as she half turned to walk away, except that she was really only doing a little pirouette to let him appreciate the full picture of her shapely figure. 'It might be a rock 'n roll. Do you jive, or rock?'

He shook his head. 'Maybe I need a teacher too. We could have the last waltz then, how about that?'

A slight pause while Carmina considered, and then, 'OK, the last waltz it is. Don't forget this time. I'll be waiting.'

'I won't forget.'

To her great satisfaction, Carmina noticed that Luc hadn't missed this little flirtatious exchange, and she cast him a glance of pure triumph as she sauntered back to her friends.

If Luc Fabriani imagined he could simply walk away and abandon her then he was badly mistaken. Once he realised what he was missing, he'd be begging her to take him back. Let him see how other boys, and even grown men of experience, couldn't get enough of her.

If her over-protective mother hadn't taken her to the doctor, the lie would never have been discovered until after they were married, which would have been far too late for Luc to do anything about it. She really had been very unlucky.

But it was only a setback, Carmina told herself as she went to see if her friends had remembered to get her a plate of supper. She was beginning to think more clearly now. All she had to do was prove the lie to be the truth. She even had an idea how to get Gina out of the picture once and for all.

Alec did not forget his promise of the last waltz, but Carmina did. She looked at him blankly when he suddenly appeared at her side.

'Our dance, I think,' he said, brushing aside the young man who'd hoped for that pleasure.

'Maybe I've changed my mind,' Carmina replied, somewhat brusquely.

She hadn't expected to have to keep this promise. She'd rather hoped that having seen what he was missing Luc would have left Gina and come rushing to her side. It hadn't happened. For all her sister's evident coolness towards him, he was still hovering about her like some love-sick puppy. And now she would have to keep her promise to dance with Alec, after all. Really, she should learn to think things through properly before being tempted by a roguish smile.

'We seem to be off on those maybes again,' he said, again with that twisted little smile.

Allowing no further argument, he took her in his arms and swept her on to the dance floor. Alec Hall surprised her still further by being an excellent dancer. He even knew the proper steps instead of just stumbling round as the other lads did.

But it wasn't his expertise with the waltz that appealed most as the way he was holding her, the heat of his body searing through her thin blouse. She could feel his hand hot and heavy in the small of her back, the pressure of his thighs against hers. She could sense his steps slowing, his mood growing languorous with desire.

Carmina was equally surprised by the effect this was having upon her. Mamma would accuse her of being wanton. Fortunately, she wasn't here to see what her daughter was up to but Carmina certainly felt wanton. What was wrong with having a bit of fun?

She eased herself closer allowing his cheek to rest against hers, his warm breath sending little shivers of excitement down her spine. She became so engrossed with the image of smooching with a mature, experienced male with whom she'd already had intimate relations, Carmina even forgot to check if Luc was watching.

'I must be the luckiest guy on the dance floor,' he murmured, flicking his tongue against her ear.

Carmina felt drowsy with lust, entranced by the fact he could have any woman, any girl, in the room, yet she was the one he wanted.

'I'd feel even luckier if you let me drive you home.'

He has a car, she thought, unlike these randy young lads who would be only too eager to take her home if they didn't have to walk quite so far. Of course, Luc had that beat-up old Morris, but Alec's car would surely be far better.

'OK.'

They passed Luc and Gina waiting at the bus stop as they drove by. Carmina waved through the window and then leant back in her seat, feeling exceedingly pleased with herself. She'd make Luc sorry for choosing her sister instead of her.

Alec didn't take her home, but then she hadn't expected him to. His car was a sporty MG Midget in British Racing Green, which Carmina loved on sight. It was so satisfying to know he could afford such a vehicle. So grown-up.

He drove down by the River Irwell and parked the car under one of the railway arches where they had a view of slate-grey water glistening in the pale moonlight as it slid under Princes Bridge. A bonded warehouse in dark red brick loomed in the background, its myriad barred windows and doors giving it the look of a prison. Carmina shivered.

It was eerily quiet here with only the distant hum of traffic in the city, as if they were in a secret world of their own. There was no movement of boat or barge, no shunting of trains on the tracks, no work of any kind taking place at this time of night. Alec turned off the engine, and the car headlights, and they both sat unmoving, staring out into the velvet darkness.

There wasn't much room in the small two-seater and Carmina was acutely aware of his warm presence beside her. She could smell the musky scent of his aftershave, a welcome change from the stink of Brylcreem that all the guys wore on their hair, mingling with the leather of the seats. It was an exhilarating combination and seemed to be having a strange effect upon her senses in the confines of the car. Still he made no move.

Carmina smiled to herself and thought, I'll count to ten. If he hasn't touched me by then, I'll get out of the car and walk home.

His voice came out of the shadows, low and husky. 'I think you're hurting, Carmina. I think you've been rejected by someone, and that's why you're here with me now. You know, of course, that I'm far too old for you. I'm thirty-five, and what are you? Sixteen, seventeen . . . ?'

Carmina interrupted him, the sound of her own heartbeat loud in her ears. 'Eighteen.' Another lie, but what did she care? If he didn't kiss her soon, she thought she might scream. 'What has age got to do with anything?'

Her eyes were growing accustomed to the gloom but she sensed rather than saw him shift in his seat and turn towards her.

'I know how it feels to be rejected, and to feel hurt inside. I've always felt myself to be a bit of a square peg in a round hole, trying to fit in. But nobody quite understands me either. I suspect you feel the same. Parents, sisters, boyfriends, how can they possibly appreciate how you suffer? Did everyone make too much fuss over Gina? Did that make you feel invisible?'

How come he knew so much about her, she thought, startled by his perspicacity.

'You're very good at putting on an act of defiance, Carmina, but I know that deep inside there's a vulnerable young girl simply longing to be loved and needed.'

She'd never heard him talk like this before, never imagined he could be so sensitive, so understanding.

A warm hand circled her knee, slid up to her thigh. Carmina held her breath. She felt the softness of his mouth on her throat, his lips searching for the pulse in the little hollow of her shoulder. His fingers unpinned her suspenders, one by one, and slid each stocking down the smooth silk of her bare skin. Then he was searching for her panties, pulling her down in the seat, his breath ragged, as was hers.

She couldn't think beyond the touch of his exploring fingers, the sensations he was sending cascading through her. Her limbs felt flaccid, weak, and an overwhelming need was growing inside her, a hunger that only he could satisfy. The memory of that other time, when he'd possessed her against her will, was quite gone from her mind. Whatever it was he did to her, she wanted more of it.

She wanted to tear off his clothes, to scratch and snarl and force him to give her whatever was necessary to make this pain go away.

And when finally he did, she cried out loud with relief. Her last coherent thought was that this would show Luc Fabriani he wasn't the only man to appreciate her.

26

Mavis, Thomas and Patsy

Mavis never went near the little house next to the pawn shop. She seemed to have washed her hands of the entire enterprise, perhaps realising Chris and Amy's minds were made up and it was fruitless to try to change them. Nevertheless, she deeply resented her husband's long absences from home.

Thomas, of course, welcomed any excuse to get out of the house, particularly of an evening when it was too dark and cold to sit in his little hut on the allotment.

'You aren't going round there again, are you?' she would say as he reached for his jacket. 'You're never away.'

'There's a great deal still to be done and we're running out of time, at least Amy is. That babby is busting to be born.'

'I really don't see the rush. Amy can have the baby here, I've already told her as much.'

'She wants to have it in the nursing home, as you well know.'

'I didn't find it necessary to go to any *nursing home* when I had Chris.'

'Things have changed. They take more precautions these days, and a good thing too. Leave 'em be, Mavis.

They have their own lives to lead and must make their own decisions.'

'That's all very well in theory,' Mavis retorted, shocked that he should dare to disagree with her. 'But only if the decisions they make are the right ones, and so far I've seen little evidence of that.'

Thomas sighed, put on his flat cap, picked up the bucket of white distemper he'd prepared, and left. Arguing with Mavis was always a pointless exercise. He had a couple of hours to spare, time enough to give the backyard walls a quick coat and make it all clean and shipshape. Then when summer came there'd be somewhere clean and decent for Amy to put the baby out in the pram. His first grandchild, eeh, he couldn't wait. He didn't care what it was, girl or boy, he'd be made up either way.

Marc thought it would be best if Patsy sold the hat stall. It had been less of a problem for her to be involved when Annie had been available to keep an eye on the accounts, even if the poor lady had been confined to the house through sickness. But the responsibility now, he said, would be far too much for her.

Patsy felt vaguely irritated by his concern, even though he was only thinking of her. 'I don't see it as a responsibility. Anyway, can we leave any decisions till after the funeral?'

It rained all day with even the heavens weeping for this feisty old lady. And, despite Annie never having had a good word to say for anyone, half of Champion Street Market turned out to pay their respects.

Clara was humbled by their support. 'Annie never believed that anyone liked her very much. But then she wasn't the easiest person to get along with, far too brusque for most people's sensibilities.'

Patsy smiled and said nothing, recalling only too well the tall, stiff-backed woman with the cropped, prematurely grey hair, her uncompromising standards and unbending manner. She remembered the many fiery exchanges they'd enjoyed over the years, and the gradual thaw that had set in when Annie had begun to see that this stroppy young orphan might have some good qualities after all. How at first she'd constantly complained about the noise Patsy made, and then bought her a record player. How she'd threatened to turn her out of the house and then offered her a home for life.

The vicar was commendably brief, perhaps aware that Annie would still be keeping a close watch that he didn't over-run, as she had so often done in life.

Friends returned with Clara and Patsy to Number 22 for the wake. Big Molly Poulson from next door was there, together with her daughter Amy looking as if she might give birth and produce the next generation before the day was out. Marc was by Patsy's side, of course, as were Papa and Mamma Bertalone, who'd always admired Annie for the courage she'd shown during the war. Winnie Holmes had never missed a good funeral yet, although Barry her husband had for some reason elected not to attend.

Jimmy Ramsay brought a plate of sausages for the repast. Joe Southworth and his wife Irma contributed one of her famous cakes, although they weren't speaking and addressed comments to each other via various friends. Even Belle Garside popped in briefly to pay her respects. All had known Annie Higginson and felt the sharp edge of her tongue on many occasions, and all were present to see that she had a good send-off.

Clara looked proud or desolate by turn, depending on whom she was speaking to. Then she would disappear for a few private moments before coming back all bright-eyed and bravely smiling. Patsy wept a few tears herself during the course of the afternoon, so was not in the mood for Marc to again harass her on the subject of her own future the moment they were alone.

They'd escaped to a quiet corner of the Dog and Duck. With its grimy exterior, hardly discernible from the once glossy black paint of the doors and window-frames, and an interior that stank of smoke, strong beer and stale sweat, the pub was nonetheless a favourite meeting point for the residents of Champion Street. Marc bought Patsy a welcome shandy and a pint of bitter for himself, then set about laying down the law yet again.

'Why would I want to sell?' Patsy interrupted when she'd heard enough of this stuck record. 'I *love* working on the hat stall. I even kid myself that I'm really rather good at what I do. Apart from anything else, it's my livelihood.'

Marc quietly pointed out that earning a living would cease to be a problem for her, once they were married.

Patsy's eyes flashed. 'And why would that be? Because you expect me to turn into a frumpy little housewife who devotes all her time to wiping down her

Formica work surfaces and baking cakes? I don't think that's quite me, do you?'

Marc smiled, 'Perhaps not, but I live in hope. I rather like the idea of you in an apron, breathlessly waiting for me to step over the threshold each evening.'

Patsy punched him, though not too hard. 'Huh, every man's fantasy. It won't happen, not unless I have a rolling pin in me hand.'

Marc sighed. 'A man can dream. Still, you might at least tell Clara that you'd have no objection to *her* selling it, should she wish to. She oughtn't to feel obliged to hang on to it just for your benefit. I mean, maybe she too feels it would be too much for her now that Annie's gone, and be glad of the chance to be rid of the responsibility.'

Patsy was thoughtful for a moment. 'If Clara wants out of the business that's her decision, and I wouldn't dream of stopping her. Although I might offer to buy it off her, assuming I could borrow the money.'

'What?' Marc looked appalled. 'You wouldn't?'

'I might, why not? Anyway, I doubt that will happen. I believe Clara will be glad of the distraction. She'll need something to occupy her mind besides grieving for Annie in the weeks and months ahead. And she too still needs to earn a living. Life goes on, as they say.'

Marc was compelled to let the subject drop, although despite his jokes and teasing, he was far from happy about the situation. Patsy, in his opinion, was working far too hard already and the situation could only get worse in the months to come.

He didn't want a wife worn out by work; he wanted

her at home with his tea on the table, his son cooing sweetly in his cot, and for her to have the energy and time to devote herself exclusively to him. What man wouldn't want that, he thought. He'd hoped that Patsy would want it too. Now she seemed to be shying away from the idea, and he really couldn't understand what had got into her.

One morning Mavis spotted Thomas coming out of Belle's Café. She instantly marched over, face like thunder. 'I thought you were working on our Chris's house? What were you doing in there talking to that hussy?'

'I were a bit peckish like,' Thomas said, his cheeks going quite pink with guilt, as if he were a naughty boy caught doing something he shouldn't.

'And you don't have a perfectly good wife to come home to, I suppose?' Mavis demanded, folding her arms across her heaving bosom.

'I don't like to bother you when I know you've just got the place all shipshape and tidy. Anyroad, it were only a ten-minute break, for a brew and a pie.'

'Pie indeed, in the middle of the morning? I never heard the like. You've already had a decent breakfast which I cooked for you at seven.'

'Aye, I know, but it's hungry work, plastering.' Recognising his mistake, Thomas attempted to back-pedal. 'It weren't so much a pie, more a toasted currant tea cake, just a snack like to keep me going.' But it was too late. Her expression was grim.

'Cutting down your working hours at the bakery is

doing you no good at all. Being at a loose end is making you eat too much.'

'I'm not at a loose end, Mavis, I'm working on our Chris's place. It's hard graft.'

'Are you suggesting I don't feed you properly?'

'Nay, I'm saying nowt o' t'sort.' Thomas knew he was getting into deep water, but for the life in him couldn't think how to extricate himself. Mavis's breakfasts were never very reliable. It could be the whole works: bacon, sausage and fried egg, or a slice of thin toast and a dollop of runny scrambled egg, all depending on her mood. Belle, however, understood about a working man's appetite and had never let him down yet.

But then she understood other appetites as well, which was the main problem so far as Mavis was concerned.

'Since you're so *peckish* of a morning, you'd better come home at eleven for coffee and a biscuit,' Mavis snapped. 'It will be ready and waiting for you. See that you're not late.'

'Yes, love.'

Watching this heated exchange from the window of her little café which looked out over Champion Street, Belle let out a sympathetic sigh. 'Poor chap,' she thought. 'Mavis never gives him a minute's peace.'

Thomas had rarely called in her café at one time, but he'd been popping in every morning for weeks now. Generally he'd ask for a large mug of strong tea and a pork pie or sausage roll, just to keep him going till lunch-time, he said. Sometimes he'd push the boat out and have the full English breakfast. That would be on the days when his wife wasn't speaking to him. Mavis always took out her revenge on her husband's stomach.

'Well, I won't see that poor blighter again.'

But she was wrong. Against all wisdom, Thomas arrived at the café on the dot of ten the next morning, as usual, looking remarkably cheerful.

'Beans on toast I think this morning, Belle.'

'Right you are, chuck. Shall I pop a fried egg on top, just to give it a bit of body?' Belle asked him, stretching her own voluptuous body as she stood close beside him. She thought he needed reminding what a good woman looked like, that they weren't all thin as a drink of water with a sour smile like his missus.

'Eeh, that'd be grand!'

She gave him a custard tart afterwards, as a treat. 'On the house.'

'You're too good to me, Belle.'

'I can always tell when a man needs a bit of spoiling.'

'I'm working hard on me son's house, so it's much appreciated. It beats coffee and biscuits any time,' he said, then glancing at his watch, 'crikey, that reminds me, I'd best be off. What do I owe you?'

'I can put it on account, if you're in a hurry. Settle up at the end of the week, why don't you? I know when I can trust a chap to deliver the goods.'

She smiled at him and Thomas gave her a thoughtful look. There was something about Belle Garside which always gave the impression she was saying much more than was at first evident. He sensed a rippling undercurrent of danger and excitement. Thomas grinned.

But then hadn't he been saying that he happen needed a bit of excitement in his life?

'See you tomorrow then.' It felt as if he'd just made an assignation and Thomas walked out of the little café with his head held high.

Unfortunately, staying talking to Belle had made him late for his morning coffee and biscuits and he could see Mavis standing on the doorstep of the baker's shop looking out for him. He waved, just to reassure her that he was on his way. He'd no appetite now for a ginger snap but it was easier to slip one down rather than create a fuss. Had she spotted him coming out of the café? No, he didn't think so. He hoped not anyroad, or there'd be hell to pay. Then just as he was about to cross the street, Belle suddenly appeared at his side.

'You forgot your cap, chuck.' And placing it on his head, she very quickly kissed his cheek. 'You'd forget your head if it were loose, you daft article,' she teased, then sashayed off, hips swinging.

Thomas's heart sank to his boots as he turned to face the blistering anger of his wife, feeling rather as Custer must have felt going into the Battle of the Little Bighorn.

27

Gina

'I know in my heart that it can't all be lies. Something must have happened between you for Carmina to mistakenly believe she was pregnant. She genuinely believed she was carrying your child.'

Here they were again, the same old argument that kept on surfacing between them like an itch that had to be scratched.

'And you believe her?'

'I do.'

Luc ran a hand through his untidy hair. 'Carmina is far more complicated, far cleverer than you might think. You're always so determined to see the best in people but life isn't like that, Gina . . .'

'Don't *you* start lecturing me about *life*,' Gina interrupted him, feeling dangerously close to tears. 'Carmina is always telling me how naïve I am, how unused to the ways of the world. That isn't my fault, you know. I've been locked away from it for nearly six years.'

'I know, I know.' Luc's heart went out to her, yet he knew she was stronger than she looked, otherwise she couldn't have got over her illness so well.

'I like people,' Gina continued, lifting her chin high, cinnamon eyes blazing. 'And I happen to think the world is a fine and beautiful place. What is so wrong with that?'

'Nothing, sweetheart,' he said, gently rubbing her arms to soothe her. 'Except that other people aren't so generous-hearted as you. Carmina is bitter and jealous because she seems to think she has some sort of God-given right over me. I really don't know why, but she does. I was always hopeful of being saved at the eleventh hour, that this wedding she was so desperately trying to bludgeon me into would never happen. Even when your father was talking to mine I was thinking, there must be a way out of this. I just couldn't believe it was happening.'

'So you'd've happily wriggled out of your responsibilities and left her to bring up your child alone, would you?'

'I never had any responsibilities towards Carmina. She wasn't ever having my child! How could she be when we didn't *do* anything to make one. It was all a complete fabrication, a figment of her warped imagination. Hasn't Doc Mitchell proved that fact beyond doubt?'

'It hasn't been proved that you didn't have sex with her, only that she was mistaken about the pregnancy.'

He looked at her aghast. Luc felt drained, and deeply unhappy, realising he was no nearer to proving his innocence. 'Why are we quarrelling? We've been through all of this scores of times. I was a fool, yes. I let things go too far, but I swear that I stopped before it got quite out of hand. Do you understand what I'm saying, Gina?'

Gina flushed bright red. 'I'm not as stupid as everyone seems to think. But you were with her, in your car, necking, petting, whatever you got up to. It was still a betrayal.'

It was Luc's turn now to redden with embarrassment. 'You're right, I did, and I hate myself for that, and for not believing in *us*. Do *you* believe in us, Gina? Can you believe in *me*?'

She looked at him properly then, straight in the eye. 'I don't know. You've hurt me badly. I don't know who to believe. Carmina is my sister. All right, so we squabble and fall out all the time. Sisters do. She's always seen me as a rival, as if she should be best in everything because she's a year or so older than me. But that's perfectly normal behaviour between sisters. She was at my side every day throughout the years of my illness. I can't forget that either. And irritating as she is, I love her.'

'And I love you. I don't want you ever to forget that.'

The only way Gina could deal with the misery that was eating away at her heart was to bury herself in her new job. She loved working for Dena in the sewing room although she kept herself to herself, rarely chatting to the other girls. She barely paused in her work, keeping her fingers flying, feet smoothly operating the treadle of the Singer sewing machine. She was grateful to at last have found something that she was good at.

But it was hard keeping her feelings bottled up inside, and while her family blithely assumed all was well her friend Amy seemed to be far more perceptive.

'Are you happy, Gina?' she asked her one day. Gina had developed the habit of popping in to see her new friend for a chat in what was to be Amy and Chris's new home.

'I enjoy working for Dena, yes. It feels so good to have a real purpose in life.'

They were sitting on upturned boxes eating egg sandwiches, and Amy set a mug of tea down beside her. The house was empty save for the two of them, since Thomas had gone off to buy more paint, and Chris was at the bakery, as usual. Amy smiled as she took a sip of her own tea. 'Good, I'm glad. And how are things at home? Are your parents happy about your decision to start work?'

'Oh, yes,' Gina agreed, eyes shining. 'Mamma was surprised when I told her, but very pleased. She tends to assume that I'd be useless at anything, or else get overtired, but then she's very protective of me, you see. Ever since . . . well, she just is.'

'You aren't useless at all. I'm sure you're an extremely skilled machinist. Dena wouldn't employ you otherwise.' Amy paused, a small frown creasing her smooth brow, not sure how to proceed. She liked Gina a lot but she was concerned for her. The younger girl might claim to be happy, but didn't look it.

'If you don't mind a friend being nosy, how are you and Luc getting on? Is it working out between the pair of you?'

Gina said nothing for some long seconds, merely gazed at Amy over the rim of her mug. In the end, she set it down and gave a philosophical shrug.

'When I say that I'm happy, I mean I love my job. I like having a reason to get up in a morning, something more to look forward to than just helping Mamma at home, or being with the children. But Luc and I . . . it's too soon to be sure. It's hard for me to forget what he did . . . hard to forgive . . . and to trust him again. That's the truth. I'm so confused yet I find it hard to pretend that things haven't changed between us.'

'Then don't try to pretend. Be honest with him. If it hurts, say so. Explain how you feel, and why. You might still be able to work things out, and be stronger as a result. Although selfish people like your sister often have an easier time of it than sensitive ones such as yourself.'

'Oh, no, that's not so,' Gina disagreed. 'Carmina is not having an easy time of it either, probably because she did lie to me at first, and maybe regrets that. She isn't happy, not at all, although she won't admit her misery is entirely of her own making. She can't bring herself to accept that she's lost Luc. And I can't accept that she's lying about – well, about what happened after those kisses. Luc swears things didn't go any further but how can I be sure?'

'Trust?'

Gina gave a rueful smile. 'But who do I trust? My sister, or my boyfriend?'

'Yet you accept she's lied once already. Why not again? Maybe Luc's right and she made up the whole thing.'

Gina gave this some thought, then shook her head. 'Why would she? It doesn't make sense to fabricate a pregnancy. I think that was a genuine concern because of what had happened between them. Anyway, I can't even find it in my heart to forgive him for kissing her, let alone anything more.'

'Have you tried talking to Carmina recently? Have you asked her, point blank, if she's speaking the truth?'

Gina gave Amy an agonised glance. 'I suppose I'm a bit afraid to ask.'

'Oh, Gina, you have to. You owe it to yourself. Don't let her walk all over you. I know it can't be easy and I don't envy you your dilemma, love.' Amy rested a gentle hand on the younger girl's shoulder. 'You can always come here and talk to me though, don't forget.'

'I know. It's good to have friends.' Particularly, Gina thought, when your closest sister has cheated on you with the boy you love.

Gina was in torment, couldn't get the image of her sister making love to Luc out of her mind. It didn't surprise her that Carmina wanted to win Luc for herself, like a prize in a raffle. And how could he resist? She was a beautiful, desirable girl.

Ever since they'd been quite small, rivalry between the two sisters had been strong.

Gina remembered once winning a certificate for reading poetry in a competition. Afterwards, Carmina had been so envious she'd 'accidentally' spilled orange juice on it. Mamma had tried to clean the stain off, and Papa had put the certificate in a lovely frame, but somehow it was spoiled, and Gina knew why. Her sister was jealous.

Her worst memory of all was of the day when her illness had been diagnosed. Gina had felt devastated, as had her parents. They both had rushed to hug her, kissing her and reassuring her that she would get well again, when suddenly her eleven-year-old sister had screamed and fallen in a fit on to the floor. Mamma and Papa had rushed to Carmina's aid then, naturally, but Gina had known, in her heart, that nothing at all was wrong with her. Carmina had fallen off her chair in order to bring the attention back to herself.

Amy thought Luc might be the one telling the truth. Yet he hadn't denied they were together in the car that night, or that he had kissed her. So how could she be sure that they didn't go all the way?

Gina could hardly bear to think of it. Unfortunately she couldn't *stop* herself from thinking about it.

'Why did you do it?' Gina had decided to take Amy's advice in one respect and ask her sister what exactly had happened, and why.

Carmina hung her head, saying nothing.

'Why did you claim to be pregnant? Tell me!'

'Because I thought I was after . . . after what had taken place between us. I was so scared,' Carmina whispered, dipping her head still further so that her face was entirely hidden behind a swathe of glossy curls.

'But why did you let him make love to you in the first place? Is it because you hate me?'

She swept back the mane of ebony hair with one hand to reveal a face ravished by tears. 'How could I ever hate you? You are my little *sister*. I *love* you! Gina, I'm so sorry for all of this, for hurting you so badly. I never meant this to happen. Luc made it very plain that he wanted me, wouldn't take no for an answer, and I simply couldn't help myself. I love him so very much, you see.'

Gina stared at her sister, dry-eyed, her heart bleeding over the pain of this confession, and the way the pair of them seemed destined to be at odds. 'Yes, I do see. But I love him too.'

'I know. Oh, Gina, what are we to do?'

'It's rather up to Luc, don't you think? He must be the one to choose which of us he wants.'

Carmina's eyes glimmered behind the stray curls that hung over her ashen face, her voice little more than a whisper. 'I suppose so. What will you do though, if he chooses me? Will *you* still love *me*? I couldn't bear it if we weren't still friends.'

Gina's heart swelled with pity, as it always did at the sight of any distressed creature, let alone her own beloved and misguided sister. She put her arms about Carmina and rocked her in her arms, as she had done many times before over the years. 'We'll never stop being friends. How can we? We're joined by birth, you and I. No matter what happens, you are, and will always be, my very dear sister.'

The very next evening Gina and Luc were walking down Oxford Road. They were going to see Elvis Presley in *Jailhouse Rock* and Gina was looking forward to it, having heard the music was terrific. She was a great fan of Elvis, even though she thought him rather dangerous. Besides, she liked going to the flicks, loved everything about it: the anticipation as you stood in the queue, the popcorn, the British Gaumont News, even the awful B-movies, followed by the excitement of the big picture.

Watching the stars on screen made her feel as if she were entering an exciting new world of glamorous people who all wore beautifully immaculate clothes. Doris Day was never short of a witty retort, John Wayne always beat the baddies and Rock Hudson always got the girl.

Luc was saying now, 'I know I've hurt you, Gina, and I want, more than anything, to put things right between us.'

'I don't want to talk about it, not tonight.'

Luc gave a gentle sigh. After a moment, he said, 'I miss you so much.'

Gina looked up at him, surprised. 'I don't understand. How can you miss me when I'm here, right beside you?'

He stopped walking to hold her gently in his arms. 'Ah, but you're not here, are you? You're millions of miles away replaying that stupid mistake I made, going over and over it in your mind like a stuck record. I can't bear it.'

When she said nothing to this, he laced his fingers in hers and they continued walking.

Was he right? Gina thought. Was she deliberately tormenting herself by trying to imagine what had gone on between Luc and her sister? Would that be the first step towards forgiveness, if she could stop thinking about them together? Hadn't she said to Carmina that he must be the one to choose? Shouldn't she at least allow him that chance?

'Amy says I've to stop pretending that it doesn't

hurt, that I should be honest with you about how I feel. Perhaps I should scream at you, or thump you.'

'Do that, if you want, I don't mind,' Luc said, his voice filled with shame. 'I probably deserve a good battering.'

Gina cast him a sideways look through her lashes. 'Screaming is more Carmina's style. I don't usually go in for high drama.'

He grinned at her. 'That's why I love you, because you're so sweet and gentle, so loving and kind.'

'I'm not always either sweet or kind. Sometimes, when my younger sisters and brothers are being noisy or a nuisance, I can get quite bad-tempered with them. And I don't exactly sulk, as Carmina does, when I don't get my own way, but I'm very independent and just hate it if people try to help me do something I'm quite capable of doing myself, or if they pity me.'

'I would never do that,' Luc said. 'Anyway, I can't really say why I love you. Because you're you, I suppose.'

This answer brought a slight flush of pleasure to her cheeks and no further words were exchanged between them but for once Gina did not remove her hand from his. She was content to allow him to hold it for the entire length of Oxford Road, and all through the time they queued outside The Regal for a cinema ticket.

When they were let in she headed for a seat in the front. Usually Gina loved sitting on the back row in the dark so that Luc could kiss her. At one time such precious moments together had been far more important to her than the actual film. Now she felt a little shy with him, and in all these long weeks since she'd discovered his transgression, she hadn't allowed him to kiss her at all. Not once.

Tonight as they sat together sharing the popcorn, their fingers sometimes touching if they both chose the same moment to dip into the bag, Gina ached to return to how they'd once been together, so content and happy.

As she'd tried to explain to Amy, she wanted to trust him, longed to forgive and forget, but found it hard. She still nursed the fear that Carmina only had to pout her pretty lips and Luc would go running to her sister's side.

She'd told him all of this and he'd vehemently denied that he would do any such thing, but how could she be sure? How could she be certain that he wouldn't leave her or cheat on her again?

Resting a finger under her chin, Luc turned her to face him. Gina could see the glitter from the flickering screen reflected in his dark eyes. He was looking unusually serious.

As if reading her mind he murmured, 'You've no reason to think I'd ever leave you for Carmina. I can't begin to imagine how I would feel if I lost you, Gina. I want to spend the rest of my life taking care of you, proving to you how much I love you.'

It was then, just as Elvis launched into his jailhouse rock number, that he kissed her for the first time in weeks. Gina didn't attempt to resist, couldn't have done so if she'd tried. His lips were soft and tender, yet compulsively irresistible, making her believe that perhaps he did love her a little, after all. Later, she was to remember this moment with a poignant longing.

28

Amy and Patsy

Buying furniture and actually moving in proved to be yet another nightmare for Amy. She bought a yellow Formica-topped table for the kitchen, a fluffy new hearthrug and a bathroom cabinet.

She'd been buying pots and pans, baking tins, cutlery and all sorts of household bits and bobs for weeks now from Carl Garside's kitchen stall. She'd bought other things off the market too: towels, bed-linen, a second-hand radio from Alec's Music Shop, plus any number of scraps of fabric from Winnie Holmes to make the cushion covers and curtains she was endlessly sewing.

She'd dreamed of being able to choose something new for the living room but Mavis seemed set on unloading some of her old-fashioned pieces on to her son and daughter-in-law: a worn-out, moth-eaten old sofa, a scratched chest of drawers and a Victorian-style dresser, a rickety gate-leg table with plush-seated chairs that had seen better days, and of course the three-quarter bed with the rattling headboard.

'It's long past time I bought myself some new furniture,' Mavis decided, casting a venomous glance at her silent husband as he stood drinking the tea Amy had made him, more paint on his overall than on the actual walls.

For some reason Amy didn't quite understand, relations between man and wife had fallen to a new low and the pair were scarcely speaking.

'I deserve a little spoiling with what I've had to put up with all these years. But there's plenty of wear left in these things yet, quite adequate for your needs, Amy dear. I'm sure you'll be glad of them. Chris and his father can carry them round later, then we won't need the expense of a moving wagon.'

Chris gave her the kind of apologetic look which told Amy that they really couldn't afford to refuse, money being as tight as it was.

And so the shabby old furniture was carried along Champion Street by father and son and set in place. Amy tried to suggest they put the Victorian dresser in the front parlour but Mavis pooh-poohed the notion.

'You haven't a stick of furniture in this middle room, and this is where you'll be living for most of the time. With the dresser, table and chairs it will be quite cosy.'

It'll look like something out of a Victorian novel, Amy thought, her heart sinking and dreams of a modern sideboard shrivelling to dust in her mind. She wondered if she could paint everything cream, with touches of Wedgwood blue, once the baby was born, as well as sew some bright new seat covers for those moth-eaten old chairs. Perhaps not, Mavis would be sure to disapprove even if the mahogany was all dark and scratched.

'Don't stand there gawping, take those drawers up

to our Chris's room,' she instructed her husband, just as if Amy didn't exist.

Mavis giving all the orders, as usual.

'We'll buy some new furniture, I promise, love. Just as soon as we can afford,' Chris told Amy later as they lay together in bed, a note of sad apology in his voice. 'Right now, beggars can't be choosers.'

Amy cuddled up to him, savouring his warmth, his strength, and tried not to let her mother-in-law's interference spoil things for them. 'There's no stopping your mam once she gets the bit between her teeth, is there?'

Chris chuckled, and, well aware of his mother's idiosyncrasies, thought how fortunate he was to have such an understanding wife. 'The bakery is going from strength to strength, and with Dad taking a back seat I've more freedom to experiment. Things can only get better. We just have to be patient.'

He said this every day and Amy believed him. How could she not when she loved him so much?

'Can we at least avoid taking this grotty old bed? I would so like us to start our new life together in a new and decent-sized double bed, with a modern headboard that doesn't rattle. I don't want this antiquated monstrosity.'

Chris kissed her in an abstracted sort of way, a small frown puckering his brow as he did a quick sum in his head that didn't quite please him. He'd been saving up in his Post Office Savings Account for over a year now, but money was pouring out of it faster than water from a leaky drain.

But he wanted Amy to be happy, and she surely deserved something new as they started life together.

'We'll buy one first thing tomorrow, even if it has to be on the never-never, and make sure it's delivered by the end of next week. All the paintwork should be finished and dry by then and the last of the papering done. I hope we can move in by next weekend and be on our own at last. As for the rest of the furniture, we'll just have to make-do and mend until we can afford to replace it with something more to our taste.'

'Something modern,' Amy agreed. 'We need to buy a cot too, but I can't bring myself to shop for the baby until he or she is actually born. I'm too afraid of tempting fate.'

Chris kissed her again, more tenderly this time. 'Don't worry, sweetheart, everything is going to be fine.'

Clara Higginson was adamant that she had no wish to sell the hat stall. 'Why would I? And with you taking the lion's share of the work, Patsy, and all your youthful energy, I can relax a little more. Although I'd be happy to take over Annie's job with the accounts, if that would help.'

Patsy agreed that it would and together they reviewed all the changes she'd made since becoming a partner, the new lines, the reorganisation of the stall itself with a much-improved fitting area.

Clara said that she approved of the new round mirror high up on the wall, which allowed them to keep a watch on what customers were up to round the back of the stall. 'But we also need a better mirror in the fitting room. That one is looking a bit fly-specked, don't you think? It must be fifty years old if it's a day, which doesn't give a good impression.'

Carmina came in while they were chatting and waved cheerily at Patsy. 'Don't worry, I'm only browsing. Just taking a five-minute coffee break. You carry on with whatever it is you're doing.'

Clara paid the girl little attention, being far too used to seeing Carmina around, and continued with what she'd been saying. She was suggesting they repaint the sign over the stall. 'Perhaps we should change it from Higginsons' Hats to Patsy's Hats, or else something new and catchy.'

Patsy shook her head. 'No, leave it as it is.'

'Wouldn't you prefer to have your name on the board?'

'No, everyone knows this stall as Higginsons'. I think it would be a mistake to change it, and certainly not just because Annie has died. You're still here, and a Higginson, after all. And I've no idea what my real name is, having only been fostered, so let's leave things exactly as they are.'

'So long as you're happy with that, Patsy, love.'

'I am.'

Patsy caught a glimpse of Carmina through the round mirror. She was round the back of the stall and she called out to her, 'Let me know if you want to try anything on, Carmina?'

'No thanks, I must get back to the ice-cream cart now or Papa will have my guts for garters. You know how he is.' Giving them another cheery wave, she swung away smiling quietly to herself, one hand clenched tight over a pair of pretty earrings which she'd tucked into her pocket. Patsy would never miss them.

'You will be there with me, won't you?' Amy said as the day of her confinement drew near. 'They said you could be, if you wanted.'

'Of course I will, nothing would keep me away.'

Chris hadn't been too sure about being present at the birth when Amy had first suggested it, but he'd gone with her to some of the ante-natal classes, although not to the one where they showed a film of an actual birth. That was one step too far for him. But maybe if he just sat and held her hand and didn't watch, it would be all right. He felt he could manage that.

His mother, of course, was horrified by the very idea.

'Men in the labour ward? I never heard of anything so preposterous! Such a thing would never have been permitted in my day. They would only get in the way, be fainting all over the place. It's not right for a man to be present. Having babies is women's business. Men have nothing at all to do with it.'

'I think I did play a bit of a part in the process, Mother,' Chris teasingly reminded her, making her blush.

'You'd be useless,' Mavis snapped. 'Tell him to stay away, Amy. And think what a mess you'll look. You don't want him to see you like that, do you?'

Amy grasped her husband's hand very tight. 'I don't mind at all. I want him by my side when our child is born.'

And so he was. As his son emerged into a bright new shining world, Chris found he had tears rolling down his cheeks and his pretty young wife had never looked more beautiful.

Bringing the baby home to their little terraced house was exciting and scary all at the same time. Chris collected Amy from the nursing home in the bakery van and it felt very strange to be moving into the house at last, and with this new little creature absolutely dependent upon her.

Amy barely slept a wink in those first few days, for fear of something going wrong. What if he should stop breathing? What if he fell off the couch or banged his head, or put something into his mouth that he shouldn't? She suddenly became aware of all the hazards around her, in this her wonderful new home, in the street, the market, the world, the very air that he breathed.

His first bath-time was a nightmare. Compelled to use the kitchen sink for want of a bathroom, Amy was terrified in case he should slip out of her wet hands. He seemed so small, so fragile, how could he possibly survive her inadequate, clumsy efforts?

'I can't cope,' Amy wailed.

'Yes, you can. You're doing fine. What we need is a proper baby bath on a stand,' Chris said. 'I'll go and buy one right now.'

'No, you won't. I'll get it,' Mavis told him, stopping him in his tracks with a firm hand. 'You'd be sure to buy the wrong thing.'

'I'm not certain there's much money left in me purse,' Amy worried.

Big Molly said, 'Ask the Bertalones. No doubt Carlotta has one she could lend you. Why go to the expense of new?'

Mavis was outraged. 'I'm not having any grandson of mine using someone else's cast-offs. Who knows where it might have been? Quite unhygienic.'

Thomas said, 'Nay, you could eat your dinner off Carlotta's floor, it's that clean. Don't talk daft, woman.'

'Who are you calling daft? It's all a matter of standards, something you might not appreciate.'

'Look, it doesn't matter,' Amy said. 'I'm quite happy to bath him in the sink. I just need a bit of time to get used to it.' And less of an audience, she thought.

But Mavis went out there and then and bought one in blue, with pictures of teddy bears stuck all around the rim, together with a stand to rest it on. Mahogany, of course.

Relations between the grandparents was not good. They seemed to be engrossed in a competition, vying with each other over who could buy the most garments, equipment, and toys for the new baby. Rarely a day passed without either Big Molly or Mavis turning up with something they'd just happened to see on the market.

Following the incident with the bath came the squabble over a cot. Mavis wished to buy one which would convert into a single bed one day, which Amy thought too big and unwieldy for a small baby. 'I'd lose him in it and he might get smothered or lost in the sheets.'

'Don't be foolish, it would make excellent sense.'

But Amy insisted it was too big as a cot, and possibly too small for a bed later when he grew. And then Big Molly arrived, followed closely by her long-suffering husband Ozzy carrying a pretty little crib with two angels dangling on a blue ribbon from a frilled hood.

Amy wasn't too sure she wanted this either, but the deed was done, the purchase made. Nor did it meet with Mavis's approval. She considered the crib far too fussy and totally inadequate for a growing child.

Next came the issue of the pram. Amy and Chris had looked in shop windows, and, being somewhat strapped for cash, been shocked by the prices on display. So they were secretly relieved when Mavis offered to buy one for them.

'It's our prerogative, as grandparents, to help provide for the baby,' she insisted. 'And I'm sure your own father couldn't manage to find such a large sum, Amy.'

Amy wanted to protest that Ozzy would give her his last penny, which was true in a way, were there any pennies left in his pocket after he'd finished paying his debts to the bookie.

But while Amy had opted for something modest in cream, Mavis purchased a Silver Cross carriage pram in burgundy with a navy hood. It looked absolutely superb, a Rolls-Royce among prams. Amy's five-foot-two form was hardly visible behind it.

But Amy and Chris had no intention of objecting or making a fuss. All they wanted was to accept these gifts with good grace so that their respective in-laws, Mavis in particular, would then leave them in peace to enjoy their baby, and married life together in their own home.

In this they were to be sadly disappointed.

With her first grandchild tucked up in a pretty crib, albeit one provided by Big Molly, Mavis resolved to keep a very close eye on what went on in her son's house. At least being situated so close she could visit every single day, and indeed fully intended to do so, even if it was next to the pawn broker.

29

Patsy and Carmina

There'd been a shower of rain earlier but now the market was basking in hot sunshine. Somewhere there was music playing. Pat Boone singing 'Love Letters in the Sand'. Belle Garside had set little tables outside her café to give it a continental air on what promised to be a lovely June day. Papa Bertalone was rushed off his feet selling ice cream. The ice-cream parlour had been busy since he opened a couple of hours ago. Now, during a short lull in trade, he was leaning on the counter happily engrossed in his favourite topic: the making of ice cream. He was telling Winnie Holmes how it had been an Italian who'd first invented the wafer.

'Before that we used to wrap the ice-a-creama in the paper which we call the hokey pokey.'

'Aye, well, at least that would be a bit more hygienic than them little glass dishes they used to have round here. Eeh, I remember those licking glasses,' Winnie said, eyes glazing over with reminiscences of her girlhood. 'It were a wonder we didn't catch summat from them what had used it afore us. We only had the ice-cream man's word for it that he'd washed the glass properly. I don't know how we survived before the war, I don't really. Not in these streets.'

Papa smiled as he switched on his ice-cream maker, its gentle hum seeming to purr with pleasure as it mixed the magic ingredients together. 'Good hygiene is essential, that is true. Making ice-a-creama is a skilled task and takes much time. It not easy. It must be smooth and creamy when it freeze, and not separate when it melts. We heat the ingredients to a high temperature and then freeze it *molto rapidamente*. Very quickly, you understand? Churning it with the rotating blades to make sure the ice-a-creama is evenly frozen.'

Winnie struggled to pay attention as she licked her lips in anticipation.

Marco smiled. 'What'll you have, Winnie? The peach melba? Coffee or chocolate gelato? Or perhaps the Strawberry Sundae? We whip in the air to make the ice-a-creama all creamy and light. That is *molto importante*! Then the mix is pumped over coolers at a strict temperature, and finally stored in these sterilised steel buckets. Of course, we must sell it quickly, you understand? Good ice-a-creama doesn't last as it . . .'

'I'm quite happy to help out there,' Winnie said, interrupting him as her mouth was watering. 'Usually I settle for a sixpenny wafer but the ice-cream cart is all shut up this morning, so I come over here instead. Happen I'll have a Knickerbocker Glory as a treat, and take the weight off me feet for half an hour.' So saying, she sat herself down at one of the small round marble-topped tables.

Papa gaped at her. 'Not open? You are saying the ice-a-creama cart is not open for business? But Carmina should be there. Where is she then?'

Winnie shook her head. 'Nay, how would I know? I'm not surprised the lass is allus late for work, Marco, with all the gallivanting she's been doing lately, off dancing every Friday and Saturday night, or so I hear. How these so-called teenagers can think above the din of that rock 'n' roll is beyond me. Do my head in, it would.'

'Ah, daughters, Winnie. Who can possibly understand them? Not a father, I assure you.'

The sun was shining, sparkling on the wet cobbles and making the pink and white striped awnings over the stalls look as translucent as candy floss as Patsy made her way to the hat stall after her coffee break that Saturday morning. She was thinking how much she missed Annie and her caustic tongue. Champion Street Market didn't seem the same without her.

Yet Patsy had made many friends on this market since the day she'd arrived as a homeless orphan.

Big Molly Poulson, with an even bigger voice, still stood at her stall happily selling pies, cheese and cold meats to a predictably long queue. Today was roast-pork day; Patsy could smell its tantalising aroma.

She could smell fish and chips too, coming from the shop owned by Frankie Morris: a large, blubbery man in a soiled apron whose bald head gleamed as if greased from the fat from his own hands. He fried fish and chips crisp and delectable on the outside, piping hot and soft within. Everyone loved Frankie's fish and chips.

Patsy smiled and nodded to Mrs Gower, a regular customer at Higginsons' Hat Stall, who had a little boy she absolutely idolised. Even now she was on her way to Lizzie Pringle's Chocolate Cabin to buy him a bag of jelly babies. She kept the child so well supplied with sweets he was as round as Billy Bunter. Why did parents spoil their children so badly?

Papa Bertalone had so spoiled Carmina the girl believed that she should have her own way in everything, even at the expense of hurting her own sister.

Patsy passed by the ice-cream cart, surprised to note that it was still shuttered and not open for business, for all it was very nearly midday. Surely Carmina should be in there by now, serving threepenny cornets and wafers to the many grubby children hovering hopefully around?

She couldn't help wondering how they would get on once she and Marc were married. And did she feel ready for all of that responsibility and family commitment? Little by little Patsy did seem to be weaning Marc off the idea of a summer wedding although he still wasn't too happy about the amount of time she spent working on the hat stall.

It was as she was entering the market hall that Patsy spotted her future sister-in-law, deep in conversation with Alec Hall.

The girl was pressed up against a wall, Alec leaning over her, his hands at either side of her head, imprisoning her between them. Carmina's lovely face was inches from his, her eyelids half closed, mouth set in a tantalising pout.

He was speaking to her in urgent little whispers and Carmina was laughing softly. Patsy hung back, making sure they didn't spot her. For one astonishing moment she thought he might be about to actually kiss the girl, but then glancing round he seemed to think better of it, and, pushing himself off the wall, walked briskly away.

Carmina stayed where she was, eyes gleaming, smiling to herself like a Cheshire cat who had swallowed the cream. Then she sauntered off in the direction of the ice-cream cart as if she had all the time in the world.

'The little madam,' Patsy said, to no one in particular. 'Now she's teasing poor Alec.'

Patsy called at the ice-cream parlour, as she so loved to do, only to discover that Papa Bertalone had already learned of Carmina's non-appearance at the ice-cream cart. He was talking to Winnie Holmes and clearly upset, a crimson stain spreading up his neck, his jaw tight.

'That girl, she so lazy. She will be the death of my business. Does she not know that competition is fierce?'

Muttering to himself, Marco expertly spooned a mixture of fresh fruit – peaches, pineapple and melon – into a tall glass, then added a few sliced grapes.

Patsy caught Winnie's eye, giving the nosy old woman a fierce glare which said, 'Why did you have to upset him?' as Papa launched into his favourite complaint: the problems of running a small business.

'Why Carmina not see we have to work in order to survive? Since the war, we have the influx of our compatriots flooding in, many from Sicily who are also anxious to make much money out of ice-a-creama. We have many vendettas, one family trying to outdo the other.'

He waved the ice-cream scoop in the air, as if it were a machete. 'Always on the rounds there are often two, three, or more vans all touting for business in the same street. It ees difficult to make the beeg profit, *sì*?'

He dropped three scoops of ice cream into the dish, one each of strawberry, chocolate and vanilla, then rapped the scoop on the counter. 'They steal my pitches all the time. And the worst offenders are the Fabrianis. Now my own daughter let me down.'

Marco was more than ready to vent his fury on this absent, recalcitrant daughter who had very nearly forcibly allied him to these hated rivals in marriage.

'Carmina, she make me mad. She still carry the torch for Luc, I think. Gina is the same. What is a father to do?' he begged of his listeners, eyes wild. 'But if my empty-headed daughters imagine there can ever be an alliance with that family, they are very much mistaken. I would see them both dead first.'

Patsy and Winnie exchanged a knowing glance. Marco often displayed this passionate, volatile temperament, but his words were meaningless. They both knew that he adored all of his children, worshipped the ground they walked on as all Italians do, so they paid no heed to his vehement remarks. Patsy smoothed a hand over his stiff back in an attempt to calm him.

'I've just seen Carmina making her way to the ice-cream cart, as a matter of fact. It should be open by now.' She made no mention of the little encounter she'd just witnessed between the girl and Alec Hall. It may, after all, have been perfectly innocent.

Drawing in a deep steadying breath, Marco added

a dash of strawberry syrup, a swirl of whipped cream, then topped it all off with a fan wafer and a few glacé cherries. Tight-lipped, he handed the dish to Winnie as if it were a gift.

'Eeh, that looks gradely,' the old woman said.

'I shall speak to her,' Marco said, darkly. 'This cannot go on.'

'And I'd better get back to my own work,' said Patsy, beating a hasty retreat.

'Why cannot you take pride in your heritage?' Papa asked Carmina, as he had a million times before. 'Why you always late for work, as you have been every morning this week?'

He'd been forced to gird his patience until Carlotta came to relieve him at the parlour for his dinner break. Only then was he able to vent his wrath on this wayward child. Father and daughter exchanged a few heated words and then she fell into some sort of daze, as if her thoughts were elsewhere.

He gave her arm a little shake. 'Stop dreaming, girl. Are you listening to a word I'm saying?

'I don't feel very well,' Carmina said, her mouth falling into a sulky pout.

Winnie Holmes, who had witnessed father and daughter in the throes of a fierce argument, waddled over to listen so that she didn't miss the concluding chapters of this little dispute. She gave Carmina a measuring glance. 'The lass does look a bit peaky, a touch under-the-weather like. Have you eaten summat that disagrees with you, girl?'

They both turned to look at the old woman, surprised to find her standing there, avidly drinking in every word of this private conversation.

Ignoring her, Marco continued, 'Mamma tell me she called you and called you, and still you late for work. You didn't even have any breakfast.'

Carmina said, 'I couldn't eat a thing. Sorry, Papa, I won't be late again, I promise.'

She was late in another respect too and had felt far too sick even to get out of bed this morning. It had happened once or twice recently and Carmina had been forced to persuade Marta, whose room she was now sharing, to fetch her a cup of sweetened tea before she could risk lifting her head off the pillow.

Her father clicked his tongue in exasperation. 'Why I employ you I cannot think.'

Carmina dimpled at him. 'Because you love me?'

He ignored this too. 'Always I hear the same excuses, and always you make the same mistake, over and over again. It is because you do not think.' He tapped his own head. 'We Italians are proud of our ability to make the best ice-a-creama in the world. Why you not proud too?'

Carmina was barely listening to him. A secret excitement was building up inside her. Nothing had been quite going her way lately, but now she thought the tide might have turned at last. Life was catching up with her dreams and Luc wouldn't be able to wriggle out of his responsibilities this time.

It seemed that whenever she told what she knew to be a lie, it had a remarkable habit of coming true.

First she'd fabricated a tale to Gina that Luc had been seen kissing other girls, and then engineered a necking session with him herself, which nicely proved her point. Her story that she was pregnant with Luc's child had sadly back-fired, thanks to Mamma and Doc Mitchell. It had been easy enough to persuade Gina to believe they really had made love, at Luc's insistence, and even been forgiven for her own part in his alleged betrayal. But she'd felt as if everything she'd dreamed of was slipping away from her.

Now it seemed fortune was smiling on her again, as she might well be pregnant after all.

Carmina became aware that Winnie was watching her, and she experienced the eerie sensation that the woman could see right into her mind. It was as if she knew everything that was going on there. But then it was well known there was little the old witch didn't miss.

Of course, there was one tiny difficulty over her situation.

Assuming she was pregnant, and in view of the fact she and Luc had not made love, and that she was involved in what might be termed an interesting, if somewhat unromantic, relationship with Alec Hall, Carmina knew well enough who the father was. It certainly wasn't Luc Fabriani, which was unfortunate.

Not that she allowed this to trouble her too much. After all, it was only her word against his what happened in his old car that night. So the father of her child could be whoever she said it was. And she would choose Luc, naturally. That would be one lie nobody could disprove, not now.

It was past three o'clock in the afternoon and she was longing to escape, but would Papa let her go?

Carmina decided to ask. 'Papa, I'm still not feeling too good, can I go home early, please?'

Marco let out a heavy sigh and shook his head sadly at Winnie. 'Daughters are never around when you need them or when there is work to be done. Always they want the time off, more money from their papa's pocket, the coat from his back.'

'Aye, some folk are expert at getting what they want,' Winnie agreed, watching Carmina walk away with curiosity in her shrewd gaze. 'But they don't allus like it when they get it.'

30

Amy and Patsy

Chris and Amy were thrilled to be in their own home at last, with their new baby, a boy whom they named Daniel. Even if the little house was an odd mix of Mavis's cast-offs and Amy's ultra-modern touches, not to mention Thomas's amateur efforts at the new D.I.Y. None of this really concerned them as they could now shut the door against the world, and against Mavis's interference. They could be completely alone and private, at least for most of the time. Mavis did manage to find some excuse or other to pop in each and every day. Thomas they rarely saw, and Ozzy stayed well clear, in case he should be asked to do something.

Amy's own mother Big Molly also popped in regularly, of course, to bounce her first grandchild on her ample knee and deposit a selection of freshly baked pies in Amy's kitchen.

'Just so's you're not dependent on that rubbish yer in-laws' bakery churns out. Tha needs summat decent in yer belly when you're breast feeding.' As if a steak and kidney pie was guaranteed to produce the best baby milk!

Amy leapt to their defence. 'I'll have you know that

Chris, my own lovely husband if you remember, works in the bakery now, and he doesn't produce rubbish.'

Big Molly made a scoffing sound in the back of her throat. Uniting the two families in holy matrimony had done nothing to banish the feud between them, not in her eyes.

The young couple spent a good deal of time holding and cuddling little Danny, and watching him breathe in and out. They would examine his tiny fingernails, all perfectly formed, his translucent skin, the down of soft hair which had a distinctly reddish tinge, clearly taking after his mother, and the curve of eyelashes that sleepily brushed his soft round cheeks. They loved the way his mouth puckered after his feed, the slight twitch which was surely his first smile, and his wide blue-eyed gaze which seemed to focus with surprise upon their loving faces.

Yet despite it being an easy birth, and Amy feeling as if she were bursting with energy and happiness, she continued to be wracked with self-doubt, fearful of the huge responsibility of caring for this new little person. The first few weeks were the worst and neither she nor Chris got much sleep during this time.

Danny was quite a good baby but small, and perhaps because of this, he tended to fall asleep before properly finishing his feed. Then two or three hours later he'd wake up crying for more.

Not that she allowed him to cry for long. Amy had carefully read and re-read every page of Dr Spock's book *The Common Sense Book of Baby and Child Care* which she followed to the letter. If Danny was crying then there must be a reason, and she would pick him up instantly to nurture and cuddle him.

Naturally, Mavis did not approve of this excessive attention. She was quite shocked by the idea of feeding the infant on demand. 'He should be fed every four hours, on the dot. His little digestive system needs a regular routine, and on no account should he be fed more frequently than that. You'll only make him fat and greedy if you give in to his every whimper, and he must certainly never be allowed to assume he is the boss.'

Fat chance of that with you around, Amy thought.

The nurse said it was nothing more than a bit of evening colic. Mavis insisted Amy had been grossly over-feeding him, but Danny simply wouldn't stop crying. Night after night he would cry till he was sick. Amy was distraught.

'He just won't feed properly. He isn't interested in anything I give him. Not his bottle, not even the breast. I'm at my wits' end.'

And if he didn't take his last feed properly, then he would wake up again two hours later, crying with hunger. Amy was lucky if she got any sleep before the early hours of the morning. She was utterly exhausted, Chris too, poor man. And he then had to get up and do the morning's baking.

Tonight, Danny was again screaming at full throttle, stiffening his little body and absolutely refusing to accept the rubber teat. Amy was in tears.

Mavis walked in right in the middle of it, without

even knocking, as was her wont. 'Cooee! It's only me,' she chirruped, and then stopped, appalled by what she saw.

'Please don't cry, Danny. Oh, what can I do?' Amy begged of her mother-in-law. 'He keeps drawing up his little legs but I've given him some gripe water. What more can I do? Why is he behaving like this?'

'You've overfed him, that's why. But you wouldn't listen, would you?'

'The nurse says it's quite normal behaviour at this age, but I don't know how to cope with it. Why won't he stop?' Amy sobbed.

Mavis watched this performance for a whole five seconds and then swept the baby up into her arms and bore him away upstairs. Seconds later she was back. Danny was still screaming, albeit at a distance.

'What have you done with him?' Amy cried.

'Put him in his cot until he calms down.'

'You can't do that. We can't ignore him. He might be sick. He might choke, or stop breathing.'

'He sounds in fine fettle to me. Once he's over his little paddy, you can feed him, calmly and quietly.'

Amy was appalled. 'But he isn't in a paddy. He has colic. He needs a cuddle. I'm going to get him.'

'Indeed you won't.' So saying, Mavis pushed Amy back down in her chair, and held her there. 'You stay right where you are. He'll stop in a minute.'

But he didn't stop. He just kept right on crying, his sobs growing louder by the minute. As were Amy's. By the time Chris arrived home from work, it was to find his mother and wife engaged almost in a wrestling match as Amy struggled to get upstairs to her screaming child and Mavis physically prevented her from doing so.

'Mother!' he shouted, above the din. 'What the hell's going on?'

Mavis let go upon the instant and Amy flew upstairs. By the time she returned with the distressed infant, Danny's sobs had subsided to a more normal tearful cry, his little mouth turned down in abject misery. Amy put him to her breast and sighed with relief as he began at last to suckle.

'You'll ruin that child. Mark my words, you'll ruin him,' Mavis announced, and marched out of the house in a fine lather, a shower of plaster falling from the ceiling as she slammed the front door.

A stream of visitors continued to arrive at the little house, all bearing gifts for mother and child. There were flowers from Betty Hemley, chocolates from Lizzie Pringle, teething rings and rattles, matinee jackets and romper suits, any number of vests, pram rugs and night-dresses, and half of Champion Street Market must be knitting bootees, Amy thought.

Dorothy Thompson, or Aunty, as she was more affectionately called, popped in for a long chat one afternoon, just to see how the young mum was coping. She gave Amy some handy tips on child-rearing without making any fuss or minding in the slightest when Danny sicked up some of his last feed all down the front of her cardigan.

'It'll wash,' was all she said, gently mopping him up.

Aunty also offered to mind him should Amy ever be

stuck for a baby-sitter. 'I've got that many foster childer, what's one more? Don't forget now, you and your lovely hubby need a bit of time on yer own now and then.'

Amy was touched. Neither grandparent had thought to offer such a thing.

Gina continued to call in regularly, following a morning spent in Dena's sewing room, and Patsy too was a frequent visitor. She would pop over for half an hour whenever she could fit it in her busy schedule, anxious to reassure herself that her friend was well. Patsy was, of course, enchanted by little Danny although firmly declaring she wasn't yet ready to embark on motherhood herself. 'Marc's the one getting broody, not me. I've told him he can have the kids himself if he's so keen.'

Amy chuckled. 'I don't think it quite works that way, Patsy love.'

'Pity. Well, maybe he could stay at home and look after them, then I can keep working on the hat stall.'

'Wouldn't you want to take time off to have children?' Amy asked, puzzled. 'I thought you wanted a family of your own.'

'I do, I do, but not yet. There are things I want to do first.'

'Having a family is important too. You can always have a career later.'

'Oh, don't you start, I thought you were supposed to be my friend. Marc is becoming a positive bore on the subject. Where's the hurry? I tell him. Though I must confess if I could guarantee to produce a baby as sweet as little Danny here, I'd be seriously tempted. Can I hold him?'

'Course you can.'

Patsy held the baby on her lap for no more than five seconds before he started to cry, when she quickly handed him back, like a parcel. 'Perhaps not.'

Amy laughed and admired the little romper suit Patsy had brought her, before tucking it in a drawer with half a dozen others. 'Thanks for getting a larger size, he's growing that fast he'll be out of his first baby stuff in no time. Mind you, I think he has enough clothes to see him through till he's four at least.'

Patsy admired what Amy had done to the house and told her about the changes she'd made on the hat stall. They chatted about Clara for a while and how she was coping, then Patsy admitted to some concern over the increase in shop-lifting she'd been experiencing lately.

'It's a real worry. I think it might be one of those new kids who have moved in below the fish market. Don't know their names but they're a bit rough, real troublemakers the lot of them.'

They went on to talk about various snippets of market gossip: of how well Lizzie Pringle was doing with her Chocolate Cabin, and that Dena Dobson was having real problems with Trudy who'd recently been involved in an accident, which naturally led back to the endlessly fascinating subject of her own child. Amy described her weekly trips to the clinic where she collected Danny's orange juice and cod liver oil.

'He put on five ounces last week. The nurse was really pleased with him.'

'Excellent,' Patsy said, trying not to sound bored.

'He'll be due for his first injections soon.'

'Make sure you give him the new polio vaccine. I'm quite certain Gina would be the first to recommend it.'

Amy nodded. 'Too right she would. She pops in when she can, although still seems uncertain about whether she and Luc will make a go of it.'

Patsy pulled a face. 'She's playing it cool, and I don't blame her. With a sister like Carmina you've got your work cut out keeping your man to yourself.'

Patsy wasn't coping quite as well as she made out. Clara was still grieving and only turned up to help on the stall a couple of afternoons a week, which meant that Patsy had less time for her hat-making and clients were growing impatient. Marc, however, was unsympathetic.

'Didn't I tell you it would be too much for you?'

Patsy gritted her teeth and made a private vow never to grumble again, not within Marc's hearing anyway. Whatever worries she had, she learned to keep them to herself.

And there were still items going missing. She daren't mention that either. Certainly not to Marc, nor to Clara who had enough to depress her at the moment with getting over the death of her sister, let alone fretting over what must surely be Patsy's incompetence. If she kept a better eye on what was going on instead of working so hard on her hat making, she'd maybe be able to catch the culprit.

Talking it over with Amy had helped a little, but her friend's only solution was to put up a mirror, which she'd already done.

But it simply wasn't possible to sit staring into it all

the time. Patsy often became distracted when she was serving, or busy sewing and wouldn't immediately notice that someone was browsing. Nor was it easy to follow a customer's every move, not without making it obvious you were suspicious. The result would be that she'd just feel uncomfortable and go away without buying a thing.

Coping with the stall single-handed wasn't easy so when one day Carmina called and offered to keep an eye on it for five minutes, Patsy was surprised but delighted. She was desperate for a coffee and toilet break.

'Oh, that would be marvellous. Thanks, Carmina. I'm starving hungry. Haven't had a thing since breakfast. I even missed dinner as I forgot to pack myself some sandwiches and I can't afford to close for lunch which is often my busiest time. I won't be longer than ten minutes, I promise. Just long enough for me to grab a cup of coffee and a doughnut.'

'Take as long as you like,' Carmina said. 'Pop in and see Amy, why don't you? No need to rush back. Can I try on some hats?'

Patsy chuckled. 'Course you can, if you're careful. Bless you,' and went off quite happily, leaving Carmina in charge. Maybe they were going to get on after all.

31

Carmina and Gina

Carmina saw no reason not to enjoy herself while she prepared her latest plan of action. So when Alec Hall invited her over to supper in his flat above the music shop, telling her his son Terry was out for the evening, she decided she'd nothing to lose. What harm could it do? The damage, as you might say, was already done.

And if she hadn't yet managed to get her hands on Luc, then Alec, she decided, would do very nicely in the meantime. He was, after all, an exciting man to be with.

Carmina couldn't seem to stop thinking about what they'd got up to in his cold, damp MG. So how much more exciting to be in the warm privacy of his flat. It almost made her feel sick with anticipation at what it must feel like to actually go to bed with a man. She'd really be a grown-up then.

He served her with a dish of what looked like stewed vegetables but were actually quite spicy. Alec called it a *kimchi*, and said it was made from cabbage mixed with ginger, garlic, pickled shrimps and green onions. This was followed with thin strips of beef cooked with mushrooms, onions, peppers, more garlic, and herbs and spices which Carmina could not identify, together with lots of rice. She thought it the strangest meal she'd ever tasted, and did little more than push the food about her plate to pretend she was actually eating it.

'Aren't you hungry?' he asked.

'I'm trying to lose weight,' Carmina lied, which brought forth the expected compliment that she really didn't need to. 'I never imagined you'd actually cook for us. I thought you'd pop out for fish and chips or something.'

'I learned to cook in Korea, though I accept this sort of thing might be an acquired taste.'

Carmina wrinkled her nose and examined the heap of food on her plate. 'What were you doing in Korea?'

'There was a war on,' he patiently reminded her.

'Oh, yes, so there was. Where is it, Korea? Is it in the east?'

Alec looked at the young girl and felt a burst of something like contempt for her ignorance. Yet why should it surprise him? What did this stupid girl know of such things, living her comfortable, selfish little life, her empty head concerned only with boyfriends and pop tunes?

Cooking in camp had consisted chiefly of self-heating cans of Scotch Broth or beef stew that gave out a sound like the crack of a gun when you activated them. Eating hadn't been about pleasure and appeal to the taste buds, not at the front. It had been about staying alive, and keeping warm. That was all that mattered. Survival.

He didn't bother explaining any of this to her. 'It

was cold in Korea and winter set in early with freezing north-east winds. Hot food was important. You dug yourself a deep hole in the ground, or "hoochie" as we called it, although if it was frozen solid a pack of explosives might be necessary to blast it deep enough.'

She looked at him, wide-eyed. 'You slept in a *hole in the ground*? Why didn't you sleep in a proper bunk in a cabin or something?'

Sexy she might be, but nobody could accuse Carmina Bertalone of either sensitivity or intelligence.

Alec could recall many miserable hours spent huddled beneath a damp blanket, when several layers of clothing from long-johns and string vest to hooded parka, thick woollen socks and heavy boots failed to keep out the freezing temperatures. When having to remove your gloves to load a rifle could lead to serious frostbite.

But then he hadn't brought her here to listen to his old war stories.

'I've got bread and butter pudding for afters, one I made myself from a Philip Harben recipe. Is that British enough for you?'

Carmina pushed her plate away. 'Why don't you put on a record then you can teach me more of those dance steps you're so good at. A slow fox-trot, or a sexy waltz.'

Alec smiled. That's why he liked her, the one thing they had in common. Sex! He'd felt a bit wary about inviting her over, knowing she was only half his age, little more than a child at seventeen, particularly following his clumsy over-eagerness that first time. But then he always found young girls hard to resist. And the encounter in the car had been interesting. She'd been like a wild cat, rampant for him, which led him to hope there might be other such episodes.

If she was woman enough to enjoy his love-making, why worry about her age? And he did find her utterly fascinating. Even if she didn't care for the food he'd prepared, or know where Korea was or why he'd been there. She had other attributes.

They danced to 'Kisses Sweeter Than Wine', a Jimmie Rodgers number. Carmina thought Alec was a sexy dancer, holding her close in his arms and whispering things he really shouldn't in her ear. After that came 'Remember You're Mine', Alec singing along with Pat Boone and making little shivers run up and down her spine.

Carmina considered telling him that she wasn't really his at all, that she belonged by rights to Luc, but he'd started to kiss her by then, his hands doing interesting things with her breasts beneath her sweater, and she really couldn't concentrate.

Later, sprawled on his bed with a tangle of sheets on the floor, there was no time for thinking at all, or much in the way of small talk for that matter. She felt oddly shy at first, being in a man's bedroom, in his bed, but then he pulled her to him and began to kiss her, quite gently at first, before deepening the kiss to explore her mouth with his tongue.

He took her by the shoulders and pushed her down on the bed, slowly unbuttoning her blouse, smoothing his tongue over each rosy nipple. He licked and suckled each one, making them spring to his touch and Carmina gave little gasps of astonishment.

She strained to pull him closer, her body heavy with desire, anxious for him to get on with it. He laughed at her eager response.

'You're like an excited little puppy. Slow down, sweetheart. These things shouldn't be rushed.'

Carmina tried to do as he bid, as she had no wish to be thought of as young and childish. Alec was so sophisticated, so experienced, like an older James Dean, hungry and dangerous. She wanted him to see her as a tantalising, seductive woman, not some silly young teenager.

But any protest died on her lips as he began to kiss her in other places, to pleasure her in ways she'd never even dreamed of. He did things with his mouth, his tongue, that set her senses reeling.

She expected it to be all over in seconds, as it usually was with the boys she knew. A quick bang, bang, then they'd light up a cigarette and go back to the dancing. Not so with Alec. He took his time, made her wait till she was almost screaming with frustration before spreading her hands above her head and taking her with more force than she'd expected, making her cry out loud.

The sensation of him moving inside her, the tremors in his lean body, the sound of his strange little grunts, even the smell of him, excited her beyond reason and she clawed at his back with her long nails, wanting more. She felt so alive! So needed and adored!

When it was over he asked her if she was all right.

Carmina was startled. No one had ever asked her that before. Of course, he'd used a johnny, he'd insisted on that.

'Better to be safe than sorry,' he'd said, smiling down at her. Carmina said nothing, merely smiled back. How could she tell him that it was already too late? He'd used one in the car too. But she couldn't remember him using one when he'd taken her the first time, by the old Roman fort. Obviously he must have forgotten then, or not come prepared, perhaps not expecting their love-making to progress quite so quickly. Neither had she. His urgency had obviously taken them both by surprise on that occasion, overwhelmed by her charms, no doubt.

And now, as a result, she was what you might call knocked up. Not that she cared, not if it got her Luc. She lay back on the rumpled sheets, making her plans, while Alec seemed contentedly asleep beside her.

Alec did not in fact, sleep well. Whenever he closed his eyes, or attempted to sleep, the nightmare came; that night of terror fresh and clear in his head.

The hills along the narrow, rutted road to Chipyong-ni were full of soldiers. Across the valley hundreds of Chinese communists gathered and he was going to have to kill as many of them as he could because they were more than ready to attack and kill him. Kill or be killed, what kind of choice was that for a civilised human being? Yet it was a philosophy of life that had become as much a part of him as breathing in and out.

An artillery barrage started pounding them, the sound of the relentless mortar attacks echoing in his ears.

He furiously fired his machine-gun into the black darkness, hoping he'd hit something, or that the enemy would simply get tired and go away.

There it was again, the smell of fear, the whine and crump of bullets. He didn't hear the one that nearly killed him.

Now he was lying in a frozen paddy field listening to the Chinese looting the dead and executing the wounded all around him. He could hear a young corporal screaming for his mother. Alec lay motionless, face down in the mud, eyes closed, barely breathing, playing dead.

It was so cold. He'd never known anything like it. Fingers going black with frostbite, his own breath turning to ice on his lips, a slick of something black beneath him that could only be his own blood, pouring from some wound he couldn't even feel. But then his friends around him were colder still in death. A part of him died too as he lay in the mud, praying the enemy couldn't hear his heart pounding.

It was pounding now and Alec jerked awake, sat up abruptly in the bed, a slick of sweat cooling on his brow.

'What is it?'

He reached for the girl beside him and buried himself in her warm soft body, ever his cure for a nightmare. What good did it do to remember? Best not to think, not to talk about it.

They'd made love the first time without bothering to undress, now his appetite seemed insatiable. Alec encouraged her to strip off for him while he lay back on the bed, stark-naked, to watch, lust and open admiration on his face.

Carmina shook back her long glossy hair and laughed, arching her body so that her breasts peaked delightfully and she heard his low groan.

'You are amazing, sweetheart. Absolutely amazing!'

It made her feel so powerful and grown-up to have a man appreciate her beauty in this way. What would her friends say if they could see her now? What would Luc say? He'd surely be jealous.

'You're like a luscious cherry ripe for the picking. I want to nibble every precious bit of you, eat you all up.'

Carmina laughed delightedly. Nobody had ever spoken to her in this way before, certainly not any of the young men she'd dated, not even Luc.

She loved the way his hands smoothed over her breasts, as if he cherished them, moving over her slender waist, caressing every part of her as if she were made of Dresden china.

'I don't deserve you, I really don't. You know I'm just an old roué, and twice your age. A rake. I've had two wives, and lost track of the number of girlfriends I've enjoyed. But then I've always thought that's what women are for, to be enjoyed and savoured like a satisfying meal or a good bottle of claret.'

Carmina wasn't too sure she cared to be compared to anything so mundane as a meal or a bottle of wine, and it flickered across her mind to object. A meal was over in minutes, after all, while a beautiful woman should be loved and appreciated for life. But then he pushed her down on to the bed and made love to her all over again so that her thoughts blurred and vanished in a haze of desire.

She couldn't get enough of him, felt the hunger burning her up inside, needing to be assuaged. He made her do quite shocking things but Carmina was so entranced by the whole adventure, she did whatever he asked of her.

When finally he lay flopped beside her, his gentle snores indicating that he had at last fallen asleep, Carmina slid out of bed and began to idly examine the room. She opened drawers and rummaged through a jumble of old photographs, one of a Chinese girl, or perhaps she was Korean. She might even be one of the wives he'd spoken of, judging by the way they were wrapped in each other's arms. She found a gold watch, and a selection of jewelled tiepins and cufflinks. Clearly Alec Hall wasn't short of money. His wallet was there too, packed with notes.

Carmina quietly opened his wardrobe door, breathing in the scent of his masculine after-shave as she riffled through the pockets of his jackets, finding nothing of any interest. He was evidently the kind of man who emptied his pockets before he put his clothes away. There was the famous velvet jacket, the pink dickie-bow tie, several of them in fact, all lined up in a mahogany tray. The shoes too were in a neat line, and shining with polish. Everything neat and tidy.

She glanced across at him, still sprawled face-down on the bed and felt a burst of fresh desire, but it was growing late and Papa would be expecting her home.

Carmina quickly pulled on her rumpled clothes, and, in stockinged feet, shoes in hand, she crept back to his bedside drawers, took a fiver out of the bulging wallet and slipped it into her pocket. With so many he surely wouldn't miss one. And didn't she deserve it?

Then she picked up her bag, and without disturbing him, crept downstairs.

Once in the shop she paused to put on her shoes, glancing idly through the stacks of records as she did so. It was hard to see what was what with only the dim glow of the street lamp shining in through the frosted glass of the shop door, but if she carried them to where a pool of light fell, she could just make out the words.

She read – 'Little Darlin'' by The Diamonds – a record she'd been wanting for quite some time. Carmina tucked it under her coat, putting the others back in the rack. Sitting on a display shelf was a delightful little transistor radio in bright red plastic. She slipped that too into her pocket.

Glancing around one last time, a smile curling her full lips, she let herself out of the little shop and ran home. All in all, it had been a most entertaining evening, and really quite profitable.

Lying in bed that night, hugging herself with glee at her daring, Carmina knew, in her heart, that genuinely pregnant or not, it wasn't going to be easy to drag Luc along to that altar. He would be shocked when he learned that she was indeed pregnant, no doubt attempt to deny the baby was his. But if she held her nerve she could get everyone on her side, the wedding back on track and he'd soon grow used to the idea.

Unfortunately he was still pining over Gina, still grovelling for her forgiveness.

So long as Gina was around, Luc would stick by her. Carmina accepted this as a fact now, although she saw the reason as more to do with guilt and loyalty rather than any love he might feel for the stupid girl. And he probably also thought Gina's saccharine sweetness would appeal to his parents rather more than her luscious, beautiful and dangerous sister. Gina would seem like the perfect daughter-in-law in their eyes, proof that their once rebellious son had been brought to heel.

In Carmina's opinion, however, it was time Luc stopped worrying about what would please his father and think about himself for a change. She was the one for him, not her sanctimonious sister.

He'd let her down badly but Carmina was determined not to simply cry over him but do something about it, something which would retrieve all she had lost. She'd make Luc regret he'd ever let her down, make him glad she was willing to welcome him back into her arms.

The moment her parents learned that the baby was a reality, they'd rush her to the altar. All Carmina had to do was make sure it was with the man of her choice.

But first she must deal with Gina.

32

Amy and Patsy

Having offloaded her outworn pieces on to her daughter-in-law, Mavis relished choosing and buying new furniture. Her taste did not run to the jazzy colours and abstract prints which Amy so favoured, but she'd bought a sleek G-Plan sideboard with matching dining table and chairs, a comfy three-piece suite in leaf-green moquette, and a nest of coffee tables. When she had her friends from the Ladies Luncheon Club round for coffee they were most impressed. She also purchased a new carpet in a swirling gold and green pattern which she had fitted wall to wall as current fashion dictated.

Yet Mavis wasn't happy. She should have been, but the initial excitement soon evaporated, leaving her feeling restless and irritable.

The problem, of course, was Thomas. While she loved to polish and dust her new furniture, he would thoughtlessly place his tea mug on it, leaving little rings on the glossy surface.

Mavis would whip the mug away and almost hit him with it. 'How many times have I told you to use a mat?'

'I can never find one.'

'They're in the top drawer, here.' She pulled out the

drawer to reveal a stack of table mats each depicting some idyllic rural scene.

'Well, why aren't they where I can see them, where they'd be some use? What do we want with a fancy new sideboard, anyroad?'

'*I* wanted a fancy new house but all I got was a few decent pieces of furniture. And you. So do try not to be too much of a liability and treat things with respect.'

She'd bought a television set, although viewing was strictly limited to the kind of programmes of which Mavis approved. She liked *In Town Tonight* and *What's My Line*, the latter because she rather admired Gilbert Harding. She quite enjoyed *Dixon of Dock Green* and *Emergency Ward 10*, particularly that Australian Doctor Dawson. But she heartily disapproved of raucous humour, the sort supplied by Benny Hill, Alfie Bass or Tony Hancock; exactly the kind of programmes that Thomas would have liked to watch. Mavis was not strong on humour.

'This is a bit dry for me,' he'd say, when *Panorama* came on, and he'd toddle off to the Dog and Duck, or to play cards with his mates at the allotment. Mavis would steadfastly sit through it, even though she didn't understand a word either.

She hated him for leaving her on her own so much, but never stopped complaining when he was around.

Mavis objected to him wearing any kind of outdoor footwear on her new carpet, even if they were his best Sunday shoes and not the smelly old boots he wore at the allotment. She would slap his feet down if he propped even his stockinged feet up on the new sofa, remove his elbow from the arm in case he should rub the fabric bare. She crocheted an antimacassar to put behind his head to prevent Brylcreem from his hair soiling the green moquette.

'Why don't you scrub me down wi' Dettol then you'd know I was clean,' Thomas told her one day, only to receive a sour smile at his flippancy. He felt a bit at a loose end, his services no longer required now that his son's house was all done up.

If he popped upstairs to use the toilet when he came back it was to find his newspaper folded and the cushion he'd creased nicely plumped up and neatly arranged. This morning she'd even tidied away his copy of *Sporting Life* into the new mahogany paper rack she'd bought. Thomas had had enough.

'Nay, I reckon I'll go for a walk,' he said, retrieving the newspaper and tucking it into his jacket pocket to read later.

'I suppose you'd rather be with your fancy woman?' Mavis snarled.

'And who might she be when she's at home?'

'Don't play the ignoramus with me. I know what you're up to with that Belle Garside.'

'Nay, I were only having beans on toast in her café, not having me wicked way with the woman.'

'Don't be rude! I won't have vulgarity in this house.'

Thomas gave a resigned sigh. There was no reasoning with her, not at the best of times, but he'd never seen her as bad as this before. He tried to explain how hard he'd been working on Chris's house, and at the allotment, which had fired up his appetite a notch, but that served only to make matters worse.

'I know what sort of appetite is being fired up, and it has nothing whatsoever to do with *beans on toast*.'

She became well nigh hysterical, screaming and screeching at him that he was showing her up before everyone.

'What, because I fancy a bacon butty now and then? Not against the law, is it?'

'Because you're bothering with that woman!' Mavis slapped him over the head with the *Radio Times* till it was all in shreds and she was near to tears. 'Now, look what you've made me do. Mess all over my new fitted carpet and I can't even read it now.'

As he said to his pals as they discussed the general merits of bonemeal or horse manure for the roses, 'The house might look grand with all the new stuff she's bought for it, but there's no peace to be found in it, no peace at all.'

Amy was deeply grateful for Thomas's efforts at D.I.Y. but fond as she was of her father-in-law, he hadn't done quite as good a job on the house as they might have hoped. Every time they shut a door, bits of plaster fell down from the ceiling. Mushrooms began to grow up the kitchen walls, and a creeping black mould spread across Amy's jazzy wallpaper. The 'bathroom' he'd allegedly built was little more than a tin shack that incorporated the old lavatory onto the end of the scullery, with the addition of a wash basin. It hadn't been possible to squeeze in a bath as well, so Amy still had to go round to her in-laws in order to have one.

Her own parents didn't have a bathroom either and went round to the public baths once a week. Amy considered buying an old tin bath for herself and putting it by the fire as her mother used to do with her when she was a little girl. But apart from the indignity of doing such a thing in these modern times, it would take an age to heat up sufficient hot water in the old back boiler, let alone fill a bath.

Naturally, Mavis had little sympathy for her plight. 'Didn't I tell you that house would be a disaster? Anyway, I really don't know what you're complaining about. We suffered far worse during the war. I remember spending hours in that damp, bug-infested air-raid shelter with all those horrid smelly people.'

'I remember that too,' Amy said. 'Just about, although I was only a nipper at the time. It wasn't so bad. I remember my old granddad singing me to sleep night after night, and there was always someone to tell me a story. But it's years since all the soldiers came home from the war, why haven't they solved the housing problem by now?'

'Because half of Manchester was bombed in the blitz, you silly girl, and it takes a lot of money to rebuild. It certainly can't be done overnight. Besides, there always was a shortage of decent housing in Manchester, even before the war. It's just that the bombing, the flood of soldiers, not to mention everybody having babies, has made a bad problem worse.'

As she said this Mavis glared at Amy, as if she personally had made matters worse by having a baby too.

Amy found her mother-in-law very strange. She still

came over every day, full of criticism and useless advice, but rarely did she offer to pick Danny up and give him a cuddle. She never volunteered to babysit, and only once had she offered to take him out for an airing, and that had been simply to show off the magnificent Silver Cross pram she'd bought for him.

Amy certainly couldn't complain about her generosity in helping to provide for the baby, but the house was another matter. It wasn't exactly the start to their married life that she'd planned. But at least they were on their own now, and she had Danny.

She loved blowing raspberries into his tummy to make him smile, and breathing in the scent of him after a bath when he smelled of soap and talcum powder. It seemed like a miracle that she and Chris could create this precious little person out of their love.

So what did a house matter? They were a family. Things could only get better.

One morning Amy tucked Danny into his pram and put him out in the backyard. At least Thomas had succeeded in making that look presentable with its white-washed walls, and pots of geraniums. Thomas loved his geraniums. Where was he these days? she wondered. Why hadn't he called in lately to see her, and to see Danny whom he adored?

The baby hadn't been out five minutes when a great gust of wind blew up. Amy heard a terrible crash and ran outside to find a length of guttering had fallen off the house inches from the pram.

'Danny could have been killed,' she told Chris the

minute he walked through the door that night. 'We have to do something.'

'What can we do?' Chris was as alarmed as she was by this near-disaster yet keenly aware that he had no spare cash to do any further work on the house. 'I can probably fix the guttering myself, with Dad's help that is. It wouldn't be worth buying new anyway, since the house isn't ours. And I certainly can't produce a new one out of the hat, sorry, love. Anyway, look at him grinning away there, he's fine.'

'He's not grinning, he's got wind,' Amy sulkily informed her husband. 'And he might not have been all right. We were lucky this time but it could happen again. Anything could happen. And I'm sure he's starting with a cold. He's very fretful and keeps sneezing and coughing. It's all this mould creeping up the walls. I keep scrubbing it away, knocking off those damned mushrooms, but they grow back in days. What *are* we to do?'

Chris could think of nothing but taking his wife to bed and loving her. It was a good start and made Amy feel much better, but wasn't particularly practical.

Amy tackled the landlord about the need for repairs, particularly the roof with its loose guttering and missing slates. He simply laughed, reminding her of their agreement that repairs were the tenant's responsibility. Besides, this was the rough end of Champion Street, so what did she expect?

There seemed little point in asking him to build on a bathroom.

The next day she went down to the council offices

to put their name on the housing list. Amy was shocked by the length of the queue since she'd imagined everyone but them must have a house by now. How wrong she was. After she'd filled in all the necessary forms she asked how long it would be before they might hope to get a council house.

'Come back in ten years or so and see how we're getting on,' said the bored clerk behind the desk.

Ten *years*! She'd be old and grey by then.

The following morning she walked the pram over Princes Bridge and visited one or two developers, asking the price of flats they were building in Salford. She came home exhausted but with a sheaf of particulars which she and Chris avidly read. They got quite excited until they came to the bottom line and saw the price. They couldn't even hope to raise the deposit, let alone get a mortgage on what Chris was earning at the bakery, so what hope did they have of ever buying a place of their own?

'We'll just have to go on renting,' Chris gloomily acknowledged.

'Then we must start saving,' Amy said, and made up her mind there and then that it was time to find herself a job. If it took ten years to get to the top of the council housing list, it surely would only take half as long to save up the deposit for a flat of their own. It was certainly worth a try. But who would employ a woman with a baby?

Patsy was again sitting amidst a muddle of baby clothes, helping to fold clean nappies while she poured out her heart to Amy. 'It's so difficult at busy times to manage on my own. Trouble is, I don't like to ask Clara to do much more than a couple of afternoons a week at present, as she's got all of Annie's stuff to sort out. She also does the accounts and all the paperwork, of course. I'd employ a girl but I couldn't afford to pay more than peanuts, so who'd come?'

'You could ask me,' Amy said, tipping another bucket-load of dirty nappies into the sink.

Patsy looked at her in surprise. 'Are you offering?'

'I might be.'

Patsy looked at her friend askance, at the milk seeping through her blouse, at her tousled hair and the dark smudges beneath her eyes. Not exactly a picture-book image of contented motherhood. 'Look, pardon me for saying so, love, but you look as if you've got enough on your plate right now.'

Amy gave a sheepish smile. 'I know, but it can surely only get better, can't it?'

'Yeah, once he's running around shoving his fingers in plug sockets and eating Tide washing powder from under the sink you'll have all the time in the world.'

'Oh, don't,' Amy laughed, cringing. 'Anyway, much as I might like to stay home with Danny and be a full-time mum, we need the money. Thomas has done a grand job, considering what he had to work with, but the house is very old and full of problems. We need to save up for a better place than this. It almost costs me as much each week for bleach to clean the mould off the walls as it does to pay the rent.'

Turning on the hot tap she began to scrub the dirty

nappies. 'And I want a washing machine too, so yes, I'm not too proud to look for work to pay for one. Danny is six weeks old now, so I'd be happy to accept peanuts if I could bring him with me.'

Patsy brightened. 'I can see your point, but I never thought to ask you. I reckoned you'd be too wrapped up in baby stuff to be interested.'

'To be honest, baby stuff, as you call it, can get a bit boring after a while. I'd welcome a few adults to talk to, and I'd make sure the pram didn't get in the way. Danny usually sleeps all afternoon, in any case.'

'I'm sure we can squeeze it in somewhere.'

'I've fixed up to do the odd morning for Lizzie Pringle too on her sweets and chocolate stall. She's no objection either to my taking Danny with me. I could do a couple of afternoons for you too, if you were interested.'

'Oh, Amy, do you really mcan it?'

'I do.'

'Then together we might catch those blighters who are robbing me blind.'

Amy grinned. 'We'll do our level best.'

'Could you manage Mondays and Fridays then, our busiest days? Clara could do Wednesdays and Saturdays, till she feels ready to take on more, which would give me the time I need to work on clients' commissions.'

'That would be fine.'

'Then it's a deal.'

And so it was agreed.

33

Carmina

Carmina kept herself amused by paying several more visits to Alec Hall's private quarters above the little music shop, whenever his son Terry was playing records at a dance, or seeing one of his own girlfriends.

She loved the secrecy of their meetings, the subterfuge. She would practically salivate with anticipation over the many thrills and little adventures Alec would devise to entertain them. He was nothing if not imaginative. He would have her dress up, or take a bath with him, try different positions or do things which made even Carmina blush. Yet she couldn't resist him. Whatever he asked of her she obeyed, because it felt dangerous and exciting.

And what did she have to lose?

She was biding her time for the right moment to make her announcement to the family that old Doc Mitchell had been wrong and she was pregnant after all. Then Luc would have to marry her whether he liked it or not. She knew he hated to be bested, that he was still soppy over Gina, but he'd come round quickly enough once he saw there was no escape.

And once Gina was no longer around.

In the meantime, Carmina was enjoying herself

hugely. Alec never again offered to make her that strange food, but he was fond of lighting candles and incense sticks which smelled funny and made her feel light-headed. And he loved to play his classical music. Sometimes he would pound into her in time with the crashing beat of the 1812 Overture. It was *so* inspiring! And she knew it was essential to keep him sweet while she put her plan into effect.

When they were both sated she would slip away into the darkness, helping herself to a few well-deserved treats while Alec slept on oblivious, as he was doing now.

She'd kept the little red transistor radio for herself, but tonight chose a blue one for Gina. It was so small it fitted easily into her pocket. As for records, so far she'd picked out 'Dream Lover,' 'Purple People Eater,' and 'Bird Dog'. She'd also taken one of Connie Francis singing 'Who's Sorry Now?' which had been in the hit chart for weeks. These, again, were for her own private use.

Now she picked out a few records at random for her sister before letting herself quietly out through the shop door.

Carmina didn't think of what she did as stealing exactly. If she cared to put a name to it at all she called it borrowing, or serving herself. She told herself that she could always put the things back, once she was bored with them. So far she hadn't done so, but it was an option.

Not that it mattered if she never did put them back. Carmina considered she deserved them for all she had suffered: her sister stealing the man she loved, Alec taking her by force that first time, and this unwelcome pregnancy. Carmina believed she'd be a fool not to take advantage of it.

And she blamed Gina for everything. Her sister was the one responsible for this situation, therefore *she* was the one who deserved to be punished.

On this particular evening as she made her way between the silent, empty stalls, the records tucked under her coat and the blue transistor radio in her pocket, she spotted Winnie Holmes. Drat it, she'd hoped there'd be no one around at this late hour.

'Hello, chuck,' Winnie said, surprise in her voice as she casually approached. 'Been dancing again, hasta?'

'Yes,' Carmina purred. 'I do love dancing.'

'What've you got there, then?' Winnie asked, nosy as ever as she eyed the bulge under her coat.

'Just a few plates Mamma lent to the dance organisers for the supper. She's very generous that way,' Carmina fabricated.

'Aye, she's a right treasure, your mam. I hope you appreciate her.'

'Oh, I do, I do.'

'Get off home with you then, chuck. Time a young lass like you was tucked up in bed!'

Carmina almost laughed out loud since that was exactly where she'd spent much of the evening. 'Good night, Winnie.'

It never ceased to amaze her how folk could miss what was going on right in front of their noses, just as Patsy missed a good deal that went on in front of hers.

Carmina had helped herself to several more little treats from Higginsons' Hat Stall too, including scarves, ribbons, earrings and a pretty bag.

Her aim was not to keep all these items for herself but to prove to Luc that Gina wasn't quite so wonderful, so honest and truthful as she made out. And in order to bring about this satisfactory state of affairs, she'd devised her cleverest scheme yet.

'Is that you, Carmina?' Papa called from the living room as she let herself into the hall.

'Yes, Papa, good night.'

'Good night, Carmina. No reading. You have work tomorrow. Go straight to bed.'

'I will.' And she obediently went up to the room she shared with her younger sisters exactly on time, as an obedient daughter should. But she didn't go to bed.

Marta and Antonia were both fast asleep, and, as luck would have it, Gina was still out. The two lovebirds were again off to the pictures, no doubt billing and cooing with eyes only for each other, completely oblivious to her own dire situation.

Carmina meant to take advantage of her sister's absence.

Whatever happened would be entirely her own fault. Had the stupid girl not selfishly tried to steal Luc from her in the first place, she would never have been obliged to do battle to win him back. Nor would Carmina ever have found the need to seek reassurance of her charms by batting a single eyelash at Alec Hall, and thus never have found herself in the mess she was in today.

Creeping quietly into the room she once used to share with Gina, Carmina hid the half dozen records in their brown paper sleeves on top of the wardrobe. No one would spot them up there, hidden as they were by the fancy fretwork all around the edge.

Next, she took from her pocket a pair of earrings and a pretty blue silk scarf. Quietly sliding open Gina's dressing-table drawer she slipped these inside, right at the back where they wouldn't easily be noticed. She was about to deposit the small bag in there too, red satin and decorated with sequin flowers, when she suddenly decided to keep it for herself. It was far too pretty to give away and would come in quite handy for dances.

She was careful not to put any of them where her sister hid her diary, or where she might easily come across them herself. Nevertheless, it proved surprisingly easy to tuck them in amidst the clutter at the back of Gina's cupboards and drawers.

She even remembered the loose brick in the old fireplace where she hid two bracelets and a pair of silver earrings. No fire was ever lit in it now, so they were quite safe.

Carmina softly closed the bedroom door, returned to her bed and thought about what she'd done.

Everyone knew how secretive Gina was, how she loved to squirrel things away and look at them in private, as she did with her china animal collection. So when the time was right, it would simply be necessary to alert the right person to look in this location, and her sister's 'crime' would be discovered.

Shop-lifting wasn't too bad though, not these days with all the kids dipping their sticky fingers into the displays at Woolies. It would do for a start, but what she really needed was something bigger, something far, far, worse. Something that would get Gina out of the way once and for all.

Later that same night Carmina heard her sister come home, heard her call out good night and creep quietly up the stairs to her room, not wishing to disturb her younger siblings. Carmina lay listening to the sounds of the house creaking, her parents switching off the lights, visiting the bathroom, checking on the younger children and then going off to bed.

When she was quite certain everyone was asleep, she slipped out of bed, still fully dressed, and let herself quietly out of the house.

Alec Hall's shop door was made up of several small panes of frosted glass, and, picking up a handy stone, Carmina hit one of the panes hard. The aim was to break it as quietly as she could but the glass proved tough and she had to bash it several times before it finally gave way. Sweat broke out on her brow as the sound echoed in the empty street and Carmina glanced fearfully around, ready to hide should anyone appear. Thankfully no one did.

Glancing up at the bedroom window above, she smiled to herself at the thought of Alec sleeping peacefully, blissfully unaware of the little plan she was putting into effect. He'd be snoring too loudly to hear anything by this time.

Tossing the stone away she let herself into the shop and took twenty pounds out of the till that she'd seen earlier. She also stole a large cardboard box which she knew contained a brand-new Ferguson record player.

Crunching the shattered glass underfoot, she hurried back along Champion Street as fast as she could, struggling a little with the bulky awkwardness of the box. All she had to do now was get it into the house and upstairs without waking anyone.

With the skill of long years of practice, Carmina eased open the door of her sister's room and slipped silently inside. As expected, Gina was sleeping peacefully, arms flung out, dead to the world. Carmina could tell by those little snuffles she made in her sleep.

Without making a sound she slid the box into the back of Gina's wardrobe and covered it with an old dressing gown. Time was now of the essence. She needed to put the last part of her plan into effect before Gina discovered them.

Smiling to herself, she crept off to bed at last.

'Chocolate, hazelnut, pistachio, raspberry, strawberry, vanilla, tortoni. What do you fancy, Winnie? The Bertalones make genuine ice cream, don't forget, not this factory-produced stuff.'

It was the next day and Carmina had been working in the ice-cream parlour all morning. They'd been so busy she'd only been allowed half an hour for her lunch. Now it was past three o'clock, her legs were aching, she was tired of Winnie taking forever to make up her mind as she had other matters on her mind.

'By heck,' Winnie chuckled, making herself comfortable at one of the small marble tables. 'Tha sounds more like yer dad every day.'

Carmina made no attempt to smile at the jest. It wasn't part of her plan to look happy, not today. She'd carefully left off any make-up so that she might look pale and wan, as if she hadn't slept. Not that she had got much sleep last night.

'He must be salting away a pile of brass, though not as much as some, eh? I heard as how them Fabrianis have a dozen motor vans, five tricycles, and a couple of hand carts. One of the fastest growing ice-cream businesses in all of Manchester. No wonder you've got your eye on that son of theirs.'

Carmina glowered. 'Ice lolly, choc ice, tub, brickette. Knickerbocker Glory. What'll it be, Winnie? The choice is yours.'

'I'll try a slice of that pineapple ice-cream cake. It's making me mouth water just looking at it.'

Carmina cut a large slice, the crushed pineapples blending with the vanilla ice cream between slices of sweet sponge cake. She piped on a swirl of fresh cream and handed it to Winnie.

'You've forgot the sauce.'

'There's no sauce with this particular dessert. Would you like a few flaked almonds instead?'

'No, put a bit of that raspberry syrup on it.'

'It might not suit the flavour of the pineapple.'

'It will if I say it will. Put it on, chuck. I like a dash of raspberry.'

Gritting her teeth to stop herself from being rude

to the old witch, Carmina did as she was told. It was essential not to lose her temper with the woman, not right now. She didn't even charge her extra for the syrup.

'And cheer up,' Winnie commanded in her bossiest voice. 'Tha looks like tha's lost a shilling and found a tanner. You've nowt to be miserable about, not like poor Alec Hall. Have you heard, he's had a break-in?'

'Oh, no!' Carmina said, as if this was the first she'd heard of it. 'When did this happen?'

'Last night. Several things have gone missing, apparently, including about twenty quid from the till.'

In an instant, Carmina manufactured sufficient tears to fill her glorious chocolate-velvet eyes. 'Oh, Winnie.'

'Nay, lass, what's up? I didn't intend to upset thee. Why would it bother you, Alec Hall being robbed? It's not your fault.'

'Oh, but it is, in a way.' Carmina glanced furtively around, as if she were about to reveal a great secret and had no wish for any eavesdroppers to overhear. 'Something dreadful has happened. Oh, I shouldn't say anything. I really shouldn't.'

Winnie sat eating ice cream as fast as she could, not savouring it with quite the delicacy she normally would as she was avid to know what the problem was. 'Nay, tha can trust me. I know how to keep me mouth shut when necessary.'

This was far from the truth, or else Winnie never had found it necessary to keep her mouth shut, which was why Carmina had chosen her as a confidante. One word in the old witch's ear and before the day was out half the market would have heard the full story, exactly as she was spreading this one about Alec's alleged break-in.

Carmina went to sit opposite her at the little marble-topped table. 'My sister's behaving most oddly.'

'Who, your Gina?'

Carmina nodded. 'You obviously know about this rivalry between us over Luc Fabriani.'

'All of Champion Street Market knows, chuck.'

'Well then, you have to understand that I've tried to be as patient and understanding as I can, even though she stole him from me. Luc and me, we're in love, and want to be together but Gina took him over when we'd had a bit of a spat one time and now she won't let him go. He feels sorry for her, of course, and has no wish to hurt her, but recently he's been trying to break it to her gently that it's all over between them. We're going to get married, Luc and me, and our Gina is devastated. As a result she seems to have run mad.'

Winnie swallowed the last spoonful of pineapple ice-cream cake and licked her lips. 'Run mad in what way, exactly?'

Again Carmina glanced around. Winnie did the same. 'She's started behaving very strangely. Secretive, you know. Most peculiar. I knew she was up to something but I couldn't work out what, not at first. Now that I've found out, I really don't know what to do about it, so I'd be glad of your advice, Winnie.'

There was nothing Winnie Holmes liked better than to give advice. 'Go on,' she urged, eager for more. 'I'm listening.'

Carmina edged closer so that they were almost nose to nose across the small table. Then dropping her voice to a whisper she said, 'Gina has started *stealing*! I think she might be the one who broke into Hall's Music Shop.'

'Nay, I don't believe it!' Winnie looked suitably shocked. Encouraged, Carmina pressed on.

'I couldn't believe it either at first, but it's true. You know Patsy's been having a lot of bother with shop-lifting. Well, I think that was Gina too. We don't share a room any more, because of this disagreement we've had over Luc. But the other evening I was hunting for some stockings I'd left behind in the dressing-table drawers and I found a stash of stuff in there, tucked right at the back where nobody would think to look.'

Winnie was agog. 'What sort of stuff?'

'Scarves, jewellery, socks, nylon stockings, all brand-new. The sort of things that Patsy claims to have been stolen. And last night when I got back from the dance, after I saw you, she wasn't in her room. Her bed was empty. What do I do, Winnie? What if Gina broke into Alec Hall's shop? What on earth do I do?'

The other woman was sitting with her mouth agape by this time. 'By heck, chuck. That's a facer, that is. Are you saying your Gina has turned criminal? That she's a thief?'

Two tears slid down Carmina's cheeks. 'Yes, Winnie, I am. I think she's lost her mind completely.'

'Then there's only one thing you can do. You have to go to the police. Tell Constable Nuttall.'

'Oh, I couldn't, I really couldn't.'

'I'll tell him for you, if you like?'

Carmina allowed more tears to slowly run down her beautiful, anguished face. 'Oh, would you do that for me, Winnie? I'd be so grateful. I just couldn't bear to shop my own sister. Isn't that what they call it when you tell on someone? It would be too terrible for words. She'd never speak to me again and I love her so much. I just think she needs help, all the help she can get. She needs to be stopped.'

'Aye,' Winnie said, her face grim. 'You might be right there. Leave it to me, lass. Leave it me.'

The police came to the Bertalone house later that same day. The whole family watched in stunned disbelief as Constable Nuttall together with two of his colleagues searched Gina's room, opening every drawer and cupboard. They took possession of various items they suspected of being stolen, including a number of records, the blue transistor radio and the Ferguson record player. They even took bricks out of the tiny Victorian fireplace and found twenty one-pound notes tucked behind a brick together with two bracelets and a pair of silver earrings.

After checking that these items were indeed stolen from Higginsons' stall, and from Alec Hall's break-in, they came back to arrest her.

Mamma and Papa clung to each other weeping as the police took away their bemused, hollow-eyed daughter to jail.

34
Amy

Mavis continued to call in most mornings, ostensibly to see if Amy required any help while Chris was busy at the bakery. Amy was feeding Danny herself and didn't much care for an audience, or for her mother-in-law telling her to 'swap him to the other side he's had enough of that one', as if she could control even the strength by which he suckled, or the amount of milk Amy's breasts produced.

This morning Mavis asked if she needed any shopping doing.

'I can manage, thank you,' Amy calmly informed her. 'I can pick up a few things when I take Danny for his afternoon stroll.' What her mother-in-law would say about her intention of going back to work, Amy didn't care to think. Best not to mention it until she'd proved she could cope.

'Dear me, it's far too wet to be taking him out today. He'll catch a chill.' It had come as an unwelcome surprise to Mavis to discover that the new young mother was suddenly less biddable than the old Amy. When it concerned the care of her child the foolish girl stubbornly refused to listen to well-meant advice. It had been this way ever since that dreadful scene over the colic. Mavis still maintained she was right, but her daughter-in-law refused to accept it.

Amy said, 'It's August, and quite warm. A short shower isn't going to hurt him.'

Mavis clicked her tongue in annoyance, hating to be bested yet again, and reaching forward she tugged at Amy's open blouse to shield her nakedness, thereby covering the baby's head too.

'Fresh air and exercise are good for him. Good for me too,' Amy said, pushing the blouse away so that she could gaze down upon her child in wonder, even if it did expose her own nakedness to Mavis's critical eye. She decided to change the subject. 'How is Thomas? More important, *where* is he? I don't seem to have seen him in ages.'

'I told him to stay away,' Mavis coldly announced. 'Since he will insist on spending so much time at that *dreadful* allotment now that he's semi-retired, he's generally covered in dust, grass cuttings and compost. Utterly revolting! I have instructed him to stay well clear of the baby. He would be unhygienic.'

Amy was devastated. 'Oh, no, poor Thomas. I really wouldn't mind, and I'm sure Danny couldn't catch anything from grass cuttings. Anyway, he could always leave his boots in the backyard.'

'I should hope so, but you can't take any chances, not where young babies are concerned. Thomas must stay away until the child is older and has developed a greater immunity to infections.'

Amy said no more, but made a mental note to visit her father-in-law in the dreaded allotment, if that was the only way she could get to see him. She certainly didn't believe that Danny would come down with some unknown disease simply because his grandfather liked to grow tomatoes.

Mavis finally deigned to sit beside her on the worn old sofa, having first removed several items of baby clothing, a towel, and a dirty nappy with the tips of her fingers. 'You should put these to soak right away.'

'I soak them in Napisan, but I don't like to disturb him till he's finished feeding.'

'How many feeds is that he's had today?'

'I can't remember,' Amy said, feeling flustered.

'I suppose you're still picking him up every five minutes. Is he sleeping through yet?'

Not wanting to admit the true facts, that sleep was something Danny still didn't do very well at all, Amy said, 'Sometimes. It's better now that I'm giving him Farex for his supper.'

'Goodness, he's far too young for solids.'

Amy sighed and said no more.

Mavis watched the baby suckling for a while, making no attempt to touch him. After a moment she let out a heavy sigh, sounding seriously put out. 'Well, I might as well go since I'm clearly not wanted. I must say I'm surprised you aren't showing a little more – gratitude – for my taking the time out of my busy day to help. Babies are hard work, as I warned you from the start. And if you continue to obstinately refuse to take advice from someone who knows better, then I can't think how you'll manage.'

'I'm coping fine, thank you,' Amy said. 'And Chris is marvellous.'

'It's not Chris's job, he has enough to do at the bakery. Looking after the baby is your job, but I fear you'll make a mess of it, as you do everything else. Still, when did you ever listen to me? I'll be on my way then, I've no wish to stay where I'm not needed . . .' Mavis stood up, hooking her handbag over her arm.

'You could put the kettle on,' Amy suggested. 'I'm gasping for a brew and I haven't had a minute today to put the kettle on.'

Deeply offended that she should be called upon to perform such a menial task, Mavis stomped off to the kitchen looking very much the martyr. She returned several moments later with a loaded tea tray, complaining she couldn't find the tea strainer.

'We don't have a tea strainer.'

'Dear me, you mustn't let standards slip just because you're feeding a baby. A tea strainer is absolutely essential if you are to avoid tea leaves in your cup. I'll buy you one this afternoon.'

'No thanks, we can afford to buy our own, if we want one. It's just that a fancy tea strainer isn't a priority right now.'

'I see.' Her mother-in-law's voice was clipped, taut with disapproval. 'You do realise that the biscuit barrel is empty. I *always* make sure I have some garibaldi biscuits in. They are Chris's favourites. Fortunately he still likes to pop home for a snack now and then.'

As much as Amy longed to say that this was Chris's home now, instead she tried to make a joke of it. 'It was Chris who finished them all off last night as a matter of fact. Greedy piggy! But then we were up half the night with me laddo here.'

She could have kicked herself. As expected, Mavis pounced.

'Good gracious, I'm surprised at you, Amy, expecting your husband to help with night-feeds. Chris needs all the sleep he can get with having to rise before dawn to bake bread, whereas you can sleep during the day.'

This made her laugh. 'Fat chance of that. I always mean to try for a snooze but then there's the washing to be done, all by hand, the ironing, a sink full of pots to be cleared and a meal to prepare, so I never quite manage even five minutes' shut-eye. Last night Danny had colic and just wouldn't settle. The doctor says that will get better after the three-month mark. Sorry about the biscuits though, I'll get some more when I go out later.'

Now she was over-explaining, something she'd promised herself she'd never do. Drat the woman, why did she always have to get under her skin?

Mavis said, 'Well, at least you're taking the *doctor*'s advice.'

Amy gritted her teeth. 'If Chris wants to help feed his son, I think that's quite a good thing. We've agreed to take turns, as we both need to snatch whatever sleep we can.'

'Good heavens, it wasn't like that in my day,' Mavis retorted, lost for any better argument.

'Things change,' Amy brightly informed her, putting Danny to her shoulder to burp him. 'And as for picking him up,' she continued, deciding she might as well be hanged for a sheep as a lamb, and make it clear from the start that she would bring up her own child as she chose. 'I see nothing to be gained by letting him cry till he's sick or gives himself wind. He might have a tummy-ache, or be feeling lonely and in need of a cuddle.'

'You'll live to rue the day if you spoil him,' Mavis snapped.

'I don't think you can spoil a child with love. Everybody deserves a bit of a cuddle now and then. I intend to make sure that my baby gets plenty of that.'

'I can see you have some very modern, radical ideas festering in that silly little head of yours.'

'Yes, I do, don't I? Love, comfort and fresh air, very radical. Oh, and the freedom for my son to explore the world and make his own decisions when the time comes,' Amy said, smiling softly as she laid Danny on the new hearthrug where he could kick his bare legs and look about him. 'No doubt you'd think that wrong too.'

The next thing Amy heard was the slamming of the front door. 'Oh, dear, Danny love. I think I might have offended her.'

Thomas was happily ensconced in his allotment shed. He'd been living there ever since the big row. It had all got very nasty. Mavis had gone on to rail and rant at him about how she'd never wanted Chris to move in the first place, and how it was all Thomas's fault for finding them the house.

'If you'd never interfered, my son would still be living at home, where he belongs.'

Pointless to remind her that their Chris shouldn't be

living with his mam and dad at all now that he was a married man. Thomas had been down that road countless times and knew it to be a cul-de-sac with a brick wall at the end.

'You've gone too far this time,' Mavis had accused him. 'If you think you can parade your fancy woman right before my eyes and shame me before everyone, you've got another think coming.' At which point she'd marched upstairs and packed his bag, which she'd then thrown out of the house. Using the back door of course, so that nobody could see.

Thomas knew when he was beaten. He'd taken his cap and jacket from the peg and moved into his shed on the allotment that same night, where he'd been ever since.

He thought he'd got away with it, that nobody knew, but now here was Amy, standing before him, her small face a picture of horror.

'So this is where you've been hiding yourself, why I haven't seen you for weeks.' Amy pulled up an orange box, looking about her in open curiosity as she made herself comfortable.

The shed was small but remarkably tidy, if very dusty and stacked high with tomato boxes, shelves of seed potatoes, and with rakes, hoes and spades hanging in a row on the wall. A paraffin lamp swung from a beam, and there was a stack of old newspapers in one corner. And among all this garden paraphernalia sat a small brown leather suitcase from which socks and shirts spilled. Amy stared at it in dismay.

'You surely can't be living here.'

'I can and I am. I had a bit of a ding-dong with Her Majesty, and she threw me out. But don't you fret about me, love. I went through worse when I were in the ARP. It were a bit parky the first night but I crept back home while she were out shopping and picked up a couple of blankets and a pillow. I'm nice as ninepence now. I've even got a friend.'

Amy couldn't help smiling as she regarded the small black cat curled up fast asleep on the old man's knee. Danny was also asleep in the pram parked outside the little hut. Thomas had oohed and aahed for a bit and commented on the lad's strength as he gripped his grandfather's finger. Now they were sitting inside and Amy was struggling against the need to express the sensation of shock rushing around in her head. How could her father-in-law be living in a garden shed? It was unbelievable. What on earth had happened to bring about this miserable state of affairs?

She tickled the cat's chin and it stretched itself luxuriously. 'What's his name?'

'Blackie,' said Thomas, imaginatively. 'He shares me dinners and he's no trouble.'

On one rickety shelf stood a small shaving mirror, brush and razor; a jug and basin balanced on the tool box beneath.

'How do you boil water?' Amy asked, appalled.

Thomas indicated a small paraffin stove with a jerk of his head. A rusty old kettle rested on top, steaming gently.

It was too much. 'Oh, Thomas, you can't possibly

live here. You can cope with that for a shave, but how do you go on for a bath? It's . . . it's . . . *awful*!'

'I go down to the public baths and manage very well, thanks. Eeh, I'm forgetting me manners. D'you want a cuppa?'

He reached for a teapot, stained from many similar brews, and began to spoon in tea leaves. Amy watched in silence as he added the boiling water. She even managed not to say a word as he wiped a couple of mugs on a grubby tea towel, then, after sniffing a half-empty milk bottle, poured a drop into each.

She accepted the tea without a murmur, although she had serious doubts about that milk. Certainly something was smelling in here: a strange mix of stale food, sweaty feet, shaving soap and ripe tomatoes.

'Where do you sleep?' She could see no sign of a bed.

'I put down me bedroll. Don't worry, I'm quite comfy.'

'Good job it's summer then, or you'd be frozen to the floorboards.'

'Wife'll happen have got over her hump by the time winter sets in.'

'And if she hasn't?'

Thomas shrugged. Ever phlegmatic he seemed to be saying that he'd cross that bridge when he came to it.

Amy wondered if she dare ask what the row had been about, but decided against it. A private argument between man and wife really wasn't any of her business. But then Thomas saved her the trouble.

'She thinks I've been playing away.'

'Playing away?'

'With Belle Garside.'

Amy nearly choked on her tea. And she'd been right about the milk. 'You must be joking. Belle Garside, and *you*?' Did that sound a bit rude, she wondered, to imply Belle would never fancy her father-in-law?

'Aye, it's a bit of facer in't it? As if she'd look in my direction, sexy lady like Belle. Mavis isn't thinking straight. It's the beans on toast which is bothering her the most, I reckon.'

Amy had quite lost the thread and decided it was perhaps time she left. She stood up. 'I've got to go. Danny will be wanting feeding again soon and I need to do a bit of shopping before he wakes up. Can I get something for you while I'm out round the market, some fresh milk perhaps?'

He grinned at her. 'That'd be champion.'

She plonked a kiss on his cheek. It felt all rough and scratchy, then she looked at the untidy heap of clothes spilling out of the suitcase. 'I could take your washing.'

'Nay, tha's enough to do wi' that babby.'

'A few more shirts and socks won't make much difference.' It would make all the difference in the world. Amy was overwhelmed by washing. Her days were an endless round of scrubbing stinking nappies, and all by hand, since they still couldn't afford to buy a machine. But she bundled Thomas's dirty clothes into the tray beneath the pram without a word. With clean socks the shed might smell a bit fresher. Anyway, the dear chap deserved clean socks, if nothing else. 'I'll fetch 'em back when they're done, but you can always come over to ours you know, if you feel like a change of scene.'

Thomas shook his head. 'Nay, I might run into our Mavis. Anyroad, I don't want to be a nuisance. You need time on your own just now.'

Amy's heart swelled with love for the old man. He was so kind, so understanding. But the idea of Thomas and Belle having some sort of torrid affair . . . Amy almost giggled at the thought. 'I'll fetch you a bit of hot pot later. I've some left over from yesterday. You can happen heat it up on that stove.'

'Eeh, tha's a star, lass. A proper star. Our Chris struck lucky when he wed you.'

'Tell that to your wife,' Amy wryly remarked.

'Nay, we communicate only by notes which she leaves stuck on the door with a drawing pin.'

Amy didn't dare ask what these missives might say. She took the brake off the pram and hurried away, not knowing whether to laugh or cry.

35

Gina and Carmina

Gina couldn't take in what was happening to her. She stood in the Magistrates Court and heard them remand her in custody for burglary under the Larceny Act of 1916. She felt numb. It was as if this were happening to someone else.

'Take her down.'

The words rang in her head and she felt nauseous, as if she might throw up all over the polished wooden floor. She looked into the eyes of the sergeant who was grasping her arm but he stared right through her, as though she didn't exist. Gina flinched as he snapped on the handcuffs, then glanced in panic across at her parents seated at the back of the court.

Her mother had her hands to her mouth and was quietly sobbing. Papa sat frozen, his face in shock. There was Luc too, half out of his seat as if he intended to leap over the barrier to reach her. She felt she'd let them all down in some way, yet she'd done nothing. She was innocent of this dreadful charge. She wanted to run to them, to cry out that she didn't do it, but it was too late. She was being led down a flight of stairs back into the cells, into a cold, unfriendly world where her only view of the outside would be through a cell window.

As the prison van bore her away, jolting over cobbles, Gina kept her eyes fixed on the view through the back window. She felt desperate for one last sight of her friends and loved ones gathered in the street, of the places she knew and loved, of sunlight but all she could see was rain beating on the glass.

When the van reached Strangeways, she passed within those same tall Victorian gates through which hundreds of others had gone before her, from petty thieves to murderers, from women who sold their bodies for hard cash, to Mrs Pankhurst and her fellow suffragettes.

How many of those poor souls had been innocent, like her?

Later, what Gina remembered most about that first day was the smell. It was dreadful! Overwhelming! Sour and acrid. Stale food and urine, vomit and fear intermingled with the paraffin and disinfectant they used to clean it all up.

And then there was the terrible indignity of it all.

She was ordered to strip, made to stand under a cold shower. Her clothes and few belongings were taken from her. Forms were filled in. No one spoke except to issue her with orders, to tell her to stand here, or there, to take this or sign that. No one treated her like a real human being. Everyone assumed she was guilty and deserved to be locked up in prison.

Gina felt as if she'd ceased to be human. She'd become an object to be pawed at, inspected, and shifted about from place to place. They gave her some sort of canvas garment that scratched against her pale skin.

Then she was marched along the wing, through a succession of clanging doors that had to be unlocked and locked again after her, taking her deeper and deeper into hell. It was terrifying, and no concession was made for her limp.

'Hurry along there, we haven't got all day,' the prison officer barked. She was a thin, weasel-faced woman with narrow eyes that turned down at each corner.

Gina did her best, feeling exposed and vulnerable beneath the hard glare of the other women prisoners who watched her go by with silent animosity, as if they resented the interruption, this reminder that there was a world outside of these cells.

Then Gina was led into her own cell, a room little bigger than three paces by four, with a tiny barred window set too high in the far wall to see out of. It was bare, bleak and empty.

'You'll have company tomorrow. Tonight you get the place all to yourself. Aren't you the lucky one?' the woman said, rattling the huge bunch of keys at her waist.

Gina thought she might never forget the sound of the heavy door closing behind her.

If she slept that night, she wasn't aware of it. She lay, hollow-eyed, a physical ache in her heart, thoughts whirling. So many questions were buzzing through her mind. How had this all come about? Everything seemed to happen so fast. Only yesterday the police had searched her room, found goods she'd never known she possessed and charged her with shop lifting and burglary. They'd accused her of breaking into Alec Hall's music shop and, to her utter dismay and disbelief, found money and the stolen record player to prove their case, *hidden in her wardrobe*.

'How did that get there?' She'd gasped out loud in horror, turning to her shocked parents and swearing that she knew nothing about it, that she'd never set eyes on the thing before. But, like her, they were too stunned to protest as the police bore her away.

Constable Nuttall had locked her up in a windowless police cell where she'd passed the most miserable night of her life on a concrete bed with nothing more than a couple of blankets to make herself comfortable. They'd given her food she couldn't eat, a plastic mug of sweetened tea that she'd had to force down her parched throat.

Now she was locked away in prison, her case to be sent to the Quarter Sessions for trial, which might not come up for months. How would she survive that long? What would she do with herself through the endlessly long hours each day? Would the other women bully her? Would the officers physically punish her? Panic gripped her, terror turning her insides to water as she tried to imagine what might happen to her in this dreadful place.

Gina had always seen herself as physically weak but mentally strong. Yet now she curled herself into a tight ball for comfort. Never had she felt so afraid, so utterly petrified. And nobody was listening to her protests of innocence. She gave herself up to despair and sobbed quietly into her musty pillow.

The moment the family were back in the house following the committal, all struck speechless with shock, Carmina made her announcement that she was indeed pregnant, that the wedding with Luc must go ahead, after all. It was several minutes before her father could focus on what she was saying. He stared at her, perplexed, a small frown puckering his brow in a face that had aged ten years in the last twenty-four hours. He turned at last to address his wife.

'I don't understand. Doc Mitchell said there was to be no baby. How can she be pregnant?'

They all looked at Luc who'd gone white to the gills. He shook his head, bemused. 'I don't believe this. I won't believe it. Tell them the truth for God's sake, Carmina, that you and I never did anything. *We never had sex*!'

'Why do you keep denying it when I carry the proof?' She patted her belly and Luc winced.

'I'm not marrying you, Carmina, not now, not ever.' So saying, he turned on his heels and stormed out of the house.

Carmina watched him stride away with a secret smile on her face, oblivious to his distress. He could protest as much as he liked but who would listen? It was still his word against hers, and now that she had a baby growing inside her it would be easy to prove that her story must be the true version. He'd come round to the idea of marriage once he saw it was inevitable.

She called after him, adopting a deliberately piteous tone, even manufacturing a few tears. 'Don't leave me, Luc. There's no need to pretend any more. Gina isn't here to hear you. You can do the right thing by me now.'

Now that her sister was safely out of the way.

Carlotta let out a terrible wail. Already, today, one

daughter had been taken from her into the unspeakable hell of prison life for a crime she surely didn't commit. Now another was telling her she was pregnant without the benefit of matrimony. It was all too much. She put her hands to her face and howled, sounding very like an animal in distress.

Marco quickly put his arms about his wife and held her tight. Hearing this dreadful noise children came running from all directions, Lela, Marta, Alessandro, Antonia and the twins, to fling themselves upon their beloved parents in a sobbing, loving heap.

Luc had walked out and Carmina had never felt more like an outsider, excluded even from the love of her own family. Yet inside beat a pulse of pure triumph. She'd achieved her object at last. Gina had been taken away and locked up where she could no longer get in the way of her plans.

Really, it had all gone far more smoothly than she could have hoped. The old witch had come up trumps and Constable Nuttall had done the rest. A few hints had been dropped, a rumour mentioned, without naming any names. Nobody but Winnie herself knew anything of Carmina's involvement. And even she was aware only of the version Carmina had given her. She was ignorant of the clever mind which had cooked up this entire scheme and put it into effect with such skill and perfection.

And having rid herself of her rival, Carmina intended to move in swiftly to claim her prize. Luc still fancied her like mad, she was sure of it. He'd get over his sulks in no time once he realised what he was gaining by marrying her: thrilling sex and a devoted slave for life.

Carmina chuckled to herself. Perhaps slave wasn't quite the right word. Nor was sex generally a subject open for discussion in the Bertalone household, save for her mother's lectures. Yet the time for such modesty was long past.

'You'll go and speak to the Fabrianis, Papa?'

Marco looked at her with dazed eyes over the heads of her siblings and managed only to give a brief nod. Carmina smiled, then coolly walked from the room and left them to their collective misery. She could relax now. There was nothing more to be done. Her little scheme had worked beautifully.

Luc would soon be her lawfully wedded husband and there wasn't a damn thing anybody could do to prevent it.

The Fabrianis were not happy. When this baby business had first blown up they'd been willing to urge their son into doing the right thing, for the honour of the family. But time had passed and they'd seen how happy he was with Gina. The situation had completely changed. But, incredibly, Gina had been arrested for shop-lifting and burglary, and the other Bertalone girl was again claiming to be pregnant with Luc's child. They were deeply suspicious and not a little upset.

This time when Marco came to discuss the necessary wedding arrangements they were less cooperative.

The post-war period for the Italian ice-cream merchants had not been an easy one. Luc's father, like the rest of his compatriots, had overcome anti-Italian feeling and devoted all his energies to building a good business, in spite of fierce competition between rival families. He'd built a modern ice-cream factory, had invested in a number of motorised vans, installed his family in a fine Georgian house on St John's Place, and was even now negotiating a new contract to buy a Mr Softee franchise. He certainly had no wish to see all of that handed over to some cheap little floozie who was no better than she should be.

They refused to push their son into anything he might later regret. Carmina might well have her wedding plans well advanced but the Fabrianis held back, insisting that their son be allowed time to consider the long term before committing himself.

This was not at all what Carmina had expected. She ranted and raved at her father, and to Luc. She wept and railed at her mother whom she felt should be more sympathetic, but nothing did any good.

'You will just have to be patient,' her father kept saying.

'How can I be patient when I have this baby growing inside me? Do you want it to be illegitimate?' she screamed, which set Carlotta off weeping all over again.

Frustratingly enough, putting Gina in jail had been relatively easy in comparison with capturing Luc. He was bedevilled by guilt, of course. And it was going to take every ounce of her seductive powers to win him round.

36

Amy

It was a hot, sultry day in August and the queue at the ice-cream cart was keeping Carmina busy. Amy bought herself a strawberry ice-cream cornet and exchanged a few pleasantries, offering heartfelt condolences over Gina's incarceration. It was hard to believe that a girl so quiet and gentle could ever get involved in shop-lifting, let alone break into a shop. She said as much to Carmina who wasn't very forthcoming, but felt that she'd at least done her best to express sympathy.

No doubt her friend Patsy would be relieved at having the puzzle of the shop-lifting solved, but Amy couldn't imagine that she'd be happy with the outcome. She was very fond of Gina.

Amy thoughtfully ate her ice cream as she browsed around the stalls. She intended to take Danny for a walk along by the river later where she might set his pram rug on the bit of grass by the lock and let him kick his legs in the sun.

She was just trying to decide whether to have cold chicken or a pork pie with the salad she meant to prepare for Chris's tea when she spotted Jeff Stockton.

He hurried straight over to ask how she was, even remembered to admire the baby. 'We've missed you at the CND meetings, Amy. When are you intending to come back?'

Amy pulled a wry face. 'I can't see me managing it any time soon, I'm afraid. Babies take up a great deal of time, and I've got myself some part-time work, as they are also very expensive.'

Jeff grinned. 'You're looking well on it though.'

'You must be joking, with bags as big as suitcases under my eyes? I keep trying to convince my mother-in-law that all is well, and then trip up over my own lies and let slip we've had yet another bad night with him. If he's slept for more than an hour in the last week or two, I haven't noticed.'

'I bet you're a wonderful mum. To be honest, I was hoping to run across you.'

Amy laughed. 'Let me guess. You want some envelopes addressing.'

Jeff looked sheepish. 'Could you fit that in, do you think, between the nappy washing and the feeds?'

He was holding out a large package and, sighing, Amy took it from him with a small smile. 'How can I refuse? But it's not work at home I really need right now, if you can understand. That's why I'm doing a few hours each week for Patsy, and for Lizzie Pringle. I'm feeling desperate to get out of the house occasionally.'

'Then come to a meeting.'

She looked at him. 'Maybe I will. When's the next one? I could perhaps manage to sneak out for the odd night.'

Jeff told her and Amy frowned, beginning to plot

how she might manage to grab herself some time off without alerting Chris's suspicions.

Strangely, Jeff seemed to read her thoughts. 'Haven't you told Chris yet that you're a member?'

Amy shook her head. 'He won't like it. Smacks too much of unions and politics for my lovely, gentle husband, and I'm not anxious for a confrontation on the subject right now. He's not over-thrilled about my working again so soon, and he's feeling pretty worn out, what with shouldering the lion's share of the work at the bakery, and suffering sleepless nights with young Danny here.'

'You're going to have to tell him soon though, if you want to keep up with your membership. We've all sorts of events planned in the coming months, which I'm sure you'd want to be a part of.'

'Oh, dear, yes I would.'

'We've another march, and a demonstration or two, which will need lots of effort on the fund-raising front. If we are to avoid another war, we can only achieve it by ridding ourselves of the means of fighting one. We need your help, Amy.'

'I will tell him, Jeff, I promise.'

'Good girl, and thanks for doing the envelopes.'

'You could sell fridges to Eskimos, you.'

He laughed. 'No, it's just your sweet, generous heart. Thanks, anyway,' and he ruffled her hair, just as he'd been doing since she was five years old, then gave her a smacking kiss on her cheek and bounded off on his long-legged stride, leaving Amy shaking her head in amused despair. Jeff Stockton was perfect at his job of persuading people to do what they really didn't have time for. Smiling to herself she pulled her shopping list from her pocket and set off in pursuit of more garibaldi biscuits to yet again restock her poor beleaguered biscuit barrel.

Mavis, standing on the street corner, having witnessed the entire scene, including the kiss the good-looking young man had given her daughter-in-law, went thoughtfully on her way. She was quite sure that she'd seen him with Amy before, on a previous occasion. And a mother's instinct told her that her son knew nothing about him.

Amy addressed all the envelopes and put them in the bottom drawer of the big old dresser where Chris wouldn't find them. She meant to hand them over the very next time she spotted Jeff around the market.

She'd been reading an article in the *Daily Mail* about how the CND intended to 'empower people to engage actively in the political process and to work for a nuclear-free and peaceful future'. Amy wanted to be empowered. If she had no say over what furniture was put in her own house, how often she fed her baby, or how many hours Danny slept, then why shouldn't she strive to change the world. It needed changing. Maybe then she and Chris would be able to afford to buy a house of their own.

The next meeting was on Thursday evening at the Friends Meeting House. Maybe she'd go along and deliver the addressed envelopes personally.

When Thursday came, Amy quickly cleared away

after supper while Chris was reading the paper, then settled Danny in his cot. She'd already secreted the package of envelopes in her basket, now she placed a minced beef pie on top.

'I'm just popping round to take this pie to your dad,' she told Chris. 'The poor man has to eat. Then I might go and have a chat with Patsy. I should think she'll be upset over Gina and this shop-lifting charge, and in need of some support right now. You don't mind holding the fort for a bit, do you?'

Chris put down his paper and pulled his wife onto his knee. 'Course I don't. Do you good to get out for a bit and talk to the grown-ups. If his master's voice pipes up again I'll give him a bottle, right?'

'Give him a cuddle first. See if he needs changing, and if all else fails try a spoonful of gripe water. He shouldn't need feeding till ten and I'll be back long before then.'

Amy kissed her husband on the lips. 'Mm, tasty. What a nice mouth you have. I must get reacquainted with it some time.'

'Mm, I agree,' Chris said, tightening his arms about her. 'That's the problem with babies. They leave you no energy for really important things, like making love.'

Amy giggled. 'We'll survive. Things can only get better.'

Chris sighed, rather over-dramatically. 'You keep saying that. Course, I could always run off with a floozie to satisfy my manly needs.'

'Don't you dare. I'd make your life a complete misery if you even considered doing such a dreadful thing.'

'Oh, good,' he grinned, kissing her again. 'Maybe we should try for a lie-in on Sunday, if Danny Boy will let us. And we can stay awake, that is.'

'Ooh, yes please. We could stay in bed all day, catch up on our rest, and other things. Only we'd have to lock the door against your mother. She'd be sure to pop in just as we were getting going.'

Chris nuzzled into her neck. 'I'll tell her we're going out for the day.'

Amy giggled. 'She'd still come round, just to check, and she'd see the lights on, or hear the radio playing.'

'We won't need any lights, and we'd be quiet as little mice. Then I shall have my wicked way with you. You could wear your black lace nightie, the one I bought you for Christmas.'

'Now you're letting your imagination run away with you, and this pie is getting cold. Let me go, there's a good lad. These manly needs of yours will have to wait till Sunday.'

He groaned, but allowed her to slip from his knee.

Thomas was grateful for the pie and gave her a few tomatoes, a lettuce and a bunch of radishes in exchange. But Amy went nowhere near Number 22 to see Patsy. Keeping to the back alleys she headed straight to the Friends Meeting House and the CND meeting.

The letter addressed to Chris arrived one morning while he was at the bakery. Amy thought nothing of it, propping it against their wedding picture on the dresser so that he'd see it when he came home. True, he didn't get many letters and she was curious, but Amy wasn't the kind of wife to steam open her husband's correspondence.

The moment their evening meal was cleared away, she gave it to him while she fetched a jug of hot water to fill the bath for Danny.

He ripped open the envelope to read it and she saw at once that something was wrong. His face went white, ashen to the lips, and his jaw set tight, the way it used to when they were hiding in Gretna Green with no food to eat and no money in their pockets.

'What is it?' she asked. 'What's wrong?'

Chris looked at her as if she were a stranger, and his voice, when he finally spoke, was cold as ice. 'I'm going out.'

'Don't you want to help with Danny's bath?'

'No, not tonight. I need a pint.' He needed time to think, to consider the implications of this letter.

She stared at him, wide-eyed. 'Are you sure there's nothing wrong, Chris?' She wanted to ask him who the letter was from, since they didn't get much post at their house, but there was something in his manner which held her back. Perhaps it was some worry over the business which he wanted to talk over with his father.

He was reaching for his jacket, making for the door. 'I'll see you later.'

'All right, don't be late.'

He swung round on that. 'At least you would know where to find me,' he said, and marched out slamming the door behind him.

Amy added a jug of cold to the hot and tested the

water with her elbow, a slight frown on her face. Now what was all that about?

Chris didn't go to the Dog and Duck, or to see his father at the allotment, he went straight round to the Higginsons' house and knocked on the door. Clara answered and he bluntly asked if he could speak to Patsy, without even exchanging the usual pleasantries.

'I'll fetch her, Chris, or would you like to come in?'

'I'll wait here, if you don't mind. What I have to say won't take long.'

Patsy came. 'I just wondered . . .' Chris began, filled with a rush of uncertainty now that she was standing on the doorstep smiling agreeably at him.

'Yes?'

He decided not to be too blunt or Amy might find out that he'd been checking up on her. They were good pals these two. He wondered if they were friendly enough for Patsy to lie for her friend. 'When my wife . . . when Amy came to see you the other evening, was it before or after she'd been to see my father?'

Patsy frowned. 'Er . . . I really can't remember. What night was that, exactly?'

'Thursday.'

She thought some more. 'No, I think you must have got the date wrong. She popped over on Friday afternoon. I remember we had a cup of tea together and gossiped a bit, as we usually do. But no, the last time I saw her wasn't on Thursday, and it wasn't evening. Why, is it important? Is there something wrong with your father?'

Chris was backing away now, desperate to be alone, to think. 'No, there's nowt wrong with Dad, except me mother who never stops going on at him. They've had a bit of a spat and he's camping out at the allotment for a bit.'

Patsy said. 'Oh, dear, I'm sorry to hear that. Nothing wrong with Amy either, I hope?'

'No, nothing wrong. Thanks anyway. I got summat wrong, that's all. Bye, Patsy.'

Patsy called after him. 'Let me know if there's anything else.'

'Aye, I will, thanks.'

She was still frowning as he disappeared round the corner.

37

Gina and Carmina

Gina's first day in prison passed in a blur of sirens, women's voices raised in argument, jeering and shouted orders, the rattle of keys and clanging of doors, endless queuing, and long empty hours alone with her tortured thoughts. Breakfast felt like Bedlam. The noise was deafening, the food uneatable and, underpinning it all, fear etched itself firmly on her soul.

Nobody spoke a word to her, except for one old woman who offered to carry her tray when she spotted Gina's limp.

'The girl can manage well enough on her own, Edith, without you hovering over her,' one of the prison officers snapped. Her would-be helper was roughly shoved aside and sent to the back of the queue where she was jostled and laughed at by the other prisoners.

Gina didn't even dare thank her for offering, in case the same thing should happen to her.

When she returned to her cell it was to find she had a new cell-mate: a woman twice her age with scrawny yellow hair and a haggard face, who told her she could have the bottom bunk. She said her name was Alice and after learning it was Gina's first day, warned her never to ask what anyone was in for.

'My crime was only to steal a few quid to feed my children. I won't ask you what yours was, so don't tell me.'

'I've committed no crime. I've done nothing.'

'Course you haven't, love. You're innocent, along with seventy-five per cent of the other women in this jail.'

'Will they realise that in the end, do you think?' Gina asked, failing to pick up the irony in the woman's tone.

The woman puffed out her lips, sat up and studied this young girl with closer attention. 'Why would they care? You're banged up. Case closed.'

'No, no, my case still has to come to trial.'

Alice made a little scoffing sound. 'A mere formality. Best set about learning the ropes, fast as you can, love. Don't worry, I'll help you. There's chores to be done: washing, scrubbing, laundry, stuff like that. Recreation, association, education classes if you're lucky, and the rest of the time you get to rest in your cell. What joy!'

Gina couldn't think of a single response to this, or why the woman's face creased into a happy smile at the prospect of such isolation.

'Just remember prison isn't a place to make friends. And don't step out of line. If anyone tries owt, thumps you like, or whatever, tell me, not the screws. There's a pecking order here, and, as a new girl, you're right at the bottom of the pile, chuck. You keep your head down and you'll be all right. Remember that, if nowt else.'

Gina felt even more muddled and confused by all of this, although it sounded wise advice. She wanted to ask questions but Alice clearly wasn't for explaining further, not right now, as she turned her face to the wall and went back to sleep.

Gina sat on her own bunk and wondered what she should do next, then realised there was nothing she could do. The empty hours stretched ahead. She could hardly begin to think how she might fill them. She longed to talk to Alice some more, to talk to anyone. The prospect of months and months in this cold cell without even a friend to trust or talk to was very frightening. And sitting in silence was making her head spin.

She hadn't even been allowed to bring a book with her, or any personal items beyond what she'd happened to be carrying in her bag and they'd taken those from her: her comb, and purse, and keys. Nothing of any importance save for a photo of Luc.

Would they let her have that back? she wondered. Did she want it? Did she still love him after the way he'd betrayed her? She remembered the way he had kissed her at the pictures, her last glimpse of him in the courtroom, the desperation in his dark blue eyes. He'd tried to reach her and a burly policeman had prevented him.

Oh, Luc, how has it all come to this?

Tears filled her lovely cinnamon eyes once more. She wondered what her parents were feeling this morning, if Luc was missing her, and, quite unable to help herself, Gina began to weep, wiping her tears and nose with her hands since she couldn't seem to find a hanky. That must have been in her bag too.

'Shut yer noise,' Alice muttered, without moving a muscle. 'Crying won't do no good. There's nobody to hear you, save me, and I couldn't give a tuppeny damn how miserable you are. Keep your mouth shut, your head down, and do your time, that's my motto. You'd do well to follow it.'

Carmina began almost at once to plan her wedding. It gave her enormous pleasure to think of her sister sitting in prison, utterly helpless, while she took her rightful place beside the man Gina had tried to steal from her. Serve the selfish little madam right.

Luc seemed slightly bemused by it all, as if he didn't rightly know what had hit him. He'd soon see which side his bread was buttered on, once they were married. Carmina intended to be a good wife to him, to never let him lift a finger. She'd do anything and everything to make him happy, look after him well and swamp him with love. And she would never let him out of her sight for a minute.

She'd bought herself a ballerina-length wedding dress in a lovely floaty tulle, very like the one she once saw at Kendals, but the wedding would have to take place quickly, before she began to show and while she could still squeeze into it. She could feel this baby growing inside her by the day.

'Do you think it should be a Register Office affair, or dare we ask Father Dimmock to do the honours?' Carmina asked Luc.

Luc simply gazed at her without speaking.

'Well, what do you think? We need to call the banns,

book the church or whatever, organise a small reception, order flowers from Betty Hemley. Weddings take a great deal of organising so what sort would you like?'

'Why would I care, it's nothing to do with me?'

Carmina let out a dramatic sigh. 'I can't get anything out of Mamma and Papa either yet decisions need to be made, and soon.'

'Quite honestly, I can't see this wedding ever taking place. We have nothing in common, we don't love each other and *that child you're carrying isn't mine*!'

Carmina laughed as she reached up and kissed his nose. 'Nobody but you and I knows that for a fact, lover-boy, and I ain't telling, so stop hankering after Gina and start thinking of the benefits.' She began to unbutton her blouse to reveal a voluptuous cleavage.

'Drat you, Carmina! No good will come of your lies, no good at all.'

'It will, if I want it to. Go on, kiss me, why don't you?' She rubbed herself against him like a cat. 'You know you're dying to. Don't you fancy a little taste of what you'll be getting every night when we're man and wife? You might as well, since everyone assumes you have already.'

'You disgust me!' And Luc walked away while Carmina laughed as if it were all a great joke.

'OK, leave the wedding arrangements to me, I'll organise everything myself. Don't you worry about a thing.'

'Please yourself, but remember the groom might not even bother to turn up,' he yelled back at her over his shoulder.

'Oh, I think he will. Stop fighting me, Luc. You know you want me, so why not admit it?'

Security, discipline and good order were, apparently, the priorities of prison life, or so Alice informed Gina, the practical application of which she found chilling in those first few days.

She witnessed one young woman being dragged to her cell by two officers, her 'crime' being that she'd made too much fuss over not being allowed to have her children come to visit her.

Another day Gina could hear the girl in the adjoining cell vomiting violently but nobody came to her aid. When someone called out to the women officers to help, their cries were met with an order to shut up and mind their own business, although not quite so politely worded.

The next morning the girl was found with her arms and legs covered in deep scratches, an injury she'd carried out with her own blunt nails.

'The poor lass is filled with anger,' Alice explained. 'She'll be put in the padded cell now, wrapped in a strait-jacket and locked up in solitary for her own good, or so they'll say, till she learns to control herself better.'

'But it's not her fault she's ill,' Gina objected.

'They'll say it was. They'll say she forced her fingers down her own throat just to get attention, like the injuries the poor lass inflicts upon herself. The screws either don't care or think what the hell does it matter, she's only a flamin' prisoner.'

'Something should be done to help the poor girl.'

Alice shrugged. 'None of our business. Like I say, love, keep your head down.'

Gina resolved to do her utmost to follow the advice advocated by her cell-mate. She swore that she would keep her own counsel and remain calm at all times. She would not engage in conversation with the other inmates, would do her utmost, in fact, to keep out of their way and avoid the possibility of trouble at all cost. Her aim was to be an exemplary prisoner in the hope that good behaviour would lead to the authorities realising their mistake, which would surely result in an early release.

But it soon became evident that making such a decision was one thing, carrying it out quite another.

On the second day as Gina stood in line to collect her soup, the woman serving her asked: 'Are you Italian?'

Thinking she was meaning to be friendly, Gina smiled and agreed that she was.

The woman spat in her soup. 'My husband were killed in Italy during the war trying to protect you lot, and all you did is join the side of our enemies.'

Gina was appalled and quickly pushed the dish away. 'Why blame me? It's not my fault. I've never even lived in Italy. Can I have another soup, please?'

'What's this, being fussy over your food, Bertalone? What do you think this is, the Ritz?' Allenby, the reed-thin woman officer with the sorrowful eyes who'd dealt with Gina that first day, suddenly appeared at her elbow.

'This woman spat in it. I can't possibly eat it now.'

'Eat it or do without. We don't tolerate fussy, toffee-nosed folk in here.'

'But . . .'

'She's not hungry,' Alice said, pushing Gina away from the counter.

'But I am, I'm starving,' Gina protested. 'It's not fair that that woman should ruin my soup.'

'This is prison, love, nothing is fair in here.'

Gina lost her appetite following this unpleasant incident. She'd never felt victimised before and it was a deeply unsettling experience. Her hunger became a gnawing ache in her belly which she did her best to ignore. In her naivety she'd imagined that prisoners would support each other against the prison officers. Alice, however, constantly drummed into her the fact that this was not so, and that as a girl from a good home she was a natural target for malice and mischief.

But if the empty days seemed difficult and friendless, the nights were even more lonely and frightening. There would be the chilling echo of slamming doors and then would come the quiet sobbing. She'd think of Mamma and Papa, her lovely brothers and sisters, of Luc, and then have to stuff the corner of the sheet into her mouth to stifle her own quiet sobs. How would she get through this? How would she survive?

Father Dimmock was more than willing to perform the wedding ceremony since he'd known Carmina from when she was a baby, and the entire Bertalone family were valued members of his flock. Her parents showed little interest in the arrangements, except to insist that it should be a simple affair with the least possible fuss.

'Your sister is in prison, remember, so it wouldn't be fitting to put on a big celebration.'

Papa asked if she had yet been to see Gina to explain to her what was happening. Carmina pouted a bit and huffed and puffed but finally admitted that no, she hadn't. She hated the thought of even setting foot in that awful, smelly place. She was quite sure that it would smell, and be full of dreadful people, all doing horrible things to poor Gina – or so she hoped.

She wanted her stupid sister to suffer, as she herself had suffered.

What she hated most though was that her parents still couldn't do enough for this precious daughter, while taking little, if any, interest in her own coming wedding, which was surely far more important. Even now that she had let them down badly, Gina was still the favourite.

'You should go and see her,' Papa was saying. 'She needs you. She needs us all. You should tell her personally about what is going on between yourself and Luc. It isn't pleasant being locked up in that place. She needs to know she's not alone.'

'It's not my fault she's in Strangeways,' Carmina retorted. Another lie, but she was too used to telling them by now to even notice. Besides, being locked up surely wouldn't greatly trouble Gina. Wasn't her sister used to being confined to her room for long periods? And she deserved to be punished. She was still a thief, after all, if not quite the kind everyone thought.

Carmina was suddenly tired of being made to appear

the guilty one. 'Why *should* I go, Papa? Gina was the one who did the stealing. She didn't just take those scarves and stuff, she stole *my* boyfriend. I've no wish to go near. I'm not sure Gina and I have anything left to say to each other. Let her stew in her own juice for a bit, that's what I say. Isn't prison supposed to teach you a lesson?'

'Carmina!' Papa looked astonished and deeply troubled by this outburst. 'I won't have you blame Gina. It not right. She is innocent, remember that.'

Carmina gave a careless shrug, put the problem right out of her mind and got on with planning her wedding.

38

Amy and Patsy

In the weeks following, Chris couldn't stop himself from continually thinking about that dreadful anonymous letter. Who would send such a thing, and why? Somebody with a malicious mind. But could it be true that his wife was having an affair? It didn't seem possible, and yet she had taken to going out on her own quite a bit recently.

And she'd changed.

She seemed ready to start up a debate about politics for no other reason than to be argumentative, so far as Chris could tell, even though Amy claimed it was no more than a desire to clarify her own thoughts.

'Did you realise that the US, Russia, and ourselves are meeting in Geneva to discuss a ban on nuclear testing?'

'No, I didn't know,' Chris would mutter. 'Should I?'

'Of course. Every right-minded citizen should take an interest in current affairs. And it's long past time they did put a curb on testing, although they're moving with the speed of a snail.'

Or she would launch a tirade against traffic problems, the new parking meters, the lack of decent housing, the bank rate, a new drug called thalidomide that was having terrible consequences, and Chris could hardly keep pace with her latest obsession.

She'd also changed her style of dress too and adopted the beatnik look. She'd taken to wearing circular skirts in jazzy colours, black tights and ballet shoes. Chris did not approve.

'I preferred the pastel colours you used to wear, the pretty pinks and blues. And what happened to all your print cotton dresses?'

Amy twirled before the mirror and told him they were quite out of date. 'Really square. Anyway, what does it matter what I wear, so long as I look good? I'm saving a few pounds each week for our house fund, now that I've got part-time work, so I'm surely entitled to a bit of spending money.'

Chris assured his wife that he had no objection to her spending money on herself, only on the clothes she chose to wear. 'And I don't like that scarf tied round your neck. It makes you look cheap.'

Amy laughed as she kissed him. 'What an old fuddy-duddy you're turning into. Don't be so old fashioned. Anyway, I haven't bought many clothes. I don't need them. I'm dead against consumer capitalism. It will ruin everything.'

'Will it?' Chris asked, not quite certain what that was.

'I feel the need to express myself, to be free to say and do whatever I choose,' Amy explained.

She'd watched her friend Patsy taking on a partnership with Clara Higginson, Lizzie Pringle running her own business as she and Aunty started manufacturing their own sweets and chocolates. Dena too had her sewing room while Amy herself felt in danger of turning into a frumpish housewife before she was even twenty-one.

'I thought you *were* free,' Chris grumbled. 'Are you saying that being married to me is tying you down?' His tone was clipped, his hurt showing.

Amy didn't notice his distress, she was too busy clasping a broad black elastic belt around her waist, thinking how well she'd lost the weight in the months following the birth. She was also thinking about the next CND meeting that very evening. They were planning a demonstration in Albert Square in a few weeks' time, which was all very exciting. She supposed she really should have told Chris by now that she'd joined, but the longer she left owning up to it the harder it became.

Even the memory of the letter which had caused her young husband such distress had quite slipped from her mind. She'd assumed it to be business related, something to do with the bakery. In any case, her own needs right now seemed to be taking priority in her thoughts.

She teasingly tweaked his nose. 'Of course I don't feel tied down by marrying you, you idiot. But you're so busy with the bakery now that your dad has largely retired, I don't see quite so much of you as I used to. I understand you have to work hard, so that we can get on and provide a good future for our child. I don't want you thinking I'm dissatisfied, but I need something other than babies to think about. I need to express myself in other ways, outside of the home. A woman has rights too, you know. I want to have a voice.'

'I thought you already had one?' Chris said, tight-lipped. 'You certainly have plenty to say, and I've never denied you any rights.'

All this talk of freedom troubled him deeply. Amy's entire behaviour was a huge worry. She'd changed so much; in her attitude, in the fact that she'd started work so soon after baby Danny had been born, even in the way she dressed. He'd tried to dismiss the letter as mischief-making, yet he was becoming increasingly alarmed that there might be something in it after all. The prospect of his lovely Amy having an affair with another man made him feel sick to his stomach. He couldn't bear it, he really couldn't.

Amy was laughing at him again, as if he were some sort of joke. 'I mean that I want a voice in our future, in what kind of a world we provide for our son. In world affairs. I care about democracy, don't you? I refuse to be dictated to by governments who think they have all the answers.'

'Why does everything always come round to politics with you? Where are you getting all of this stuff from?'

He knew his tone was cold and sharp, as it so often was these days, but he felt so confused, and deeply unhappy. He'd followed her once or twice, to see where she went, but hadn't yet seen her with any strange man, hadn't seen her go anywhere of interest at all. But then he was often stuck in the house babysitting when she was out gallivanting of an evening, and he couldn't follow her then, could he? His mother would play pop if she caught him wheeling the baby out in the damp night air, even if it was summer.

But Chris didn't care to be dubbed as a fuddy-duddy, or old- fashioned simply because he disapproved of her dressing like a beatnik, even though she still looked lovely. He wanted his own sweet Amy back. He wanted to hold her and kiss her and not be forever embroiled in difficult discussions about consumerism and democracy.

And they still hadn't got going yet on their Sunday love-making sessions, as they'd planned. Somehow, he didn't have the heart to start, not since he'd received that letter.

'Did you know that Chris has been checking up on you?'

Patsy and Amy were sitting in the ice-cream parlour enjoying a banana split. Scoops of strawberry, vanilla and chocolate ice cream had been smothered in chopped pineapple, whipped cream and maraschino cherries, and liberally decorated with crushed nuts, coconut and strawberry syrup. Really quite delicious.

Amy looked up in surprise. 'When? Why?'

Patsy grinned. 'Perhaps he thinks you're having an affair with Jimmy Ramsay.'

Amy almost choked on a pineapple chunk. 'Don't be daft, with the fat butcher? Never!'

'Oh, then you don't dismiss the idea of an affair quite out of hand then?'

She laughed. 'You know I'm a one-man girl, but go on, tell me what it was Chris really wanted.'

Patsy licked cream from her spoon then slid another piece of banana into her mouth, making little satisfied humming noises. After a lengthy moment to savour the delicious flavour she admitted that she'd no idea. 'He asked if you'd been round to ours on some evening or othcr, a Thursday, I think it was. I said no, he'd got it wrong, that it was a Friday afternoon when we usually got together for a bit of a crack.'

Amy's face paled. 'Oh, dear.'

Patsy stopped eating to give her friend a quizzical look. 'What is it? Is there a problem?'

'There might be. I did say I was with you one Thursday evening so Chris wouldn't find out where I really was.'

Patsy's eyebrows met the fringe of her silver fair hair. 'Don't tell me you really are having it away with Jimmy Ramsay?'

'Stop it, this isn't a joke, this is deadly serious. The truth is I've joined the CND, and I can't pluck up the courage to tell Chris because I know he won't approve. Worse, he'll make me give it up and I really have no intention of doing so.'

Now it was Patsy's turn to say, 'Oh, dear.'

'I know, it's all got a bit out of hand. The longer I leave it, the harder it is to tell him.'

'It's not a good idea to keep secrets, particularly from a husband. Tell him the truth, Amy. And tell him soon.'

'I will,' Amy agreed, staring into her ice cream. 'I will, I promise.' But both girls knew there was little conviction in her words.

* * *

Mavis remained a thorn in Amy's side. She objected strongly to her daughter-in-law going back to work, accusing her of neglecting her child for all that she took Danny with her. 'I want no grandson of mine growing up as a "latch-key kid".'

'He's not yet three months old. How could I give him a key?'

'Exactly,' Mavis said, as if she'd proved her point. 'Haven't I been shamed enough by Chris's father?' This was always the way she referred to her husband nowadays, ever since he'd set up home in his allotment shed.

'How is Thomas?' Amy asked, although she knew perfectly well since she visited him most days, taking him a plate of dinner, or collecting his dirty washing.

'I really wouldn't know,' Mavis sniffed, and then spotting a row of her husband's socks hanging on the clothes rack, added frostily, 'I hope he isn't taking advantage of you.'

Amy smiled and shook her head. 'Not at all.' Not half so much as *you* used to, she might have added, but managed to hold that acid comment in check. 'I do at least have running hot water, which he doesn't.'

'I've never refused to do his washing for him,' Mavis snapped, voice rising in high dudgeon. 'Nor did I suggest he live in that nasty little hut.'

'Hopefully he'll come home before winter sets in,' Amy said. 'Maybe you could suggest that he does. We don't want him catching pneumonia, do we?'

The expression on Mavis's face darkened, but no such promise was forthcoming. Switching the line of her argument, she returned instead to the inadequacies of Amy's housekeeping, running her finger along the edge of the mahogany dresser.

'It could do with a good wax polish, dear. I used to do it every week, remember? And this is a respectable street,' Mavis reminded her daughter-in-law, offcring her sour smile. 'I couldn't help noticing that you haven't donkey-stoned your doorstep, or the window-sills either. And don't forget to polish the letter-box. Standards must be maintained.'

'I've a new baby,' Amy patiently reminded her, elbow deep in soap-suds as she scrubbed nappies, baby vests and her husband's work overalls. They still hadn't got round to buying a washing machine, she'd been up half the night with Danny again, Chris was still in a sulk over something or other and she really wasn't in the mood for her mother-in-law this morning. 'I haven't time for such niceties.'

'Which exactly proves my point. You should never have removed my son into a slum like this. With your background, is it any wonder that you are quite incapable of looking after things properly?'

Right, Amy thought, that's it. I've had enough.

'Where are we going?' Chris grumbled, curiosity overcoming his black mood for a moment as a day or two later Amy dragged him along Champion Street and on to a bus heading for the city centre.

'You'll find out soon enough when we get there,' giving him a sly wink which once would have made him chuckle. He'd always loved Amy's teasing sense of humour, now he felt infuriated by it, as if she had no right to be happy.

Amy wasn't interested in her husband's sulks today, only in bettering her own lot in life. Thomas was showing no inclination to return either to work or to his wife. His semi-retirement seemed to have turned into full-time, and he did little more than dig his plot and play cards with his friends. He also obstinately refused to say how he would cope when the nights started drawing in and the days grew colder. And if all of this meant that Chris was overworked, overtired and worried, well so was she.

She took Chris to the Electricity Showrooms where a young woman was holding a demonstration of a new washing machine. Chris was instantly alarmed and whispered furiously in his wife's ear.

'We don't need a washing machine. We can't afford one.'

'We *do* need one, and we'll *have* to afford one,' Amy insisted. 'I can't go on like this, washing everything by hand, not and hold down a job as well.'

'You don't have to work,' Chris protested. 'That was *your* idea.'

'It's a necessity,' Amy patiently pointed out, 'if we are ever to get out of this house your mother calls a slum.'

'Take no notice of her, she over-dramatises everything. Come on, we're going home.'

He took hold of her arm, about to march her out of the shop when the young woman clapped her hands to welcome them to the demonstration, announcing she was about to show them something truly wonderful.

'Now, gentlemen, which would you prefer to come home to, an exhausted wife and a house full of wet sheets and nappies, or a beautiful wife content with her lot, dinner on the table and the laundry already dried, folded and put to air?'

Chris paused to think about this for a moment and Amy took advantage of his hesitation to gently push him nearer to the front.

She could see how the demonstrator flirted unashamedly with the husbands, appealing to their desire for comfort and no hassle in their lives. And as she fluttered her eyelashes at the men, and told them how economical a Hoovermatic was to run, she managed to give sideways smiles and little winks to the women, to prove that she was really on their side.

She talked of 'superlative water washing action that gives the cleanest, quickest and most thorough wash', of a full family wash taking only half an hour; of automatic timers and controls for all types of fabric. She pandered to the men's love of technical details while assuring the women the machine would be easy to operate and the stainless-steel tub wouldn't rust or chip.

It all worked splendidly and at the conclusion, when the startlingly white shirt had been put through the spin dryer and hung up on a hanger to air, Chris was easily persuaded to sign a hire purchase agreement on the promise that one of these marvellous machines would be delivered to their door the very next day.

'Can we just take a peep at these new electric cookers

while we're here?' Amy suggested, thinking it was worth a try as she seemed to be on a winning run.

But that was one step too far for Chris who instantly hustled her out of the shop before she spent any more money he didn't have. Still, it was a start, Amy thought with secret joy. No more scrubbing messy nappies by hand. Utter bliss!

Let her mother-in-law find fault with that!

39

Gina

September came in balmy and mild, the trees by the River Irwell rich with scarlet berries and the smell of bonfires. Each morning Betty Hemley's stall was bright with chrysanthemums, the market bustling with huge lorries bringing potatoes from Norfolk, apples from Kent, oranges and lemons from the continent. Small vans carrying local produce edged their way between the stalls to deposit crates of cabbages and leeks, peas and carrots from the farms of Cheshire and Lancashire, or fish from Grimsby and Whitby.

Gina had loved to watch all of this activity from her bedroom window. She missed looking out upon the familiar stalls with their iridescent display of mackerel, cod and salmon, the cries of the fishmongers calling out their wares as they gutted and sliced. She missed the sound of canvas flapping in the rain, of people laughing and shouting, the cheerful banter that was a focal part of any market.

Even when she'd been ill and confined to her room, she'd never felt quite so isolated as she did now.

She was struggling to learn the rules and to toe the line. She'd put her name down for any number of education courses and workshops from basketwork to

Egyptian history, from cookery to embroidery. Anything to fill each long day, to help maintain her sanity. Perhaps then prison wouldn't be quite so bad, she thought. Losing her liberty was bad enough without losing her mind too.

Unfortunately things didn't quite work out as she'd hoped. More often than not the class would be cancelled. She would be called upon to do kitchen duties, work in the laundry, or to sew the coarse prison dresses, or simply be left with yet more empty hours to fill.

She soon learned that while much was offered in theory to rehabilitate and educate the prisoners, little took place in practice. Wisely, she made not one word of complaint. She'd learned that lesson too.

Discovering that the prison housed a library, Gina tried to fill her time with reading. She borrowed countless books, gobbling them up quickly at first, as she would at home, eager to finish one story and move on to the next. Experience, however, taught her to slow down, as there were times when the library would be locked, possibly for days on end, for no apparent reason, or perhaps because something had happened to displease the staff and it was considered necessary to inflict punishment upon them all. Once again she would be left staring into space for hours on end, with nothing to read and too afraid to risk borrowing a book from another inmate.

And every morning she would queue for what seemed like hours in the hope of a shower, or better still a bath, and not complain if she missed out, which very often she did. The other women, the old hands who'd been here for months or even years, would shove ahead of her in the queue, steal her soap, or trample on her towel, and Gina never dared to object.

She kept her head down, as instructed by Alice, and said not a word. But the endless empty hours were stultifying, leaving her mind numb with boredom and paralysed by fear.

Gina discovered that some of the staff appeared friendly enough, one in particular, a plump woman known as Wilcox with dark curly hair, cut excessively short, very like Gina's younger brother, Alessandro. She made a point of talking to Gina and asking her how she was settling.

Gina admitted that she was finding it difficult. 'There's no one but Alice willing even to talk to me.'

Wilcox laughed. 'You'd be wise not to trust our Alice. Very fond of dipping her fingers into shop tills and other folk's pockets.'

'Yes, she told me, but only in order to feed her children.'

The woman laughed. 'Those would be the same two children who were taken into care when they were found abandoned while she plied her trade, would they?'

'Trade?'

'I surely don't have to draw a picture. Among her other many talents, our Alice is a prostitute.'

Gina was shocked. She tried not to be. She strived to appreciate that she'd entered a different world, and that Alice possibly had good reason for doing what she did. Yet a part of her shuddered at the thought of letting men do as they wished with you, quite unable to imagine ever being quite so desperate.

Even so, she stoutly defended her new friend. 'Oh, but she seems so nice, and has really been very helpful.'

'Don't try making friends in here, love,' Wilcox warned, oddly echoing Alice's own advice. 'Particularly since you're obviously from a decent home background and this place is a den of thieves, prossies and women not quite right in the head. Someone like you shouldn't be in a place like this.'

'I know. I keep saying I'm innocent but nobody will believe me.'

'Poor love!' The woman stroked Gina's smooth cheek, looked deep into her lovely dark-fringed, tear-filled eyes. 'Is there something I can do for you? Some little personal item you might need, for instance, to make life more comfortable?'

'Oh, yes, please. I've a photo of my boyfriend in my bag, but they took it from me at reception.' She still wanted it with her, still loved Luc, despite his betrayal. She couldn't seem to help herself. In any case, they'd been getting along so much better, ever since he'd kissed her in the cinema when they were watching Elvis sing 'Jailhouse Rock'. Their choice of film seemed almost prophetic in a way, she thought bleakly.

The woman officer smiled. 'I'll see what I can do, love.'

The picture was returned to her later that day.

'Oh, thank you so much,' Gina cried, hugging it to her, deeply grateful for this small act of kindness.

Wilcox squeezed her arm, her breath warm on Gina's face, smelling faintly of the rice pudding she'd eaten at dinner time. 'I'll think of a way you can repay the favour one day.'

Alice appeared, seemingly out of nowhere, and drew Gina firmly away. 'Are you stupid, or what? Don't mess with old Wilcox, for God's sake. What was she after? You don't get owt for nowt in this place.'

'She's let me have my boyfriend's photo back,' Gina said. 'I don't mind doing her a favour in return.'

'You will when you find out what it is.'

And by the time Alice had finished filling Gina in on some facts of life which had hitherto passed her by, she knew there was indeed nobody she could trust in this place, not here in Strangeways, nor back in Champion Street Market. She was on her own.

One morning during what was known as association when the cell doors were unlocked and the women were free to move about for a while, to play cards, attend a class if there was one, listen to the radio or simply chat, four women suddenly appeared at the door of Gina's cell, crowding in, filling the small confined space.

'So this is the new girl, eh?' said one, clearly the leader. She was taller than Gina by several inches, athletic and strong with a long, narrow face framed by greasy blonde hair, a high forehead and green, heavy-lidded eyes that seemed to rake over Gina with cold distaste. Her mouth was all dry and cracked, and running with sores.

'Me name's Lorna Griffith but you can call me Griff.

Everyone else does. Have you explained how things work in here?' she demanded of Alice, without taking her gaze off Gina who was visibly shaking. The three girls who accompanied her were poking about in the cell, riffling through their few belongings and throwing things around; turning back the sheets and blankets on her bunk, stripping the pillow case off Gina's pillow, searching through her clothes. Gina hated them for this intrusion.

'She came in wi' nowt,' Alice told them. 'Yer wasting yer time. She's clean as a whistle.'

'Oh, dear, nothing to contribute to the Griff fund then? I'm sorry to hear that.'

'She doesn't even smoke,' Alice said.

Gina said nothing. She'd no idea what they were looking for but prayed they'd soon grow bored and leave.

'Maggie, add her to the sheet,' Griff instructed a small wiry woman with red hair and a beautiful heart-shaped face. Her mouth was a perfect cupid's bow, seeming to curl up at the corners as if she were smiling over some secret known only to her.

The expression on Griff's own face might have been classed as a smile, if you considered a slight stretching of her sour cracked mouth worthy of the word. 'A girl like you needs looking after. I dare say Alice here has explained? Sadly, some girls take more looking after than others. With a lovely face like yours, you'll be very popular with the bent screws, and hated by the old lags, if you catch me drift.'

She stepped closer to tower over Gina, her voice

dropping to a hissing whisper. 'I'll be generous though, since it's your first week, and settle for a shilling a day.'

'I don't understand. A shilling a day for what?'

'Nay, Alice, You said you'd told this lass the facts of life, in prison terms, that is, though perhaps not quite clearly enough, eh? A bob a day my little innocent, is for protection.'

'But I haven't any money,' Gina protested, hating the whining note in her own voice but fear was overwhelming her for she really didn't know how to deal with this frightening woman, or what she was offering to protect her from.

'Your family isn't short of a bob or two, I'll warrant, and they'll be only too happy to make your life as comfortable as possible during your stay here. Have a word with them when next they visit.' Turning back to Alice, she said, 'Fill her in on the fine details, love, and do it properly this time. You know I don't like to be messed about.'

Then pinching Gina's cheek, she showed off a row of bad teeth in an evil smile. 'Who else is there to look after you, chuck, but good old Griff? And by the look of you, scrawny thing that you are with that limp, you'll need a lot of attention, wouldn't you agree, Alice me old chum? A cripple always costs extra.'

Griff and her band of mischief-makers turned to go but Gina's face had turned crimson. Something had snapped inside her, that part of her which hated to be referred to as a cripple. 'I'll pay you nothing, not a bean! I won't be bullied just because I have a limp, and don't you dare call me names!'

The silence following this unwise outburst was terrible to behold. The woman's green eyes seemed to blaze, her entire body swelled and puffed out, her face turning purple. Gina was certain, in that moment, that Griff, as she termed herself, would lash out and strike her. A part of her almost wished that she would, then she could hit back and get rid of some of the pent-up anger that had built up inside without her even realising it.

Instead, Griff burst out laughing then perched herself on Gina's bunk, pulled down her knickers and urinated on the mattress that had been stripped bare by her friends. They seemed to find this highly amusing and roared with laughter while Gina looked on, her face a mask of horror.

When she was done, the girl calmly pulled up her knickers again and said, 'Oh, dear, you seem to have wet your bed, chuck. What a shame! And getting someone to dry it for you in this rotten hell-hole is well nigh impossible.'

How Gina would have dealt with this she was never to discover as they were interrupted at this point by Wilcox. 'Visitor for you, Bertalone. Hey, what's going on here?'

Gina's heart leapt at mention of a visitor as it always did when her parents came to see her. They represented her only contact with the outside world. She snatched up a comb to start dragging it through the snarls of her tousled hair.

Alice took a hasty step forward to block the officer's view of the wet mattress. 'Nowt's going on. They were just going.'

'Aye, we were,' Griff agreed. 'Come on, girls, let's leave our new friend to her visitor. We'll talk again later, Gina love, after they've gone. Don't forget what I said now. I'm always ready to help a newcomer.'

'That would be a first,' Wilcox drily remarked. 'Get on your way, Griffith.'

Gina stood, comb frozen in her hand at the thought of a continuation of this difficult conversation, while the girl and her trio of malicious helpers strolled nonchalantly away, clearly attempting to make the point that they were leaving of their own free will and not because Wilcox had told them to.

The woman officer gave Gina a shove, breaking her out of her terrified paralysis. 'Stop that titivating and look sharp about it. We haven't all day.'

Gina was marched along the wing, Alice's parting words ringing in her ears. 'Sometimes, it's hard to keep your head down low enough.'

It wasn't Papa or Mamma waiting for her in the empty visitors' hall, but Luc. He stood up when she appeared and Gina's heart sang as she saw the expression on his face. He did love her, after all. It was written there for all to see. She thought she could tolerate any amount of abuse in this hateful place if she could be certain that he still loved her and would wait for her.

She half ran towards him but Wilcox put out a hand and made her sit across the table from him, instructing the two lovers not to even think of touching each other, or he'd be sent packing.

Gina bleakly nodded. Wilcox moved back a few paces

but her looming presence made her realise that they weren't even to be granted the luxury of a few private moments.

Luc too seemed unnerved by the large woman. He cleared his throat, clenched and unclenched his hands, desperately wanting to grasp Gina's but not quite able to find the courage to defy the officer. He looked beseechingly at the girl he loved, his gaze telling her how much he wanted to hold her and kiss her while his voice calmly said, 'How are you?'

'Fine.' She'd never felt less fine in her life.

'Are you getting enough to eat?'

'Yes.' She was almost permanently hungry, not trusting any food prepared for her following the incident of the woman spitting in her soup.

'And your cell, is that OK?'

Gina nodded, quite unable to answer. How could she tell him that right now it looked as if a tornado had hit it and a fellow inmate had just peed on her mattress? 'How are *you*?' she managed. 'And Mamma and Papa?'

'They're coming next week, as usual. They want you to know that they are doing everything they can to get you out of here. Your father says he'll prove your innocence if it costs him every penny he possesses.'

Gina's eyes brimmed with tears. 'Tell them I love them . . . that I miss them . . . and my brothers and sisters.'

Luc nodded. 'I will. They were desperate to see you this week too but I persuaded them to let me come. There's something I need to tell you . . . something important . . . and I didn't want you to hear it from anyone else.'

Gina's heart now flipped in the opposite direction, sinking to her boots. 'Something bad has happened, hasn't it? Is it to do with Carmina?' She saw how he avoided her probing gaze. 'You're back with her, aren't you?'

'No . . . well, yes . . . at least she thinks so, but not in the way you mean. It's difficult to explain but the fact is . . . Drat it, Gina, there's no easy way to say this, Carmina *is* pregnant, after all, so . . .'

He got no further. Gina was on her feet in a flash, walking away from him. 'Goodbye, Luc. Don't bother to come again.'

Luc leapt to his feet and called after her in desperation, 'Noooooo! Don't go, Gina, don't go till I've explained. *Listen to me*!'

But she wasn't listening to anyone, certainly had no wish to listen to Luc Fabriani ever again. Wilcox was at her side in a second, ready to unlock the door and allow Gina back on to the wing. Luc was left punching his fist into the table, his last hopes and dreams shattered.

40

Amy and Chris

The very next time Amy said she was going out for the evening, Chris made secret plans to acquire a babysitter. He arranged for Dorothy Thompson, Aunty of any number of foster children, to look after Danny for a couple of hours. He needed to be completely free to follow his wife and see exactly where she went. He wanted this matter resolved, once and for all, even if she was seeing another man. Not knowing for sure was doing his head in.

'You don't mind me going out this evening, do you, love?' Amy asked him as they lay together in their lovely new double bed. Since Chris was always up before dawn to bake bread and Danny kept them awake half the night, Amy had taken to joining her husband when he took a nap in the afternoon. With luck, the baby would also sleep for an hour or two.

Chris assured her, with as much conviction as he could muster, that he didn't mind in the least. 'Why ask me? You must do as you please, you generally seem to.'

Inwardly flinching at his indifferent tone, Amy cast him an anxious glance. She was growing increasingly concerned by this coolness towards her. A distance seemed to be growing between them and she couldn't work out why that was. Danny was over two months old now and they still hadn't re-established marital relations. It was getting almost as bad as when they were first married. Except then they'd felt inhibited by the close proximity of his mother on the other side of paper-thin walls. Now they had their own home, so what was the problem? Determined to change all of that she tugged back the sheets, climbed astride him and started kissing him very passionately.

'What are you doing?' he cried, as if a wife had no right to be kissing her husband.

'I'm trying to show you that I'm not as tired as I once was, and that I'm in full working order again. Also, if you've noticed, there's no sound coming from Danny's cot yet, so we could make the best of what time we've got, eh?'

Chris started. 'Maybe we should go and check on him.'

'I already have and he's fine.' She peeled off her nightdress so that he could enjoy the rosy fullness of her breasts. 'I've really filled out, don't you think?' she teased.

Chris swallowed. He couldn't ever remember her looking more lovely, and he loved Amy so much. More than anything he longed to make love to his beautiful wife but the memory of that anonymous letter held him back. Amy had said that she was going out this evening, yet she hadn't told him where. Nor had he asked. Perhaps he should.

'Where are you off to tonight then?'

Amy was peeling off his baker's T-shirt and kissing his chest, her toes scrabbling at his shorts in an effort to pull those down too. She longed to be completely honest and casually remark that she was actually attending a meeting of the CND. She'd been riddled with guilt for a while after Patsy told her that Chris had tried to check up on her. And she'd tried to tell him, she really had. Many times. She would deliberately steer the conversation round but he always managed to change the subject. He hated it when she talked about politics. And this certainly wasn't the right moment. This was the nearest they'd got to love-making in months.

'Has anyone told you that you talk too much? Come on, Chris, we haven't got long before Danny wakes for his next feed. Touch me. Kiss me. I can't do this on my own.'

She was running her fingers through his hair, flicking her tongue over his mouth. She blew a few hot breaths into his ear and Chris could resist her no longer. With a low groan he snatched her to him and began to kiss her hungrily, swiftly turning her on to her back so that he could make love to her properly. It felt so wonderful to be holding Amy again, to be loving her. He cried out as he sank into her, so needing to be a part of her.

'Cooee, anyone in? It's only me.'

Chris was out of bed in seconds. Amy pulled the sheet over her head in silent agony.

Amy dressed for the meeting as she always did in something bright and trendy. Tonight she chose her red Capri trousers and a striped top, and she couldn't fail to notice how Chris appraised her as she came downstairs. His eyes seemed to be asking why she was making herself so pretty just to chat with Patsy.

She might have told him then but, perhaps because of the disastrous afternoon love-making session, Amy felt even more need than usual for some free time of her own, out of the house.

Her mother-in-law had stayed for at least an hour, drinking tea, talking to her son and complaining about Amy's Madeira cake. Too heavy, and not enough cherries. Amy hadn't expected the woman to actually enjoy it, but it was annoying that Mavis didn't seem to appreciate the effort it took even to find the time to produce something home-baked when she was run off her feet with a baby and two part-time jobs. Amy wondered why she bothered at all when she was married to a baker, except that she was also trying to find some way to please her husband and to lighten his load. Thomas still hadn't set foot in the bakery for weeks.

They'd had words after Mavis had gone, Amy blaming Chris for never locking the front door and Chris arguing that his mother would think it odd if he did.

'Who cares what she thinks, we surely deserve some privacy?' Amy had argued.

'You know she always likes to pop in for a cuppa of an afternoon and see little Danny after he wakes from his nap. How was I to know you were going to jump on me like that?'

'I shan't bother next time,' Amy had yelled right

back, tears welling in her eyes as she stalked off upstairs to get ready for her night out. He'd followed her, of course, and they'd both calmed down after a while, although it was sad that at one time after a quarrel they couldn't wait to make up in wild passionate love-making.

This afternoon Chris simply went to make them both a cup of tea. So unromantic.

Amy despaired of ever getting close to him again. She'd thought everything would be wonderful once they were in a house of their own, but it didn't seem to be working out that way. What with the baby exhausting them both, and her mother-in-law's interference, the last thing she needed right now was an argument about a radical peace movement of which he'd be bound to disapprove.

She kissed his brow. 'I won't be late.'

'Where will you be should I need you?' he asked, again with that coolness to his tone.

Amy hesitated, guilt bringing a flush of colour to her cheeks. She turned away to fuss with her bag and comb her hair. 'Why would you need me? Danny is asleep and will hopefully stay that way. Put your feet up and listen to the wireless. Isn't there a match on? I'm popping over to see your dad for a start, to take him the rest of my failed Madeira cake, then I shall find someone to gossip with. Don't I always?'

Five minutes later she was out in the street, breathing in the cool night air, an uneasy feeling in her chest that this secret was beginning to weigh heavier than that flipping cake.

Before she'd reached the end of the street Chris had rushed upstairs, collected Danny and was hurrying round to deposit him with Dorothy Thompson. By the time Amy had finished chatting to his father, he'd be free to follow her and make one more effort to discover whether what the letter had told him about his wife was true.

Thomas was sitting in his hut, as always, with the cat, Blackie, on his knee, smoking his pipe when Amy tapped on the door.

'Come in, it's a shop,' he joked.

'I've fetched you a piece of cake,' Amy said, setting the tin down on an upturned orange box. 'Although Mavis says it's a bit heavy and doesn't have enough cherries in it.'

'Eeh, that's all right, chuck, I'm not too fussed about cherries but I do love soggy cake.'

'Bless you. Shall I put the kettle on?'

They sat companionably together, drinking tea and eating deliciously moist Madeira cake which Thomas declared wasn't half bad for an amateur. Outside, in the cool of the autumn evening, Chris huddled beneath a tree, waiting.

'Chris misses you at the bakery,' Amy said. 'Do you think you might feel up to helping him occasionally, when he's particularly busy?'

Thomas regarded her in all seriousness. 'Happen, but it's his business now. Better he make his own way. He doesn't want his old dad hanging round his neck all the time. He gets enough of that from his mother.

How're you getting on with my missus these days? Is it easier now you have a place of yer own?'

'Better, I think,' Amy agreed, with only the slightest hesitation in her voice. 'She's still very critical of my taking a part-time job, and played pop when she heard I was off out again tonight. She seems to think that a woman should never leave her own fireplace, or show any sign of a brain.'

Thomas reached for another slice of cake and chewed on it for a moment in silence. 'So where are you gallivanting off to this time? A bit of a chat with your friend Patsy, is it?'

Amy hesitated. She hated to lie. Of course she'd kept secrets before, like the time she hadn't told her parents that she and Chris were planning to elope to Gretna Green. But that was different. She and Chris had carried the weight of that secret together, and it had been an important one.

But she'd never kept a secret from her lovely husband before, nor told a lie in her life, not as such. Not even over this CND thing. She'd simply avoided telling Chris that she was involved with the organisation. When she said she was off to gossip with some friend or other, she nearly always managed to do just that, if not for quite as long as she claimed, although obviously there had been one or two occasions when she'd been late and had dashed off straight to her meeting. Guilt ate at her soul. Had that made it into a lie? Had Chris recognised it as such and was that the reason he'd apparently checked up on her with Patsy?

'Nowhere special,' she told Thomas now, prevaricating as usual.

'Well, so long as our Chris knows where you are and doesn't mind, what business is it of my wife's?'

Amy nibbled on her lower lip, then cast her father-in-law an anxious sideways glance. Did he too know she was keeping a secret? She'd come to love this old man. He was her friend and she hated to deceive him, hated to deceive Chris, had never meant to, not really. She'd been a coward and perhaps it was time she owned up.

Setting down her mug, she said, 'Actually, I was wanting your advice on this very subject, as a matter of fact,' and Amy began to tell Thomas all about her newly acquired passion.

She was late arriving at the meeting hall, rushing in all flustered and apologetic. Jeff Stockton made a space for her beside him and Amy quickly concentrated on what was being said. Jeff's girl-friend, Sue, was absent for once, but Jeff and his colleagues were well into planning the nuts and bolts of their next demonstration. Once she'd caught the drift of their argument, Amy was more than ready to voice her own opinions on the subject, often disagreeing with them.

'I don't think we need a band,' she protested. 'It's just an extra expense.'

'But we had one at Easter and it worked well. It certainly caught everybody's attention.'

'A silent vigil could be just as effective now though.'

Someone said, 'She's got a point. We've a serious

message to get across. We don't want to look as if we're just out for a good time.'

They thrashed the subject out thoroughly, along with several others about posters and banners, of trying to get an interview in one of the local papers, or even on the radio. In the end, as always, their decisions were governed by cost, so there was to be no music, and the banners would be home-made. Amy even found herself offering to make some handbills to push through letter boxes, although how she would manage that without alerting Chris to what she was up to, she'd no idea.

Yet hadn't she just promised her father-in-law that she would be honest and tell him about this secret passion of hers?

Amy's chat with Thomas had taken longer than she'd expected but his advice had been exactly the same as Patsy's. 'Don't keep secrets from your husband, it'll only rebound on you.'

Right at that moment, had she but known it, Chris was outside the Friends Meeting House, hiding behind a wall. He'd quietly followed her from the allotment, keeping well back so that she wouldn't see him, but he had no idea why she'd come to this place. Had she suddenly got religion? he wondered, and become a Quaker, although he knew that many clubs made use of these rooms so it could be any one of a number of women's organisations she was attending. She might have joined the WI, or the WVS, or a mother and baby group. Something perfectly innocent.

He was still there when Amy came out, and he saw at once what he had most feared. She was talking to a young man. He was tall and lanky with a shock of untidy brown hair. Chris wasn't close enough to see his face but his wife was standing right beside him, laughing up at him in that way he knew so well. The young man was laughing too, then cupping her face between his palms he growled at her, as if he were pretending to be a dog, or a man needing a woman. Then he affectionately ruffled her curls.

'You always were an argumentative soul.'

The young man's laughing voice carried clearly across to where Chris hid in the shadows.

He felt sick. He saw at once that it was all true what that letter had said. His wife was indeed having an affair, and this was her lover.

41

Carmina and Patsy

Carmina could hardly believe that September was here already, still with no firm date fixed for her wedding, although after a great deal of effort she had most of the arrangements in place, much to her satisfaction. The banns had been called, Father Dimmock easily persuaded to officiate, and the reception was to be held at the Co-operative Rooms. Not the most tasteful choice perhaps but since Papa had insisted on no fuss, there seemed little alternative.

She looked down at the list in her hand, ticking items off one by one. The flowers were ordered: white lilies with sprigs of orange blossom. Her gown was hanging in her wardrobe and she'd even warned Joyce that she would be needing a very special hair appointment.

'Isn't it fortunate, Mamma, that my sisters already have the bridesmaids' dresses you made?' Carmina said.

Carlotta glanced up from her needlework, surprised. 'But those are for Patsy's wedding, later in the autumn.'

'I'm sure she won't mind if the dresses are worn for my wedding too, particularly considering there is so little time.' Carmina patted her stomach with a meaningful smile, and Carlotta shuddered.

Only a few items on her list lacked a tick, indicating

the last remaining matters needing to be dealt with, the date being the most pressing. She really must speak to Luc, and try once more to pin him down on that.

He was still playing the reluctant groom. She was furious about his sulks, found it deeply embarrassing to be so snubbed. Her parents would give her questioning, quizzical looks whenever they asked if they might hope for a visit from their future son-in-law soon. Carmina nevertheless convinced herself that he was looking forward to the day every bit as eagerly as herself, just stubbornly refused to admit it.

It was no more than guilt that he felt for Gina now, and a misguided sense of loyalty.

Carmina also made a point of avoiding Alec Hall. She had no wish to see him, and he was the very last person who needed to know what was going on and why. Her parents had taken little persuasion to keep her delicate condition quiet while she made the necessary preparations, so by the time Alec discovered the facts, it would be too late. She and Luc would be man and wife.

'I will ask Patsy how she feels about that,' her mother tartly commented, pressing her lips together in a tight line, making it perfectly clear that she wasn't happy about any of this.

She'd deliberately left the arrangements entirely to Carmina, which was a great disappointment in a way. Carlotta had looked forward to arranging her own daughters' weddings for years. First there had been Maria, and next would come Carmina and Gina, but nothing was turning out quite as she'd hoped.

Everything was wrong. She wished she could put her finger on when things had started to go awry, how Gina came to be in that horrible prison, but she couldn't work it out. It was all too frightening and dreadful.

'Why do we need to ask *her* permission?' Carmina sneered. 'I shall be married long before she is, and there isn't time to make a fresh set, so it's perfectly reasonable that my sisters should be allowed to wear their own bridesmaids' dresses.'

Carlotta sighed and promised she would do her best.

Patsy was puzzled. Everything seemed to be happening so fast. First Carmina was pregnant and rushing into a hasty marriage with Luc. Then she wasn't pregnant after all. Most strange.

Things had suddenly started going missing from her own hat stall, swiftly followed by the break-in at Hall's Music Shop and then, quite out of the blue, Gina was arrested and sent down on remand awaiting trial. How had that come about for goodness' sake? Gina was the last person on earth Patsy would have considered as a possible culprit of such a crime. The whole thing seemed incredible.

While his younger siblings moped about with long faces, Marc was beside himself with grief, talking of employing a top-rank lawyer to defend his sister.

All the Bertalones were naturally devastated except for Carmina, the sister closest to Gina in age, who seemed to be happily engrossed planning the wedding of the year.

Carmina alone seemed content, positively bubbling

over with happiness. She still served on the ice-cream cart, still helped Papa for a few hours each day in the ice-cream parlour when he was making his famous peach gelato or rum tortoni, and gave a very good impression of a cat who has swallowed a whole tub of ice cream.

Yet Luc, the supposed bridegroom, the man who had jilted Gina for her more beautiful sister, never came near. Patsy hadn't set eyes on the young man in weeks. He never called at the house, either to discuss the arrangements or even to see his bride. Most strange!

Patsy couldn't quite put her finger on what it was but something was badly wrong; something about this entire scenario smelt very fishy indeed.

When next Patsy came for supper, as she often did on a Friday, the sensitive subject of the bridesmaids' dresses was tactfully broached by an embarrassed Carlotta, except that she became so agitated that she reverted to rapid Italian.

'I wonder – in view of the circumstances – whether you would mind very much if the bridesmaids' dresses were worn at Carmina's wedding too? If you do mind, then they can wear something else, of course. We can buy them something new, if necessary. I really have no wish to spoil your wedding, Patsy.'

When this had been translated to her by Antonia, Patsy looked stunned for a moment but soon rallied. 'No, of course I don't mind. You certainly mustn't go to any expense on my account.'

The entire household seemed strangely muted. No

longer did Gabby and Giovanni happily squabble over Sorry! or Ludo. Marta no longer bossed anyone around, Antonia seemed to be constantly staring into space instead of being absorbed in a book, and Lela sat sucking her thumb in a corner. It was a scene far removed from the happy, bustling, loving family she'd come to know so well. There wasn't a jigsaw or marble in sight.

Patsy smiled at Carlotta, noting how the older woman's face had become lined with worry. 'By all means let the girls wear the dresses. Marc and I can't even think about our own wedding with all of this going on.'

Carlotta hugged her. 'You are like another daughter to me. So kind, so thoughtful, always thinking of others, just like my Gina.' Whereupon, she fled to her room in floods of tears.

Patsy sighed. 'It must be so difficult for her.' Then, as she thoughtfully considered Carmina, her future sister-in-law, she quietly added, 'I'm surprised you have the heart to organise a big fancy wedding in the midst of all of this?'

Carmina was not in the mood for one of Patsy's lectures. She thought she might go round and see Luc instead. They certainly needed to talk, to start making serious plans for their future together such as where they were going to live. And she fully intended to insist he work in the family business as they had a family to think about now. Yet she hadn't set eyes on him for days. Dear, darling Luc was still stubbornly doing his utmost to avoid her.

Carmina smiled to herself. He wouldn't be able to

do that for much longer. Not now they were indeed about to become man and wife. Her plan had worked even better than she'd hoped. Quite inspired. Her timing was perfect. All she'd really needed was to get rid of Gina.

'My wedding isn't going to be either big or fancy, but the fact that my sister is in jail is difficult for me too,' Carmina whined, reaching for her handkerchief and casting Patsy a sideways glance to see if she was convinced by this charade of misery as she dabbed at her eyes.

'Of course it is. It must be unbearably difficult for you, as it is for us all. Even more so considering your particular circumstances. I do understand your distress, Carmina. And how unfortunate, strangely coincidental in a way, that your pregnancy should be confirmed just as Gina is arrested.' Patsy gave her a quizzical look.

Carmina ground her teeth together but said no more. She merely shrugged her shoulders in that expressive way she had and walked away.

Patsy watched her in silence, making a private vow to keep a close eye on the situation.

It was one hot afternoon of this blissful Indian summer when Patsy was idling across the market in search of a strawberry ice to cool herself that she again spotted Carmina in deep conversation with Alec Hall.

This time they were clearly engaged in an argument, a fierce row in fact. Patsy stopped in her tracks, not wishing to draw too near and appear as if she were eavesdropping. She half turned away and pretended to be examining a collection of pretty buttons on a nearby stall. Even so, she couldn't help but overhear some of what was said.

'This is all your doing,' Alec spat the words at the girl and Carmina put back her head and laughed. He said something else that Patsy couldn't quite catch and then shouted, 'But I thought that was all over.'

Carmina made as if to turn away but he grabbed her arm and gave her a little shake.

Patsy didn't catch his next words either but whatever it was soon wiped the smile from Carmina's face. She blanched, then she was spitting back at him, her fury such that her voice rose to a pitch which carried easily back to Patsy.

'I don't care what *you* want! It's what *I* want that matters.'

Patsy half smiled to herself when she heard this. Wasn't that ever the case where Carmina was concerned? Now she was shaking herself free of his grip and stalking away, head held high. Alec stood where he was, clenching and unclenching his fists, the steam of his rage seeming to radiate around him.

Now what was all that about?

Patsy found the whole situation deeply troubling. Why would Carmina suddenly find herself pregnant just as Gina was arrested? The timing might not be important, yet somehow Patsy was convinced it couldn't be coincidence.

What if Luc's claims that he was innocent were justified? If so, then they needed to look elsewhere for the father of this child. Could it possibly be Alec? Patsy recalled witnessing that kiss, and now a furious row. No one exchanged such heated words unless they'd once been close. How close had Alec and Carmina *really* been?

Could this whole terrible mess of Gina being charged with burglary be yet another of Carmina's lies?

A chill ran down Patsy's spine at the thought. Dear Lord, surely even Carmina wouldn't go so far as to have her own sister arrested so that she could get her thieving little hands on the man she coveted?

When Marc came to collect her after work that evening, he found Patsy in a thoughtful mood as she tidied away after a busy day on the stall. He watched in silence for a moment as she locked away the hat trimmings, ribbons and sewing materials that she'd been using. Then, as she pulled down the metal blinds, carefully locking each one with a large padlock against intruders, he quietly reminded her that October was just around the corner and no decision had yet been made about their own wedding.

'At least Carmina's marriage plans seem to be coming along, even if ours aren't.'

He again begged her to at least come and view some flats with him. But with her mind still on the fierce argument she'd witnessed between Carmina and Alec, Patsy put Marc off yet again, making some excuse about being too busy preparing the autumn collection.

'So finding time for us isn't high on your list of priorities then?'

He sounded so bitter, so sad, that Patsy longed to

fall in with his plans but in her heart she felt this wasn't the right time to be thinking of their own happiness. 'Perhaps we should consider postponing our wedding for a little while.'

Marc looked at her, his face grim. 'Oh, Patsy, I really don't want to do that. I want us to find a nice flat together, enjoy a simple ceremony then settle down happily as man and wife. I don't want any of this other stuff, all this worry about Gina being in prison, unwanted pregnancies or Carmina stealing Luc from her. And my little sisters are so looking forward to wearing those dresses Mamma has made them.'

Patsy clicked the last padlock in place. 'They're going to wear them at Carmina's wedding instead.'

Marc was startled into silence, then his shoulders seemed to droop, his dark good looks to turn almost grey, if that were possible. 'Why is all this happening? It's dreadful!'

Patsy put her arms about his broad shoulders and kissed him, her eyes filling with a rush of tears to see this strong man she loved so much bowed by worry over his family. She wondered if she should voice her suspicion that these two events could be linked, that she believed Carmina might have played a major part in Gina's arrest?

She hadn't been fooled in the slightest by Carmina's display of emotion over Gina's plight. Those were nothing more than crocodile tears, and she still hadn't visited her sister in prison.

Dare she tell Marc about the row she'd witnessed between Carmina and Alec? And if she did, could she prove its significance? She had no proof, not a scrap, only a bad feeling growing ever stronger inside.

But Patsy's courage to broach this difficult issue failed her and, instead, she said, 'I don't understand what's happening either, love, really I don't. I only feel that right now Gina needs you more than I do. Our happiness can surely wait for a little while, perhaps till the spring? Of course, you could always call the wedding off completely if you wanted . . .' she began, but Marc quickly put a finger to her mouth.

'Don't even think such a thing, let alone say it. I just don't want you working too hard on this flippin' hat stall, that's all. But I accept that perhaps we shouldn't rush into starting a family too soon. You've every right to concentrate on your job and wait until you feel ready before having babies. There is, as you say, plenty of time.' Marc chuckled softly as he tweaked her nose. 'And I'm well aware that you're a very independent-minded young woman, and have every right to be so.'

'Oh, Marc, I do love you so much.'

'And I you. I want only to look after you.'

Patsy laughed. 'Now don't spoil it by robbing me of the independence you've just now assured me is my right. I'm not looking for a minder, only a husband, remember. So kiss me again. We can still do that, at least.'

'I want to do so much more,' Marc groaned, pulling her roughly into his arms. 'I hope this trial comes up quickly and my lovely sister is sent home soon, then we can get married and I can show you in every possible way how much I love you.'

He made a pretty good attempt right then, in the empty market hall, leaving Patsy all tousled and flushed. Then they walked slowly home, arms wrapped about each other, trying to hope for the best but each lost in their own sad thoughts.

42

Thomas, Amy and Chris

The heat of summer with its lazy days of eating ice cream and browsing amongst the stalls was finally over. Christmas was still too far distant for the market committee to have started putting up fairy lights or the big tree which by tradition stood in the small square. The air was filled with typical autumnal scents of chestnuts roasting and hot baked potatoes, home-made mint chocolate from Lizzie Pringle's Chocolate Cabin and the rich tang of oranges from Barry Holmes's stall.

A cold north-east wind blew in through the big double doors of the old Victorian iron-framed building. It whistled round folks' legs and made old ladies shiver and think longingly of their own firesides as they swiftly filled their shopping baskets with onions and potatoes, a few leeks and carrots from Holmes's Fruit and Veg, and a couple of chump chops from Ramsay's Butchers to make a nice lamb hotpot for tea.

Thomas was sitting in Belle's Café enjoying a bacon butty, as he so often was at this time of a morning. He had his copy of *Sporting Life* spread out on the blue-checked tablecloth before him, happily reading about likely winners for the two-thirty when a familiar voice at his elbow rudely interrupted his contentment. 'I thought I'd find you here.'

He was so startled he nearly knocked his mug of tea flying but managed to catch it just in time. 'Mavis, I didn't see you come in.'

His wife folded her arms across her corseted chest and looked down her long nose at him. 'Why would you, when you're too busy feeding your face?'

'A man has to eat.' Nevertheless, Thomas set down the bacon sandwich, unwilling to continue partaking of his breakfast beneath her eagle eye. 'Were you wanting summat?' he bravely enquired.

Thomas was surprised to note that she was wearing a different-coloured lipstick, a soft pink shade instead of her usual dark crimson. And her sagging cheeks, marred by a few over-large freckles, had been coated with a thick foundation cream instead of the usual dab of her favourite Goya face powder. It turned her face a sort of dull orange.

Mavis settled herself in the seat opposite, which surprised him even more. She set her handbag on her lap, folded her gloved hands on the table and regarded him with the kind of expression he could recall his old primary school headmistress giving him when she'd caught him climbing out of the classroom window one day, hell-bent on escape. He had a great longing to do something similar right now.

'I thought we'd have a few words.'

Thomas felt completely at a loss, wondering which particular words she might have in mind. He couldn't think, offhand, of anything he'd done wrong of late to offend her. Hadn't he been keeping well out of her way?

'I can take no more of this daft nonsense.'

Thomas didn't move a muscle.

'I decided it was long past time I put me foot down.'

And then she smiled at him. At least he assumed it was a smile. It had been so long since he'd witnessed such an expression on his wife's face that he couldn't be entirely certain.

'I was wondering when you were thinking of coming back home?' Mavis spoke through a mouth set so tight it seemed as if the question had been torn unwillingly from her lips.

'Eh?' Not an intelligent response, but the only one Thomas could come up with right at that moment.

'I thought with winter coming on . . .' She left the sentence unfinished. They both did. Thomas certainly had no inclination to predict where this conversation might be heading.

Blinking rapidly, Mavis took out her lavender-scented handkerchief and blew her nose upon it, leaving the tip of her nose all red and with a smear of orange foundation on the linen fabric. Then she dabbed at her eyes and gave a loud sniff. If it had been anyone else performing these actions Thomas would have said the woman was close to tears, but this was Mavis.

He cleared his throat, since some reply seemed to be expected of him. 'I don't quite understand what yer on about? I'm quite comfortable.'

'You can't possibly be comfortable. You can't spend

all winter living in that hut,' Mavis snapped. 'It wouldn't be right. And what will folk think?'

'Folk can think what they like, I don't much care.'

Mavis glowered, but seeing that she was making no progress she remembered how she'd promised herself to be patient with him, how strangely silent the house was without him. There seemed no purpose to her life any more, no focal point to her day without a husband to cook for, or tidy up after. She even resented the fact that her daughter-in-law was doing his washing for him.

However infuriating Thomas might be, he was still her husband. They were man and wife, bound together through life for better or for worse. And if she would have preferred a bit more of the former and a bit less of the latter, well, that couldn't be helped. It was a wife's duty to grin and bear her lot, whatever that might be. She couldn't bear the silence of waking up alone in that house any more, that was certain.

She reasserted the smile. 'It'll do your chest no good at all. You'll get bronchitis again.'

'I might, I might not. I'm sure I can cope. Anyroad, I'm staying put.'

Now she was deeply troubled, for he didn't seem in the least concerned. What on earth could she say to persuade the daft fool to see the error of his ways if he didn't care about the gossip permeating through the market about their quarrel, nor even about his own health?

But Mavis knew well enough who to blame for this state of affairs, this late rebellion in her normally docile husband.

'Staying put indeed. We shall see about that,' she said, putting away her handkerchief and closing her handbag with a loud click.

Belle Garside was talking to Sam Beckett from the ironmongery stall while he ate his egg and bacon breakfast. She had her arms folded, pushing up her magnificent breasts above the low-necked blouse she wore. And while she fluttered her eyelashes and flirted outrageously with him, as she so loved to do since Sam was a good-looking bloke, she was keeping half an eye on the little scene taking place in the far corner.

Mavis had been aware of the other woman's interest for some moments, and, getting briskly to her feet, marched right over. 'If you think I don't know what's been going on then you've another think coming. I'm no fool, so don't take me for one.'

'Excuse me?' Belle said, confused by this unexpected attack, coming quite out of the blue.

'It's about time you got an husband of your own, if you can find one, instead of pinching other folks.'

Two swift steps took her behind the counter where a large pan of Heinz baked beans was bubbling on a small stove. Mavis grasped it with both hands and before anyone could stop her, deposited the entire contents on top of a range of apple pies, custard tarts and cream cakes set out on a glass shelf.

'I'll give you beans on toast,' she said, thrusting the hot pan into Belle's trembling hands. 'You'll find *your* toast burned to a crisp if you ever lay one of those scarlet fingernails on my poor husband again.

'And as for you,' Mavis said, turning her ire on the

man in question, 'you can get off home this minute, you daft lummock, before I really lose my temper.'

'By gum,' Thomas said to the gaping diners. 'What a woman!'

Amy couldn't understand it. Mavis had changed. Her usual dour expression had vanished, her whole demeanour seemed to have been transformed from glum and over-critical to sunny and what could only be described as happy. Amy had never heard her mother-in-law singing before, but she did that all the time now as she hurried off to do her shopping following her usual daily visit. She'd even managed to sit for a whole half hour chatting without once finding fault. Amy wondered if she was ill, or if she was growing senile perhaps, as old folk often did.

But then she discovered that Thomas was happy too, and no longer living on the allotment.

'What's happened to your mother and father?' she asked Chris one day. 'Your mother's like a dog with two tails. She came and collected all your father's washing the other day and told me he was back home now and that she'd be doing it herself in future. Not only that, but, according to Thomas, she's waiting on him hand, foot and finger, which she always said she'd never do. She's even letting him watch football on the new telly. What's going on?'

But Chris only grunted from beneath lowering brows, which was the biggest puzzle of all. While his parents seemed to have resolved their matrimonial difficulties, Amy discovered that she'd acquired a whole new raft of her own, and she couldn't understand why.

Chris had never been so unhappy in his life. It was all true, what that anonymous letter had said. Amy did indeed have a fancy man. He'd seen the bloke with his own eyes and Chris hadn't the first idea how to deal with the situation. Should he confront her and demand to know what was going on, or hope that it would all blow over and she'd come back to him?

But did he still want her if she'd betrayed him with another man? Chris groaned. What he wanted was for it not to be happening at all.

In the days following that dreadful discovery, he seemed to be walking around in a dream. He couldn't concentrate on anything, couldn't think. He certainly couldn't talk to Amy properly, could hardly bear to even be in the same house with her. He would go and sit in the bakery in the dark, with his head in his hands in total despair, or go for long walks alone down by the canal, talking to himself like a man demented.

Once or twice he'd caught her writing something but when he asked what it was, she'd pushed all the papers out of sight, flushing a guilty pink, which inflamed his suspicions still more. Was she writing him love letters too, on *his* kitchen table?

What should he do? What *could* he do if she no longer loved him?

And why was she doing this to him? Why had she done this terrible thing? That's what he couldn't work out. Why would she want to? What had gone so badly wrong with their marriage that she would even think to look at another bloke? He'd managed, albeit with difficulty, to provide her with a home of their own to live in, one he and his dad had done up and improved as best they could. Of course, he hoped to find her something a bit better one day, but at least they now had the privacy they'd always craved.

And they had little Danny. He worked hard, handed his money over every week, so where had he failed her?

Was it in the bedroom department? he wondered with a pinch of guilt. Amy was a lovely young woman with a healthy appetite for loving. Chris considered all the times when he'd put her off, when they'd been interrupted, even in their own home, by his mother.

Had he been wrong to allow Mavis to march in whenever she chose? Should he start locking the door? Should he tell his mother to knock, or to stay away altogether unless invited? Nay, that would cause ructions, yet more trouble just when his parents seemed to have patched up their differences.

Yet if he didn't do something, he'd lose his lovely wife whom he adored.

She was always talking about politics and world affairs, teasing him because he didn't join in her debates. Did she want him to be more a man of affairs? Chris wasn't sure if he could manage that. He thought of the beatnik-type clothes that she'd started to wear. Did she find him boring? Did she see him as dull and predictable?

And who was this other bloke, anyroad? That's what he needed to know. Where had they met? They'd seemed very cosy together, really quite close, even intimate by the way he'd held her face and teasingly growled at her then ruffled her hair. The pain in Chris's chest intensified, a physical band of iron clamping his heart.

Amy had betrayed him, cheated on him with another man.

He started, jerked out of his thoughts as Susie Southworth, the sixteen-year-old who served behind the counter in the shop came marching in with a mug of tea.

'Morning, I thought you'd be gasping for a cuppa by this time,' she said, rewarding Chris with her wide, beaming smile.

Susie was bright and cheerful and very pretty with fluffy blonde hair and big blue eyes. As she set the mug down on the scarred surface of his desk, Chris allowed his gaze to travel over her neat little figure, her pretty face. She was wearing a tight-fitting white blouse which emphasised her pert young breasts, and a short black skirt beneath her apron that showed off a pair of shapely legs.

Maybe he should give Amy a bit of tit-for-tat. That would make her sorry. It had been a long time since he'd chatted up a girl, couldn't ever remember needing to with Amy. They'd just fallen for each other on sight.

Chris smiled at the young girl. 'You're looking very pretty this morning, Susie.'

The girl looked slightly startled, saying nothing as she set down a plate of biscuits.

'I expect you've got a boyfriend. Several, I shouldn't wonder, chasing after you,' he added, giving her a broad wink.

She glanced at him sharply, sudden panic in her blue eyes. 'Ooh, Mr George, I'm sorry Frank come round the other evening. He weren't meaning to be no trouble. I've told him not to come near but he will insist on walking me home now the nights are drawing in.'

Chris was deeply embarrassed. She'd taken his little attempt at flirtation as some sort of criticism. 'No, no, that's not a problem. Quite right that he should walk you home when it's going dark. I was just . . . well, I was simply making a compliment, that's all. Thank you for the tea, Susie. Don't worry about . . . about Frank. Get along with you now.'

And she fled. Chris put his head in his hands, his pride battered even more. Even the young girls who worked for him thought him too old and boring to see him as a man they might fancy. No wonder his wife was looking elsewhere.

43

Patsy

There were days, like today, with its lowering skies and the threat of rain, when the market seemed perpetually dismal and dirty. The fish stalls stank, the walkways were littered with rubbish, the women slatternly and the men rough and grimy. A scene which entirely suited everyone's mood as Gina's trial approached.

Some of the stallholders, like Jimmy Ramsay, Barry Holmes and Betty Hemley looked hollow-eyed and unusually bad tempered, but then most of them had been on the go since the first flush of dawn, long before their customers even knew it was morning. Buying early was the only way to secure fresh products at a good price.

Even Chris George looked like a man gone wild these days. Clearly young Danny was giving them precious little sleep.

Patsy too had suffered a sleepless night, tormented by her suspicions, and whether she should mention them to Marc.

On impulse, she called to see Clara, her surrogate mother and business partner, and poured out her heart to her. Patsy spoke with anguish about the problems she and Marc had been experiencing recently. She also told how he kept asking her to look at flats with him but she was too busy to go.

Clara listened carefully to this rush of confidences and smiled as she kissed Patsy's cheek. 'You're very hard on yourself at times, love. You need to meet Marc halfway. Take more time off and give proper attention to your own personal life. It would be a mistake to take this nice young man for granted.'

'You're right, I know you are. He grumbles that we've lost the chance to rent two flats locally already because I wouldn't take time off to look at them with him.'

'There you are then. You have Amy coming in now, and I can help too.'

There was a small silence, and then Patsy said, 'One minute he's trying to rush me into marriage and babies, the next he's fretting over his sisters. It's so difficult. But since we can't find anywhere to live, and there's all this worry and fuss over Gina's trial coming up, not forgetting Carmina's wedding, I wonder if perhaps we should postpone our own for a while.'

'You must discuss that with Marc, not me.'

Patsy chewed on her bottom lip. 'The trouble is, marriage, babies and flats aren't my only worry. I have serious doubts over this whole situation between Gina and Carmina. The question keeping me awake at night is whether I should voice my suspicions to Marc? He's so infuriating, won't hear a word said against her. Yet she's evil, that girl, and I suspect she's the one who has created this entire mess.'

Clara frowned. 'I'm not sure I wish to hear this.'

'That's all it is at this stage, a suspicion, a gut feeling which has grown while watching the way she behaves with certain people, one man in particular.'

Clara put up a hand. 'Please don't tell me who he is, I don't want to know.'

'All right, but tell me this. If you saw two people kissing, then the next minute she's flirting outrageously with him while he's finding any excuse to watch her, or be with her, isn't that significant? And if they have a humdinger of a row, doesn't that seem to prove that they must once have been very close? They say hate is very close to love.'

'Leave it,' Clara advised with a little shake of the head. 'Say nothing. Let things be.'

'Even if this whole shot-gun wedding thing is based on a lie? Even if Luc is innocent and losing him breaks Gina's heart?' Patsy asked her adopted mother.

'Even then. Concentrate on yourself, on your own future, Patsy, and leave the Bertalones to sort out such problems for themselves. If you were to say something and Marc disagreed or took offence, you could lose him. You know how close that family is. He'd be bound to put them first, even the treacherous Carmina.'

Amy too agreed with Clara's assessment of the situation when they got together for their usual Friday afternoon chit-chat over coffee and cake in Belle's Café.

'But what about justice for Gina?'

'Leave that to the solicitors and her family.'

'Mind your own business' seemed to be the general opinion of her friends, which Patsy was beginning to get the feeling she must obey.

'And pay more attention to your own life,' her friend gently scolded her. 'He's a lovely man is Marc and, as Clara says, you don't want to risk losing him. You can't solve everybody's problems, love, much as you might like to. Put yourself first for a change.'

Patsy thought of Gina, locked up in that prison cell and firmly shook her head. 'I don't see how I can do that until Gina is free.'

On Saturday afternoon Patsy finally, and reluctantly, agreed to close the hat stall early and go with Marc to view the new flats he'd mentioned, which were being built at Kersal. As they sat cosily side by side on the upper deck of the bus he told her they were going to be eleven storeys high. 'How do you fancy that? You'd be able to see right over Manchester.'

She looked at him, an apology in her eyes. 'I'd prefer to stay close to Champion Street and the market.'

'You may change your mind when you see them.'

Patsy shifted her gaze to the wilderness of streets through which they were passing, trying to imagine travelling this journey every day. It did not appeal. Besides, she loved the hustle and bustle of the market, she always had. She couldn't imagine living anywhere else.

'Are there going to be shops too? If so, I suppose I could always try renting one of those and branch out a bit,' she said, without too much enthusiasm.

'I thought the idea was for you to take a break from work?'

Patsy said no more. They got off the bus and went

to look at the flats, and the shops, although it would be several months yet before they'd be completed.

'Well?'

She shook her head. 'I don't think so.'

Without a word they climbed back on to the next bus and returned to the city centre, getting off at Whitworth Street. They remained silent throughout the journey, seeming to have nothing left to say to each other. In deep gloom they crossed over Albion Street Road Bridge and headed for the towpath, walking on past an old textile warehouse and Albion Mill with its façade of decorative cast-iron window frames.

It was almost dusk and Patsy could hear the distant hum of city traffic, a clock striking the hour, and she couldn't help but think of Gina and how each minute must feel like an hour to her. They made their way back towards Champion Street, bought fish and chips which they ate looking out over the Rochdale Canal, their own future suddenly seeming as bleak as the landscape.

Days later Patsy saw Alec Hall crossing the market. He looked harassed and distracted, constantly running his hand through his hair which brought her suspicions to the fore once more. He was about to go back into his shop when he spotted Patsy and strode over. Ignoring all pleasantries he came straight to the point.

'You're very close the Bertalone family, do you know the full story of what's going on over there?'

'Er . . .' Patsy was dumbfounded. Had he noticed her loitering the other day, when they were arguing? There was an abruptness about his manner and a wild expression in his grey eyes. How much did he know? How much dare she tell him? Would Carmina consider the pregnancy to be private information? 'I'm not sure that I'm the right person to ask,' she hedged.

'You are if you're in possession of all the facts, which I clearly am not. Is it true that Carmina is about to marry Luc Fabriani, and if so why? I understood he was courting the other sister, Gina. I'm surprised he's turned against her, even if she is in jail. But then I'm surprised Gina was arrested in the first place. She never seemed the sort to take up thieving.'

'I agree,' Patsy cried, relieved that even the injured shopkeeper should take this lenient attitude. He had been the one most affected, after all. 'Apparently the proof was irrefutable, or so the police say, since they found the record player stolen from your shop, along with other items, hidden away in her wardrobe. The case comes up for trial soon.'

Alec frowned, and after a thoughtful moment nodded. 'Yes, so they told me. I never thought they'd actually send her down for it though. And why would Luc so swiftly drop her? Carmina and I . . .' He stopped, gave a small smile and a shrug. 'I thought it was all over between her and Luc.'

Patsy's mind was whirling. What was he trying to say? Was that almost an admission that they had indeed once been intimate? She'd never been afraid to take risks in her life, and these last words of Alec's decided her. No matter what Clara and Amy said, she really couldn't leave Gina to stagnate in that dreadful place without doing something to help.

Besides, she knew how it felt to be confronted by secrets about your past that you couldn't uncover. Was it fair to this unborn child to allow it to face life on the strength of a lie? And if she was forced to choose between Luc and Carmina over which of them was telling the truth, it was no contest.

Patsy glanced around at the rush and helter-skelter of the market, and drew Alec behind a large display of handbags, in case anyone should be watching, Carmina in particular.

'I expect it's because of the baby,' she quietly remarked.

'Baby?'

'You did know that Carmina was pregnant? Lord, if you didn't, then for goodness' sake don't let on that *I* was the one who told you.'

Alec's expression now looked more shocked than irritated. 'I won't let on,' he mumbled. 'You're saying that Carmina is pregnant? By whom?'

Patsy looked him straight in the eye. Carmina would kill her for this, if she knew. This was interference of the highest order. 'She's certainly pregnant by someone. She says Luc, but he denies it. Yet who else could it be?'

Alec drew in a long shaky breath and let it out quite slowly. Then he spun on his heel and walked back into his shop, closing the door with a sharp click and turning the sign to closed.

Oh dear, now what had she done?

Patsy was a regular visitor to the prison. She took her friend treats: a few chocolates from Pringle's Chocolate

Cabin, an orange and apple from Barry's stall, or a home-made cake she'd baked herself. These items were all taken from her at the gate, and she wondered sometimes if Gina ever got them.

'I haven't hidden a file in it,' she joked on one occasion, only to receive a sour look from the woman concerned. She never risked it again.

'Does Carmina never visit you?' she once asked Gina, but Gina only turned her head away and refused to answer. Patsy took the hint and quickly changed the subject. Relations between the two sisters had never been so low.

Only once had the coming wedding been mentioned. Gina had quietly asked if it really was going ahead and Patsy had told her that she believed it would be some time soon.

'What about your own wedding?'

Patsy had laughed, joking about how she'd won that little disagreement with Marc. 'I doubt it will even be an autumn wedding, as I originally planned. None of us are in the mood for celebrating,' she said, feeling that it was wrong to even discuss such happy things while Gina was incarcerated in prison. 'We may well postpone it till the spring, till you're able to be there as chief bridesmaid. In fact, I insist upon it.'

Gina smiled but her eyes remained bleak.

Patsy constantly asked her how she was being treated, how the food was, and what her cell-mate was like, although her answers were never very satisfactory. She thought her friend looked dreadful, her face ash-pale, beautiful brown hair all lank and greasy. And her lovely cinnamon eyes bore dark purple bruises beneath, seeming to stare into some abyss no one else could imagine.

'It will all be over soon,' Patsy would assure her. 'You must be strong. Remember that we're all praying for you. Marc is organising a lawyer, the best defence money can buy, although he says you're not to worry about the cost as they expect you to be granted legal aid. This mix-up will soon get sorted out, I know it will, love. It won't be long now before the trial comes up, then you'll be out of here. You just have to stay strong, right?'

Gina would say little by way of response, merely give a thin, meaningless smile. She seemed to have withdrawn into herself, to some secret place in her head. The most conversation she volunteered was to ask after Mamma and Papa, and her beloved brothers and sisters. Then she would walk back through the door into the terrible hell-hole beyond, and Patsy would leave the prison feeling hopelessly inadequate and useless.

Today, as Patsy approached, she was thinking over Carmina's strangely unfeeling reaction to her sister's incarceration. But then she'd been behaving oddly right from the day Gina was arrested, if not before. So full of herself, so indifferent to her sister's plight. And to spring her pregnancy on her parents on Gina's first day in prison seemed too cruel for words.

Patsy went over Alec's reaction too in her mind. She'd swear he knew something, that there'd been something between them.

Her suspicions were aroused, and she fully intended

to pursue the truth and get to the bottom of the matter. There must be something she was missing, some evidence which hadn't yet come to light which could free Gina. She would begin this very day by asking her a few leading questions. Her trial was just days away, after all, so time was of the essence.

But as she neared the all-too-familiar Victorian entrance of Strangeways Prison Patsy could hear the sound of klaxons going off. By the time she joined the long queue forming outside the office, a straggled line of weary men and women patiently waiting to see their loved ones, it was obvious something was amiss.

Instead of the queue being ushered inside, people who'd already been admitted were being rudely ejected, prisoners apparently being sent back to their cells despite it being well past the hour for visiting. And somewhere in the background frantic sounds could be heard. A car drew up and a man carrying a black bag jumped out to be hustled through the door. An ambulance came next, tearing into the prison yard, its own klaxon taking over from the silence left in the wake of the other.

'What on earth's going on?' Patsy asked of no one in particular.

'One of the prisoners has tried to hang herself, apparently,' said the woman in front. 'I'd bleedin' do the same an' all, if I were ever locked up in that hell-hole.'

An ice-cold hand gripped her heart as some terrible instinct told Patsy that this person was Gina.

44

Gina, Patsy and Carmina

The Indian summer was well and truly over and trade on Champion Street Market was busy, everyone rushing to buy winter scarves or woollen hats. The ice-cream parlour was closed, not as a consequence of the time of year, but because Father Dimmock was saying special prayers for the Bertalone family.

Gina had spent several days in hospital but was now back in prison under strict supervision. At least she was alive, her family cried, lighting more candles in thanks for her survival.

Patsy had attended the eight o'clock Mass with them at St Mary's in Brazennose Street. Luc too had been present, much to Carmina's delight.

Even she seemed subdued by the horror of her sister's attempted suicide. Yet she was looking as beautiful and voluptuous as ever. Pregnancy seemed to suit her. Her blue dress was straining somewhat over the bloom of her burgeoning figure, glossy ebony hair tied back with a matching chiffon scarf.

It fleetingly crossed Patsy's mind that the scarf looked oddly familiar, and she wondered if she'd seen Carmina wearing it before somewhere.

On their return to Champion Street, Carlotta retired to her bed, where she'd been ever since she'd learned the terrible news. Gina's parents had been allowed to visit their daughter only once since her attempted suicide, although Carlotta had wept to see her darling child lying sick in a hospital bed, unable to speak properly and one hand shackled to the bed post. It was all too troubling and shaming.

Now, as the younger children gathered about their mother, Patsy made her excuses and left.

It was a difficult time for them all, waiting for the trial, not least for Gina. She was back in her prison cell with Alice, but never left alone for a moment. If Alice was absent then Wilcox, or Allenby, the reed-thin woman officer with the down-turned eyes who'd dealt with Gina on her first day, kept watch at the door. She hated their constant presence but understood why it was necessary.

For a time after she'd recovered consciousness to find herself in hospital she'd been filled with anger that she was still alive, hated everyone and longed for the comfort of that enveloping darkness, with all her soul. She'd lost Luc, was about to be consigned to prison for years, her reputation was tarnished, what could she possibly have to live for? But now, as a good Catholic, she saw that she'd committed a mortal sin and was filled with shame. Every morning she went to Mass and prayed for forgiveness.

Gina had reconciled herself to misery and despair. No matter what the trial might bring, no matter if she was compelled to live her life without Luc because of his betrayal with her sister, then so be it. She must deal with it.

Despite the fact she was never left alone there was still far too much time for her to reflect on what had happened to her and why. Ample time for Gina to work it all out fairly accurately.

She realised that the only person, beside herself, who knew about the loose brick in the old Victorian fireplace, was Carmina. And her sister had far more opportunity to steal from Patsy's stall, and from Hall's Music Shop, than herself.

It was only in recent months, after all, that she'd begun to get about more, most of her time spent helping Mamma in the house until she'd started working for Dena. Gina had rarely visited the hat stall, and couldn't remember the last time she'd even browsed through the records at Hall's Music, let alone bought one. And it went without saying that it would never cross her mind to actually steal one.

So who had, and why would Constable Nuttall even consider searching her bedroom unless someone had tipped him off to do so? Despite her inner struggle against facing the truth, it was now perfectly clear to Gina that she'd been manipulated by Carmina.

Late one night she confessed these suspicions to her cell-mate, Alice, who told her the correct term was 'framed'.

Whatever the word, the fact that Carmina could do such a thing filled her more with grief than fear. How could a loving sister behave with such cruelty? All those years when Carmina had supported her through her illness. Had that been a lie too?

'You'll have to shop her,' Alice said. 'You'll have to tell the beak when you go to trial.'

When Gina had translated this, she was horrified. 'I could never do such a thing. How could I tell on my own sister? She would then be the one locked up.'

'And a good thing too. Doesn't she deserve to be, if what you say is true? She certainly had the opportunity, and I assume she had the motivation.'

'Oh yes, I'm afraid she did indeed have the motivation, of course she did.' Carmina's reasons were all too clear, had been from the start, only Gina had failed to take proper notice. 'She wanted Luç, my boyfriend, and was clearly determined to get him at any price. Well, it looks as though she has. She's won. Carmina will marry Luc now.'

'And you'll get two years if you don't speak up, maybe more,' Alice calmly informed her.

This prediction proved to be entirely accurate. When Gina's case came up for trial a few days later, two years was exactly what she got, and there seemed little hope of an appeal.

After all that had happened Patsy really did not feel inclined to take Clara's excellent advice. Perhaps if she'd spoken about her suspicions earlier Gina might never have attempted to do such a terrible thing as trying to take her own life, might not now be facing two years in prison. Patsy felt deeply responsible. Unfortunately, she still possessed no proof that her theory was the correct one.

Her next visit to the prison was heartbreaking. To see the bleak acceptance, the desolation in those lovely cinnamon eyes, sent a chill down her spine. Gina might have survived her act of desperation but to see this lovely young girl in such despair was almost more than Patsy could bear. She seemed to have given up all hope of a happy future, believing she'd lost everything.

Patsy offered what little comfort she could, pointing out that although the sentence was tough, it wouldn't last for ever. 'There'll be time off for good behaviour, and one day you *will* be free. Maybe there'll be an appeal. You mustn't give up hope. I know your parents have been to see you, but has Luc been since the trial, or since you . . . ?' Patsy stopped, lost for words.

Gina looked right through her, seemingly oblivious to her friend's embarrassment as she gazed into some private hell. 'I refused to see him so he wrote me a letter.'

'What did he say?'

'That he'd be there at the gate on the day of my release.' Her voice was cold, expressionless.

'And?'

Gina shrugged. 'I didn't write back. What is there to say? He's marrying my sister.'

As Patsy walked away from Strangeways that day, the chill of fear for her young friend changed to a burn of anger. Why should Carmina profit from her lies? Why should she be allowed to get away with her evil schemes? It wasn't right.

She decided someone needed to speak to Luc. Someone should ask him straight out what was the truth of the matter. And the lad surely had the right to say which sister he truly loved and wanted to marry? Someone also needed to speak to Carmina. And surely the best person to do all of this was Marc.

Patsy wasted no time. Immediately following her visit, she met up with Marc on his way home from work and took him to Belle's Café where they were doing a roaring trade in hot buttered crumpets, although mainly to the stallholders themselves.

Over a frothy coffee, with the juke box playing 'Sweet Little Sixteen' in the background, she told him of her visit to the prison that afternoon. Patsy expressed her deep concern over Gina's state of mind: how she still seemed deeply depressed, was refusing to see Luc or even reply to his letters, and to have completely lost heart. But before Marc could respond to this, she ploughed right in with her suspicions.

'The point is why would Luc be willing to wait for her if he didn't love her? I mean, can we be absolutely certain that he is indeed the father of this child Carmina is carrying?'

Marc stared at her, eyes widening in disbelief as he folded his arms across his broad chest. 'What are you saying?'

'I believe that he isn't, that he's entirely innocent.'

'So who do *you* say the father is then, if not Luc?'

Patsy put up a hand by way of apology. 'I accept that Carmina would kill me if I even attempted to interfere, but I do believe this to be another of her lies. I'm not sure she can stop herself from lying, it's almost compulsive with her now.' A pause while she took a steadying breath, trying to pay no attention to the glowering frown gathering on her fiancé's face. 'Actually, to be honest, I've already interfered, in a way. I've told him that she's pregnant. It was obviously news to him, so Carmina evidently hadn't done so.'

'Told *who*? You're speaking in riddles.'

Patsy's expression was soft with sympathy as she faced Marc's ire. 'Alec Hall, of course. I saw them once having a terrible row and the other day he asked me to tell him what was going on, so I did. I told him Carmina was marrying Luc because she claimed to be having his baby, but that Luc denies it's his. He was completely shell-shocked. It was quite obvious that something had been going on between the pair of them.'

The moment these words left her mouth, it seemed to dawn on Patsy that Clara might have been right, after all. That this was indeed a very dangerous path she trod.

Marc actually gasped, then snorted his derision. 'Alec Hall? You think *Alec* is the father of Carmina's child?'

He was glaring at her now in cold fury and Patsy felt an intense discomfort as she realised she'd perhaps gone too far this time.

'I don't believe it. I won't believe it!' He wagged a finger inches from her face. 'You have absolutely no proof. It's purely malicious gossip and I wouldn't advise you to take this any further. You're the one spreading wicked lies, about *my* sister! Whoever the damned father is, it certainly couldn't be Alec Hall with his velvet jackets and pink dickie-bow ties. He's years older than her. And I fail to see what damn business it is of yours.'

There was a small silence, then Patsy quietly remarked, 'I thought that it might be my "damn business" because I love you, and because I'm going to become a member of your family.'

'That doesn't allow you to add to all the rumours already circulating about my family,' Marc shouted, making the cups and saucers jump as he pounded his fist on the table. Then he marched out of the café, stamping his rage across the cobbles.

Belle came over to her at once. 'Are you all right, love?'

Patsy blinked the tears from her eyes. 'Yes. Yes, I'm OK.' But she wasn't at all. She saw now the true wisdom of Clara's words. Patsy very much doubted Marc would be pressing her to view any more flats after this. It was most unlikely that there would be any wedding for them now.

Carmina had endured what she considered yet another long, boring day serving strawberry, chocolate and vanilla ice cream from the cart. How she hated it. How she loathed the children who took forever to choose between a cornet or a wafer, an orange iced lolly or a choc ice. She would be glad when Papa put the ice-cream cart away for the winter. Of course, the parlour would still be open, and Papa would serve hot Vimto as well as cold drinks with the desserts and Sundaes. She hated that too, all the chopping and peeling of fruit, the stirring and smiling and serving and being nice to people.

There had to be a better way to spend her days.

Once she was married into the Fabriani family there'd be no necessity for her to work at all. She could sit back and let others get on with it. She fully intended to insist that Luc join his father in the business. That was essential if one day they were to inherit all those riches, as was only right and proper for any son.

And since the Fabrianis were quite well off, she would also be able to afford to employ someone to help look after the baby. Carmina certainly had no intention of allowing a snotty-nosed kid to curtail her freedom in any way.

Carmina had expected to be married by this time yet here they were already in October and still Luc was prevaricating. If she didn't watch out this stupid baby would be born before ever she got him to that altar.

She found the delay over her wedding deeply irritating. With Gina's trial out of the way and the verdict she'd hoped for in place, she'd believed that all her troubles would be over. Of course she'd been shocked by her sister's attempt to take her own life, but really it was a very stupid thing to do. A couple of years and she'd be out of that place. And why she should imagine that Luc would be there waiting for her at the end of it, Carmina really couldn't imagine.

The triumph over Gina's sentence had palled instantly when still Luc insisted on standing by the girl, which was utterly ridiculous. What a waste of time that would be. Gina wouldn't be coming home for a long, long time, she'd told him. He'd looked stricken but she knew he didn't really mean what he said. It was only because he felt sorry for her, filled with a guilty sort of loyalty. Or else he was trying to avoid his responsibilities.

This was how Carmina saw it, that Luc was entirely responsible for her current predicament. She'd quite shut out of her mind the fact that he'd done no more than kiss her on that night at the dance, stubbornly refused to remember that her attempts to seduce him had failed. So far as Carmina was concerned everything was proceeding as planned. All she needed was a firm date for the wedding and her triumph would be complete.

As she ran up the steps of the tall terraced house that evening, her intention was to grab a hasty supper then go in search of him. Luc had agreed to see her tonight, and she meant to have it out with him once and for all. She would insist he name the day.

So it came as something of a shock to find Alec Hall seated in the Bertalones' living room, engrossed in deep conversation with her father.

'Ah,' Papa said, as Carmina burst through the door, 'the very person we want to see. Alec has been filling me in on some very interesting facts. Why don't you sit down so that we can discuss them together.'

Carmina was incandescent with rage. The interview with her father had been the most difficult, the most shaming, that she could ever remember. Worse, Papa had largely ignored her protests of innocence. Now she and Alec were standing beneath the street lamp at the foot of the house steps and he was looking at her with that little smirking smile which irritated her so much.

'Absolutely not! No, I will not marry you. *I will not*,' she screamed. 'Never! How dare you march in and talk to my father without my permission. How dare you attempt to interfere in my life and *ruin all my plans*!'

'I don't think you're in any position to refuse, do you?'

'I most certainly am.'

Alec shook his head, then moving closer he stroked Carmina's softly rounded belly in a flagrantly intimate gesture. 'Think about it, my love, you and I know for a fact that this child must be mine. Even if you did once have sexual intercourse with Luc Fabriani, that was a long time ago. Too long. And you admitted to me, if you recall, that it didn't happen the night I saw the pair of you in his car. There's no question but that you are carrying my child, and I mean to father it.'

His tone became brisk. 'I've arranged the licence, as I was just explaining to your father, and we can be married Saturday week at the Register Office.'

Carmina gasped. 'You'll have to drag me there bound and gagged.'

'If necessary, but I don't think it will be, do you?' He jerked her into his arms, pressing her body hard against his so that she could smell the onions and rice on his breath from one of those strange Korean meals he liked to cook.

'You and I *also* know who the thief really is, don't we? It certainly wasn't pretty little Gina who rummaged through my records. I've fought in and survived two wars, do you really imagine that I sleep soundly?' He laughed, a coarse, bitter sound. 'Sadly, I have too many dreams, too many nightmares, for that to be the case. Soldiers learn to sleep with one eye open, particularly when young girls are ransacking their room, or their shop. So if you don't want to take your sister's place in that miserable little prison cell, you'd better start considering changes to your little scheme, a new groom to stand by your side on that happy day. Do you understand what I'm saying to you, Carmina?'

Sadly, she did, and although Carmina didn't like what she heard one little bit, she was struck speechless. For once in her life her mind was a complete blank. She could see no way out.

Within seven days it was all over. The marriage took place, as arranged, at the local Register Office. Carmina wore a pale blue suit since she could no longer squeeze into her ballerina-length wedding gown. She carried white lilies for her bouquet although they looked rather stark and funereal rather than exotic, and there was no orange blossom available at this time of year. Nor did her sisters act as bridesmaids. Carlotta was too ashamed to even allow them to attend.

And the groom standing by her side was not Luc Fabriani.

In order to secure her freedom, Carmina had been compelled to submit to Alec's blackmail. Instead of marrying into one of the richest Italian families in the neighbourhood, to a man who had occupied every waking moment of her life for over a year, she became plain Mrs Hall. She was now the wife of a man nearly twice her age who owned nothing more exciting than a little music shop on Champion Street Market. A man she didn't even love.

45

Chris and Amy

Chris couldn't quite pluck up the courage to confront Amy and tell her what he had seen. He couldn't even mention the anonymous letter accusing her of cheating on him, and the reason for his reticence was perfectly simple. He was terrified of what her answer might be. He had no wish to hear her say the words that she no longer loved him, that she'd found someone else. Even to contemplate a life without his lovely wife was unendurable. But he couldn't go on like this. He had to do something.

Unable to decide between his many possible choices, Chris opted for the lot.

His intention was to become a more dynamic, interesting person, particularly in the bedroom. At the same time he was so hurt, so angry by her betrayal, that he thought he might punish her by having a bit of a fling himself. Of course it was really Amy he wanted, not some other woman, but she clearly didn't give a fig about their marriage vows and the love they'd once shared, so why should he?

All he had to do was spruce himself up and find a likely candidate, although he was a bit nervous about how he would proceed should he actually find one.

Chris began the new regime by telling his mother not to call at the house unless invited, indicating that they found it inconvenient having folk popping in and out whenever they fancied. And although her jaw dropped, she surprised him by making no real protest. In fact, she seemed far more interested in herself than her son, for once.

'I've no time, anyroad, to be running round after you and Amy any more,' as if she ever had done such a thing. More often than not it had been the reverse. 'Your father and me are planning a little holiday, and then we have a few other plans on the go.'

'So Dad's not thinking of coming back to the bakery then?' Chris asked, his expression bleak.

'You must ask him that yourself. I can't speak for your father.' Thereby denying a lifetime's habit.

Thomas confirmed that his retirement was indeed permanent, and that if it became necessary Chris should employ another baker, or train an apprentice. His only son would be entirely in charge of the bakery from now on, which meant he would also need to learn how to do the accounts.

Chris bought himself a book on the subject, also one on modern politics. He read it under the bedcovers when Amy was asleep, using a torch, or while he was waiting for the dough to rise and he should really have been mixing the next batch of tea cakes.

What amazed him most was his wife's general air of innocence. She seemed not to notice how upset he was, how miserable, but carried on exactly as before, humming and singing to herself as she went about her chores, chattering away as if she hadn't a care in the world. He came dangerously close to hating her for this casual disregard for his feelings.

But how could he ever hate his lovely Amy, no matter what she had done? He loved her to bits. Loved the bones of her. It was that bloke he hated, the one who had stolen her from him.

He would just have to try harder to be a better husband.

He stopped buying the *Daily Express* and bought the *Financial Times* instead, although it wasn't nearly so interesting, and didn't give the football results. Then he tried out a few random remarks on various topical issues in the hope of livening up their conversation of an evening. Chris would say how much he agreed with the philosophies of Martin Luther King. He would air his views on the troubles in Cyprus, or Fidel Castro, or comment on the new bank loans being made available. He even voiced an interest in who might be the new pope since Pope Pius XII had died following a stroke.

'Why would it matter to you?' Amy asked. 'You aren't even a Catholic.'

'I'm entitled to my opinion, same as anyone else. Like you spouting on over consumer capitalism or nuclear disarmament.'

Amy frowned, listening bemused to this new side to her husband, more accustomed to his views on the test match, or who would win the cup. But his mood was so black, his tone so cold and distantly sarcastic that she wasn't able to take this new interest in current affairs as a good sign. Something was bothering him, and she couldn't for the life of her think what it might be.

Next, and quite at odds with the image he was developing of himself as a man of affairs, he bought himself a pink shirt, a maroon Slim Jim tie, and a long draped green sports jacket which fastened with a single link button. He even bought some dark grey trousers that tapered at the ankle. Amy looked at him aghast when he first put them on.

'By heck, are you turning into a Teddy Boy?'

An angry flush stained his neck and jaw. 'I thought I'd brighten up my wardrobe a bit.'

'Well, you've certainly done that. They'll see you coming a mile off. I thought you didn't like pink shirts?' She was referring to the time when they'd used to giggle over her habit of letting pink socks get mixed up with the whites in his mother's wash boiler. 'I'm sorry, no, don't look like that. I didn't mean it. I quite like the shirt, now that I come to look at it properly. I would've come with you though, if I'd known you were wanting new clothes.'

She looked hurt that he hadn't thought to ask her, and troubled by this new show of independence. He could tell by the little pucker of anxiety between her eyes. But Chris didn't apologise or explain. He simply told his wife that he was off out for a pint with his mates then clamped his mouth tight shut, not even saying which pub that might be. Let her worry where he was for a change.

But he was making no progress on the romance front.

He might now look the part of a lothario but he couldn't quite pluck up the courage to actually chat a woman up. He certainly didn't fancy any of the women in the bar of the Dog and Duck. They weren't a patch on his lovely Amy. And if one should come near while he was enjoying a pint, he would be overcome by panic. His tongue would cleave to the roof of his mouth and his brain would empty of any witty or flirtatious remark. He'd want only to tell them to go away and stop bothering him; that he was a happily married man, thank you very much, and not interested in other women.

Deciding to play Amy at her own game was one thing, actually carrying it out quite another.

Puzzled though she might be by her husband's increasingly odd behaviour, not for a moment did Amy ever suspect him of chasing girls. Perhaps she knew him better than he knew himself, but, in her view, Chris simply wasn't the type. He loved her far too much to be interested in anyone else. And didn't she feel exactly the same way about him?

If he'd taken to wearing trendy clothes and going out a bit more, well, didn't he deserve it, working as hard as he did? She knew he'd been worrying about his father a good deal lately, and the responsibility of running the bakery on his own. Amy also wondered if he'd perhaps fallen out with his mother, and that was why Mavis hadn't been round lately.

At least their Sunday morning love-making sessions had been re-established, which must be a good thing. And if she would have liked him to talk to her a bit more, before and after, well, she must be patient. Chris wasn't very talkative at the best of times. He was overworked and often tired, which was probably the reason why it sometimes felt different, a bit more mechanical than usual.

But things were improving generally for her, for them both. Danny was sleeping better at nights so she had more energy to give to her two part-time jobs: helping on the hat stall for a couple of afternoons a week, and working for Lizzie Pringle for the odd morning when needed. Which in turn meant that she was able to put a bit by each week. She'd opened a Post Office Savings Account and hoped one day, maybe in a year or two, to have saved enough to put down as a deposit on a flat or little house of their own, one that didn't have creeping damp.

She was thankful that Mavis seemed to be keeping her distance for a change, and that Thomas was back by his own fireside. It was a huge relief that her in-laws seemed to have patched up their differences. And Amy was thrilled with her new washing machine which had transformed her daily routine and meant she didn't spend hours every day elbow-deep in soap suds, scrubbing.

She was also very excited about the coming CND demo.

Life was good, except for being filled with guilt over still not having confessed to her husband that she was a member of this rather radical organisation, and the longer she left it, the harder it was to own up. And she certainly had no wish to add to his worries right now.

Amy still shuddered at the recollection of the day he'd come home early and caught her writing out handbills which members of the Peace Movement intended to push through letter boxes so that people knew about the rally next week. It surprised her in a way that Chris hadn't asked her what she was doing, although he'd remained in a black mood for days afterwards.

Following this scare, Amy had learned to take care not to do any work appertaining to the CND when there was the slightest possibility Chris might pop home for any reason. Although that wasn't easy to predict.

Jeff Stockton had pointed out that they needed to be more professional and offered to buy her a second-hand typewriter but Amy had refused. How could she ever have explained one of those in the house?

Then one afternoon Jeff called to say his uncle had volunteered to print a few hundred handbills for them and could he please have one to copy?

'That would be marvellous!' Amy agreed. 'It would save me so much work and produce far more than I could ever print by hand. And there's no point in holding a demonstration rally without an audience.'

She was so thrilled by the idea that she left Jeff standing on the doorstep while she dashed into the house to find one there and then. Without thinking he followed her inside, still talking about their plans, and about the posters Sue had painted and stuck up everywhere.

'I think the rally will be well attended, and several reporters from local newspapers have promised to come along. There are a few more I intend to ring up before next week, so we should get good press coverage.'

They were standing in the hall with the front door ajar when Mavis's head suddenly appeared around it.

'Cooee, it's only me. I don't mean to intrude but I saw the door open and . . . Oh, I didn't realise you had company,' in that tone of voice which clearly indicated that she knew perfectly well. She'd obviously seen Jeff standing on the doorstep and had come to investigate.

To her intense annoyance Amy felt her cheeks start to burn, and couldn't think of a thing to say. She was deeply aware of something very like a glint of triumph in Mavis's pebble-hard eyes as she studied the young man. Just as if she'd found them stark naked in bed having mad passionate sex instead of engaged in a civilised conversation in the little hall. Amy expected nothing less than an inquisition once he was gone.

Jeff seemed completely unabashed, offering Mavis his most winning smile. 'Don't worry about me, I was just leaving.' He took the papers from Amy's hand, which to her shame she found to be shaking, thanked her and made as if to head for the door, except that his exit was blocked by Mavis.

They performed a little dance of trying to avoid each other and then Mavis backed out the way she had come. 'You don't need to go on my account, I'm the one who's arrived uninvited. I can see now why I need to make an appointment to see my own grandchild.' An the door slammed shut behind her.

'Oh, dear,' Jeff said. 'I don't think my being h went down too well, did it?'

Amy attempted to laugh the incident off. 'Don't worry about my mother-in-law. I can deal with Mavis.'

That was the first lie, Amy realised, that she'd ever knowingly told.

Mavis often popped downstairs for a loaf of brown bread or a couple of currant tea cakes, and would slip into the bakery at the back of the shop to talk to Chris. This particular afternoon she took great pleasure in asking him what Amy was up to today, knowing what she had witnessed with her own eyes earlier. The urge to see the expression on his face when he learned of his wife's infidelity was overwhelming, but Mavis managed to hold herself in check. She had no wish to fall out with her own son, and there were more subtle ways of getting the information across. She had a letter tucked in the bottom of her basket, which would reveal all.

'I haven't seen your Amy for days. I suppose she's too busy with that new job of hers to spare any time for friends and family. Is she ever home? Does she pay you any attention at all? I'm sorry, but I think she's very neglectful, of you and the child. I really don't know how you put up with it.'

'Don't start, Mother.'

Chris went over to check on the progress of the latest batch of bread in the big side flue oven. The blast of hot air as he opened the door would account for the angry flush on his cheeks. He certainly had no wish to discuss the state of his marriage with his own mother.

Mavis flounced out, calling at the post box on her way to Ramsay's Butchers.

The next morning Chris found the letter among a

pile of bills waiting for him at the bakery. He opened it without thinking and there it was in black and white, the shocking evidence of Amy's betrayal.

'*Your wife has been seen entertaining her lover in your own house. She's a shameless hussy! Are you really going to put up with that?*'

Chris stared at the words in stunned disbelief, then he screwed up the letter, little more than a note, and threw it to the far side of the room.

He found that his legs would no longer support him and he sank down on to a chair, head in hands. He felt as if he were drowning in despair, as if everything he held dear was falling away from him. Chris thought of his son, his efforts to provide a good home for his family, the responsibility of this business that had landed unasked on his shoulders, and of the future he'd dreamed of for them all, and silently wept.

Like all strong, caring men he didn't cry easily. Hard, brittle sobs seemed to be torn out of him against his will, jerking his shoulders, bringing a grinding pain to his chest.

Then he crossed the room in three short strides, picked up the note again, smoothed it out and tucked it into his pocket. No, he certainly wasn't going to put up with it. Something had to be done.

The vision of his wife's lover in *his own house*, possibly in *his lovely new bed* with *his wife*, haunted him for the rest of that day and night, and those following. Chris couldn't think, couldn't eat. He lost all interest in trying to 'improve' himself or chat up other women. Amy was his wife and he loved her. And if he lost her, if she no longer wanted him then he didn't know what he would do. He wouldn't have any reason to go on.

So it was that when Amy set off for Albert Square on the night of the planned rally, Chris deposited young Danny with Aunty Dot, as usual, and set off after her. He was determined, once and for all, to confront the bloke who had stolen his beloved Amy and deal with him, man to man.

46

Patsy and Carmina

Patsy hadn't seen much of Marc lately, not since she'd spoken of her suspicions over Alec being the father of Carmina's child. As it turned out she'd been proved to be entirely correct in this respect. But although she and Marc had attended the small civil ceremony together, relations between them had remained cool, almost as if he blamed her for the situation. He certainly didn't seem willing to apologise for disbelieving her.

This irritated Patsy somewhat, but at the same time she was sympathetic over his confused state of mind. They agreed on one thing at least, a refusal to accept Gina's fate and he was entirely caught up in furious discussions over the possibility of an appeal.

She was surprised and pleased when, late one morning, he suddenly popped his head around the curtain of the hat stall, as he used to do so often in those blissful first months together.

Patsy had been stitching a beaded silk ribbon around the rim of a velvet beret but happily set it aside to allow him to place a tender kiss on her brow and then full on her lips.

'How's my favourite girl?'

She smiled. 'Do you have many?'

'Only you.'

'I'm glad to hear it. So, how did it go?' she asked, referring to the latest meeting with Gina's solicitor.

Marc rubbed the flat of his hands over his face. He looked tired, she thought, and desperately sad. 'Not good. He sees no grounds for an appeal, claims she was given a fair trial. He can't seem to see the disparity of a two-year sentence when she is so clearly innocent.'

Patsy put a hand on his arm. 'The problem is proving it.'

'I know. I just wish I could get my hands on the real culprit. Do you think it could be one of that new family who've moved in below the fish market?'

She hadn't planned to speak her mind. She'd already learned to her cost the result of interfering in Bertalone matters. They closed ranks, leaving her on the outside. Perhaps it was the pain in his tortured, beloved face, or her fondness for Gina that made her once again recklessly jump in with hobnailed boots on, heedless of how they might muddy the water.

'Of course, there is one way to get Gina released, and that is to persuade Carmina to confess she is really the guilty party.' The words came out of her mouth quite of their own volition.

Jerked out of his gloomy thoughts Marc stared at her in silence for several terrifying moments. His eyes narrowed dangerously. 'Have I heard you correctly? Are you seriously suggesting that *Carmina* was in fact the thief?'

Patsy quailed before his steely gaze but desperately

held on to her nerve. 'Actually, I've been wanting to discuss this with you for a while, Marc. I backed down from saying what I thought the last time we talked about this, and perhaps that was a mistake. I should have gone for broke then. The fact is, I don't believe for a minute that Gina stole those things, any more than you do, but I do suspect that Carmina did.'

Marc's tone was glacial. 'On the grounds that Carmina must be guilty of everything, is that it? You're accusing her of deliberately getting her own sister locked up so that she could steal her boyfriend? How many B-movies have you been watching lately?'

'Yet she very nearly succeeded in catching Luc, didn't she? Would have done so had I not – interfered – and told Alec about the baby she was having. OK, I should've kept my nose out of it, but I couldn't sit back and see Gina's heart broken for no reason, or Luc's for that matter. And Alec certainly seemed to agree with my assessment of the situation, didn't he?'

Marc was silent once more, his brow creasing into a deep frown.

Patsy let out a heavy sigh. 'Maybe Carmina didn't plan the shop-lifting, maybe it all came about by chance, or accident. I accept that I could be wrong about the entire thing.'

'You certainly are wrong if you believe *my sister* capable of planning something so horrendous.'

Too late, Patsy recalled telling Clara how infuriating Marc was for refusing to see any wrong in Carmina. Furious would be a more appropriate word now, Patsy thought, as she met his livid gaze.

Marc was on his feet, spitting out words as if he hated her. 'You think that Carmina would stand back and do *nothing* while her innocent sister is arrested for something *she* had done? For God's sake, Patsy, what's got into you? I know the pair of you don't get on, but you must be sick in the head to even suggest such a thing.'

Patsy picked up her sewing with trembling fingers and made an effort to get on with it. 'I found it hard to believe too, at first, but I think that's exactly what she did.'

'Why?' The snap of ice in his tone should have warned her to say no more.

She let the sewing fall to her lap with a resigned sigh. 'Because she's manipulative and wicked. She's certainly selfish enough, and a greedy little magpie. She wants everything she sees. It's exactly the sort of thing she would do, to get one over on me by stealing something from the stall right in front of my nose. She'd think it funny, I expect. I noticed she was wearing a blue chiffon scarf in church the other morning, and I remember now where I saw it before. Hanging on a clip on my stall, from where she must have stolen it. She certainly didn't pay for it, and I didn't give it to her.

'The rest of it, the thieving from Alec Hall, well, she certainly had the opportunity if she and he were embroiled in an affair. And as for the goods found in Gina's wardrobe? All carefully staged to implicate her, I'd say. Oh, yes, I'm quite certain that Carmina is the guilty party. It all adds up. She wanted Luc, and was prepared to do anything to get him. The girl is evil.'

Marc gave an ominous growl deep in his throat. 'You think my sister is *evil*?'

Patsy looked him square in the eye. 'Yes, I do. And an inveterate liar.'

She thought for one terrible moment that he might be about to hit her, but he was far too much of a gentleman to ever strike a woman. To Patsy's mind, he might just as well have done so for his next words hit her with the kind of rage she would never forget as long as she lived.

'I don't think you and I have anything left to say to each other, do you?' And Marc turned on his heel and strode away.

So far as Alec Hall was concerned his decision to marry Carmina was proving to be the worst mistake of his life. Almost overnight she had turned from a sexy little minx into the wife-from-hell.

If he asked her to do anything useful such as clean the house, which had become increasingly untidy and filthy since he'd dispensed with his housekeeper, she would fling her clothes on the floor, leave dirty plates in the sink, burn the food she was supposed to cook for him and generally be as uncooperative as possible.

Like a spoiled child she was lazy and selfish and all she seemed to want to do was spend his money, lie in bed all morning, laze about all afternoon and go out every night. He soon put a stop to that, although she flew into a veritable tantrum when he locked the door and refused to allow her out of the house.

'*You can't keep me prisoner here!*' she screamed at him.

'I can do as I please. You're my *wife*, and I choose not to have my wife making an exhibition of herself on some dance floor with other men. I need you to stay home and be nice to me.'

'I never asked to be your damned *wife*, so why should I do anything to please *you*?'

He smiled at her. 'Because the alternative is a real prison, not a locked door, which is surely far worse? Think of your poor sister behind bars, and all because of you.'

'I don't give a damn about Gina, I care about *me* and what you've done to me. You've robbed me of my one chance of happiness.'

'Would you like some *kimchi*?' he asked, setting a plate of rice and spicy stewed vegetables in front of her.

'*No!*' Carmina picked the dish up and threw it at his head, hating him all the more when he ducked and the missile fell harmlessly to the floor. Then she flounced off to bed and sobbed her heart out in a lather of self-pity.

Later, when Alec joined her, he really had to be quite firm with her to make the girl understand what a wife's duties were. No longer did she respond to his kisses and teasing as she had before the wedding. She absolutely refused to remove her clothing in front of him so that he was compelled to rip them from her body.

When he slid a hand over her inner thigh, she didn't moan and sob for him to take her as she once did. She fought like a tiger, bit and scratched and clawed at his face in a vain attempt to prevent him from having her.

Alec found this rather excited him and, laughing in her face, simply spread her legs, captured her flailing wrists and took her anyway. She was his *wife*, for God's sake, whatever other useful purpose did she have?

All of this high drama was simply because she hadn't got her own way. Alec realised now that he had been but a pawn in her plan to trap Luc, a plan that had badly back-fired.

He found himself thinking more and more of his lovely Joo Eun, his silver pearl. Why had he ever deserted her? He hadn't really expected her to follow him when the army had withdrawn from Korea. He'd left her in tears without a second thought. He must have been mad. Was it a flaw in him that once he'd had a woman he soon grew bored with her and started looking around for another? If so, then his other flaw was to marry far too many of them. Marrying this one had been the worst mistake of all.

Patsy was distraught. Marc wasn't speaking to her. She hadn't set eyes on him in days, except at a distance across the market when he would look at her coldly and walk away in the opposite direction.

There was no talk now of an autumn wedding, nor even a spring one. So far as Patsy could see, it was all over between them and she was heartbroken. She'd lost everything she loved and valued simply because she had this great urge to save other people from their misfortunes.

At least, unlike Amy, she wasn't trying to save the world.

Weeks went by and she continued to visit Gina in prison, watching sadly as she withdrew further into her own private, silent world. The laughing girl with the glorious eyes who had battled with and defeated a devastating illness was now a mere shadow of her former self. She was painfully thin, positively gaunt, with lank hair, pallid grey skin and fingernails chewed to the quick.

Trying to make conversation with her across the table in the visitors' room was heartbreakingly difficult, if not well-nigh impossible. Patsy wanted to hug her, and did take her hands to give them a little squeeze only for a large, formidable prison warden to bark at her that contact with a prisoner was not allowed.

Gina seemed locked in her own world so Patsy would chat about some inane nonsense, such as how Terry Hall had bought one of those new Isetta bubble-cars, or the fact she'd acquired a new line of nylon stockings in jazzy pinks and blues to sell on the stall, but Gina never responded. She wasn't in the least interested, and why should she be? She wasn't able to ride in such a car, or wear a pair of powder-blue nylon stockings herself.

Patsy said nothing about her own problems with Marc. Where was the point? Dreadful though they might be, they were nothing by comparison to Gina's troubles.

It was one Friday after she'd returned from such a visit that Carlotta came hurrying across Champion Street to gather Patsy in her arms and press her to her warm breast.

'Patsy, at last I find you. Where have you been hiding yourself? I not see you for ages!'

'I've been a bit taken up with the hat stall, as usual,' Patsy said, by way of excuse.

'I know you still go visit my girl.' Tears stood proud in Carlotta's lovely brown eyes as she pressed her hands to her trembling mouth. 'I thank you so much for your loyalty and your kindness. We all do. If we cannot get her out of that place, then at least she know she not forgotten, eh?'

Patsy couldn't meet the other woman's eyes. How she longed to tell Carlotta what she suspected but knew she could never do that. If Marc had believed her, then he might have been able to discuss the matter with his parents, but he'd believed that Patsy was only out to make mischief.

How could he even think such a thing of her? Despite claiming he loved her and wanted to marry her, Marc would still allow her no say on family matters.

Patsy kissed the older woman on the cheek, told her that she'd just left Gina and she was well, considering, then made to walk away. Carlotta stopped her.

'Don't go. I want you to come to supper tonight. The children miss you.'

Patsy was embarrassed. 'Er, I can't, sorry, not tonight.' How could she when Marc wasn't speaking to her?

Carlotta dismissed her protest with a flap of her hands. 'I know there is big problem between you and Marc. He is like the bear with the sore head for weeks now. Don't tell me what it is, I don't want to know. But he love you, you love him, it time you make up. You come to supper tonight. It is Papa's birthday and I will have no more pain, no more sulks. Carmina is coming too, with her new husband. Tonight, we want all our family round us. Seven o'clock, no excuses.'

47

Amy and Chris

When Chris arrived at Albert Square, dominated as it was by its neo-Gothic Town Hall, and the gloomy monstrosity that was the Northern Assurance Building, he didn't, at first, appreciate what was happening. It was a cold October evening, already quite dark and the entire area was packed with parked cars, buses, and people hurrying to catch one, dashing to a cinema or to the Lyons Corner House. He paid little attention to the huddle of people gathering by the railings, all carrying something that looked like placards or banners. Nor did he pause to admire the fine spire above the movement to Prince Albert, Queen Victoria's consort, for whom the square was named.

His gaze was fixed upon Amy, his heart full as he watched her run over to a young man whom Chris instantly recognised as the one he'd seen her with on that previous occasion. She didn't kiss him, he noticed. Nor did he touch her, as he had done before. But then there were other people around this time, one of them a young girl who was leaning against him. Could that be the young man's wife? Had she been equally betrayed? he wondered, feeling a rush of sympathy for the poor girl.

He began then to take more notice of the rest of the group. They seemed to be a mixed bunch, comprising people of all ages. They were organising themselves into some sort of orderly fashion, with lines two or three deep to form a procession while the neighbouring statue of Gladstone gazed stonily down upon them, holding aloft an admonishing finger.

Chris began to grow curious. What was going on? He realised he was very far from alone in his interest. The number of spectators had grown to a sizeable crowd, some of them quite noisy.

The procession suddenly brightened as torches were lit and he saw then what it was all about. He read the words set out in bold print on the home-made banners. 'Ban the Bomb.' 'CND.' 'Save our children.'

The young man suddenly put an arm about Amy, and one around the other woman too, urging them both forward as the procession began to slowly move. Chris moved much quicker. He crossed the short distance between them at a run, reaching the group just as they climbed the steps surrounding Albert's monument.

'Hey, you,' Chris shouted. 'Keep your flamin' hands off my wife.' And lunging straight at the young man Chris socked him one, right in the jaw.

Chris and Amy were back home in the safety of their own living room, a fire blazing and the kettle singing as Amy put Germolene on Chris's skinned knuckles.

'I can't think what came over you. Whatever possessed you to think such a thing? Me having a love affair with Jeff Stockton indeed, the very idea. He's an old school chum, that's all, soon to be married to Sue. If you hadn't lunged at him you might have noticed she was flashing an engagement ring. They're very happy together, as I thought we were.'

Shame and relief flooded through Chris in equal measure like a rush of hot breath. He didn't mind how much she berated him, how foolish he'd been, all that mattered was that Amy wasn't having an affair at all. All she'd done was join the Peace Movement. She'd become a radical, a member of the CND, and hadn't dared upset him by admitting to it.

Unfortunately, the rally had ended in something of a fracas, with the trouble-making elements of the crowd taking his blow at Jeff as a sign for a free-for-all. Within seconds there'd been utter mayhem. Things had turned a bit nasty and when they heard the sound of police whistles and running feet, the Peace Movement members had been forced to take to their heels and run for it, Jeff and Sue, and Chris and Amy included. He was sorry for wrecking their rally, but so very glad that he hadn't lost his wife.

'I thought we were happy too, till I got that letter.'

Amy sank to her knees at his feet to gaze up into his face, her own puckered with fresh anxiety. 'What letter?'

'The one that told me you were having an affair. It came ages ago. It wasn't signed.'

Amy blinked. 'You mean you preferred to believe a malicious, anonymous letter, rather than the word of your own wife? Why didn't you tell me about it? Why didn't you ask? Why didn't you at least give me the chance to defend myself?'

Chris hung his head in shame. 'I suppose I was too afraid of what I might hear.'

'So you didn't trust me? You'd rather take the word of a nasty letter.'

Chris shook his head, grasped her hands in his. 'It was hard not to believe what it said. Whoever it was who wrote it seemed to know so much about us. Let me show it to you.'

He pulled the letter from the inside pocket of his jacket and passed it to her. It had clearly been well read as it was falling apart at the folds. Amy read the cruel accusation, printed in large capitals, her heart thumping painfully in her chest. Someone had seen her talking to Jeff on the market, on more than one occasion, seen him chuck her chin or ruffle her hair, and jumped to the worst possible conclusion.

Chris then handed her a second note, and this time her eyes grew wide with shock, the words seeming to leap off the page.

'Your wife has been seen entertaining her lover in your own house. She's a shameless hussy! Are you really going to put up with that?'

Jeff Stockton had set foot in her house only once, the day he'd called for a sample handbill which his uncle was going to print up for them. And only one person could have seen Jeff standing in the hall. Mavis! Her busy-body mother-in-law had taken it into her nasty little head to get her own back for all the imagined slights she'd suffered at Amy's hand. Presumably because she'd grown in confidence and independence, obstinately resisting all interference and daring to remove Chris from his mother's suffocating care. This was her revenge for Amy stealing her beloved son.

She looked up at her husband with pity in her eyes. 'I know who wrote this, and you aren't going to like it one little bit.'

She was right, Chris didn't like it. He'd never really had a major row with his mother, always backing down at the last moment from real confrontation, but he did so now and it was terrible to behold. Mavis sobbed and begged for forgiveness, Thomas stood by white-faced, one minute backing up his son, the next defending his poor broken wife.

'Tell him to leave me alone, he's making me ill,' Mavis cried, weeping into her husband's shoulder.

'I can't believe you would send me such malicious, nasty letters. Have you gone mad?' Chris asked.

It was Amy, in the end, who called a halt to the devastation. 'That's enough! I'm calling time on this argument.'

'*I* shall decide when this discussion is over,' Mavis screamed, instantly forgetting her grovelling apology the moment it was made. 'Chris has absolutely no right to speak to me like this.'

'I have every right, because you deserve it, you interfering old bag,' Chris yelled right back. 'You almost ruined my marriage!'

'Hey up, hold on, son,' Thomas shouted at his son.

'She might have made some bad mistakes but it were your welfare she cared about.'

Amy stood before them all, her child in her arms and a very determined expression on her young face as she calmly addressed them all. 'I said, that's *enough*! This subject is now closed. We've all made mistakes. Mavis clung on to her son too long, and maybe, one day, I might do the same thing.' She rubbed her cheek against Danny's head. 'It must be hard to let go, and suddenly stop being a mother.

'Thomas made the mistake of leaving it too long before he stood up to his wife's bossiness.' Mavis again started to protest but Amy silenced her with a look.

'And even then he chose to run away and hide in his shed while Chris sat on the fence and tried too hard to please everyone. As for me, well, I foolishly started to keep secrets from my lovely husband, and was then forced to tell lies to cover them up. So we've all made mistakes and we're all sorry for them. I suggest we never refer to this matter ever again and behave much better towards each other in future.'

Chris came to stand beside her, his arm protectively about his wife and son. 'I want everyone to know that I feel I'm the luckiest man on earth to have Amy and I'll not hear another word against her, ever. I know things aren't perfect, Mother, that the house is still a mess, but we're going to carry on loving each other, caring for our lovely boy, and working hard to save up for a better one.'

Then smiling into his wife's eyes, he finished, 'Things can only get better.'

Mavis cleared her throat and everyone looked at her with something like trepidation on their faces. It was a great deal to ask of this difficult woman that she never again boss her husband, give orders to her daughter-in-law or fuss over her son.

She looked at her husband and Thomas gave a barely discernible nod, then she gave what might have been a smile. 'You don't have to save up to buy another house. You can have this one. Your father has bought us a new one, in Thornton Cleveleys. You can move in here any time you like now you've taken over the bakery. There's a sum of money deposited in the bank to help with the business, and to do the place up to your liking. You can, of course, choose your own furniture, Amy. I shall be taking mine with me, fitted carpets and all. You might also like to help your husband by working in the business with him. I used to once upon a time, until we could afford more staff. You might find you enjoy working together, as we always did, didn't we, Thomas?'

'Aye, love, we did,' Thomas said, with a gleam in his eye.

'Perhaps I missed being involved more than I realised. Anyroad, retirement beckons and we shall be content now to walk on the prom and listen to the band. We might both take up bowls. I hope you'll come and visit now and then but what you do with this house, this business, is entirely up to you. We won't interfere. We'll keep our noses out, won't we, Thomas?'

'I certainly will, though I think yours is growing a

bit longer already, like Pinocchio's did when he told a lie,' Thomas said, and they all laughed.

Hearing their merry laughter, young Danny decided to join in with a chuckle, which was such a thrill to them all they forgot their differences at last and became what they should have been all along: a united happy family.

48

Patsy and Carmina

The atmosphere in this once lively, noisy household could have been cut with the proverbial knife. No one spoke as they all took their seats around the big dining table. Everyone was on their best behaviour. Papa Bertalone sat at the head, of course, with his wife opposite. The children were arranged in between according to age: Alessandro, Antonia, Lela next to Papa, as she so loved to be, then Marta and the twins. They were all neatly scrubbed and brushed, strangely silent with their hands in their laps, evidently under strict instructions to behave.

Patsy took her usual place next to Marc, although he didn't so much as glance in her direction, let alone pull out the chair for her, as he would normally have done.

Looking around her, the one thing that hit Patsy most forcibly was the vacant chair where normally Gina would be seated. There it stood, empty of its rightful occupant. In Patsy's eyes it represented a testimony to jealousy and sibling rivalry.

Not only was Gina not present, nor was Luc. Sadly, there was no reason for him to attend Bertalone family functions, now that he wasn't about to marry either daughter.

This unwelcome thought brought Patsy's gaze finally to Carmina, seated opposite, her new husband beside her. At six months pregnant she didn't appear to be exactly blooming, although her face was fuller and flushed by the wine she was drinking. Nor was she exactly bubbling with the kind of joy one would expect from a new bride. Patsy guessed this must be the first time Alec Hall had joined a Bertalone family gathering since the wedding, as he too was looking decidedly uncomfortable, even a little nervous. She didn't blame him. She felt very much the same herself. The sad thing was that it could all have been so very different.

She and Marc should be married by now, the young Bertalone girls allowed to parade and show off in their specially made bridesmaids' dresses on what would have been a joyous occasion.

Gina and Luc could have been quietly courting and getting to know each other, perhaps with a view to an ultimate engagement and marriage. Carmina herself, the architect of the disasters which had befallen this family, certainly in Patsy's mind, could still have been enjoying life as a single girl. Instead of which she was pregnant, and married to a man twice her age whom she clearly did not love.

Patsy had a theory on why the girl had agreed to marry him, but again, had no proof.

Jealousy and lies had led them to this place of distress and misery, had broken her mother's heart and sent her sister to jail. But poor Carlotta was doing her utmost this evening to rouse her family into some sort of celebratory mood for the sake of her husband's birthday.

They ate chicken liver pâté with home-made ciabatta bread, pasta shells with a salmon cream sauce, followed by lasagne alla Bolognese, and naturally some of Papa's finest ice cream. They managed a little desultory conversation, all excessively polite. Carmina never once glanced at, or addressed Alec, although he fussed charmingly over her, placing food on her plate which she neither asked for, nor ate.

'I don't want any salmon,' Carmina hissed at him.

Alec smoothed a curl behind her ear, as if trying to calm her. 'Remember you're eating for two now, my love. You must think of what's good for the baby.'

'I don't give a damn about the baby,' she snapped right back, a remark which caused Mamma to click her tongue severely at Carmina, and even the children stopped eating to stare at their sister wide-eyed. Patsy could sense Marc's tension as he seemed to stiffen beside her.

'Raise your glasses to darling Papa,' Carlotta announced into the midst of the ensuing silence, and obediently everyone did just that.

The entire meal was so stilted, so very difficult and embarrassing that Patsy couldn't wait for it to be over so she could escape back to the blessed peace of Number 22 and Clara. Marc hadn't spoken a single word to her all evening. Patsy could hardly bear it, could hardly do justice to the wonderful food as her throat felt choked with emotion.

But now Carlotta was bringing out a cake with lighted candles and the children were cheering and singing, not perhaps with their usual vigour, but doing their best to show their love and loyalty for their beleaguered parents.

Alec glanced at his wife's flushed cheeks and said, 'I think you've had enough wine, darling. You know you aren't supposed to be drinking at all really, although I don't object to your having one glass, since it's your father's birthday.'

'I'll drink as much as I wish,' Carmina retorted, oblivious to the shocked glances her parents and siblings were exchanging.

Alec said, 'I don't think you will,' and removed Carmina's glass from her hand. Alessandro snorted with laughter and Antonia nudged him in the ribs, which made him laugh all the more.

'Children, children, behave,' their father remonstrated with them.

'You see how cruel he is to me, Papa? See how you've forced me to marry a bossy, cruel man.'

Marco gave his daughter a measuring look but addressed his remarks to her husband. 'You do well, sir, to keep her under control. I'm afraid I never could.'

Whereupon Carmina burst into tears, although how real these were Patsy couldn't decide. They seemed more temper than genuine distress. Then reaching beneath her chair Carmina drew out her bag, took out a hanky and began to mop up the tears, manufactured or not. The children watched, goggle-eyed. Seeing their open curiosity Carmina gave a cry of anguish and fled to the bathroom.

Patsy was feeling fairly goggle-eyed herself. She sat for some long moments in stunned shock. That bag.

Red satin with a silver clasp, she would have known it anywhere. Hadn't she stitched those sequinned flowers on herself? The last time she'd seen it was when she'd put it out on display, and within hours it had vanished, as had the chiffon scarf and the earrings before it.

When Carmina returned, Patsy excused herself and also left the room. But she didn't go to the bathroom, as everyone assumed. She crept quietly upstairs to the room Carmina had most recently shared with her younger sisters.

It took less than three minutes for her to find a box of nylon stockings of the very same brand Patsy sold on the stall, together with two pairs of silver earrings, several records and a small red plastic transistor radio, secreted away in the bottom of the big wardrobe. She'd clearly not wished to part with these things yet perhaps hadn't quite known what to do with them when she left to get married. She could hardly take the records and radio into her new marital home, whence she had stolen them.

Patsy gathered all these things together, took them downstairs and laid them out on the table before Carmina for everyone to see. Of course, she was interfering yet again, but Patsy was beyond caring now. She'd lost Marc anyway, so what did it matter any more? Gina had tried, and thankfully failed, to take her own life, but was still serving two years for a burglary she didn't do. She, at least, deserved to know the truth.

'I believe these are some of the items you stole from

my stall, Carmina, as well as that red satin bag you have there, which I stitched with my own fair hands.'

After the silence came the noise, like the build-up of a great storm, the kind the Bertalone family were only too familiar with. Papa was shouting, Mamma was weeping and wailing, Lela was crying and Carmina herself was screaming at the top of her voice. The children clung to their parents, bemused and white-faced, in great distress, until Patsy had the presence of mind to shoo them into the front parlour to play Sorry! or Happy Families, which seemed entirely appropriate.

Marc was the only one who sat unmoving in stunned silence while mayhem erupted around him. When he finally did speak, his was the voice which broke through the hubbub, the one everyone listened to.

'What did you do, Carmina?'

Silence.

'I want you to start at the beginning and tell us the truth for once.'

Carmina turned her face away, folded her arms and ignored him.

'Is it true what Patsy says?'

Carmina threw Patsy a venomous glare. 'That little whore should learn to keep her nose out of my affairs.'

Marc got to his feet in a rush of anger. 'Don't speak about Patsy in that way.' And while his shocked parents looked on, Marc persisted with his questions. 'Tell us, Carmina, did you lie about this pregnancy at first in order to trap Luc into marriage? Did you steal this bag, and other things, from Patsy's stall and from Alec's shop? Did you deliberately set out to get your innocent sister arrested? Answer me, Carmina, did you?'

'*Yes!*' Carmina screeched at the top of her voice. '*Yes, yes, yes!* Are you satisfied now?' And she lunged at Patsy, may well have struck her had not Alec and Marc leapt to prevent her. It certainly took both of them to force the near-demented girl back into her seat while Carlotta rushed for a damp cloth to cool her daughter's brow, urging her to think of the baby she carried, as if Carmina were capable of caring about anyone but herself.

The day Gina was released from prison the sun cast golden rays over all of Manchester. This special day brought the kind of radiance and joy to Champion Street Market that hadn't been seen since VE Day, or the Coronation, or maybe when Amy and Chris had returned home safe and well from Gretna Green.

Gina heard the clang of those huge gates closing behind her for the last time, heard the scrape of a key against a lock, knowing she was on the outside, and not in. She lifted her face to feel the sun's soft warmth and let it caress her face. An idle breeze ruffled her newly washed hair, and she noticed how loud the birds sounded as they chirruped happily in the trees on this mild winter's day which she was now free to enjoy.

Free! What magic there was in that simple word.

She was instantly aware of her family waiting for her, their happy faces smiling in delight. There were her loving parents, her brothers and sisters, and Patsy and Marc with their arms wrapped tight about each other. But her gaze was focused most particularly upon one face.

Many hands pushed Luc forward, not that he needed any encouragement. He strode quickly across to the shy young girl standing uncertainly with paper bags at her feet, and gathered her hands gently in his.

'I'm still here, Gina, still waiting for you, as I promised I would be.'

She didn't ask him this time about Carmina. The story of how her sister's obsession had grown beyond her control had already been carefully explained to her.

Following Papa's disastrous birthday party it had been agreed that justice must prevail. Constable Nuttall had been called immediately, and the truth told.

Carmina was now the one serving time; her marriage, and her life, in ruins. Alec Hall had seemed surprisingly unconcerned to lose his new bride so soon.

'I am fond of her, and I certainly wanted the best for my child, but I confess the marriage wasn't really legal anyway,' he admitted to Papa Bertalone. 'I'm still married to a Korean girl, assuming she's still alive. Who knows? She was my third wife, my first died during World War Two and my second ran off with a merchant sailor in nineteen forty-eight, or was it forty-nine? So even my marriage to Joo Eun might not have been strictly legal, come to think of it. I'd be quite happy to care for the baby though, once it is born.'

Papa told him with barely disguised contempt that this was a decision only Carmina could make.

But no one was worrying about any of this now. No one wanted to be miserable on this special day. The children were noisy and giggly, Mamma was beside herself with joy, Papa stood tall and proud. Marc and Patsy were not only speaking again but kissing and happily making plans for a spring wedding in which all the Bertalone girls, Gina included, would act as bridesmaids. Marc's apology to Patsy for his lack of faith in her had been readily made and absolutely sincere.

Now, Gina slipped her hand into Luc's and smiled up at him. 'I knew you'd come for me one day. Let's go home.'